Read what the experts are saying about
THE GIRLS OF MISCHIEF BAY

An Amazon Best Book of the Month

"Once again, Susan Mallery has created an inviting world that envelops her readers' senses and sensibilities. Fans of Jodi Picoult, Debbie Macomber, and Elin Hilderbrand will assuredly fall for *The Girls of Mischief Bay*."

—*Bookreporter*

"Mallery skillfully depicts three very different women in different stages of their romantic relationships who enter into unbreakable friendships... Will appeal to fans of women's fiction, especially such friendship books as Karen Joy Fowler's *The Jane Austen Book Club*."

—*Booklist*

"Fresh and engaging... There's a generational subtext that mirrors reality and the complexities of adult relationships...filled with promise of a new serial that's worth following."

—*Fort Worth Star-Telegram*

"Romance superstar Mallery begins a new women's fiction series with a novel that is both heart-wrenching and warmhearted... A discerning, affecting look at three women facing surprising change and t*** powerful and uplifting impact of friends."

***s

"You will become totally inves*** characters and their strug*** ending. Can't wait for t*** Mallery and *The Girls*** ***ction

"Mallery's series debut is *** ***on in triumphs and tragedies to*** ***ic eloquent style... Her exceptional han*** *** the climactic hard knocks and joyful events, and her tiny canine co-star, rocked."

—*RT Book Reviews*

For a complete list of titles by Susan Mallery,
please visit SusanMallery.com.

SUSAN MALLERY

The Girls of Mischief Bay

ISBN-13: 978-0-7783-1975-7

The Girls of Mischief Bay

Recycling programs for this product may not exist in your area.

For questions and comments about the quality of this book, please contact us at CustomerService@Harlequin.com.

www.MIRABooks.com

Printed in U.S.A.

Dear Reader,

Welcome to Mischief Bay! This book is the first in what I hope will be a long-running series. I love creating a world that readers step into and experience fully. I'm hopeful it will be one you'll want to return to again and again.

While I love coming up with a fictitious place and discovering all the ways it can be as real as possible, there are challenges. One of the biggest ones is figuring out the types of businesses my characters will encounter and then naming them. Last year, when I was starting this book, I was suddenly and overwhelmingly stymied by the prospect of having to go through that. Realizing that sometimes it does indeed take a village to make a village, I turned to the people I adore most. My friends and readers at Facebook.com/susanmallery. I asked for suggestions and you came through. I was amazed by the response, even though I really shouldn't be. You're always there for me.

So, with gratitude, I dedicate this book to those of you who took the time out of your busy lives to help a struggling author. I hope you love Mischief Bay as much as I do. Special thanks to these Mischief Makers:

Alicia H, Oklahoma City, OK; Andie B, Woodstock, ON; Ann L, Pittsburgh, PA; Cat J, Johnson City, TN; Cheryl H, Auburn, MA; Dale B, Ocala, FL; Jennie J, Monroe, TN; Joyce M, Orange, TX; Karen M, Exton, PA; Kelly M, Corvallis, OR; Kelly R, Oregon City, OR; Kimberly C, Corning, NY; Kriss B, Chassell, MI; Kristen P, Westfield, NJ; Krystle P, Smithfield, PA; Linda H, Glen Burnie, MD; Lindsey B, Nestleton Station, ON; Lisbeth G, Honesdale, PA; Lora P, Papillion, NE; Melanie O, Chico, CA; Melissa H, Versailles, KY; Patricia K, Ashdown, AR; Phyllis G, Holbrook, MA; Roberta R, Berne, NY; Sandy K, Tucson, AZ; Sherry S, Jane Lew, WV; Susan P, DeValls Bluff, AR; Susan W, Morganville, NJ; Suzanne V, Rockaway, NJ; Suzi H, Kansas City, MO; Tina M, Warner Robins, GA; Tracy A, Rochester, NY; Yvonne Y, Edmonton, AB.

Love,

Susan Mallery

The Girls of Mischief Bay

One

"Did Tyler make that for you?"

Nicole Lord turned to look at the picture she'd posted on the wall of Mischief in Motion, her Pilates studio. Three large red hearts covered a piece of pink construction paper. A handprint had been outlined over the hearts. The hearts were wobbly and highly stylized, but still recognizable. Not bad, considering the artist in question was not yet five. The handprint had been traced by one of his teachers.

"He did," Nicole said with a smile. "I promised him I would bring it to work and show everyone."

Her client, a thirtysomething fighting her way back from a forty-five-pound pregnancy weight gain, wiped sweat from her face and smiled. "He sounds adorable. I look forward to when my daughter can do more than eat, poop and keep me up all night."

"It gets better," Nicole promised.

"I hope so. I'd always assumed once I started having kids, I'd want six." The woman grimaced. "Now one is looking like more than enough." She waved and walked toward the exit. "See you next week."

"Have a good weekend."

Nicole spoke without looking, her attention already back on her computer. She had her noon class, then a three-hour break before her late-afternoon classes. Which sounded nice until she thought about all she had to get done. Grocery shopping for sure—they were out of everything. Her car needed gas, there was dry cleaning to pick up and somewhere in the middle of all that, she should eat lunch.

She glanced at the clock, wondering if she should text Eric to remind him to pick up Tyler from day care at four. She reached for her phone, then shook her head and sagged back in her chair. No, she shouldn't, she told herself. He'd only forgotten once and he'd felt awful about it. She had to trust him not to forget again.

Which she would, she told herself. Only these days he was forgetting a lot of things. And helping less around the house.

Marriage, she thought ruefully. It all sounded so romantic until you realized that hey, you not only had to live with someone else, but there would also be days when they actually thought you were wrong about things.

She was still trying to figure out in which order she was going to run her errands when the door to her studio opened and Pam Eiland strolled in.

"Hey, you," Pam called cheerfully, an oversize tote hanging off one shoulder.

Anyone who didn't know Pam would assume she had a clutter problem if she needed to haul around that much stuff in her bag. Those who did know Pam were privy to the fact that her actual handbag was fairly small and that most of the space in the tote was taken up by a soft blanket and a very weird-looking dog.

Right on cue, Lulu poked her head out of the tote and whined softly.

Nicole stood and approached them both. After giving Pam a hug, she reached for Lulu. The dog leaped into her arms and snuggled close.

"I see you're in pink today," she said, stroking Lulu's cheek, then rubbing the top of her head.

"We both felt it was a pink kind of day," Pam told her.

Lulu, a purebred Chinese crested, had white hair on the top of her head, by her ears and on her tail and lower legs. The rest of her spotted body was pretty much naked and an unexpected shade of grayish pink with brown spots. Her health issues were legendary and what with having no fur, she was chronically cold. Which meant Lulu had a collection of sweaters, jackets and T-shirts. Today's selection was a lightweight, sleeveless pink sweater trimmed with shiny gray ribbon. With money tight and her own clothes threadbare, Nicole found herself in the embarrassing situation of envying a dog's wardrobe.

Lulu gave her a quick puppy-kiss on the chin. Nicole held on to the warm dog for a few seconds more. Her relationship with Lulu was the least emotionally charged moment in her day thus far, and she was determined to enjoy it.

Pam, a pretty brunette with an easy smile, wore a loose short-sleeved dress over her leggings and workout tank. Unlike the other clients who came in for the noon class, Pam didn't walk over from an office. Nicole knew the other woman had held a job at her husband's company years ago. She understood how a small business worked and often gave Nicole sound advice. Aside from that, Pam seemed to have her days to herself. Right now that sounded like a dream come true.

"Who's coming today?" Pam asked as she pulled the blanket out of the tote and folded it before setting it in a corner of the room. Lulu obligingly curled up, with her long legs tucked gracefully under her body. Nicole knew the dog wouldn't budge until class was over. She supposed the sweet temperament and excellent manners made up for Lulu's odd and faintly sci-fi appearance.

"Just you and Shannon," Nicole said, clicking on her computer's scheduling program to confirm. She was actually relieved to have a smaller class. Lately she was so damned tired all the time. Pam and Shannon could have run the workout themselves, so there wouldn't be pressure to stay on top of every move.

Even better, all three dropouts had come in early that morning. The studio had a strict twenty-four-hour cancellation policy, which meant she was going to be paid for five students regardless. She accepted her momentary pleasure even though the thought made her a bad person, and vowed she would work on her character just as soon as she figured out how to fix what was going on with her marriage and got more than four hours of sleep on any given night.

Pam had slipped off her sandals in preparation for class. But instead of putting on her Pilates socks, she turned to Nicole and grinned.

"Want to go to lunch?"

Pam's smile was infectious. Her hazel-green eyes crinkled at the corners and her mouth curved up.

"Come on," Pam teased. "You know you want to."

"Want to what?" Shannon Rigg asked as she walked into the studio. "I've had a horrible morning dealing with a misogynistic idiot from the bank who insisted on continually asking to speak to my supervisor. When I explained I was the CFO of the company, I think he had a seizure." She paused, her blue eyes dancing with amusement. "I offered to send him a scanned copy of my business card, but he declined. Then I told him that if he didn't get his act together, I would be moving the company's four-hundred-million-dollar account to another bank." She paused for dramatic effect. "I think I made him cry."

Pam held out her arm, hand raised, for a high five. "You both constantly impress me. Nicole juggles her husband, her five-year-old son and her growing business. You're busy frightening men who really should know better. I, on the other hand, will pick out my dog's wardrobe for tomorrow and make biscuits from scratch. It's sad."

"I don't even know what you put in the bowl to make a biscuit," Shannon admitted as she gave her friend a high five, then turned to Nicole. "Do you?"

"Flour, water, something else."

Shannon laughed. "Yeah, that's where I would get lost, too. It's the something else that always gets you."

Nicole thought about how Pam had described her. Juggling sounded so perky and positive. Unfortunately most days she found herself cleaning up what had fallen and shattered rather than keeping her plates spinning in the air.

Okay, that was a confused and slightly depressing analogy. She really needed to think more positively. And maybe learn how to make biscuits.

Shannon had on a tailored sleeveless dress and three-inch pumps. Her legs were bare and tanned, her hair a glorious tumbling mass of auburn waves that fell past her shoulders. She wore expensive watches and elegant jewelry. She drove a BMW convertible. If Nicole could pick, she would want Pam for her mother and to be Shannon when she grew up. Only at thirty, Nicole had a feeling she was about as grown-up as she was going to get.

"Wait," Pam said as Shannon headed for the small dressing room next to the restroom. "I thought we'd go to lunch instead of working out."

Shannon already had her exercise clothes out of her gym bag. She turned back to Pam. "Not exercise?"

"Sure. We're the only two today. It's Friday, my friend. Live a little. Have a glass of wine, mock your uninformed banking friend and unwind."

Shannon looked at Nicole and raised her eyebrows. "I'm in," she said. "What about you?"

Nicole thought about her to-do list and the fact that she was behind on the laundry and had a stack of bills to pay and a husband who had walked away from a successful career in computer software to write a screenplay. She thought of the spinning and falling plates and how she spent her life exhausted.

She pulled the tie from her blond ponytail, shook her hair loose, grabbed her keys and her handbag and stood. "Let's go."

McGrath's Pub had been around nearly as long as the Mischief Bay pier and boardwalk. Shannon remembered coming here when she'd been a teenager. The drive in from Riverside had taken about an hour, if there wasn't any traffic. She and her girlfriends had spent the whole time talking and laughing, imagining the cute boys they were going to meet. Boys who lived by the ocean and surfed and had sun-bleached hair. Boys not like those they knew in high school.

Because back then all it took to get her heart beating faster had been sun-bleached hair and a retro convertible. She liked to think that in the past twenty-plus years she'd matured.

As she followed her friends into the pub, her gaze strayed to the sand and the ocean beyond. It was midday and low tide. No surfers out there now. As it was also a weekday in February, there weren't any people playing volleyball. Despite the fact that it was probably seventy degrees.

McGrath's was a three-story building with outdoor dining on the main level. Inside there was a big, open bar. Pam led the way directly to the stairs. They bypassed the second-floor dining room and went up to the top-floor eating area.

"By the window?" Pam asked, already heading in that direction.

The big windows offered a view of the Pacific. Today they were partially open, allowing in some fresh air. When temperatures dropped to anything below sixty-five they could be closed and in the summer, they were removed completely.

Shannon sat across from Nicole. Pam settled next to Nicole and put her tote on the floor next to her chair. The perfectly trained Lulu would stay hidden until they left.

The first time the three of them had played hooky and gone to lunch, Shannon had spent the entire time freaking out about Lulu. Now she saw the strange creature as the mascot for their friendship—odd, unexpected and over time, very comforting.

She turned her attention from thoughts of a Chinese

crested to the restaurant location. The view should have captured their attention and left them speechless. Taupe-colored sand led the way to midnight blue water. A couple of sailboats leaned in to capture the light breeze, and in the distance container ships chugged toward the horizon and the exotic ports beyond.

But this was L.A. and amazing views existed around every turn. Whether it was a star sighting at a Whole Foods or the lapping waters of the Pacific. Instead of talking about the beauty of the moment, Pam passed out menus.

"There's a burger special," Pam said with a sigh. "Did you see it? If I get that, will someone eat some of my fries?"

"I will," Nicole told her. "I get the protein plate here."

Pam wrinkled her nose. "Of course you do."

Shannon knew the protein plate consisted of broiled fish and shrimp with a side of steamed vegetables. Healthy, sure, but the low calorie count was of more concern to the body-conscious, bikini-clad locals.

"I'll have a couple of fries, too," she said. They would nicely round out the salad she generally ordered.

Pam poked Nicole in the upper arm. "You're a stick. You should eat more."

"I eat plenty."

"Roots and grubs. Have a burger." Pam leaned back in her chair. "Enjoy your metabolism while you can. Because one day, it's all going to hell."

"You look great," Nicole said easily. "You're in terrific shape."

Pam's brows rose. "If you say 'for a woman my age' I'm pitching you out the window."

Nicole laughed. "I'd never say that. You're nowhere near a certain age. That's old."

So spoke the thirty-year-old, Shannon thought wryly. Time was going faster and faster every day. She couldn't believe she was only a few months away from turning forty, herself. She glanced at Pam and Nicole's hands and saw the wedding bands and diamond engagement rings winking back at her. Not for the first time, Shannon considered the fact that somewhere along the way she should have gotten married.

She'd meant to, had always thought she would. Only her career had been her first priority—a fact that the men she knew didn't like. The more successful she got, the harder it was to date. Or at least find a man who didn't resent her devotion to her career. Lately, finding someone interesting and appealing had started to seem nearly impossible.

She briefly toyed with the idea of mentioning that. All the articles she read said that she had to put herself out there if she wanted to meet a great guy. She had to be willing to tell all her friends that she was serious and looking. Of course, she had a sneaking suspicion that many articles in women's magazines were written by people who had no idea what they were talking about. Besides, she wasn't keen on pity. She was a successful, vital businesswoman. Hell, she was the chief financial officer of a company grossing more than a billion dollars a year. She didn't need a man in her life. Which wasn't to say she might not like having one around.

"How's my favorite young man?" Pam asked.

Nicole smiled. "Tyler is great. I can't believe he's turning five in a couple of months. It's going so fast. He'll be in kindergarten in September." She paused. "In a way, that will be nice. There'll be less day-care juggling."

As she finished speaking, her smile faded and a muscle twitched in her cheek. As if she were clenching her teeth.

Shannon hesitated, not sure if she should ask what was wrong. Because she already knew the answer. The three of them had been in the same exercise class for nearly two years. While she and Pam were faithful participants, the same couldn't be said for anyone else. For some reason, the Friday noon class tended to attract the flakier clients.

Which meant it had often been just the three of them. They'd talked between Pilates moves, had shared various ups and downs. Shannon knew that Brandon, Pam's youngest, had been a wild teenager—to the point of driving so drunk, he'd wrapped his car around a tree. Now he was a sober, determined student in medical school. She'd listened as Nicole had tried to explain her bewilderment that her stable, hard-working husband had quit his job to write a screenplay and surf. In turn, Shannon had shared the tribulations of her own personal life. Everything from the challenge of being the only female executive at a tech company to the difficulty finding a Mr. Right who supported her career goals.

While Shannon searched for a delicate way to ask if Nicole's comment meant Eric was still determined to conquer Hollywood, Pam plunged right in.

"He continues to be an idiot?" she asked.

Nicole wrinkled her nose. "He's not an idiot. He's..." She hesitated. "Confusing. I know it's been six months, so I should be over it, right? It's not that I didn't know."

Pam angled toward her friend. "Honey, everyone *says*

they want to write a screenplay or be on *American Idol* or something, but no one takes them seriously. There are dreams and then there's real life. Eric has a wife and a son. He walked away from a great job to type and surf. Who does that?"

Nicole winced. "He's writing, not typing."

"Details. He's not contributing financially or in any other way."

"He helps," Nicole said, then sighed. "Sort of. I don't know what to do. You're right. Everyone says they want to be rich or famous, and that's great. But I don't know. When he walked in and told me he'd quit his job…" She raised her shoulders. "I still don't know what to say."

Shannon got that one. She had been just as shocked as her friend and she didn't have to live with Eric. She supposed a case could be made for everyone having the right to follow his or her dreams, but in a marriage, shouldn't both parties get a vote? That was what had been so stunning about Eric's decision. He hadn't mentioned it or negotiated or anything. He'd simply walked away from his job and told his wife after the fact.

"While I don't recommend this for every situation," Pam said slowly, "have you considered smothering him with a pillow?"

Nicole managed a soft laugh. "Not my style."

"Mine, either," Pam admitted. "I'm more direct. But it's an option."

Shannon grinned. "This from a woman who carefully dresses her dog so she won't be cold? You talk tough, but on the inside, you're a marshmallow."

"Don't tell," Pam said, glancing around, as if afraid they would be overheard. "I have a reputation to protect." She touched Nicole's hand. "All jokes aside, I know this is difficult for you. You want to shake some sense into him and right now you can't. Hang in there. You two love each other. That'll get you through."

"I hope so," Nicole said. "I know he's a good guy."

"He is. Marriage is like life. Just when you think you have it figured out, it changes. When I stopped working, I felt guilty that John was carrying the whole financial load. But we talked about it and he finally convinced me he liked having me home. I take care of things there and he handles bringing in the money."

A world she couldn't imagine, Shannon admitted, if only to herself. It was as if Pam was from another planet. Or another era. Shannon knew there were plenty of stay-at-home moms. The difference was she didn't know any of them. Not as friends. The mothers she knew were like Nicole—always scrambling to keep up.

Although now that she thought about it, there were a couple of friends who had left their jobs and become stay-at-home mothers. Only once that had happened, Shannon had lost touch with them. Or maybe they'd lost touch with her.

"There are always rough patches," Pam said. "But if you remember why you're together, then you'll get through it."

Two

Pam walked through from the garage to the main house, Lulu keeping pace with her. In the mudroom they both paused. Pam fished her small handbag out of the tote, then hung the larger bag on a hook.

The open area served as a catchall for things that otherwise didn't have a home. There was a built-in storage unit with plenty of hooks, shelves and drawers. The latter were mostly filled with Lulu's various clothes.

Now Pam eyed the lightweight sweater her pet wore and decided it would keep the dog warm enough until bedtime. Like the rest of the family, Lulu wore pj's to bed. Pam didn't care if anyone laughed at her for that. She was the one Lulu cuddled next to under the covers and she wanted her dog wearing something soft when that happened.

They continued through the house to the kitchen. Pam pulled her cell out of her purse and stuck it on the side table by the hall, then checked on the Crock-Pot she'd left on that morning. A quick peek and stir confirmed the beef burgundy was coming along. She added the vegetables she'd already prepared and stirred again, then went out the front door to collect the mail.

The day had warmed up nicely. February in the rest of the country could mean snow and ice. In Southern California there was every chance it would be sunny and seventy. Today was no exception, although she would guess it was closer to sixty-five. Hardly reason to complain, she told herself as she pulled the mail out of the box and started back toward the house.

Mischief Bay was a coastal community. Tucked between Redondo Beach and Hermosa Beach, it had a small pier, plenty of restaurants, a boardwalk and lots of tourists. The ocean regulated the temperatures and the steady light breeze made sure there wasn't much in the way of smog.

She and John had bought their sprawling ranch-style home ages ago. Jennifer, their oldest, had been what? Three? Pam tried to remember. If Jennifer had been three, then Steven had been a year and she'd been pregnant with Brandon.

Oh, yeah. She *had* been pregnant all right. There'd been the charming moment when she'd thrown up in front of the movers. Brandon had been a difficult pregnancy and she'd been nauseous a lot. Something she brought up every so often—when her son needed a little humbling. As all children did, now and then.

She paused to wait for Lulu to do her business by the bushes and studied the front of the house. They'd redone much of both yards a few years ago, when they'd had the house painted. She liked the new plants that edged the circular drive. Her gaze rose to the roof. That had been replaced, as well. One of the advantages of having a husband in construction—he always knew the best people.

Lulu trotted back to her side.

"Ready to go in, sweet pea?" Pam asked.

Lulu wagged her feathered tail and led the way. Pam glanced down at the mail as she walked. Bills, a letter from an insurance agent she'd never heard of—no doubt an ad—along with two car magazines for John and a postcard from the local high school.

Pam frowned at the postcard and turned it over. What on earth could they...?

Lulu walked into the house. Pam followed and automatically closed the door. She stood in the spacious foyer, afternoon light spilling onto the tile floor.

But she didn't see any of that. She didn't see anything but the stark words printed on the postcard.

Class of 2005. Fellow Cougars—save the date!! Your 10-year high school reunion is this August.

There was more, but the letters got blurry as Pam tried to make sense of the notice. A ten-year high school reunion? Sure, Jennifer had graduated in 2005, but there was no way it had been ten years, had it? Because if Jen was attending her ten-year reunion, that meant Pam was the *mother* of a woman attending her ten-year high school reunion.

"When did I get old?" Pam asked, her voice a whisper.

Involuntarily, she turned to stare at the mirror over the entry table. The person staring back at her looked familiar and yet totally wrong. Sure the shoulder-length dark hair was fine and the irises were still hazel-green. But everything else was different. No, not different. Less... firm.

There were lines around her eyes and a distinct softness to her jaw. Her mouth wasn't as full as it had been. Ironically, just last November she'd turned fifty and had been so damned proud of herself for not freaking out. Because these days fifty was the new thirty-five. Big deal, right?

John had thrown a huge party. She'd laughed over the gag gifts and had prided herself for achieving the big 5-0 with grace and style. Not to mention a pretty decent ass, thanks to the three-times-a-week classes she took at Nicole's studio. She hadn't felt…old. But that was before she had a daughter who had just been invited to her ten-year high school reunion.

Sure, she'd had kids young. She'd married John at nineteen and had Jen when she'd turned twenty-two. But that was what she'd always wanted.

She and John had met at Mischief Bay High School. He'd been tall and sexy, a star player on the football team. His family had a local plumbing company. One that worked in new construction rather than fixing stopped-up toilets.

John's plans had been set. He was going to get his AA in business from Mischief Bay Community College, then work in the family firm full-time. He would start at the bottom, earn his way to the top and buy out his parents by the time he was forty.

Pam had liked how he'd known what he wanted and went after it. When he turned his blue eyes on her and decided she was the one to share the journey, well, she'd been all in.

Now as she studied her oddly familiar and unfamiliar reflection, she wondered how the time had gone by so quickly. One second she'd been an in-love teenager and now she was the mother of a twenty-eight-year-old.

"No," she said aloud, turning away from the mirror. She wasn't going to freak out over something as ridiculous as age. She had an amazing life. A wonderful husband and terrific kids and a strange little dog. They were all healthy—except for Lulu's ongoing issues—and successful and, best of all, happy. She'd been blessed a thousand times over. She was going to remember that and stay grateful. So what if she wasn't firm? Beauty only went skin deep. She had wisdom and that was worth more.

She headed into the kitchen and flipped on the wall-mounted TV. John got home between five fifteen and five thirty every day. They ate at six—a meal she'd made from scratch. Every Saturday night they either went out to dinner or had an evening with friends. Sunday afternoon the kids came over and they barbecued. On Memorial Day they held a big party, also a barbecue. It was LA. When in doubt, throw meat on a grill.

She automatically collected the ingredients for biscuits. Self-rising flour, shortening, sugar, buttermilk. She'd stopped using a recipe years ago for nearly everything. Because she knew what she was doing. John liked what she served and didn't want her to change. They had a routine. Everything was comfortable.

She measured the flour and told herself that comfortable wasn't the same as old. It was nice. Friendly. Routines meant things went smoothly.

She finished cutting in the shortening, then covered the bowl. That was the trick to her biscuits. To let them rest about twenty minutes.

Lulu sat patiently next to her bowl. As Pam approached, the dog wagged her fluffy tail and widened her eyes in a hopeful expression.

"Yes," Pam told her. "It *is* your dinnertime."

Lulu gave a bark, then followed her to the refrigerator, where the can waited.

Lulu's diet was an on-going challenge. She was small so didn't need all that much. She had allergies and skin conditions, not to mention a sensitive stomach. Which meant she ate prescription dog food, consisting of a "novel protein" diet. In her case, duck and sweet potato.

Pam stuck a quarter cup of water into the microwave and hit the start button. After measuring out the right amount of canned food, she swapped the plate for the measuring cup, then started the microwave again. Hot water was stirred into kibble. Lulu had delicate teeth and couldn't eat regular kibble. So hers was softened with hot water.

They went through this ritual every night, Pam thought as she held out the bowl. Lulu immediately sat, as she was supposed to, then lunged for the bowl and devoured her meal in less than eight seconds.

"You do remember you had breakfast this morning and a snack after lunch, right? You act like we feed you weekly."

Lulu was too busy licking her bowl to answer.

Pam rolled out the biscuits and put them on the cookie sheet. She covered them with a clean towel and started the oven. She'd barely finished setting the table when she heard the faint rumble of the garage door opener. Lulu took off running down the hall, barking and yipping in excitement.

A few minutes later John walked into the kitchen, their ridiculous dog in his arms. Pam smiled at him and turned her head for their evening kiss. As their lips touched, Lulu scrambled from his arms to hers, then swiped both their chins with her tongue.

"How was your day?" John asked.

"Good. Yours?"

"Not bad."

As he spoke he crossed to the bottle of wine she'd put on the counter in the butler's pantry off the kitchen. It was a Cab from a winery they'd visited a few years ago on a trip to Napa.

"Steven's working on a bid for that new hotel everyone's been talking about. It's right on the water. Upscale to the max. He said they were talking about the possibility of twenty-four-karat gold on the faucets in the penthouse. Can you believe it?"

"No. Who would do that? It's a hotel. Everything has to be scrubbed down daily. How do you clean gold?"

"I know." John opened the drawer to pull out the foil cutter. "It's a bathroom. They're idiots. But if the check clears, what do I care?"

As they spoke, she studied the man she'd been married to for thirty-one years. He was tall, just over six feet, with thick hair that had started going gray. The dark blond color meant the gray wasn't noticeable, but it was there. Being a man, it only made him look more appealing. A few months ago he'd asked why she wasn't going gray, too. When she'd reminded him of her visits every six weeks to her hair person, he'd been shocked. John was such a typical guy, it had never occurred to him she colored her hair. Because he thought she was naturally beautiful.

Silly man, she thought affectionately, as she watched him.

He had a few wrinkles around his eyes, but otherwise looked as he had when they'd first met. Those broad shoulders had always appealed to her. These days he claimed he needed to lose ten or fifteen pounds, but she thought he looked just fine.

He was handsome, in a rugged kind of way. He was a good man. Kind and generous. He loved his wife and his kids and his routine. While he had his faults, they were minor and ones she could easily live with. In truth, she had no complaints about John. It was the her-getting-older thing she found faintly annoying.

He pulled out the cork and tested it with his thumbnail, then poured them each a glass of Cab. She slid the biscuits into the oven and set the timer.

"What are we having?" he asked as he handed her a glass.

"Beef burgundy and biscuits."

His mouth turned up in an easy smile. "I'm a lucky man."

"Even luckier. You'll be taking leftovers for lunch tomorrow."

"You know I love me some leftovers."

He wasn't kidding, she thought as she followed him through the kitchen. His idea of heaven was any kind of red meat with leftovers for lunch the following day. He was easy to please.

They went into the sunroom off the back of the house. In the cooler months, the glass room stayed warm. In the summer, they removed the glass and used the space for outdoor living.

Lulu followed them, then jumped up on the love seat where Pam always sat and settled next to her. Pam rubbed her dog's ears as John leaned back in his chair—a recliner with a matching mate in the family room—and sighed heavily.

"Hayley's pregnant again," he said. "She told me this morning. She's waiting until three months to make a public announcement."

Pam felt her mouth twist. "I don't know what to say," she admitted. "That poor girl."

"I hope this one takes," John said. "I don't know how much more of her suffering I can stand."

Hayley was John's secretary and desperate to have children, but she'd miscarried four times over the past three years. This would be try number five. Rob, Hayley's husband, wanted to look into adoption or a surrogate, but Hayley was obsessed with having a baby the old-fashioned way.

"I should send her a card," Pam said, then shook her head. "Maybe not." She took a sip of her wine. "I have no idea how to handle this."

"Don't look at me. You're in woman territory."

"Where if you stray too far, you'll grow breasts?"

"Damned straight."

"I'll write a note," she decided. "I can say we're rooting for her without a you're-having-a-baby message. Did the doctor say she would be okay if she could get to three months?"

Her husband forehead furrowed. "I don't know. She probably told me, but I barely want to know if she goes to the bathroom. Baby stuff is too intimate."

"You're not a complex man, are you?"

He raised his glass to her. "And that's why you love me."

He was right. She did love that he was dependable and predictable. Even if every now and then she wanted something different in their lives. A surprise trip to somewhere or a fancy bracelet. But that wasn't John's style. He would never plan a trip without talking to her and as for buying jewelry, he was more of a "go buy yourself something pretty" kind of man.

She didn't object. She'd seen too many of her friends endure surprises of the not-very-pleasant kind. Ones that involved other women or divorces. John wasn't looking for more than she had to offer. He liked his routine and knowing that gave her comfort.

"Jen got mail from the high school today," she said. "An invitation to her ten-year reunion."

"Okay."

"You don't think it's stunning that we have a daughter old enough to have been out of high school ten years?"

"She's twenty-eight. So the reunion is right on time."

Pam sipped her wine. "I was shocked. I'm not ready to have a daughter that old."

"Too late to send her back now. She's used."

Despite her earlier distress, Pam laughed. "Don't let her hear you say that."

"I won't." He smiled at her. "And you're not old, sweetheart. You're barely in your prime."

"Thanks." She heard the timer chime and stood. "That's our dinner."

He scooped up Lulu and followed Pam back to the kitchen. As Pam went about serving the meal, she reminded herself she was a very lucky woman. That a bit of sagging and a few lumps and bumps didn't change who she was as a person. Her life was a blessing. If there weren't any tingles anymore, well, that was to be expected. Wasn't she forever hearing that you couldn't have it all?

* * *

It's just drinks, Shannon told herself as she pushed open the door that led into Olives—the martini bar/restaurant where she was meeting her date. Her online date.

She wanted to pause and maybe bang her head against the wall. Why did she do this to herself? It never went well. Dating wasn't her strong suit. It just wasn't. She was a successful businesswoman. She earned mid six figures and fully funded her 401K every single year. She had friends, she had a beautiful condo with an ocean view. Okay, there had been a string of boyfriends over the years and she'd been engaged twice, for no more than fifteen minutes each time. But no marriage. Not for her.

The truth was, she didn't have good romantic relationships. Maybe it was her, maybe it was men, but she had to accept the truth that having it all simply wasn't going to happen. Not to her. So why was she back dealing with the nightmare that was dating? Worse—online dating.

The only saving grace was that ProfessionalLA.com was a halfway decent site that actually screened subscribers. So the guy was going to look like his profile picture and wouldn't have any felony convictions in his past. But the distance from that to happily-ever-after seemed insurmountable.

Still, she was here. She would go in and say hi. She would be pleasant and as soon as she was able to duck out without seeming wildly rude, she would run back to her office, get her car and head home. One glass of wine, she promised herself. She could survive that. Maybe what's-his-name would be great.

She paused for a second, as panic set in. What was his

name? Crap. Double crap. She kept moving even as her
brain hustled toward whatever synapses stored short-term
memory. Andrew? *A* something. Adam? Right. Adam.
Adam something she would never remember. He sold
cars maybe. He was about her age, divorced and possibly blond?

She made a mental note to spend a little more time
with the profiles, even as she scanned the people in the
bar and hoped to find someone who looked vaguely familiar.

A man rose and smiled at her. He was about six feet,
with dark hair and eyes and a crooked smile. He was
tanned and fit, but not in a look-at-me kind of way. And
he was staring at her as if she had a monkey on her head.

She did her best to appear casual as she glanced over
her shoulder to make sure she wasn't being followed by
Taylor Swift or someone else who would cause a grown
man to simply stare. There wasn't anyone of note. So she
kept moving toward him and hoped for the best.

"Shannon?" he asked as she got closer.

"Yes. Hi."

"I'm Adam." He held out his hand and they shook.
"Thanks for meeting me."

He continued to look at her in a way that made her
wonder if she'd forgotten to check her teeth or had grown
a wart on her nose in the five minutes it had taken her
to walk from the office to the bar. It couldn't be that she
looked different from her picture. She'd used a business
head shot. Nothing that would overpromise.

They sat down.

Olives was the kind of place that catered to locals
and tourists alike. The bar was well lit, without a diner
feel. Tables were spaced far enough apart that you didn't

have to worry about everyone listening to your conversation. The restaurant was upscale-casual, with an eclectic menu. Except for a few paintings of olives and martini glasses on the walls, they hadn't gone crazy with the motif.

Shannon liked it for a first date because she came here just enough to be familiar with the staff and all the exits. If a first date went bad, she could easily call for help or bolt. It was also within walking distance of her office, which meant she didn't have to worry about a second drink before driving. If it was time to leave, but she wasn't ready to get behind the wheel, she simply returned to her office and did something mindless until she was ready to make the six-minute commute to her condo.

Adam's gaze was steady. Shannon couldn't stand it anymore.

"You're staring at me," she said, trying to keep her voice as friendly as possible. "Is something wrong?"

His eyes widened, then he glanced away before returning his attention to her. "No. Sorry. Jeez, I'm being an idiot. It's just…you. Wow. You sent a picture and it was so great, I figured there had to be a mistake. Then when I saw you just now and you were even more beautiful in person…" He verbally stumbled to a stop, then cleared his throat.

"Can we start over or do you want to leave?"

His expression was both chagrined and hopeful. Shannon tried to remember the last time anyone had been so rattled by her looks. She knew she was pretty enough and when she made an effort, she could up her game, but she wasn't the kind of woman who left men tongue-tied. Or staring.

She smiled. "We can start over."

"Good. I'll do my best not to be scary." He smiled. "It's nice to meet you, Shannon."

"Apparently."

He chuckled and motioned to the server. "What can I get you to drink?"

She ordered a glass of the house red while he chose a Scotch. He added the fruit and cheese plate to the order. When they were alone again, she leaned back in her chair.

He was nice, she thought. A little awkward, which meant he didn't date a lot. At least he wasn't a player. She didn't need any more of them in her life. Divorced, if she remembered correctly.

"So, Adam," she said. "Tell me about yourself."

"What do you want to know?"

Everything that had been in his profile, she thought, wishing she'd paid just a little more attention. The thing was she didn't like online dating. She counted on the service to screen the men and then moved fairly quickly to a meeting. For her, emails and a couple of calls didn't provide any insight into how things would go in person.

"Do you live in the area?" she asked.

"Sure." The smile returned. "I was born and raised right here in Mischief Bay. Most of my family is still in the area, which means it's hard to get away with anything."

"Do you try to get away with things?"

The smile turned into a laugh. "I gave that up when I was a teenager. I'm a bad liar and if I cross the line, I get caught. So I don't bother with either anymore."

His smile faded. "You're not in to bad boys, are you?"

She had been, and had the heart scars to prove it. "Not anymore. They're great in theory, but life isn't about theories. It's about real people who take the time to show up."

"I agree."

They were on opposite sides of a small table. Adam leaned toward her. "You're in finance?"

"Yes. I'm a CFO for a software company."

She tried to speak normally, knowing that when she mentioned her job she tended to be both defensive and proud. An awkward combination at best.

The problem was some men resented her success and some men were intimidated by it. A few had seen her as a way to the easy life, but fortunately they weren't usually very subtle about their hopes of being kept. The ones who accepted that she'd done well and worked hard were often the keepers, albeit rare and therefore hard to find.

"Are you in line to be president next?" he asked.

She smiled. "No. I'm comfortable being the queen of the checkbook. I like the financial side of things." She shifted toward him and lowered her voice. "Software is not my thing. I'm better than most on a computer, but it's never been easy for me. You should see some of the college kids we hire every year. They're brilliant. What about you?"

"Not brilliant."

She laughed. "Thanks for the share. I meant, tell me about your work."

"Oh, that. My family's in construction. Large projects, mostly. Office buildings, hotels. I'm the foreman on a hotel we're dealing with now. It's just south of Marina del Rey. It's high-end, twenty stories."

Impressive, she thought. "Foreman sounds like a lot of responsibility."

Adam grinned. "I stand around and tell other people what to do. It beats a real job."

Their server arrived with their drinks and the cheese plate. Adam raised his glass.

"To unexpected surprises."

She touched her glass to his and thought he was certainly that and more. She'd had no expectations for their date, but here she was, having a nice time. So far Adam was funny and charming. There had even been hints of his being genuinely nice. She knew better than to get her hopes up, but the evening was turning out better than she'd anticipated.

"Tell me about the family that doesn't let you get away with anything," she said.

"I'm one of five kids and I could practically walk to four of their houses from here. Same with my parents." He shrugged. "My youngest brother is back east, but then he's always felt he had something to prove."

She stared at him. "You're one of five?"

"I know. I told my dad they figured out what causes pregnancy, but he said he and Mom always wanted a big family. I have to say it was a fun way to grow up."

"And loud," she murmured.

"Yeah, there was noise."

"How many boys and girls?"

"Three boys, two girls, and we alternate. I'm in the middle. My older brother was never interested in the family business. He's a graphic designer. Very talented. My older sister always wanted to be a veterinarian, so by the time I was six or seven, Dad was starting to get nervous that no one was going to go into the business. Fortunately my idea of a good time was building things. I got my first job at the company when I was fourteen."

He took a piece of cheese. "I know. Not very exciting."

"Exciting is highly overrated," she murmured. All this and stable, too. So what was the flaw? Emotional unavailability? A secret life as a serial killer? There had to be something, because to be honest, her luck simply wasn't that good.

"Where did you grow up?" he asked.

"Riverside. I'm an only child, so I can't relate to your noise. My house was always quiet."

"Were you the smartest girl in the class?"

"Sometimes. I liked math, which made me unacceptable to most groups. But I wasn't brilliant enough to major in it. Finance seemed like an interesting way to spend my days."

His brown eyes crinkled with amusement. "If I had a nickel for every time I looked forward to spending time working on the company's financial records…"

"You wouldn't have a nickel?"

"Something like that."

She smiled. "Your profile said you're divorced?"

He nodded. "Nearly a year now. We were separated before that." He shrugged. "It wasn't anything dramatic. We were married young and over the past few years realized we didn't like spending time with each other."

There was something about the way he spoke that had her leaning forward. As if there was more to the story.

"That's no fun," she said quietly.

"Tell me about it." He looked at her, then swore softly. "Hell. Okay, she cheated. I don't like to say that because it makes me look like an idiot. I didn't know. She came to me one day and said she'd been having an affair and that she'd fallen in love with the guy. She didn't want to marry him or anything, but she'd realized that if she could be in love with someone else, she wasn't in love with me anymore."

He moved his glass back and forth on the table. Tension pulled at his mouth. "I was shocked and hurt and didn't know what to do. I grabbed some stuff and moved out that night. About a month later, when my pride and ego weren't so much in the way, I realized we'd been growing apart for a long time."

"That must have been hard," she said, thinking that if he was telling the truth, then she was liking him more by the second.

"It was. We have two kids. Charlotte is nearly nine and Oliver is six. We share them. One week on, one week off. Tabitha and I live about two blocks away from each other. Slightly awkward for us, but easy for the kids." Humor returned to his eyes. "Of course, my parents and three of my siblings live in the neighborhood, too, so I'm going to go out on a limb and say it's way more awkward for her than for me."

"As long as it works," Shannon told him.

"And you?" he prompted.

Yes, the inevitable questions. "No kids, no ex-husband. I was engaged twice, but never quite made it down the aisle."

"Who made the decision?"

"One time him, one time me."

She'd also had a long-term on-again, off-again relationship with a music producer, who'd been very bad for her, but there was no reason to mention him. At least not on the first date.

"What do you do for fun?" Adam asked.

"I love to travel. Take two or three weeks and go somewhere I've never been."

"Like?"

She smiled. "I've been on every continent except Antarctica. I was thinking of taking one of those ships there, but after one got stuck a couple of years ago and made headlines, I changed my mind."

"What's your next trip?"

She laughed. "You're going to be shocked."

"I doubt that."

"Okay. Machu Picchu."

His eyes widened slightly. "Remind me to listen to you next time. That's Peru, right?"

"Yes. I'm going with a girlfriend and it's going to be great. We'll be hiking the Inca Trail. The ruins are at seven thousand feet above sea level so I'm a little worried about my athletic ability. I'm—"

A familiar ringtone drifted from her purse. She reached for her bag.

"Sorry," she said as she pulled her phone out of its pocket and glanced at the screen. "It's work. I need to take this."

She was already standing and heading out of the restaurant. When she stepped onto the sidewalk, she pushed Talk.

"This is Shannon."

"Len Howard in the Seoul office. Sorry to bother you but we have a problem with the South Korean finance minister. He's insisting on speaking with you."

Shannon glanced back at the bar and saw Adam glancing her way. Adam, who appeared to be pretty darned close to perfect.

"Based on my other conversations with him, I'm guessing he wants me to phone him in the next few minutes."

"If possible."

Because he was a man of power and she needed his help with some banking regulations. Nolan, her boss, wanted their Asian headquarters in Seoul, which meant Shannon had to make nice with the finance minister.

"Please tell him I'll call him back in fifteen minutes," she said. "From my office."

"Will do."

She walked back into the restaurant. Adam rose as she approached the table.

"Everything all right?" he asked.

She shook her head. "I'm so sorry. I have to get back to work. There's a crisis in South Korea and I need to be on the phone in fifteen minutes."

"I'm sorry to hear that. I was hoping we could grab dinner. Should I wait?"

She wanted to say yes. He was an unexpected find. But once she was done calming things down, she would have to call her boss and do paperwork.

"It's going to be a late night." She gave him a smile. "But I enjoyed meeting you."

She wanted to say more. She wanted to ask him not to be intimidated by what she did. She wanted to say it would be great if he mentioned he wanted to see her again. Instead, she reached for her wallet.

"No way," he told her. "I've got this. Go make your call."

"Thank you."

She waited a second, hoping he would say more. When he didn't, she smiled. "It was so nice to meet you."

"You, too."

She walked to the door and out into the cool evening.

Her office was only a few blocks away. She would make it back in time with no problem.

Thoughts swirled and competed for her attention. If only, she thought, then pushed the words away. She'd wanted her career. She'd wanted to be successful and know that she could always take care of herself, no matter what. And she had that. There was no way she was going to feel bad about what she'd accomplished.

It was just that sometimes, she found herself wanting more.

Three

Nicole turned on the coffeemaker and leaned against the counter to wait for it to work its magic. It was early still. Quiet. The time of day she liked best—except when she was exhausted, which was most of the time.

She told herself that eventually the situation would get better. That she would figure out a schedule that worked, that Tyler would get older and need her less, that Eric would get a real job and start helping support the family again.

The last thought made her feel both guilty and angry. Not a happy combination. Because as much as she loved her husband, there were times when she didn't like him very much.

No, she thought. She didn't like what he'd done. There was a difference.

Back before he'd quit his well-paying, very steady software development job to write a screenplay, things had seemed more balanced. She'd been comfortable in their roles. But lately…not so much.

She told herself she had to be fair. That he had the right to follow his dream. Only it wasn't the dream she minded as much as the fact that he hadn't asked her first. Instead, he'd announced what he was doing. And that announcement had come two days after he'd already resigned.

She closed her eyes against the memory, but it crowded into the kitchen, anyway. It had been a Friday morning. She'd been standing in the kitchen, just like she was now. Eric had walked in to the room, wearing shorts and T-shirt.

"Don't you have to get dressed for work?" she'd asked.

He'd taken her hand. "I have to tell you something. I've quit my job. I'm going to write a screenplay."

There had been more talk. She was sure of it. But she hadn't heard anything beyond the keen screaming of fear that had filled her head.

Quit? How could he quit? They had a mortgage and she was still paying back her old boss for buying out the exercise studio. They had a four-year-old and college to save for and nearly no savings. They'd put off having a second kid because they couldn't afford it.

The coffee flowed into the mug Nicole had left in place. She waited until it was nearly full, then expertly shifted the mug out of the way and the carafe into its spot without missing a drop. She inhaled the perfect earthy scent before taking her first sip of the day.

"Mommy?"

She took another quick sip, then turned as Tyler walked into the kitchen. He was tousled and still half-asleep. One hand held his battered, red stuffed toy, Brad the Dragon. The well-loved plush dragon was based on the popular series of children's books. The author must make a mint from all the merchandising, she thought as she put her mug on the counter, then bent down to scoop up her son.

She wrapped her arms around his waist. He settled his around her neck, while hanging on with his legs. She pretended to stagger as she lifted him.

"You grew!"

He giggled at the familiar comment. "I can't grow *every* night," he told her.

"I think you can."

She kissed his cheek and breathed in the scent of his skin. Whatever else went wrong in her day, Tyler was always right.

"How did you sleep?"

"Good." He snuggled close. "Brad had bad dreams, but I said he was safe with me."

"That's very nice of you. I'm sure he appreciated having you to protect him."

She carried Tyler over to the table. He released her to stand on his chair. With a quick, graceful movement, he settled into a sitting position.

Based on how athletic he was and how well he did in preschool, Tyler seemed to have inherited the best from her and Eric. Nicole could only hope. She'd wanted to enroll him in a dance class, but Eric had nixed the idea. For a while he'd wanted his son to attend a computer camp. But that interest had faded when he'd started writing his screenplay last year. She supposed they could agree on drama camp or something. Assuming Eric didn't stop writing his screenplay to follow another surprise dream.

She walked over to the pantry. "Oatmeal and berries?" she asked.

Tyler looked at Brad the Dragon, then nodded. "We like that."

Because Brad was consulted on most decisions.

Nicole would have been worried about her son's constant companion, except Brad stayed home when Tyler went to preschool or day care and from everything she'd read, his attachment was completely normal. She was sure having a couple more siblings would ease his dependence on the stuffed toy, but there was no way that was happening anytime soon. She was barely able to keep them financially afloat as it was. If she got pregnant... She didn't want to think about it.

Not that it was much of an issue. She barely saw Eric these days. They passed in the hall and their brief discussions were generally about logistics regarding Tyler. Sex wasn't happening.

As she measured out the oatmeal, she mentally paused to wonder if Eric was cheating on her. He was by himself every day. She didn't know how much time he spent writing. She wasn't here to see for herself and he didn't volunteer the information. Once he was done surfing for the day, he could be seeing anyone.

Her stomach tightened at the thought, then she turned her attention back to getting breakfast for her son. She had to get Tyler fed and dressed with one eye on the clock. Once she got him to preschool, she had a full day of classes to teach, payroll to run for her two part-time instructors, groceries to buy and life to deal with. Worrying about Eric's possible affairs was way down on her list.

As she carried the oatmeal over to Tyler, she thought maybe her lack of concern was the biggest problem of all. The question was: What, if anything, did she do about it?

Pam wrapped her towel around her body and reached for the tube of body lotion. While she stuck to a fairly faithful regimen for her face, when it came to body products, she liked to mix things up. Right now she was enjoying Philosophy's Fresh Cream—a vanilla-based scent that made her feel like she should have chocolate-dipped strawberries for breakfast.

But for once the thick lotion didn't make her smile. Probably because she was fully aware that while she was applying it, she was doing her best not to look in the mirror.

The shock of Jen's impending ten-year high school reunion hadn't gone away. It had faded, only to return. Telling herself age was a number and she was a lucky, happy woman wasn't helping, either. It seemed as if every time she turned around, there was yet another reminder that her days of being a hot thirtysomething were long over.

She put down the tube, braced herself for the horror and tossed the towel over the tub. Then she stared at her naked self in the very wide, very unforgiving mirror in the master bath.

She wasn't fat, she told herself. She'd gained the most weight with Jen when she'd thought pregnancy meant a license to eat. And she had. Yes, her daughter had been a robust eight pounds and the rest of the associated goo had some weight and volume, but it didn't excuse the seventy-five pounds she'd packed on.

Losing them had been a bitch, so with her next two pregnancies, she'd only gained a reasonable thirty. Still, her body bore the battle wounds—including stretch marks and a definite doughlike puddle where her once-flat tummy had been.

Her breasts were worse. More tube socks than mammary-shaped. She got by with a good, supportive bra. Of course at night, when she just had on a sleep shirt, they eased back into her armpits. On the plus side, getting a mammogram wasn't a problem. Her breasts oozed into place on the tray. Still, there'd been a time when they'd been full and round and damned sexy.

There were a handful of spider veins on her legs, a distinct lack of firmness to her jaw and—

"Kill me now," Pam muttered out loud, then reached for her panties. What was the point in all that self-assessment? It wasn't as if she was going to get any kind of plastic surgery. She worked out three days a week at Nicole's studio and walked on the treadmill at least two other days. She was fifty. She'd better get used to not being anything special. She had a feeling it was only downhill from here.

She finished dressing, then combed her hair off her face. At least it was still thick and had a nice wave. She kept the length just past her shoulders and layered, to take advantage of the waves. Color and a few highlights in summer meant no one had to know about the en-croaching gray.

The thing was, she thought as she applied her anti-aging serum—the one that didn't seem to be doing its job as well as it had a couple of years ago—there wasn't any warning. Sure, everyone knew that old age was in-evitable. It was that or death and she was willing to admit she was pretty happy to be alive.

But what about the rest of it? AARP had been chasing her for the past six or eight months. In addition to their chronic invitations to join, they should send a heartfelt letter that told the truth. Something along the lines of "enjoy it now—in ten years, you're going to look in the mirror and see your grandmother staring back at you."

Perhaps not the most effective marketing campaign, but at least it would be honest.

She patted the eye cream into place, then used her fingertips to pull at her skin. What about a face-lift?

She studied the results, liking how pulling her skin up and back gave her a nice taut look. She didn't want to be scary—one of those women who almost seemed plastic. But maybe a little nip and tuck wouldn't hurt.

She dropped her arms to her sides and watched her face return to its normal position. Who was she kidding? She wasn't ever going to have a face-lift. Surgery on her face for vanity? No way. She wasn't some megarich celebrity. She was a normal woman freaking out about the unkindness of time and gravity.

She leaned closer to the mirror. Although maybe she could get some kind of injection. A filler or BOTOX. Didn't everyone do BOTOX these days?

She left the bathroom and walked into the bedroom. Her morning chores awaited. John had left for the office nearly an hour before, but there was still plenty to do. Make the bed, throw in some laundry, clean up the kitchen dishes. She had a once-monthly cleaning service come in. Those hardworking women always made her feel guilty, but she still let them scrub her floors.

After preparing the marinade for the chicken pieces they would be barbecuing that night, Pam collected a light jacket for herself and a violet knit shirt for Lulu. She let the dog out for a quick potty break, then picked her up and tucked her under her arm. They had an appointment with the vet.

While Lulu was a sweet, loving, well-behaved little girl, she came with several expected Chinese crested issues. She had skin allergies and soft teeth, luxating patellas and tummy problems. They were lucky in that her eyes were fine. And her moving kneecap didn't seem to be a problem yet. John said it was because the dog never walked anywhere.

"You're cute," Pam told her pet as she carried her to her small SUV. "Of course people want to carry you."

Lulu was six years old and had a veterinary file so thick, it was broken up into two folders at the vet's office. Pam had a feeling that a lot of other families wouldn't have been able to afford her chronic medical costs, but she and John were blessed. For all his complaints that Lulu cost as much as sending any one of their kids to college, the truth was, he adored her.

Now Pam climbed into the driver's seat of her SUV. Lulu scrambled into her doggie car seat. Pam put her in her harness and made sure it was attached to the restraining leash, then confirmed the air bag was off.

"Ready to see Dr. Ingersoll?" she asked.

Lulu wagged her tail in agreement.

The drive was only about ten minutes. Come summer, it would take three times that long. Tourists loved Mischief Bay. Despite the fact that it was often warm and sunny all winter long, most visitors didn't bother their little community until Memorial Day weekend. Which made it nice for locals.

Pam drove along T Street and then turned right into the parking lot of Bayside Veterinary. Lulu whined until she was released from her harness, then jumped into Pam's arms for the short carry inside.

"Hi, everyone," Pam said as they walked into the foyer.

The two receptionists smiled at her. "Good to see you, Pam. How's our favorite girl?"

"Doing well on the new cream."

Pam set Lulu on the ground. The slightly pink dog with the dark patches raced behind the counter and greeted the two women.

There was much skittering of nails on linoleum and yips of excitement as she was given her soft cookie. When Lulu finished munching, she returned to Pam and waited to be picked up.

Heidi, one of the techs in the office, appeared with Lulu's file. "He's just finishing up with another patient. Let's get her weighed and in a room."

Pam carried Lulu to the scale in the hallway. Lulu sat obligingly until she was told she could move.

"Exactly ten pounds," Heidi said, making a note. "Same as always. I wish I could maintain my weight as well."

"Me, too," Pam admitted.

"We're in room two."

Lulu jumped off the scale and led the way through the open doorway. Pam picked her up and put her on the examination table while Heidi went through the usual visit stats. Seconds later she left Pam alone and a few minutes after that, Dr. Fraser Ingersoll walked in.

"How's my best girl?" he asked with a smile.

Pam knew he was asking the question of Lulu, but every now and then she pretended it was addressed to her.

Dr. Ingersoll, a tall, slim, dark-haired man in his early forties, radiated sex appeal. Pam couldn't explain it, nor did she want to. It was one of those things best left undefined.

She was sure half his female pet parents had a mad crush on him, and she was comfortable adding herself to the ranks of the swooning. Vivid blue eyes stared out from behind adorable glasses. He always had an easy smile ready, along with a quick touch of reassurance. Sometimes, it seemed to her, that touch lingered.

While she loved John and would never do anything to screw up her marriage, every now and then she allowed herself a little daydream. One involved a request from Dr. Ingersoll to meet for coffee. She would reluctantly agree, he would suggest a place outside of Mischief Bay and she would pretend not to know why. Over lattes and muffins, he would confess his attraction to her and while she would be genuinely tempted, in the end, she would let him down as gently as she could. After all, she was a married woman. She might not have been a virgin on her wedding day, but John was the only man she'd ever been with. She wanted to *fantasize* about Dr. Ingersoll, not actually sleep with him.

Still, those little moments helped when her day was tedious or she was annoyed by always having to take care of everyone.

But now she was less sure of her crush. Did Dr. Ingersoll see her as a sexy, slightly older, vital woman? Or was she simply Lulu's old and wrinkled pet mom?

"How's the new skin cream working?" the vet asked. He stroked Lulu as he spoke.

"She's scratching less."

"Her skin looks clear."

Pam watched him pet her dog and noticed that while the backs of his hands were smooth and taut, she'd developed a few age spots on hers. She held in a sigh. She didn't like this, she admitted to herself. Not the questioning or the concerns. Not the self-absorption. She'd always considered her life to be one that was blessed. She was lucky. Lucky people didn't get old and wrinkly, did they?

Which brought her back to what the AARP really should be doing for their future members—warning them about the coming apocalypse of old age.

Shannon finished the quarterly reports and hit the send button. She would meet with the CEO later to discuss the actual results, but she wasn't worried. The numbers looked good.

She'd recently revamped the timetables and discounts in accounts payable. Cash flow was better, which meant the company's expansion could be funded internally. When interest rates were low, taking out a loan made sense, but she had a feeling they were going to start climbing. Better to keep the money at home.

While a lot of finance people saw the products their companies produced as interchangeable "widgets," she didn't agree. Every company was different. The challenges to produce a physical good varied between industries and even within them. Cars were different from furniture and software was nothing like envelopes. Her attitude had been the key reason she'd been hired nearly five years before. Nolan could have hired any one of a dozen applicants, but he'd chosen her. She had a feeling her rant on the fact that manufacturing products shouldn't be reduced to the pejorative term "widget" was a part of the reason.

She glanced out the big window by her desk. The sun had set a while ago. There was no hint of light coming from the sky—not counting the bright lights from around the office building, of course. She'd been at the office since six thirty and except for taking a class at Mischief in Motion during her lunch break, she'd pretty much been chained to her desk.

She saved her files and began to shut down her computer. She would stop for some Thai food on her way home and spend a quiet evening by herself.

Because she didn't have a date. Certainly not with Adam, who had yet to call after their single meeting.

She'd been hopeful, she thought as she watched her computer move from saving to shutting down. Hopeful that he was man enough to accept her success, her career demands, to respect them, even. But he hadn't and that meant he wasn't for her. But being logical didn't help the dull ache she'd learned to recognize as loneliness.

Sure there were friends she could call. With Eric so busy with his screenwriting, Nicole was often up for dinner out. Tyler came with her, which was fine with Shannon. She enjoyed hanging out with the charming, happy little boy. Or she could see if Pam and John wanted some company for an after-dinner glass of wine. No doubt there would be delicious leftovers for her to dine on.

But while she loved her friends, she wasn't lonely because of them. Every now and then, she wanted to find "the one." That ridiculous concept she'd been unable to shake, no matter how she tried. Sometimes Shannon worried that all the talk about pair bonding in humans just might be true.

She pulled open the bottom desk drawer and removed her handbag. She reached for her cell only to have it buzz with an incoming call.

The screen flashed with the icon she'd linked with the name. A skull and crossbones. Humorous, but also a warning. Because hearing from Quinn was never good.

She considered letting the call go to voice mail. Mostly because that was the safest action. He wouldn't leave a message. No doubt she wouldn't hear from him for weeks. But if she did answer…

She grabbed her phone and pushed the talk button.

"Hello?"

"Gorgeous."

That was all it took. A single word in that low, smoky voice. Her tension eased, her breathing slowed and between her legs she felt the telltale combination of hunger and dampness. She could talk all the successful-career, self-actualized crap she wanted, but at the end of the day, she was little more than Quinn's bitch.

"Hey," she murmured, even as she glanced at the clock on the wall and calculated how long it would take her to drive to Malibu at this time of the evening.

"Come over."

Quinn didn't ask. He instructed. He took charge. It was the same in bed, where he decided what they were going to do and who came first. She should have resented it, but she didn't. There was something to be said for a man who took charge. She relaxed around him because there was no point in fighting the tide.

"I can't stay," she said—a feeble attempt to take control. But she'd learned the hard truth. Better to get what she wanted and escape than spend the night.

"No problem."

There was a soft click. She knew the call had been disconnected.

She dropped her cell into her handbag, then crossed to the private bathroom that came with her C level title. After using the bathroom, she freshened her makeup and brushed her teeth. Then she left and headed for her car.

The drive to Malibu was simple. Head north on Pacific Coast Highway, which became Sepulveda and a half dozen other streets through Marina del Rey and Venice. She picked it up again in Santa Monica, then followed the road until she reached Malibu.

When people thought of that town they pictured beachfront mansions and star sightings. Both were plentiful, but much of the community was also old and a little worn around the edges. Tiny restaurants favored by locals nestled against the larger, more famous attractions, like Gladstone's.

Shannon turned onto a small street. In one of those weird L.A. ironies, the most beautiful homes often had completely deceptive entrances. There was a garage, a secured gate and what looked like the beginning of a modest thousand-square-foot bungalow. All of which concealed eight or ten million dollars' worth of luxury living and incredible views.

Quinn's house was similar, although his gate kept anyone from pulling into the driveway. Shannon punched in the code. In that split second before the heavy iron gate swung open, she wondered if it would. Because she knew there would come a day when her code would no longer work. She often told herself that would be a good thing. Some days she even believed herself.

But it wasn't tonight, she thought as she drove into the open garage and parked next to his Maserati.

She got out and walked inside.

Quinn's house was built on the side of a cliff. The tri-level home was probably about five or six thousand square feet with an unobstructed view of the ocean from all three levels. During the day, the rooms were filled with light. At night, electric blinds protected the privacy from those who would try to capture a glimpse of how the beautiful people lived.

Shannon left her shoes in the foyer by the garage door and walked barefoot through the living room. Music played. She didn't recognize the man singing, but she was sure he was one of Quinn's latest finds.

A couple of lamps had been left on to guide her, but she could have found her way blindfolded. She ignored the elegant furniture, the expensive artwork, the too casually arranged throw pillows and headed for the stairs.

Down a floor was the kitchen and another living room. This was where Quinn spent most of his time. The upper floor was for entertaining. A dumb waiter allowed whatever catering service he was using to deliver food quickly and easily.

Instead of elegance, this level was all about comfort. Oversize leather furniture and a giant TV on the wall dominated the room. The electronic equipment could probably intimidate a NASA scientist. Being a successful music producer paid well.

Shannon circled to the final staircase and took it down a floor. She passed a small guest room and walked into the master.

The glass doors were open. Cool night air and the sound of the ocean mingled with the scent of wood burning in the fireplace. There was a large, custom bed, a couple of chairs and a man. Her attention zeroed in on the latter.

Quinn had been reading. He put down his e-reader and rose as she approached. His blond hair was too long, his blue eyes slightly hooded. He was the kind of man who took what he wanted and he looked the part. Despite the loose cotton shirt and chinos, he was dangerous. Like a beautiful, yet venomous snake—the more appealing the appearance, the more you had to beware.

She dropped her bag onto the carpet. He removed his shirt by simply pulling it over his head and tossing it aside. His pants followed. Being Quinn, he didn't bother with underwear.

Shannon studied the honed lines of his body. Defined muscles swooped and hollowed. The man was pushing forty and yet could have easily been hired as a butt double for stars half his age.

He was already aroused.

She hesitated. Just for a second. It was like being in the first week of a diet when cravings were insistent and tempers ran high, and someone offered you a brownie. Did you accept it and promise to start again tomorrow, or did you do the right thing, take the empowering step and walk away?

She knew she'd already made her decision. Answering the call had been the equivalent of picking up that brownie. Now all she had to do was take that first bite.

She walked over to him. Quinn drew her close and kissed her. With the stroke of his tongue, she surrendered to the inevitable and promised herself she would do better tomorrow.

Four

"And hold," Nicole said, her tone encouraging. "Five seconds more."

Pam stayed in the plank position. Every muscle in her body trembled with the effort, but she was determined to make it the entire minute. The image of her naked self still haunted her. The least she could do was give her all in exercise class.

"Time," Nicole called. "And you're done, ladies."

Pam collapsed onto the mat for a second to catch her breath. Her stomach muscles were still quivering. She would be sore well into tomorrow, which was kind of depressing considering she did three classes a week.

She rose and staggered over to the shelf that held the cleaner spray and the towels, and wiped down her mat and the equipment she'd used. The other students did the same. She kept her eye on Shannon, wanting to make sure they had a chance to talk. She figured of all the women she knew, Shannon was the one most likely to have a referral. Or at least be able to get one.

"She's trying to kill us," Pam said, moving next to the annoyingly firm redhead.

"I think that, too."

They collected their personal belongings from the cubbies by the waiting area. Lulu stood and stretched. Pam stuffed the blanket Lulu had been on into her tote, then walked toward the door. Lulu walked along with her.

When they were outside and heading for their cars, Pam scooped up the dog and wondered how exactly she was supposed to bring up such a personal topic.

"Do you have a second?" she asked.

Shannon stopped and faced her. "Sure. What's up?"

Pam took a second to admire the other woman's smooth face. No saggy jawline for her. And her skin was really bright. Pam had noticed a couple of dark spots on her cheek and forehead. All that time in the sun when she'd been a teenager was coming back to haunt her. Day by day her complexion was moving from human to dalmatian.

"I don't mean to imply anything," Pam began, wishing she'd planned this better. "Or be insulting. It's just… I don't know who else to ask."

Shannon's mouth curved into a smile. "I suddenly feel like you're going to ask me if I've had a sex change operation. The answer is no."

Pam tried to smile. "It's not that. I was thinking about maybe getting some BOTOX and wondered if you knew anyone who ever had or something."

"Oh, sure. That's easy. Of course I can give you a name. I have a person."

Pam frowned. "A person who does it?"

"Sure."

"Because you get it?"

"I have for about five years."

Pam's frown deepened as she studied her friend. "But your face is so smooth and natural looking."

"Which is kind of the point," Shannon told her. "I've been using it to prevent wrinkles."

"They can do that?"

"They can." Shannon moved her hair off her forehead. "I'm trying to scowl. Any movement?"

"Not much."

"So it works. I'll email the contact info for the place where I go. They're very good. The shots hurt—I won't lie. But after it's done, it's no big deal. Then about a week later, you have fewer wrinkles."

"That sounds easy," Pam murmured, even as she wondered if she'd left it too long. She was years past preventative care.

"I love it," Shannon told her. "But I will warn you, it's a slick road to more work. I'm flirting with the idea of injectable. Maybe a little filler in my lips, that kind of thing."

"Filler?" Pam's stomach got a little queasy. "I'm not sure I'm ready for that."

"So start with BOTOX. The rest will be waiting."

"Thanks."

They chatted for a few more minutes, then headed to their cars. As Pam strapped in Lulu, she sighed.

"I was kind of hoping she would tell me I didn't need anything done," she admitted.

Lulu wagged her tail.

"Be grateful," she told the dog. "You'll always be a natural beauty."

Nicole walked into the house at 6:28 p.m. Not a personal best, but pretty darned good, she thought. She ignored the ache in her back and her legs and how all she wanted to do was sleep for the next twenty-four hours. At least tonight was one of her early nights. Tuesdays and Thursdays she worked until eight.

"Mommy's home! Mommy's home!"

Tyler's happy voice and the clatter of his feet as he raced toward her made her smile. On Mondays, Wednesdays and Fridays she didn't get to see him in the morning. Her first class started at six, which meant she was up and out by five thirty.

She dropped her bag on the floor and held out her arms. Tyler raced around the corner and flung himself at her. She caught him and pulled him close.

"How's my best boy?"

"Good. I missed you. I practiced my reading today and Daddy made sketty for dinner."

"Spaghetti, huh? Sounds yummy."

"It was." He kissed her on the lips, then leaned his head against her cheek. "I love you, Mommy."

"I love you, too, little man."

She lowered him to the floor. Tyler headed back to the living room and she walked into the kitchen. There were dishes everywhere. The plastic container that had contained the "sketty" Tyler had enjoyed, along with everything from breakfast and lunch.

The pain in her legs moved up to her back. Frustration joined weariness. She walked into the bedroom and saw the laundry she'd sorted at five that morning still in piles. Hadn't he done anything?

Eric walked into the kitchen and smiled at her. "Hey, hon. How was your day?" As he spoke, he stepped close and kissed her. "I know you're going to say fine and that you're tired, but I gotta tell you, you look hot in work-out clothes."

The compliment defused her annoyance for a second. "Thank you and my day was fine. Long, but good. How was yours?"

"Excellent. I rewrote a scene three times but now I have it right. At least I hope so. I'll find out at my critique group on Saturday. In the meantime, I have class tonight, so I'll see you later."

She stared at the man she'd married. He was so similar to the guy she remembered and yet so totally different. He still wore his hair a little too long and had hideous taste in loud Hawaiian shirts. But the old Eric had taken care of the details of their life, while this guy didn't seem to notice anything beyond his screenplay.

She told herself to breathe. That yelling never accomplished anything.

"I'd love to read the new scene," she told him.

"You will. When it's perfect."

The same answer she always received. Because he'd yet to let her read a word of his work. Which sometimes left her wondering if he was writing anything at all. Which made her feel guilty, which led to her wanting to bang her head against the wall in frustration.

"I gotta run." He kissed her again, then straightened. "Well, shit. I forgot to do the dishes. Leave them. I'll do them when I get home. Or in the morning. I promise."

"Okay," she murmured, knowing she would do them herself. Something inside of her made it impossible to relax with a sink full of dishes sitting around. "Any chance you got to the sheets today?"

His expression turned blank. "Did I say I would?"

"Yeah, you did."

"Oh, man. I'm sorry."

"I appreciate that, but Eric, we need to talk about this. You're excited about your screenplay and that's great, but lately it seems you're doing less and less around here."

"I'm not. I do the grocery shopping and take care of Tyler when he's not in day care. I forgot the dishes, but I'll do them. And the laundry." His expression tightened. "You have to understand. It's all about the writing for me. I've got to focus. That's my job. I know it's not paying anything right now, but it will. When I'm working, I'm as committed as you are at your job. I need you to respect my time."

"I do." Sort of, she thought grimly. "I need to be able to depend on you."

"You can. Trust me." He glanced at his watch. After picking up his backpack, he headed for the door. "Tomorrow. I swear. I'll get it all done. Gotta go. Bye."

And he was gone.

She stood alone in the kitchen and let various emotions wash over her. Annoyance, confusion, exhaustion, regret. They churned and heated until they formed a large knot in her belly.

Respect his time writing while she busted her ass to support them all? She closed her eyes. No, she told herself. That wasn't fair. He was working. At least she hoped he was.

The changes in her relationship with her husband had started so quietly, in such tiny increments, that she'd barely noticed. Excluding his decision to quit, of course.

At first he'd taken care of stuff around the house. The laundry, the grocery shopping. But over time, that had changed. He forgot to get everything on the list. He put clothes in the washer, but not the dryer. He didn't pick up

Tyler at day care. Now he wasn't cleaning up the kitchen as he'd promised.

She thought about going after him to talk about what was happening, then shook her head. He would be focused on getting to class. Soon, she promised herself. She would sit down with him and talk about what was wrong. She didn't want to have a roommate, she wanted a husband. Someone who was invested in their family, and not totally focused on his own dream.

Did he really think he was going to sell a screenplay? The odds against that were what? A billion to one? Talk about ridiculous. And yet there was a part of her that wondered if he would make it happen.

The knot in her stomach didn't ease. But that wasn't important right now. She picked up the empty laundry basket. Prioritize, she told herself. She could probably stay awake through two loads, so which were the most important?

Five minutes later their old washer was chugging away. She turned the radio on to an oldies station and danced with Tyler as they worked together to tidy the kitchen. Or rather she worked and he shimmied while "Help Me, Rhonda" played. By seven the dishes were in the dishwasher and the food put away. Tyler had had his bath the previous night so they had a whole hour before his bedtime.

She sank onto the floor in front of her son and smiled at him. "What would you like to do? We could play a game, or watch a show." She didn't offer to read a story, because that went without saying. Except for the two nights she worked late, she always read him a story. Usually some adventure about wily Brad the Dragon.

"A movie!"

"There's only an hour."

"Okay."

Tyler took off running toward the family room. His shows and movies were on a lower shelf where he could browse on his own. She walked to the refrigerator and opened the door. Nothing much inspired her, although she knew she had to eat. She picked a blueberry yogurt and an apple.

"This one," Tyler told her, holding out a familiar and battered DVD case.

Nicole studied the grainy picture on the front. It was sixteen years old. She'd been all of fourteen and this was a copy of her audition performance for The School of American Ballet in New York. For their summer session.

Not the actual audition. No one was allowed to watch, let alone record that. But she'd re-created the dance for her mother. On the same DVD were a half dozen other performances.

"Honey, you've seen that so many times," she reminded her son. "Don't you want to watch something else?"

He thrust out the DVD—his small face set in a stubborn expression she recognized.

"Okay, then. Dancing it is."

She put in the DVD, then settled on the sofa. Tyler cuddled up next to her. She offered him some of her yogurt, but he shook his head. On the TV, the picture flickered, then familiar music filled the room.

Nicole watched her much younger self perform. She was all legs, she thought, without the usual gangliness of adolescence. Probably because she'd been studying dance since she'd been Tyler's age.

She'd made it into the summer program only to be

told at the end that she didn't have what it took to make it professionally in ballet. At the time she'd been both heartbroken and secretly relieved. Because her being a famous ballerina had been her mother's dream for her.

Nicole's mother had cried for two days, then come up with a new plan. There were many kinds of dance, she'd informed her only child. Nicole was going to conquer them all. There had also been acting classes and voice lessons. She'd barely managed to get the grades to graduate from high school because she was always attending some coaching session or another.

On the screen, the scene shifted to yet another performance. Nicole figured she'd been about seventeen. It was the year her mother had started complaining of headaches. By the time Nicole had received word of a full dance scholarship at Arizona State University, her mother had been diagnosed with an inoperable brain tumor. The funeral had been the Saturday before Labor Day. Nicole had already started at ASU.

So many choices made that weren't really choices at all, she thought, pleased she'd reached the point of only sadness. For a long time she'd tasted bitterness, too, when she'd thought about her past. Maybe watching the DVDs with Tyler helped. He only saw the beauty of the dance. There weren't any emotional judgments. No history fogged his vision.

Nicole hadn't been so lucky. Her mother had wanted her to be a star. The origin of the dream wasn't clear. Something from her own childhood perhaps. But they hadn't talked about that. Instead, their most intimate conversations had been about how Nicole could do better, be better. Always strive for more, her mother had told her. How disappointed she would be today.

Sometimes Nicole wondered if she was disappointed, too. How different things would have been if she'd been just a bit better. A hair more talented. Not that regrets helped, she reminded herself. They only wasted time and energy because regrets didn't change anything.

She stared at the screen and watched her younger self dance with a grace and confidence that seemed to be lacking these days. While she didn't regret not being famous, she knew that somewhere along the way she'd lost something important. All the elements of a happy life were there—a growing small business, a husband, a wonderful son, friends—but somehow they didn't come together the way they should. She accepted the exhaustion. That came with the territory. It was everything else—the sense of never having quite found what made her happy, the wondering if she'd made a mistake somewhere along the way. That was what kept her up nights.

Sunday morning Pam double-checked the contents of her refrigerator. The whole family was coming over for dinner later that afternoon and she needed to make sure she had all she needed.

Sunday dinners were an Eiland family tradition. When the kids had been younger, they were all required to be home by four, regardless of whatever fun they might be having somewhere else. Exceptions were made for travel, of course, and now, vacations. But otherwise, Sunday dinners were required.

During the summer, they were casual affairs, mostly outside with barbecued whatever as the entrée. Come September, there was usually a football game playing and when favorite rivalries were on the line, dinner became a buffet in the family room.

For today Pam had decided on prime rib. She'd ordered a large one so she and John could have plenty of leftovers. The rest of the menu was simple. Mashed potatoes and green beans. Steven, their middle child, had requested her jalapeño-corn biscuits. She'd made pies yesterday. Custard and chocolate. She liked to do as much in advance as possible so that when her kids arrived, she didn't have to spend all her time in the kitchen.

She wandered into the dining room and walked to the built-in hutch along the far wall. She opened the cabinet doors and studied the stacked dishes. There were three sets of them, all inherited from grandmothers. One was only used for special occasions. She looked at the other two and picked up a side plate with blue-and-green swirls. She put it on the table, along with a tablecloth and a stack of napkins. John would set the table later, using what she'd set out.

There would be six of them today. Jen and her husband, Kirk, Steven and Brandon. Steven used to be allowed to bring a date but he went through women like most people went through chewing gum. Pam had grown tired of liking girl after girl only to have them disappear. It was discouraging. Now Steven was under a very strict rule. No girlfriends allowed at family functions until they'd been together for at least six months. Which meant they hadn't met anyone he'd dated in the past three years.

She told herself he would grow out of it. He was only twenty-six. Which seemed young. How funny. John had only been twenty-two when they'd gotten married. But times were different now. People were different.

The doorbell rang and Lulu took off toward it, barking excitedly.

Pam followed her. "You know, I can hear it, too."

Lulu was unimpressed by the information and continued to bark until Pam scooped her up and opened the door.

Hayley Batchelor held out a plate of cookies. "Hi. I haven't seen you in forever. Is this a good time?"

"Sure."

Pam stepped back to let in her neighbor and John's secretary. Hayley set down the plate of cookies and held out her arms. Lulu made an easy jump from one cuddler to the other.

"How's my favorite girl?" Hayley asked.

Lulu snuggled close and gave a quick chin kiss.

"So sweet," Hayley murmured. "Why did your mom get you fixed? There could have been more Lulus in the world."

"Given her health issues, I don't think that's a good idea," Pam told her. "Come on. I have herbal tea in the kitchen."

"John told you," Hayley said.

"He did. Congratulations. You must be excited."

"I am. It's going to be different this time. It has to be."

Pam admired her determination and belief. Hayley had suffered a series of miscarriages in her quest to get pregnant. She'd been probed and tested and there didn't seem to be any specific reason for the problem. She wasn't allergic to her husband's sperm—or so she'd shared with Pam a year ago. Pam hadn't known such a thing could happen. Allergic to sperm? What were their bodies thinking?

The plumbing all worked and was in the right place, the hormone levels were good, she wasn't lacking in any vitamins or minerals. But Hayley was unable to carry a baby past twelve weeks.

With the last pregnancy, she'd gone straight to bed rest the second she'd found out she was pregnant and that hadn't helped, either.

Now Hayley sat in one of the stools at the bar-level counter while Pam put water on to boil. She pulled out her tea tray and chose her friend's favorite—a white tea with pear.

"How far along are you?" she asked.

"Seven weeks. Only five more to go."

"You feeling okay?"

"I feel great."

Pam nodded. So that wasn't different. Hayley always felt perfectly healthy right up until she started bleeding.

"I wish I could help," Pam told her. "Give you something."

"You offering to be my surrogate?" Hayley asked, her voice teasing.

"God, no."

Hayley laughed. "I figured." Her humor faded a little. "I appreciate what you're saying, though. I'd like some of whatever magic it is that so many other women get to take for granted."

Pam nodded. She'd been pregnant three times and had three healthy children to show for it. She'd suffered bad morning sickness with Brandon, but otherwise, the pregnancies had been uneventful. She'd never considered how many other women had to deal with so much more.

"How's Rob doing?" she asked.

Rob, Hayley's husband, worked two jobs to help pay for the various fertility treatments Hayley wanted them to try. He was a good guy and Pam knew he worried about his wife.

"Good," Hayley said brightly. "Excited I'm pregnant again."

Pam nodded without speaking. She would bet Rob was a whole lot more worried than excited. She knew he wanted Hayley to stop trying. To give her body a rest. Not that Hayley listened.

Pam poured boiling water into two mugs and passed one to Hayley, along with the tea bag and spoon. She dropped a bag of Earl Grey into her mug just as John strolled into the kitchen.

"Hey," he said as he walked around to Hayley and gave her a quick hug. "How's my favorite secretary?"

"Good."

"I see you brought cookies. I've always liked you. Remind me to give you a raise on Monday."

Hayley grinned. "I will."

John winked at Pam, took a couple of cookies from the plate and headed for the garage. Lulu, sensing the possibility of a snack, followed her dad.

"John is about the nicest man I know," Hayley said when the door had closed. "Everybody at work loves him."

"I was lucky to find him," Pam said, knowing that nice was more important than exciting and after thirty years anyone—even George Clooney—could seem less thrilling. It was simply how life worked.

Hayley mentioned something about the hotel project the company was working on. Pam mostly listened. The light had shifted and she noticed a subtle glow to her friend's skin.

Hayley was what? Thirty? Thirty-one. She had a firm jaw and no wrinkles at all. Her hands and arms were so smooth. Pam drew in a breath as she realized that except for John, she was nearly always the oldest person in the room. And while she should probably be happy that so many young people wanted to hang out with her, she would rather it was because she was young, too.

She mentally gave herself a firm shake. She had to stop thinking about herself all the time. She was becoming obsessed and tedious.

She tuned back in to Hayley's conversation and laughed over a comment about a client.

"I should head home," Hayley said, coming to her feet. "Thanks for the tea and the company."

"When does Rob come back?" One of Rob's two jobs involved business travel.

"In a few days."

"If you need anything or get scared, just grab your pillow and come over," Pam told her. "You're always welcome. We have that guest room sitting empty."

Hayley nodded, then hugged her. "Thanks. It helps to know you're right across the street."

"And down two houses. You go across the street, you'll find yourself at the Logans' and they have those really mean cats."

Hayley laughed. "Good point."

Pam walked her out. When she turned to go back to the kitchen, she saw John and Lulu walking toward her.

"Everything okay with her?" he asked.

"So far." She drew in a breath. "I don't want to send a message to the universe or anything, but I have a bad feeling about this. Why can't the doctors figure out the problem? And when are they going to tell her that all these miscarriages are a bad idea?"

She'd bled a lot with the last one and Pam had ended up insisting she go to emergency.

John put his arm around her. "She really wants a baby."

"And I want her to have one. Just not like this."

Her husband squeezed, then released her. "Jen texted me. She and Kirk are coming over an hour early. They want to talk."

Pam pressed her lips together. "Why didn't she text me?"

"Probably because she knew you would ask questions."

"Didn't you? Is something wrong?" A thousand possibilities, all of them horrible, flashed through her mind. "You don't think one of them is sick, do you? Or maybe Kirk shot someone and is going to be indicted for murder." She pressed a hand to her chest as her breathing hitched. "Oh, God. What if they're getting a divorce?"

Her husband chuckled. "I have to admire your ability to see disaster in every situation. You think they'd tell us that together, before Sunday dinner?"

"Probably not."

"Then maybe stay calm until we hear what it's about. For all we know, they want to move in with us to save money."

Pam rolled her eyes. "Don't even joke about that." Her mind stopped swirling with disastrous possibilities and she tried to think of good ones. "I wonder if they're getting that puppy they've been talking about. Jen called me last week to ask about how long it took to house-train Lulu. A puppy would be nice."

"I'm sure they're getting a puppy."

"I don't know if that's a great idea. They both work, so they're gone all day."

John kissed the top of her head. "You are the queen of finding the cloud in every silver lining."

She smiled. "Okay. Point taken. I'm going to get the roast ready."

"Need any help?"

"No, thanks."

She returned to the kitchen, Lulu walking beside her. The dog curled up in her kitchen bed while Pam set the roast on the counter. She would let it warm up for about an hour before popping it in the oven. In the meantime she could peel the four hundred pounds of potatoes they would be eating tonight. Unlike a lot of their friends, she and John saw their grown kids a lot. They'd stayed close geographically and seemed to like hanging out with their parents.

So far they'd been blessed with their children. Jen, their oldest, had been sweet and funny. Steven had been a typical boy—always getting into trouble. But he had a good heart and lots of friends. Brandon, their youngest, had been more difficult. He'd been moody and attracted to trouble. High school had been hell. He'd skipped class, hung out with horrible kids and discovered he liked to party. The summer he turned seventeen, he'd wrapped his car around a tree.

Angels had been with him, Pam thought, as she peeled her potatoes. The crash should have killed him, yet he'd walked away with nothing more than some bruises and a broken arm.

She and John hadn't known what to do, so they'd erred on the side of tough love. They'd sent him to rehab for six weeks. Not one of those touchy-feely kinds with meetings where you shared and did crafts, but one with a boot-camp philosophy and lots of lectures from people in recovery. Brandon had quickly realized he was far from the biggest, baddest dog in the pack. He'd come home older, wiser and, most important, sober.

He'd completed his senior year with a 4.0 GPA and had made what had seemed like the impossible decision to be a doctor. But he'd stuck with it and was now in his second year of medical school.

"My son, the doctor," Pam murmured.

They were all in a good place right now. She would be grateful and not borrow trouble. Although she did think that Jen and Kirk might not be ready for a puppy.

Five

Pam sat next to John on one sofa while Jen and Kirk sat on the other. Her daughter, a pretty brunette, smiled broadly.

It didn't *seem* like there was anything wrong. They both looked happy. Kirk was relaxed, which he probably wouldn't be if he'd shot someone in the line of duty and was going to prison. Plus, they would have seen it on the news.

Pam glanced at the clock. It was barely two—probably too early to make herself a Cosmo. Although she would like to point out that it was already five in New York and probably tomorrow in Australia.

She reached for John's hand. He gave her fingers a reassuring squeeze.

"All right, you two," he said. "You've kept us in suspense long enough. What's going on? Is it a puppy?"

They were moving, Pam thought, looking at their faces. Kirk had gotten promoted or something. No, that wouldn't work. He was on the Mischief Bay police force. It wasn't as if they were going to relocate him to San Francisco.

Jen glanced again at Kirk, then turned back to her parents. She drew in a breath and laughed.

"No puppy. We're pregnant!"

Pam felt her mouth drop open.

"What?" John stood and crossed to them. "Pregnant? How far along? Did you plan this? Pregnant!" He pulled his daughter into his arms. "My baby's going to be a mommy. That's great, honey. We're so happy for you."

Pam felt the room shift a little. As if one side of the house had suddenly dropped a couple of feet. She managed to stand and felt her face moving, so guessed she'd smiled. Kirk walked up to her and she hugged him because it was the obvious thing to do.

Jen pregnant. There was going to be a baby. She loved babies. Adored them. She couldn't be happier for her daughter and son-in-law. There was only one unbelievable catch.

She was going to be a grandmother.

The Farm Table was an upscale, organic, locally sourced restaurant. The kind of place completely at home in the beachy, LA-vibe quirkiness that was Mischief Bay. Everything in the restaurant was either sustainable or re-purposed. The floors were bamboo, the tables and chairs rarely matched and the dishes were all old Lenox, Spode and Wedgwood patterns. But the odds of any one table getting two place settings that were the same were slim.

Eclectic didn't begin to describe the decor. A combination of elegant, shabby chic and country, with a rabid interest in recycling to the point that the restaurant kept a pig and two goats to eat any food leftovers that couldn't be given to a local organization that specialized in feeding the homeless. The food was extraordinary.

There was generally at least a three-week wait to get a reservation. Which meant getting a call from Adam inviting her to dinner was only half as shocking as hearing his suggestion as to where they would go. The man obviously had some pull, she thought as she stopped in front of the valet and handed over her keys.

She tucked her clutch under her arm, walked into the restaurant and glanced around. Adam was already there, standing in the foyer. He smiled when he saw her—a warm, welcoming smile that made her feel just a little bit giddy.

She was willing to admit she had been more than a little pleased to hear from him. She hadn't thought she would. Now, as she moved toward him, she saw his gaze drop to take in what she was wearing. The sudden widening of his eyes added to her sense of anticipation.

She'd put a lot more thought into what she would wear on this date, as opposed to the last one. Despite the fact that it was late February, this was still Southern California and evening temperatures weren't going to dip below fifty-eight. She'd been able to wear her favorite outfit and bring a pashmina as a wrap.

The dress was one of her rare clothing splurges. An Oscar de la Renta silk cloqué cocktail dress. The fabric—a textured silk—was simply tailored. A scooped-neck tank style, front and back, fitted to the waist, then flaring out. She'd left her red hair loose and wavy, and added diamond studs for her only jewelry. She'd left her legs bare, with only a hint of a shimmery lotion to add a glow, then finished off the outfit with a classic pair of black pumps.

Honestly, she'd been hoping for some kind of a reaction and Adam didn't disappoint. He crossed to her and took both her hands in his.

"I know this is going to get old, but wow."

She smiled. "Thank you. You're looking very handsome yourself."

Dress at The Farm Table was generally nice to fancy. Adam wore a suit and tie. Men had it easy, she thought. Give them some decent tailoring and they look great.

He excused himself and gave his name to the hostess, then returned to her side.

"It'll just be a few minutes."

"Thank you." She stared into his dark eyes. "I was surprised to hear from you."

His brows drew together. "Why?"

"I didn't think our first date went very well."

Genuine confusion tugged at his mouth. "Seriously? I thought it was good. We were getting to know each other. If you thought it went badly, why did you say yes to dinner?"

She touched his arm. "I meant I thought I wouldn't hear from you because I got called back to work. I'm not saying it happens all the time, but when it does, I have to take care of the problem."

There it was—her career out there. So far she liked Adam. He made her hope in a way she hadn't for a long time. But she wasn't going to pretend to be other than who she was for anyone and she wanted to make sure he got that.

He relaxed. "Oh, that. It's okay. You have a job with demands. I do, too. Would you have a problem if I had to cancel because of a crisis at the job site?"

"No."

"So we both get that we have responsibilities."

As easy as that? "It's my turn to say wow."

He chuckled. "If that impresses you, then I'm doing a whole lot better than I thought. Makes me glad I called in all those favors to get the reservation here."

"I am impressed by you and the venue. So it's a win-win."

"I like that in a date."

His gaze dropped to her mouth for just a second longer than was polite.

Shannon knew it was silly to let the man's obvious attraction win her over. She had to be feeling it, too. But she had to admit it was pretty nice to be wanted.

A voice in her head pointed out that Quinn also wanted her. Only it was on his terms, his way, on his schedule. Theirs wasn't a relationship. It was some kind of twisted addiction. Adam just might be the right antidote.

The hostess led them to a small table by a window. They were tucked into a private alcove, a little bit away from the other diners.

"Have you dined here before?" she asked.

They both said they had.

"Then you know how our menu works. The chef has some very special dishes in store for you. Enjoy."

The Farm Table's menu was information, not a choice. The items changed every week and there were a few vegetarian options for main courses. Otherwise, you ate what was put in front of you. They were taking a stand and Shannon could respect that.

She glanced at the five-course menu and was grateful she hadn't put on Spanx. At least she would have some extra room for all the yummy food.

Adam picked up his menu. "What's a squash blossom and how do you put salmon in it?"

"It's a plant."

"You're guessing."

"No, I'm sure it's a plant-based thing that has an opening or can be stuffed or something."

He looked at her, his brows raised.

She sighed. "Fine. I have no idea what it is. I'm sure it's delicious. Do you know what sorrel tastes like? We have sorrel sauce in our third course."

"Not a clue."

"Then I guess we'll find out together."

He nodded and put down his menu. "Want to go with the wine suggestions?"

"Sure."

"Me, too." He leaned toward her. "I really was okay about the job thing."

"I get that now."

"I didn't call right away because I was away on business. The guy who's building the hotel insisted I fly to Denver to meet with him personally. He doesn't like email updates."

"Not a problem."

"I didn't want you to think I was flaky. Or not interested." He leaned back and smiled. "I see the biggest problem here is that you're too attractive. I'm not sure I can see you as a person."

"What would I be if not a person?"

"An object." The smile faded. "All joking aside, Shannon, I'm not in this to get laid. I'm not that guy. Don't get me wrong. Of course I want to sleep with you. I'm breathing, right? I guess what I'm trying to say is I'm a divorced father with two kids and the thought of playing the field exhausts me. I want to find somebody special.

Somebody I can care about and share things with. A relationship, I guess."

He paused and grimaced. "That was sure more than you needed to know. Sorry. Did I mention I'm not the greatest first date?"

"This is our second date."

"That, too."

He looked embarrassed, but she wasn't put off by what he'd said. It was honest, and lately it seemed honest men were hard to find.

He wasn't looking to play games or torment her or be totally in charge. He wanted to connect on a level that was meaningful.

"I appreciate what you've said," she told him. "And I get it." She did her best not to smile. "Especially the part about not wanting to sleep with me. Because every girl longs to hear that."

He groaned. "Of course I want to sleep with you. I said that. I made that really clear."

Their server appeared. If she'd overheard what they were saying, she didn't let on.

"Good evening and welcome to The Farm Table. I'll be taking care of you tonight."

Despite the fact that it was a set menu, it still took a good three or four minutes to perform the niceties and order the wine. After their server left, Shannon stretched out her hand, palm up.

"It's okay," she told Adam.

He put his hand on top of hers. "Yeah?"

"Yeah. I'm not going to sleep with you tonight."

He sighed. "Would you have before I said anything?"

"Not a chance."

He brightened. "Now we're getting somewhere."

"You are very strange."

"I've been told that before."

The server returned with their first glass of wine. When she left Adam raised his.

"To the most beautiful woman I've ever gone out with and the fact that she won't sleep with me."

"At least tonight," she added, before touching his glass with hers.

Adam cleared his throat. "Temptation. I like it."

She laughed and sipped her wine. "I'm going to have to time my tempting moments. You have children and shared custody. How does that work?"

"Friday is our exchange day. My week starts when they get out of school. I have the kids this weekend, but they're spending a night with my folks."

"So no curfew."

"Don't. You're only teasing."

"Yes, I am."

Conversation shifted to his work and the big hotel project. As he described it, Shannon felt as if she'd heard a conversation like this before.

"Do you know John Eiland?" she asked.

"John? Sure. His company is installing all the plumbing. Why?"

"I know them. Pam and I are friends and I hang out at their house every now and then. I've been to the big Memorial Day barbecue they have."

"No way. Was last year your first one, because it's the only one I've missed. I've been going since I was a kid and I would have remembered you."

She laughed. "It was my first. I met Pam at Mischief in Motion. It's an exercise studio. We take a class together three days a week."

He shook his head. "What I would pay to see you work out."

"Really?"

"Too much? Sorry. I'll get my mind back in the game. John's a great guy. And Pam's a sweetie. She reminds me of my mom."

"What are your thoughts on Lulu?" she asked. "Cutest dog ever or frightening genetic experiment?"

"A test. Okay, I'm good at these. Um, great personality, very well trained and the weirdest-looking dog, ever. What's up with the clothes?"

"She's naked. She gets cold." Shannon sipped her wine. "And I agree with you. I love Lulu, but the spots, the pink skin. It's not natural. Dogs should shed. It's nature's way of keeping us humble."

Their first course arrived. Caviar on some kind of leaf with three drizzled sauces. There were also tiny shaved white things—turnips, so they said.

Adam stared at the dish. "You first."

She grinned. "So you're not the wild adventurer type."

"I can be. But turnip and caviar? Who thought that up?"

"The famous chef in the back." She lifted the leaf and took a bite. The saltiness blended with the faint bitterness of the leaf, while the shaved turnip piece was surprisingly sweet.

"It's really good."

Adam looked doubtful but followed her lead. He chewed and swallowed. "I don't hate it."

"Then you need to write a review." She looked around the restaurant. "Pam and John came here for their last anniversary. They are such a great couple. I love watching them together. It makes me believe that true love is possible."

"Otherwise you don't believe?" he asked.

"Not exactly. I think it's hard for people to stay together. I've never gotten married. You're divorced. My friend Nicole, she's the owner of Mischief in Motion, is having trouble in her marriage right now."

"That's never easy," Adam said. "What's going on?"

"Her husband decided to write a screenplay. Only he didn't discuss it with her first. He just quit his job. He hasn't worked in nearly a year. They have an almost five-year-old and Eric barely helps out at all. I feel so badly for her, and I have no idea what to say. It's hard."

"You're a good friend."

"Thanks. I try. Now, tell me about your kids," she urged.

He smiled. "They're great. Char—Charlotte—is going to be nine in a couple of months. Sometimes I swear she's pushing thirty instead. She's bossy and she would draw blood to protect her little brother. She loves anything princess-related and can't wait to start wearing makeup. She's beautiful and I'm terrified to think about her starting to like boys."

He paused. "Oliver is my little man. He's all boy. He likes trucks, building things and breaking things. He's six. He'll be seven this summer."

She could hear the love and pride in his voice, which was very appealing. She'd dated plenty of guys who didn't seem that interested in the families they'd already created. "Do you like having them half the time?"

"I'd rather have them all the time, but I accept the compromise."

"Are you and your ex friendly?"

"We get along. I regret that my marriage failed, but I don't miss our relationship, if that makes sense."

"It does. I like that you don't call her names."

"Why would I? I married her and chose to have children with her. Calling her names means I'm the moron."

Their server appeared to remove their plates. Conversation flowed easily throughout the rest of the meal. It was after ten when she and Adam left the restaurant. He handed her ticket to the valet, then pulled her to the side of the waiting area.

"I had a great time tonight," he told her.

"Me, too."

"Next time maybe you'll let me pick you up. You know, like a real date."

She smiled. "Next time I will." She leaned in and lightly kissed him. His mouth was firm and warm. She drew back. "You have the kids this week, right? So we'll keep in touch by text?"

He looked startled. "You're okay with that?"

"Sure. It's way too soon for them to know about me."

"Thanks for understanding. Or to repeat myself... wow."

She laughed.

He put his arm on her waist and drew her against him. "About that sleeping together thing."

"Not a chance."

"You're amazing."

"You are the only man I know who would say that after being told he *isn't* getting laid."

"I'm special."

"You are."

She had more to say but he kissed her and suddenly talking seemed highly overrated. His mouth lingered.

Had they been anywhere else, she would have wanted a little more. But they were outside at a valet stand, waiting for their cars. This wasn't the time to get into tongue.

She heard a car engine and stepped back. "That's me," she said, pointing at her convertible. "I'll talk to you soon."

"Promise."

Shannon got in her car and drove away. As she headed for home, she thought about the tingles and the quivers. How just being with Adam made her feel good. This was so much better than the post sex-with-Quinn drive of shame. Something she had to remember.

Pam typed quickly on the laptop in Nicole's small office, while Nicole sat in the chair beside the desk and waited for the news.

When she'd first bought Mischief in Motion, she'd only been able to afford basic remodeling and had put every penny into the studio itself. Her small down payment had been supplemented by money from a business angel network called Moving Women Forward. They'd given her advice along with start-up funds.

With no money left over for something as frivolous as an office, she'd made do with what she had. Her six-by-eight work space was little more than a human cubby, with a desk, two chairs and an overly bright light fixture.

Not that it mattered much to her. She was in her office as little as possible. Technology allowed all her clients to sign up for classes online. Once they created an account, they could purchase sessions individually or in packages. She received a report every day, the money was automatically deposited in her account and, best of all, she didn't have to pay for a receptionist. That savings meant that she'd been able to hire a couple of part-time instructors and cut her work hours down to sixty instead of eighty.

About a year ago, she'd been struggling with her accounting software. She'd casually mentioned it and Pam had offered to help. Now her friend spent about an hour every couple of weeks going over the books and making sure Nicole stayed on top of things like taxes and the mortgage. Because she hadn't just bought the business, she'd also bought the building. An expense that sometimes had her lying awake at night, wondering if she was ever going to feel that they were financially stable.

"You're in great shape," Pam said as she looked up. "And I'm not just talking about your ass."

Nicole smiled. "You're sure?"

"Yes. I haven't had to correct any entries for at least a couple of months. With the automatic payment reminders in place, you're able to hold on to your money as long as possible and still get the bills paid on time. You, my dear, are turning into a tycoon."

"I think tycoons take home more than what I do."

"It's all a matter of perspective."

Nicole wished she had her friend's confidence in herself. Pam had worked in her husband's company for years so all this came easily to her. She'd also most likely paid attention in school. Nicole had grown up with the idea that an education was for other people and that she needed to focus on her *art*. All fine and good until the moment when art ended and the real world began.

Pam tilted her head. "Are you all right? You really are doing well. You're putting aside money for taxes and into savings every month. The monthly costs are fairly stable and the business is growing. So why aren't you smiling?"

"I'm smiling on the inside." Nicole shifted in her chair. "I'm sorry. I really appreciate the help and you're right. The news is great. I'm just tired."

Pam nodded, but didn't speak. She was good at that, Nicole thought. Knowing when to ask and when to keep quiet. Was it a mom thing? Would she develop the skill as Tyler got older?

The silence stretched on a few seconds more. Nicole gave in to the inevitable and sighed.

"Eric and I aren't seeing much of each other these days," she admitted. "I'm always heading to work and when I get home, he's going out to his critique group or his screenwriting class. It's hard."

What she didn't mention was that her husband was getting home later and later, often smelling of beer. She understood that a few people in class wanted to go out afterward, but Eric had a family to come home to. She didn't understand what was happening to him. To them. And the unknown scared her.

"I know it's hard," Pam told her, her tone caring and warm. "I don't know how you haven't killed him. I swear to you, if John came home and told me he was quitting his job to write a screenplay, I'd back the car over him."

"John would never do that. He's a responsible guy. Predictable."

Pam body tensed a little, then relaxed. "You're right. And most of the time, that's a good thing."

"When isn't it a good thing?"

Her friend shrugged. "After thirty years of marriage, a little unpredictability would be nice."

"Is everything okay?" Nicole asked. Because self-ishly, she needed Pam's marriage to be better than her own. Somehow knowing Pam was okay gave her a safe place to be.

"We're fine," Pam assured her. "It's just…" She drew in a breath. "I'm fifty."

Nicole waited for the revelation. When Pam didn't say anything else, she searched for some kind of meaning. "I was at your birthday party last fall. You've been fifty for a while."

"I know, but I didn't feel it before." She waved her hand. "You're thirty and gorgeous and you won't understand, but trust me. One day you're going to look in the mirror and wonder what happened. It's not that I'm unhappy with my life. I get the blessings. My kids are still talking to us and coming over to dinner every Sunday. They're happy. John and I are healthy and I'm pleased to see him at the end of the day. It's just I didn't think it would happen so fast. Me getting old."

"Pam, you're not old. You're fantastic. You're one of my best students. You can keep up with anyone. You're in terrific shape."

"You haven't seen me naked," Pam muttered. "It's nothing like what it used to be."

Lulu wandered into the office. Pam bent down and picked her up, then petted her.

"All I can tell you is pay attention to what you're doing, because you're going to blink and it's going to have been twenty years."

Nicole wasn't exactly sure what she meant, but she nodded, anyway. "I can see that with Tyler. He's growing so fast. He still thinks watching my old performances is great fun. In a few years he'll pretend he doesn't know me."

"They do go through that stage." Pam cradled Lulu

in her arms. "I'm glad you had all those tapes put onto DVD. You'll always have them."

"They're not all that great to watch."

"To you, maybe. I've only seen a couple, but they were beautiful. You're a talented dancer."

A few months ago talk during class had turned to her former dancing career, such as it was. Pam and Shannon had insisted on seeing proof of her claims to have danced professionally and she'd brought in a DVD.

After graduating from ASU, she'd done what every other self-respecting dancer did. She'd headed for New York. Armed with determination, a lifetime of her mother telling her that she had to be a star and recommendations and introductions from her instructors, she'd started the arduous process of going to auditions.

It had taken two brutal winters for her to realize that she simply wasn't Broadway material. Or off-Broadway. She managed to get hired for two different Rockette shows and had danced for free for a few small productions that no one had seen. But she hadn't had whatever it was that got dancers noticed. At the end of those two years she'd returned to LA, where at least she could be poor and hungry in a sixty-degree winter.

She'd been down to her never-to-be-touched emergency five hundred dollars. It was all that stood between her and finding a bed at a shelter. A sign outside of Mischief in Motion had said the owner was looking for someone to teach a dance-based exercise class. She'd been desperate enough to try.

Nicole had found that she liked the work. Over the next couple of years, she'd gotten certified in several kinds of fitness instruction, including Pilates. Now six years later, she owned the studio. So at least that part of her life was doing well. And she had Tyler. As for her marriage, well, maybe that was a problem for another day.

"I like what I do now," Nicole said, knowing that she had been luckier than most. "I just need to get better at juggling."

"Balance is never easy. I'm not sure it's possible." Pam rose, Lulu still in her arms. "Trust me. I think it's like those fake holidays created by the greeting card industry. We pay attention to different things at different times in our lives. Sometimes we get it right and sometimes we don't."

"Always with the wisdom," Nicole teased. "Can I be you when I grow up?"

Pam smiled. "You're already grown-up. See? Everything happens when we're not paying attention."

Six

"I never get tired of that DVD," John said as he turned off the TV.

"It's a good one," Pam agreed.

They'd just watched *The Bourne Identity* for maybe the four hundredth time. She didn't mind the movie repeats. It gave her a chance to catch up on her magazine browsing. John didn't require her to pay attention so much as he liked her to be in the room.

She set her unread magazine back in the basket by her side of the sofa. The ones she'd gotten through would go into recycling. Lulu, curled up in her bed on the other end of the sofa, raised her head, as if asking if it was time.

"Ten o'clock, baby girl."

Lulu stood and stretched. Ten o'clock was the phrase that meant "last time to pee before morning" or however the dog translated it in her head.

John got out of his recliner—because yes, they were that couple. The ones with a recliner in the family room. At least they weren't at the stage of having two recliners. John had suggested it, but Pam knew she wasn't ready. She was sure the time would come, but not today.

"You going to take her out?" he asked, which he did every night.

Pam wanted to ask when he let the dog out. Not that he wouldn't if she asked. But the routine was him asking and her doing it.

How did things like that happen? she wondered. How did people get stuck in ruts? It must be part of the human condition—a need to not think about everything, maybe. So the brain found routines and being in a routine was oddly comfortable. Until it became a rut, at which point it wasn't comfortable anymore.

Pam smiled at her husband. It wasn't his fault she was thinking too much these days. "I'll take her out."

John nodded and walked past her. As he did, he paused to lightly pat her butt.

She would guess he didn't even know he was doing it. That if she mentioned it, he would look at her blankly. Which was so like him, and mostly endearing. It was yet another routine. A signal that the outside observer would never catch, but that a wife of thirty years knew intimately.

Later, when he finished in the bathroom, he would look at her expectantly. The question would hang in the air until she nodded and said something along the lines of "I'd like to." Because the butt pat was John's signal that he was interested in sex that night.

Pam and Lulu walked to the back door. She opened it for her little dog, then waited while Lulu took care of business. They walked back to the bedroom.

When Steven had moved out, they'd done a remodel of the rear of the house. They'd expanded the master and added a second bathroom, while redoing the first. They'd also enlarged the closet. Pam didn't mind sharing any part of her life, but she'd always wanted a completely girly bathroom and a few years ago, she'd gotten it.

There was a huge shower with a built-in bench so she could shave her legs easily. She had an oversize tub, a single sink with long countertops on both sides and as much storage as the makeup department at Macy's.

John's bathroom suited his needs, as well. There was a TV so he wouldn't miss any part of a game if he had to pee, a steam shower and a vanity that was several inches higher than usual.

Now she went into the closet and pulled out the drawer designated for Lulu's pj stash. The little dog had already gone over to the bed and used the pet stairs to make it onto the high mattress. Pam selected a soft T-shirt—pink, of course.

"All right, little girl," she said softly as she sat on the bed.

Lulu dropped her head as Pam removed the light sweater. The garment slid off easily. Then Pam held out the T-shirt. Lulu stuck her head through the opening and raised her left front leg to step into the arm hole. She always tried to do the right one, too, but usually missed. Pam got her shirt on. Lulu went up to the decorative pillows on the bed and burrowed in behind them, where she would stay until the humans got into bed.

Pam retreated to her bathroom where she removed her makeup, applied three kinds of serums and creams, then brushed her teeth. As she performed the familiar rituals, she tried to think sexy thoughts to get herself into the mood. But she couldn't seem to summon any energy about it.

Sex with John was fine, but it wasn't exciting anymore. She remembered how it had been at the beginning. The thrill of seeing him naked. The constant need to make love. How every touch had been arousing. Time and familiarity made that difficult to maintain. Add to that three kids and busy lives and it just wasn't the same.

But she loved him and wanted him to know that. While the words were always welcome, he also needed her to desire him. Something she'd figured out the second decade of their marriage when she'd been caught up in the exhaustion that came from having three active kids in the house.

She slipped on her nightgown and returned to the bedroom.

John was already there, sitting up, reading. He wore reading glasses—something that he'd resisted until any kind of printed material had become impossible. Lulu was on his lap. When she spotted Pam, she jumped up and came over to her side.

She put the dog in her bed in the corner. John put down his glasses and e-reader, then flipped back the covers and patted the mattress invitingly.

She climbed in next to him and studied his familiar face. She knew everything about this man, she thought. How he talked and laughed and thought. She knew his scent. When he put his arm around her waist and drew her close, she knew how their bodies would go together.

They kissed as they always did. She tried to ignore the thoughts whipping through her brain, but they were insistent. Somewhere in the back of her mind a bored voice announced the next step in the process. *Three tongue kisses, two nibbles on her neck. Right breast, left breast, then down to the promised land.*

Pam moved against him, searching for a spark to focus on. But she was thinking too much, and for her that was always trouble. She could feel what he was doing, but couldn't find the sex in it. After a moment she felt his erection pressing into her thigh.

When he was done, he rolled off her and cleaned up, pulled on his briefs and then returned to her side.

"What about you?" he asked, sliding his hand along her thigh. "Want to do it the old-fashioned way?"

Because he always knew if she'd had an orgasm or not. And her pleasure was important to him. Yet another excellent quality when it came to a husband, she thought. If she asked, he would touch her until she found her release. He knew how—they'd done it a thousand times before. Or maybe ten thousand.

"I'm in my head tonight," she admitted.

"You sure?" he asked, even as he withdrew his hand. "I am."

"All right. I love you." He kissed her, then stretched out on his side.

Pam pulled on her nightgown and retreated to the bathroom to wash up. As she closed the bathroom door she wondered when he'd stopped pressing her to try a little before giving up. A year ago? Five?

She wasn't complaining, but she was curious. Was she really "in her head" so much that he'd given up convincing her otherwise? That wasn't good.

She finished and returned to the bedroom. John was already asleep. The sound of his steady breathing calmed her, as did his solid presence.

She collected Lulu from her dog bed and carried her into the people bed. Lulu dove under the covers and waited until Pam lay on her back, then curled up next to her.

The tiny ball of warm life was familiar. Just like John

and her routine and their lovemaking. Familiar and comfortable and safe and boring. No, she thought. Boring was too harsh. It was something else.

Dusty, she thought as she stared into the darkness. Her life was dusty. She'd been given so much, so if she wasn't happy, then she was the problem.

"So you like him," Nicole said late Saturday morning.

Shannon tried to play it cool, but she couldn't help smiling. "I do. Adam's really nice. We've been out three times since our first date."

All three evenings had gone well. The last one had been the previous weekend when they'd gone sailing on a friend's boat and then had eaten at Gary's Café. He'd driven her home and they'd ended up making out in his car like teenagers.

She'd been tempted to invite him in for something more adult, only a part of her was enjoying the anticipation.

"And he's with his kids this weekend?" Nicole asked.

"Uh-huh. Last night until next Friday morning."

They stood by the carousel at the base of the Mischief Bay pier, otherwise known as Pacific Ocean Park. The original "POP" had been built in Santa Monica in the fifties and torn down in the 1970s. When Mischief Bay had rebuilt the pier, they'd named it the POP, to continue the tradition.

The town was big on old things. Several of the city's outdoor sculptures had been purchased from other places and relocated here. The carousel itself had been rescued from an east coast boardwalk that had wanted to put in more modern rides. Residents had formed a joint task force with city officials to raise money and bring the hundred-year-old carousel to the pier. It had been restored and put into use.

Nicole waved as Tyler rode around on a black horse. A leather strap held him securely in place. He was a cute kid, blond, with his mother's eyes. He was friendly and sweet. Being around him made Shannon wonder what it would be like to have a child of her own. And when that happened she would remind herself that she'd always wanted to go the traditional route. Husband, then kids. Which hadn't seemed possible.

Only now that she'd met Adam, she was starting to wonder if maybe it was. If maybe now she *could* have it all. While she knew it was way too soon to be thinking that, the thoughts wouldn't go away.

"It wasn't that long ago that Tyler still wanted you to stay with him," Shannon said, mostly to distract herself.

"I know. He's growing up so fast."

"Soon he'll be wanting to borrow the car," she teased.

"Don't even go there. I can't stand to think about it." Nicole pulled her cell phone out of her pocket and pointed it toward the carousel. "I'm still trying to accept the fact that he's going to be five."

Tyler circled into view again. Nicole snapped his picture and Shannon waved.

"Speaking of his birthday," Shannon said, "you'll never guess what I saw the other day."

Nicole groaned. "If you say Brad the Dragon supplies, I'm going to slit my wrists."

"Not something any of us wants."

Shannon waited while Nicole put her phone away. The other woman squared her shoulders, as if gathering strength. Nicole then tossed her blond hair over her shoulder and nodded.

"Give it to me straight."

Shannon laughed. "What do you have against Brad the Dragon? He's a pretty low-key guy." She knew. She'd read several of the books to Tyler the few times she'd babysat. "Doesn't he grow from a toddler to a young dragon in school?"

"Yes, which means I can never escape him. I have no idea why he bugs me, but he does. So what did you find?"

"There's a gift store in Hermosa. They have an entire selection of Brad the Dragon party supplies. Plates, napkins, goodie bags and a few games. There's a Brad the Dragon bean bag toss, Brad the Dragon pin the tail on the…dragon, I guess."

"Kill me now," Nicole murmured.

"You're not going to check them out?" Shannon found herself a little disappointed. She figured Nicole would ask her to help with the party and to be honest, she was looking forward to a Brad the Dragon birthday celebration.

Her friend groaned. "Of course I am. And then I'll buy them and Tyler will be the happiest little boy there is. Which is what I want. After all, it's his birthday. Dear God. Brad the Dragon. I swear, if I ever meet that author, I'm going to strangle him with a Brad the Dragon stuffed animal, wrap him in a Brad the Dragon blanket and throw his body out to sea."

"Someone needs to scale back on the caffeine," Shannon murmured.

Nicole laughed.

The ride came to an end. Nicole stepped on to talk to Tyler, because there was every chance he wanted to go again. This was only his second time and he was usually good for three or four sessions.

Shannon watched how mother and child interacted, their blond heads nearly touching as they laughed together. They were so close, she thought wistfully. So happy with each other. She wanted that. Not that she was all that sure she would be very good at it. When she'd been growing up, her mother hadn't ever given her a birthday party. Not with friends invited. There was a special dinner at home and a couple of presents, but nothing to compare with a Brad the Dragon extravaganza.

Different styles, she told herself, even though she knew in her gut that the real problem had leaned a lot more toward indifference.

The ride started up again.

"Hello, Shannon."

She turned and was startled to find Adam walking toward her. He had two children with him. A dark-haired daughter with ribbons in her curls and a younger, light-haired boy.

Thoughts crowded in her brain. Obviously these were his children and they'd both agreed it was too soon for them to meet her. So what was he doing? Thinking?

"Hi," she said, feeling both children staring at her.

"This is my friend Shannon. Shannon, these are my kids. Charlotte and Oliver."

She smiled at them. "Nice to meet you both. And this is my friend, Nicole. Her son is Tyler and he's riding the carousel."

Nicole shook hands with Adam.

"We love the pier," Charlotte said, her dark eyes the same as her father's. She was a pretty girl. Almost nine if Shannon remembered correctly. "Daddy, can we ride the carousel, too?"

"Sure. Let's go get tickets." He glanced at Shannon. "I'll be right back. Don't go anywhere."

"He's cute," Nicole whispered when he reached the ticket booth. "Cute kids, too."

"I don't understand. He said it was too soon. I said it was too soon. Why did he introduce me to his kids? Is this weird?"

"No. Come on. He saw you at the pier. You're a friend. It's not like they walked in on you two doing it." Nicole grinned. "Have you done it?"

"Not yet."

"Do you want to?"

Shannon watched him lead both children up to the carousel. Charlotte chose a white unicorn with painted flowers in her mane, while Oliver took the black horse next to Tyler. Adam pointed to him and Nicole waved.

"That one's mine," she confirmed, before turning back to Shannon. "Do you?"

"Yes," Shannon hissed. "I want to sleep with him. Are you happy?"

"Not as happy as you're going to be. Look. Here he comes. Act natural."

Great advice except she didn't feel she was acting unnaturally.

"Hey," Adam said as he approached. "You okay with this?"

"Meeting your kids? Sure. But I thought we'd agreed on the timing."

"We had, but then I saw you with your friend and figured I'd introduce you as someone I know. The pier isn't that big. You were bound to see us and I didn't want you feeling like you had to avoid me."

She had to admit that would have been awkward

and potentially comical. "Can I be someone you know through work?" she asked.

"Sure."

Nicole laughed. "I'd forgotten all the intrigue that goes into dating. I'm both envious and relieved I'm not dealing with it."

"Kids add a layer of complication," Adam admitted. "We were going to get lunch after this. Want to join us?" He nodded at Nicole. "Oliver and Tyler seem to be getting along."

Shannon glanced at the carousel and saw the two boys were talking and laughing.

"Sure," Nicole said. "We'll be your beard. Or is it your shill?"

"I think it's beard," Shannon told her.

After two more rides on the carousel even Tyler was ready for lunch. The six of them made their way to The Slice Is Right, where Shannon and Nicole claimed a table while Adam and the kids went to order the pizzas.

"He's nice," Nicole murmured as they sat down. "And cute."

"You already said he was cute. You're pressuring me."

"I know. I can't help it. I can feel the sexual tension radiating between you. It sizzles. Now I know what Pam says when she complains about feeling old."

"You're younger than me by years."

"But I'm married. There's a lot less sexual tension now."

Shannon watched her friend as she spoke and saw something in her eyes. Before she could ask what was going on, Charlotte walked over.

"Daddy's ordering three pizzas," she informed them.

"Cheese, pepperoni and one with vegetables." She shuddered visibly. "He wants to know if that's okay and what you'd like to drink."

"The pizzas are great," Shannon said as Nicole nodded. "Iced tea for me."

"Me, too."

Shannon touched Charlotte's arm. "Thank you for taking our orders."

The girl beamed. "You're welcome. I'm the oldest, so I'm responsible."

"Apparently so."

She walked back to join her father.

"Adorable," Nicole whispered. "Don't you just want to hug her?"

Shannon nodded. Sure it was early hours, but she had to admit she liked what she'd seen so far. Not to be one of those scary it's-been-one-date-can-I-see-myself-married-to-you? women, but maybe being a stepmother wasn't as bad as a lot of her friends claimed. Some of the pain and suffering was determined by the personalities of the children.

Adam collected a tray of drinks and led the three kids back to the table.

"I hope it's okay," he told Nicole as he approached. "Tyler said he was allowed chocolate milk when he ate out."

"He's right and he is," she said, scooting over to make room for her son.

Adam settled next to Shannon. They were just close enough that she could feel the heat of his body and there was no impediment to her sliding close to get her touching fix. Not counting his two children, her friend and

Tyler, of course. Suddenly, it seemed her life had gotten, as Adam had described the situation earlier, complicated.

Nicole turned to Charlotte. "You're in the third grade?" she asked.

"Yes."

"Do you like school?"

"Uh-huh. My teacher's nice and I'm reading above my grade level so she gets me extra books from the library." Charlotte snapped her attention back to Shannon. "Are you married?"

"No. I'm not."

"Do you have children?"

"No."

She opened her mouth as if she was going to ask another question, but Shannon got there first.

"I like the ribbons in your hair."

"My mom put them in yesterday." Charlotte gave an exaggerated sigh. "My dad's not good with girl stuff, but he tries."

"I do try," Adam added.

"Dad can do stuff Mommy can't," Oliver said loyally.

Adam put his arm around the boy. "Thank you for defending my honor."

"What's honor?"

"My mommy bakes cookies and reads to us every night," Charlotte added. "Even if she's busy."

Shannon tried to wrap her mind around the subtext. She had no way of knowing how the divorce had played out at home. Given how cautious Adam was with his kids, she wondered if they'd ever seen him with another woman. So even though no one had said anything about her and Adam dating, she might still be a potential threat.

She kept her smile easy and her expression friendly.

"She sounds great. You're lucky to have such a caring mom. Nicole is like that, too. Moms are the best."

Charlotte studied her for a second, then seemed to relax. Adam watched his daughter, but under the table Shannon felt his knee bump into hers. He kept it there for a second before moving it away.

She told herself not to read too much into the gesture or the conversation. One friendly disarmament did not a relationship make. But maybe a little smugness was allowed.

Seven

Tuesday evening Nicole told herself not to panic as she pulled into the garage. The fact that Eric's car wasn't there didn't mean he'd forgotten Tyler. If that had happened, she would have gotten a phone call from the day care. They wouldn't close and simply leave her son there alone.

Maybe they'd gone to the store. Or Eric had thought this was a late night for her and had taken their son out to dinner. Although these days he didn't seem interested in anything but surfing and his screenplay. While she couldn't imagine him taking Tyler out, that didn't mean it hadn't happened. Because the alternative...

She grabbed her bag and raced into the house.

"Tyler? Tyler!"

"Mommy."

Her little boy came running to greet her. She dropped her bag and fell to her knees, her arms open wide. He thundered into her. She held him so tight, she was afraid he couldn't breathe, but for that second, she simply couldn't let go.

"Hey, you," she said as she relaxed her grip and smiled at him. "How are you?"

"Good. I like Ce."

"See what?"

Tyler giggled. "That's funny."

"He means Cecilia. The name seemed to be causing him trouble so I told him he could call me Ce."

Nicole looked at the petite, curly-headed teenager standing in her kitchen. While she looked harmless enough, Nicole had never seen her before.

She resisted the urge to lunge for a knife from the block, then stood and carefully positioned Tyler behind her. "Hi. Who are you?"

Cecilia pointed to the refrigerator. "Eric left a note. He knows my brother. They're in a screenwriting class together. From what I heard, the two of them got invited to some lecture by some screenwriter guy. My brother asked if I could emergency babysit. He promised Tyler, my man here, would be in bed by eight, and I could study as much as I wanted. So here I am."

Nicole scanned the note. It said basically the same thing and was in Eric's writing. Which should have relieved her, but didn't.

She forced a smile for the teen. "Thanks, Cecilia. I really appreciate you helping out like this. How much do I owe you?"

"I haven't been here very long." Cecilia waved her hand. "You know what? This one's on me. I'll leave you my number. If you want to do this again, I'll text you some references."

Because Nicole probably hadn't done a very good job of concealing her horror on finding someone she didn't know with her son.

She waited while the teen collected her belongings. There really was a chemistry textbook and a notebook, along with an iPad and headphones. She and Tyler walked "Ce" to the door.

"I had fun," Tyler told her.

"Me, too," Cecelia said.

Nicole fished a twenty out of her jeans pocket. "Thanks so much for helping us out."

"You bet." She stared at the money, then shrugged. "I won't say no. I have expenses."

Nicole grinned. "I'm sure you do."

She waited until Cecelia got into her battered Corolla before closing the door.

"That was fun," she lied. "Did you get dinner?"

"Daddy and me went to McDonald's. I had a burger and fries."

"The dinner of champions," she murmured, making a mental note to make the fruit and veggie smoothie he liked for breakfast in the morning. She wasn't sure if that was going to be before or after she killed her husband, though. She would have to play the timing by ear.

In the hour before Tyler's bedtime, she vacuumed, then they played the tickle game. She also got through the first load of laundry. After reading him not one, not two, but six different Brad the Dragon books, she was able to attack the kitchen. She scrubbed the stove and sink until they gleamed, sorted through the crap mail that always collected on the island and wiped down the table.

Next she used her bubbling anger to fuel cleaning both bathrooms, including taking a stiff brush to the tiles in the shower in the three-quarter bath. By the time she heard the garage door open, it was nearly midnight. The house smelled of lemon and verbena. The laundry was done and put away and she was more than ready for a fight.

She positioned herself in the center of the sofa, which would force Eric to the lower, less comfortable club chairs, and waited.

He walked in, humming under his breath. When he saw her, he jumped in an almost comical exaggeration. She might have laughed if he'd tripped and hit his head, but no such luck.

"Nicole, jeez, you startled me. I didn't think you'd still be up. It's after midnight. Don't you have an early morning?"

"No, that was today. I was home by six thirty."

"Oh, I guess I got the days mixed up. Why are you still up?"

For a second she only looked at him. Looked at the man she'd married and had a child with. Eighteen months ago, she would have said she knew everything about him. That he was a nice guy. Friendly, funny, smart, dependable. She would have said he was a good father and provider. She would have said they were a team.

Their marriage hadn't been perfect. Sure, there were times when they looked at each other as if there was nothing left to talk about, but so what? Every marriage had its issues.

She would have said no matter what, Eric would be there for her, just like she would be there for him. But she never, ever would have guessed or believed he was capable of quitting his job to write some goddamn screenplay and then leave their child with a stranger!

"I met Cecelia."

She'd expected a little panic, or maybe some shame. Instead, he grinned. "I know, isn't she great? I took her information so we can use her again. Tyler really seemed to like her."

"You left him with someone I don't know," she said between gritted teeth. "You left him with someone *you* don't know."

"It's not like that. She's Ben's little sister. I've known Ben for over a year. He's a good guy. The family is cool."

"I don't care about the family. I care about my child and the fact that you didn't call me or text me. I came home to find your car gone and Tyler being looked after by someone I don't know from a rock. What the hell is wrong with you?"

He dropped his backpack onto the chair and narrowed his gaze. "Nothing. I had a chance to attend a lecture at the Writers Guild. A private lecture. Do you know how rare that kind of invitation is? Do you know who I got to meet? You were working. I would have called, but you get pissed when I interrupt one of your classes."

"Then text me. Do something."

"I left a note," he yelled, his brown eyes bright with anger. "I left a fucking note. What do you want from me?"

"I want you to think about someone other than yourself. I want you to do something around here other than eat food and sleep and work on your screenplay."

He rolled his eyes. "Okay, here we go." He folded his arms across his chest, then used his right hand to motion her forward. "Come on. Let's hear it. You've got a whole list of things you want to complain about. Let's get to it."

His complete dismissal of her before she'd said anything made her want to throw something. Or him.

She stood and glared at him. "You're an asshole, you know that? You can pretend this is me being me, but you're wrong. Completely wrong. You're rarely here anymore. We don't ever see each other. You make promises you don't keep—like helping around the house or buying groceries. You do nothing to keep this household going. I work, I bring in all the money and I have to do almost everything around here."

She sucked in a breath. "Sometimes you won't even help with Tyler. He's your son, Eric. Your child. Why won't you be there for him?"

Eric stared at her for a long time. She watched anxiously, hoping for something that wasn't anger. His jaw twitched, his mouth twisted. Remorse? Could she possibly have gotten through to him?

"This is all your fault," he said quietly.

She blinked. "What?"

"You did this. You made this happen."

Her mouth dropped open. "What are you talking about?"

He waved his hand at the room. "All of this. If you're unhappy, then you only have yourself to blame. I took it, Nicole. For as long as I could. What about me? What about what I want? But none of that matters to you. You don't care that I was unhappy with my life. You don't care that I wanted more than what we had."

She couldn't have been more surprised if he'd sprouted a second head and started breathing fire.

"Are you drunk?"

"No. I'm completely sober and I know exactly what I'm saying." He took a step toward her. "Before you and I met, I'd been saving every penny I had so that I could quit my job and write a screenplay. It was something I'd always wanted to do."

"What? That's not true. You talked about it maybe

twice the whole time we were dating. You never said anything more until the day you quit your job."

"That's because I knew you'd mock me. I knew you wouldn't be supportive. Or believe in me."

She opened her mouth, then closed it. What was she supposed to say to that? Realistically, the odds of him actually selling a screenplay were tiny. But if she pointed that out, she fell into the unsupportive camp. Because Eric had a dream and nothing else mattered.

"I'm sorry you think that," she said instead. "Eric, I want you to be happy, but I also need you to be a part of our marriage. Our family. I feel like we're living separate lives."

"I have to do what I'm doing," he told her stubbornly. "This my time. My dream. You lost yours. You couldn't make it, but at least you had the chance to try. It's like you don't want me to have my shot. Because what if I'm talented? You'd hate that."

It took her a second to figure out what he was talking about. "My dancing? I let that go years ago."

"Because you had to. I don't. And you resent that."

"My God, do you really think that about me?" Pain sliced through her. Could it be that they'd never really known each other at all?

"You've never once asked to read my screenplay."

"No," she said firmly. "That is not true. I've asked and asked. You keep saying it's not ready. You won't let me read it until it's perfect. We just had that conversation a couple of weeks ago."

He shifted and looked away. "All right. I guess that's true."

"You know it is. Just like you know you never really

told me how much you wanted to write until the day you quit. You didn't ask, you didn't negotiate. You just did it."

"I knew you'd say no."

"Neither of us know what I would have said. What happened to negotiating? To writing on the weekends."

"I wanted to just go for it."

"And damn the rest of us? Where does that leave us?"

"Nowhere." He spoke flatly, as if he didn't care what he was saying.

She didn't know what to say or do. They had the same argument about him quitting at least once a month and here they were again. Back where they'd started.

"You might be nowhere," she said with a sigh, "but I've got a thousand places to be and a to-do list that goes on for miles."

She was about to say that she wanted them to work as a team, to be in a marriage again, when he turned suddenly and stalked out.

"Then I'll leave you to it," he said, before he stepped into his office and closed the door behind him.

Nicole sank back on the sofa and covered her face with her hands. She waited for the tears, but there weren't any. Just a knot the size of Ecuador and the heaviness that came with a strong sense of foreboding.

Pam lay on the padded mat and waited for her insides to stop quivering.

"I think that was a personal best," she gasped, barely able to raise her head to stare at Nicole.

"I second that," Shannon called from two mats away. "I'd raise my arm in solidarity, but I don't think I can."

The two other women in the class simply groaned.

"Too much?" Nicole asked anxiously. "Sorry. I didn't mean to…"

Pam heard something in her voice and forced herself to sit up. Her stomach muscles screamed in protest. Pam knew that they wouldn't be all that was screaming come morning. She wondered if she could get in for a massage.

"What?" she asked when she was upright.

Nicole gave her a slightly off-center smile. "Nothing. I'm fine."

Uh-huh. A likely story. The truth was she probably didn't want to mention it in front of her other clients.

Pam shifted to her knees, braced herself and stood. Her thigh muscles actually trembled. For a second she wasn't sure she could stay standing.

"Lulu," she called.

Her little dog got up from the blanket and obediently trotted over.

Pam pointed to Nicole. "Go say hi." She looked at her friend. "Pick her up, please, and hold her."

Nicole did as she requested. Lulu cuddled close, then reached up and licked the bottom of her chin.

Pam started for the water dispenser. Nicole trailed after her.

"Why am I holding Lulu?"

"So you'll feel better. You obviously need a hug. Until the other clients leave, it's the best I can offer."

Nicole's eyes filled with tears. "Thank you. Can you stay a few minutes? I would like to talk."

"No problem."

Pam got a glass of water and sipped it slowly. She was gratified to see the other clients walked just as gingerly. One of them pressed an arm into her stomach, as if trying to support the muscles.

Shannon walked over. "That was a killer workout."

Pam eyed her. "Uh-huh. You obviously don't care. How's the new boyfriend?"

"Adam? He's great." She ducked her head. "He sent me flowers. Because of how things went this past weekend. With his kids."

Pam nodded. On Monday Shannon had told her all about the random meeting on the pier. She'd practically glowed as she talked. Which was nice. Shannon didn't tend to glow that much when she talked about her various boyfriends.

She was nearly forty and still single, Pam thought. A concept that was so foreign to her. No husband, no kids. She did what she wanted, went where she wanted, answered to no one.

Pam supposed a case could be made for how appealing that was, just not to her. She *liked* knowing John was coming home every evening. She *liked* her kids. While she complained from time to time and whined more than was probably funny, the truth was, she liked her life. Even the impending doom that was being a grandmother came with a really cool perk. Namely a baby.

"Did I tell you I know him?" she asked.

"Adam? He's worked with John, right?"

"Yes. They're building that hotel. It's going to be beautiful when it's done, but getting there is a mess. Anyway, we know Adam and his brothers and sisters, along with his parents. They're great people. Very friendly."

Pam nearly pointed out that Adam's parents were much older than her and John, but figured there was no point. Her demons wouldn't make sense to anyone else.

"I'm glad about the flowers," she added. "He's a good guy."

"I'm getting that." Shannon glanced at the clock. "I need to get back to work." She turned to Nicole. "You made me sweat today. You know how I feel about that!"

Nicole faked a smile back.

By the time Shannon collected her things and left, the other clients were gone, too. Nicole sank down on one of the mats, forcing Pam to do the same. She tried not to wince as she wondered how on earth she was going to get up again.

Lulu immediately crossed from Nicole to Pam and climbed onto her lap.

"Tell me," Pam said gently.

Nicole nodded, then started to cry. She covered her face with her hands and her shoulders shook with her sobs.

Pam waited, stroking Lulu and breathing slowly. Three kids and a combined total of twenty-one teenage years had taught her that if she stayed calm, the other person tended to stay calm. It was all about controlling the energy in the room.

Nicole hiccupped a couple of times, then sniffed and raised her head.

"It's Eric."

"I guessed it was him." The little pinhead.

"We had a big fight. I came home to find he'd left our son with a teenager I'd never met."

"Are you kidding? How could he do that?"

"I don't know. She's the sister of one of his writing friends. She seemed nice enough…" Her voice trailed off.

"It's not about her being nice," Pam pointed out. "It's about not talking to you first. It's about being a parent and a husband. I swear, I want to slap him."

Nicole brightened. "Me, too." Her shoulders slumped again. "It's just hard right now."

Pam couldn't begin to imagine. While she was sure there were two sides to what was going on in their marriage, there was no excuse for acting the way he was. He had responsibilities and it was time for him to deal with them.

None of which would be news to Nicole, or the least bit helpful.

"I'm going to take Tyler," Pam announced suddenly.

"What?"

"For a couple of days. He and I get along great. Lulu loves him, as does John. Honey, you need a break."

"Pam, that's too much."

"I've had him before. Overnight."

"Once and I couldn't ask."

"You're not. I'm offering. Seriously. I'll take him for two nights. If he gets upset, I'll call, but I think he'll be fine."

Nicole's eyes filled with tears. "You're so good to me."

"I know. And later, you can walk in front of me while throwing rose petals at my feet."

Nicole chuckled. "That would be very strange."

"Yeah, but I like it when I make people talk." She staggered to her feet and rubbed the front of her thighs where the burn was the worst. "Just tell me what time to be at your place."

"I'll bring him to you. It's the least I can do."

Nicole stood and hugged her. Pam returned the embrace and realized except for the angry muscles, she was feeling pretty good. This was what she needed, she told herself. To think about someone else. It was good for her.

Eight

Friday afternoon Shannon left work at four. Her assistant tried not to show her surprise and failed miserably.

"You can head out, too," Shannon told her. "Start the weekend early."

"Thank you."

Shannon told herself that her good mood came from her satisfaction with work and the blue sky and a bunch of other crap she didn't believe. Because she knew the truth. She was happy and bouncy and okay, giddy, because she had a date with Adam that night.

She tried to remember the last time she'd been so excited to see a guy. Nothing came to mind. Maybe it was because they were taking things slow. They hadn't done more than kiss, which she kind of liked. Not that she wasn't interested in taking things to the next level. She was. Very much. But anticipation had its place.

She was home by four fifteen and rode the elevator up to her condo. The space was considered a one-bedroom, plus. There was an alcove off the living room that she used as her home office.

Sunlight spilled into the living room as she stepped

inside. She was on the fifth floor of the six-story building, with a northwest-facing unit. She had a view of the Pacific to her west and the pier and beach beyond to her north. The wide balcony wrapped around from the living room to the bedroom. There was lots of storage, a huge closet in the master and a laundry room big enough for her washer and dryer to sit next to each other rather than stack.

When she'd bought the place four years ago, she'd worried about paying the mortgage. But the lifestyle Mischief Bay offered had made it worth the gamble. Two raises later, she was paying down her mortgage with a little extra every month and still having some left over for savings and retirement. Life was very, very good.

She stepped out of her shoes as she entered the bedroom. She was going to shower and redo her makeup and revel in her anticipation.

She set her phone in the docking station by her bed and selected a playlist. While easy jazz filled the bedroom, she walked to the kitchen and poured herself a glass of wine, then returned to the bathroom.

After her shower, she dried her hair, then set it with hot rollers. She wanted lots of girly waves for tonight. Her wardrobe would take a little more thought. Sexy, but not obvious, she thought. Adam was taking her out to dinner. What were her options?

One hour later, she opened her door to let in Adam. She'd chosen a simple strapless empire waist dress that skimmed her curves. It wasn't fancy, it wasn't supersexy, but the color brought out the blue of her eyes and the only thing holding it up was one long, easy zipper. She wasn't sure Adam would notice that fact and be distracted by it, but a girl could dream.

He wore jeans and a long-sleeved shirt. Simple. Easy. And he still got her heart to fluttering just a little.

"Hey," she murmured, stepping back to let him in.

"Hey, yourself."

He looked her over, then shook his head. "How'd I get so lucky? You're gorgeous, smart and funny. There's got to be a catch."

"I used to be a spy, so I know fifty ways to kill you."

He chuckled, then pulled her close.

She stepped easily into his embrace. She wrapped her arms around his neck and let her eyes drift closed. He kissed her. Softly at first, but then with growing intensity. She parted her lips and felt the first stroke of his tongue.

Heat poured through her. Wanting followed, leaving tingles and aches in all the most interesting places. Before she could decide if she wanted to take things further, he stepped back and sucked in a breath.

"Have I said *wow* yet today, because I should."

She laughed. "You're really sweet to me."

"I'm trying to be a good guy. You make it tough."

His compliments were handed out so easily, she thought, amazed by the lack of game-playing. Adam thought she was pretty and sexy and he told her. There was no payment for the information, no expectation. She couldn't remember the last time she'd experienced that. Maybe never.

"You're nice to say that, but I have plenty of flaws."

"Not that I can see. Why aren't you dating George Clooney?"

She laughed. "Because he's too old for me." She stepped close to Adam again. "You know what I would really like for dinner?"

"What?"

"Pizza. We could have it delivered and just stay in."

"I'd like that, too."

"Good." She put her hands on his chest and stared into his eyes. "I'm thinking we can order in about an hour."

Confusion drew his eyebrows together. But before he could ask what they were going to do in that time, she very deliberately stepped out of her shoes and then raised herself up on tiptoe to kiss him.

He responded in kind, moving his mouth against hers. She stepped closer still, pressing her body against his and felt the exact moment he figured out what she was offering. His arms came around her, his kiss deepened and she felt his fingers reach for the zipper at the back of her dress.

Friday Nicole arrived home at her usual time. She was surprised that Eric's car was in the driveway. He hadn't been around much since their fight, and when he was, he tended to avoid her. He'd been sleeping on the futon in his office and heading out long before she was up. Quite the trick considering when she had to get up for her early classes.

But she hadn't said anything or even left a note. Probably because she was as reluctant to talk to him as he was to talk to her.

Their fight had rocked her. Mostly because he seemed to want to assume the worst about her. Like his claim that she didn't want to read his screenplay and his assumption that she wouldn't be supportive. That hurt her and left her not sure what to do next.

Now she carried her tote and gym bag into the house. "Hi," she called.

"Mommy!" Tyler came running down the hall. "You're home! You're home."

She dropped everything on the floor and kneeled down to catch him when he flung himself at her. Love washed through her, reminding her what was really important. Whatever she and Eric had going on, they had to protect Tyler. He had to come first.

She stood and collected her bags, then walked into the kitchen. Eric sat at the table. His gaze was wary, as if he expected her to start yelling at him. Instead, she offered a calm hello.

"I'm going to put my things away, then start dinner. Are you eating with us tonight?" she asked. Because lately he'd been gone for most evenings.

"My critique group doesn't meet until eight tonight," he said. "I can stay."

"Good."

She noticed there were a lot fewer dishes in the sink than there had been that morning and that the dishwasher indicator showed the load was clean. But because of their recent fight, she wasn't sure if she should say anything or not.

She started the oven. A few months ago she'd turned to the most likely candidate for domestic goddess that she knew and had asked for help. She'd explained how she was always tired and running from place to place and never sure what to do about dinner.

Pam had told her to set aside an afternoon to cook for the week. She'd also offered a few easy recipes for casseroles and the Crock-Pot.

Nicole had taken her advice to heart. But rather than give up an afternoon every week, she tried to do two or three weeks of food at a time. She doubled and tripled their favorite recipes. She'd bought smaller casserole dishes that suited the size of their family. Instead of one time consuming lasagna, she made four smaller ones—two meat, two vegetable. They were big enough for dinner and for her to have for lunch the next day. Eric didn't do leftovers and something like that was too hard for Tyler to have at preschool.

She made chili and dozens of chicken recipes. She also made it a habit to steam double amounts of vegetables and freeze the extras. They either had them later or she used them in soup.

After she'd put her things away, she pulled a casserole out of the refrigerator and popped it in the oven.

"Dinner's in thirty minutes," she said. "I'm going to take a shower."

Before she headed for the bathroom, she tossed in a load of laundry. To her surprise, she saw that there were towels in the dryer. So he'd done a load today. That was an improvement.

She hurried through her shower. When she was dressed again, she combed her wet hair, then pulled it back in a braid.

When she returned to the kitchen, Tyler was gone.

"He's watching one of his shows," Eric said as he set the table. "I thought we should talk."

"Okay."

He set down the last fork, then faced her. "This is important to me, Nicole. What I'm doing. The screenplay. I think it's really good. But it's not just me. It's my critique group and a couple of other people who have read it. I'm making contacts all the time. Networking. I can do this. I need you to believe in me."

All of which would have been nice to hear during one

of their fifty thousand fights, she thought grimly. Not that it would have changed much.

She wanted to say it wasn't fair. That he was basically holding her hostage. That she'd never been given a choice. But her head told her this was one of those times when she had to suck it up and do what was best for them rather than what was best for her.

If only they could be the same thing. But they weren't. So far, she'd rarely found a time when they were.

"I do believe in you," she told him. "And I have asked to read your screenplay. A lot."

"I know. I was wrong to say that. I'm sorry." He looked at her. "I need to do this. I need to have my shot. I should have explained all this before, I guess. That one day my boss was talking to me about a new project and I realized this was my life. This was all it was ever going to be. Work I wasn't sure I liked, let alone loved. I couldn't do it. So I quit."

Without warning. No, she told herself. She'd said that too many times already. They were here, now. They had to deal with this current reality.

"Okay," she said slowly.

"All my energy is going into creating this right now. I'm sorry I don't have enough left over for you and Tyler, but it's an all-or-nothing thing for me. This is my shot. I can feel it. I have to put a hundred percent of what I have into the screenplay."

"Except for surfing."

The words burst out before she could stop them.

She waited for him to get mad, but he only shrugged. "The surfing helps. It clears my head. So it's kind of part of my process."

Seriously? "I'm guessing housework doesn't clear your head?"

One corner of his mouth twitched. "Okay, good point. I'm trying to help out more."

"I appreciate the laundry you did and running the dishwasher."

He nodded. "Thanks. I know it shouldn't all be you."

The timer dinged.

"I'll go get Tyler," he said and walked out of the kitchen.

Nicole stared after him. She had thanked him for pushing a couple of buttons on the dishwasher and throwing in a load of towels. When did she get thanked for everything she did, including supporting their damned family? When did she get to go surfing to clear her head? How come she had to be the only grown-up?

She shook her head and reminded herself she had to focus on what was important. Eric wanted to try. That was something. But what she didn't know was if it was enough.

"You are such a girl," Adam said, his tone teasing.

Shannon sat on the sofa, her wineglass in her hand. She felt good. Satisfied and happy and full. It was a nice combination. She tucked her feet under her. The action caused her robe to fall open a little. But she decided showing a little of the girls wasn't a bad thing. Adam had certainly appreciated them earlier.

The lovemaking had been good. Hot and fast the first time, then slow and sensuous the second. He'd explored her body with a combination of skill and enthusiasm, and expressed his appreciation of every inch of her. Afterward, they'd ordered pizza and opened a bottle of wine.

She watched him peruse her movie collection and realized the piece that seemed to be missing. Drama and pain. She didn't worry that he was going to try to push her away by being mean, or want to point out that despite what they'd done, she didn't matter to him. He wasn't self-absorbed or difficult.

Bad boys played well in fiction but in real life they were what the name implied. A sucker bet she always lost.

"I thought my being a girl was something you really liked," she murmured.

He winked at her. "It is. But this movie collection. It's sad."

"Too many chick flicks?"

"Way too many. Where are the action movies? Men with guns driving fast cars?"

"Oh, right. Well, now you've found a flaw."

He returned to the sofa and sat next to her. He took the wineglass from her hand and set it on the table then leaned in and kissed her. At the same time he slipped his hand under her robe and cupped her breast. Tendrils of desire curled through her.

"It's an easy flaw to live with," he whispered, then kissed his way down her neck.

She pulled her robe open and shifted so she was lying beneath him.

He didn't need to be invited twice. They went from playing to serious in less than a minute. When he entered her, she arched against him, wanting all of him. Her still-tingling body was coming by the third thrust.

Later, when they were semiclothed again, she leaned against him. He had his arm around her and kissed the top of her head.

"You're amazing," he told her. "Why aren't you married?"

She looked up at him. While this wasn't the first time she'd been asked the question, she generally deflected it. "You mean why hasn't George Clooney snapped me up?"

"I know about your thing against George. He looks good, though."

"He does." She stretched her legs across his lap and decided she was okay having this conversation with Adam. A testament to how different he really was from her usual fare. Or Quinn. Talk about a disaster relationship.

"I'm not married because I've never found anyone who could get past my commitment to my career." She waved her hand. "I'm talking about the past ten years. Not when I was younger. From what I've found, men say they're fine with it until I have to cancel a date or a weekend and then it becomes a problem."

"Then they're idiots. What about kids? Do you like them?"

"Sure. I've always liked kids." She thought about mentioning how she was shocked to find herself turning forty and not yet a mother, but that might sound weird. Or like she was pressuring him.

"I would still like to have children in my life," she continued. "In the meantime, I make do with my friends' kids. Like Tyler. He's great."

"Oliver liked him a lot."

"I'm glad. Tyler has this thing for Brad the Dragon."

"I'm familiar with the character."

Shannon laughed. "You have that same tight voice Nicole gets when she talks about him."

"There's a cultlike quality to the series," Adam admitted. "I can't figure out how the author does it, but kids get obsessed."

"I know. Tyler's going to be turning five soon. I'm helping Nicole with his party. I found a store that carries Brad the Dragon everything. She can't decide if she's going to go for it or not."

He pretended to shudder. "I share her pain."

"You should. I think Nicole is going to invite Oliver to the party. Which means if she goes all Brad the Dragon, you're in trouble."

He grinned. "So you have a dark side."

"You know it."

He drew her against him and kissed her.

Adam stayed until about two in the morning. Shannon thought about inviting him to spend the night, but decided she needed the space. Maybe next time. For now, the physical intimacy had been enough.

He'd been gone all of ten minutes when her phone buzzed with a text message.

"You're such a romantic," she said as she reached for the phone.

But it wasn't Adam. Instead, the message was from Quinn.

Whatsup?

The single word was his way of asking her to a booty call.

She dropped her phone onto the sofa and walked into the bedroom without looking back. As she got ready for bed, she reminded herself that she couldn't take credit for being a stellar person. It wasn't as if she'd grown in the character department and decided to end a relationship that was totally bad for her. Instead, she'd had a great night with Adam. There was a difference.

Still, she should accept the victory, regardless of its cause. Maybe romance *was* all it was cracked up to be.

Nine

"We're going to take a picture of the left side of your face," the woman in the white coat said. Her name—Anne—was stenciled on her coat.

She was tall, thin and looked maybe thirty, which was intensely annoying.

"We do the left side," Anne informed her with what Pam was pretty sure was a smug smile, "because that's the side that gets all the damage when we drive. Unless you've always used sunscreen."

Another smug smile that told everyone that Anne knew for a fact Pam *hadn't* used much sunscreen.

Pam had been asked to show up at her consult/BOTOX appointment without any makeup. Being seen in daylight bare-faced should be enough of a punishment. She was committed to have a lethal neurotoxin injected into her face. Wasn't that enough on the pain and suffering scale? Anne of the white coat didn't seem to think so.

The medi-spa was tucked into a corner of an actual medical building. There were plenty of dentists and internists and even a practice devoted to cardiac care. So this place must be okay. It was the one Shannon had recommended. That had to matter more than Anne's attitude.

"All right," Anne said, positioning her in front of a white cone. "Keep very still."

Pam did as she was instructed, then was left to wait for a few minutes. She had a feeling the images were instantly available. They were digital after all. No doubt the extra time was for her to fully embrace her lack of sunscreen shame.

Anne returned and sat in front of her computer. She typed a few keys and an awful purple-and-green-spotted picture of the side of Pam's face appeared on the large television mounted on the wall.

The side of her nose was covered in massive craters and dark blotches. Her cheeks looked as if they were as uneven as the surface of Mars. Her forehead was a battleground. She nearly ran for the nearest exit.

Anne, her power firmly restored, gave her a sympathetic smile. "It's not as bad as it looks."

"Oh, good."

"You have significant sun damage. Here, here and here." She pointed as she spoke, touching the screen on the picture's nose, cheeks and forehead. "Your number is forty-five."

That wasn't so bad, Pam thought. "So I have the skin of a forty-five-year-old?"

"No. The scale takes a hundred women your age and tells you how many have better skin and worse skin."

"Oh. Which is better? A hundred or one?"

The sympathetic look appeared again. "Your sun damage is less than forty-four of the women."

Rats. "So higher is better."

"Yes. Now on to inflammation."

Thirty minutes and a half-dozen pictures later, Pam thought seriously about simply slitting her wrists. It would be faster and cheaper. And maybe embalming would make her look fabulous.

"I'm mostly interested in BOTOX," she told Anne.

"Of course. You mentioned that when you made your appointment. I agree."

"You do? You don't want to talk me in to some injections?"

Anne studied her face for a second, then shook her head. "No. BOTOX will smooth out your forehead. We'll do the bunny lines, as well."

"Bunny lines?"

Anne pointed to the mirror. "Wrinkle your nose."

Pam did as she was asked. Her brow lowered and horizontal lines appeared on the bridge of her nose.

Anne pointed. "Bunny lines."

"Right. Like a rabbit."

"Yes. As for the rest of it, injectable will get expensive and won't give you the results you want."

Pam didn't like the sound of that. "What would?" she asked before she could stop herself.

Anne rose. "A face-lift. Now if you'll come with me, I'll introduce you to Reveka. That is who you requested."

Pam followed automatically. Reveka was who Shannon had recommended. She entered a treatment room with an adjustable chair and some scary looking lasers. But none of that registered. She was too busy trying to keep breathing after hearing the dreaded *F* word.

Pam arrived home in one piece. She was extra grateful not to have been in an accident. Not only had the BOTOX hurt like hell—not just needles piercing her face, but the actual stuff burned as it oozed into her muscles—but Reveka had also told her not to lie down for at least four hours. All Pam could think after that was if she was in a car accident, she was going to have to tell the paramedics to simply leave her in place until her BOTOX had set.

She greeted Lulu and let her out, then walked into the kitchen. Her face still hurt a little. One of the injections had hit a capillary, which Reveka had said wasn't uncommon. The downside for Pam was she would have a little bruise.

She thought longingly of a glass of wine or a very large vodka tonic, only she wasn't supposed to drink for twenty-four hours. What on earth had she been thinking?

Lulu walked back inside and raced over. She assumed her pick-me-up position. Pam squatted, rather than bending over, and was careful to keep her body lower than her head. After straightening, she cuddled her dog and tried to take comfort in Lulu's familiar warmth.

Her phone buzzed. She fished it out of her bag and glanced at the screen. Brandon, her youngest, had texted to say hi.

She stared at the phone for a second. Her twenty-four-year-old son in medical school had taken the time to text her to say hi. Steven was thriving working with his father. Jen and Kirk were having their first baby.

She was married to a wonderful man who loved her, took care of her and who had never once been unfaithful. She had a beautiful house, great friends. In truth, she'd been blessed in every way possible. Why was she suddenly so obsessed with how she looked? So she was fifty. It was just a number. A meaningless number that only had the value she gave it. By itself it was powerless.

She walked into her small office and booted her computer. When it was ready, she sat down and settled Lulu in her lap, then raised her hands to type. Then she paused.

What was she looking for? What did she want? Not counseling. Not really. She wanted…

She wanted to be excited about marriage again, she decided. She wanted to feel like she had even twenty years ago. When they'd been a young family. Or like when they'd first started dating. That would be fun. Like she'd thought to herself the other night, their marriage wasn't broken but it sure was dusty.

She typed into the search engine. The first few tries got her nowhere, but eventually she stumbled onto several sites that promised to refresh a strong marriage.

Are you looking to put passion back in the bedroom?

Pam clicked on the link and stared at the picture of a nice resort in Palm Desert. The information on the site promised small classes where "laughter and passion are the keys to renewing the bonds of love."

As long as it's not stand-up and bondage, Pam thought. She glanced at the date and saw it was the following weekend. "What's the worst that could happen?"

She clicked on the registration link and saw there were still spaces available.

"If nothing else, we'll have a weekend away." She quickly filled out the form and typed in her credit card number. As soon as she got the confirmation, she called her daughter to see if she could take Lulu.

"It's just a weekend in Palm Desert," Pam said. "Your dad and I haven't been away together for a while."

"I think it's great," Jen told her. "We're happy to take her. She's such an easy dog. Maybe I can practice my diapering skills on her."

"Or maybe not," Pam said. "Thanks, honey." The

phone beeped. "Jen, it's your dad. I'll talk to you later, okay?"

"Sure, Mom. Bye."

Pam toggled to the second call. "Hi. Guess what I just did."

"Pam." John's voice was heavy and sad.

She caught her breath and put her free hand on Lulu's warm back. "Oh, God. What?"

"It's Hayley. She miscarried last night. She just got home. Rob called this morning to tell me what had happened and that she wouldn't be in to work. I asked him to let me know when she was back. I knew you'd want to go over."

"I do. Thanks for letting me know." She paused. "I feel so bad for her."

"I know. Me, too. I'm not sure how many times she can keep doing this."

"I know. Okay, I'll go see her right now. Thanks for letting me know."

"Sure thing. I love you."

"I love you, too."

She hung up and printed out their confirmation, then logged off her computer.

"Come on, pretty girl. We have to go help a friend."

She detoured to the laundry room, where there was a spare upright freezer. After checking what she had prepared, she chose a lasagna and a chicken broccoli dish she knew that Hayley liked.

She put them in a large tote, along with a couple of bottles of wine, then picked up her keys and cell phone and headed for the front door. Lulu trotted along with her.

Pam had the dog do her business before they crossed the street and walked down two houses. When she reached the front door, she knocked twice, then let herself in.

"Hey, it's me," she called.

"We're in here."

The voice, familiar, but not Hayley's, caused Pam to pause for a second. She told herself that it was nice for Hayley to have family around, even if that family was Hayley's slightly overbearing sister. Rob would have dropped off his wife and then returned to work. Because he had two jobs to deal with, thanks to his wife's determination to have a baby.

The logical side of Pam's brain understood that every woman had to figure out what would make her happy. But her heart ached for her friend and what she was putting herself and her wonderful husband through.

Pam closed the front door behind her. Lulu took off at a run, headed through the foyer and turned right into the family room. Pam detoured through the kitchen, where she left the chicken casserole on the counter to thaw faster and stuck the lasagna in the refrigerator. She wrote instructions for heating both on a Post-it and stuck the note on a cupboard door. Then she, too, headed for the family room.

Hayley sat curled up in a corner of the sofa. She had a blanket draped across her lap and a box of tissues by her side. Lulu had already curled up next to her, her brown doggie eyes watching anxiously.

Morgan, Hayley's sister, sat in one of the club chairs. She smiled brightly as Pam walked in.

"You're so sweet to come by. I appreciate it. I don't think Hayley should be alone right now, but I have my kids to deal with. Amy has a cold and the other two are…" She trailed off. "It doesn't matter. The point is I'm superbusy."

She was picking up her purse as she spoke. "Hayley, hon, if you need anything, you know you only have to call, right? I can be here in ten minutes. I swear."

Hayley nodded.

"Good. I hope you feel better."

With that, Morgan waved and was gone. Pam waited until the front door closed before she walked over to Hayley and hugged her.

"I counted six *I*s in less than ten seconds," she said by way of greeting. "What number did you get?"

Hayley smiled. She started to laugh, then the humor turned into tears and she covered her face with her hands and cried. Pam scooped up Lulu and sat in her place, then set the dog on her friend's lap. The little dog trembled slightly, as if undone by all the emotion. She leaned in and licked the back of Hayley's hand.

Hayley raised her head and sniffed. She was pale and had dark circles under her eyes.

"I hate this," she admitted, stroking Lulu. "It's wrong and unfair."

"You know it. Why does Morgan get to pop out kids like she's a toaster and they're waffles? She's so annoying. You, on the other hand, are lovely and everything about this situation sucks."

Hayley continued to cry, but she was smiling, too. "You're my weirdest friend and I love you so much."

"I love you, too." Pam hugged her. "I'm so sorry you're going through this again."

Hayley pulled Lulu close and kissed the top of her fluffy head. "Me, too. I was so sure this was the one. That I was going to be fine." She sucked in a breath. "The doctor says I can't keep doing this. You know last time I lost all that blood. This time was better, but she's worried."

"We're all worried."

Hayley shook her head. "I know. It's just… I don't want to spend the day crying. Please, please distract me."

Pam grinned. "You know, I can do that. I can make you totally forget how sad you are."

Hayley tilted her head. "That isn't possible."

"I had BOTOX today."

"What?"

"I did." She moved her bangs so her friend could see the puncture marks. "It takes about a week to work and I'm not supposed to lie down for four hours. So if I have a heart attack or stroke, keep me propped up until two."

Hayley was wide-eyed. "I can't believe you did that. Did it hurt?"

"Yes. A lot."

"BOTOX. Wow. Impressive."

"I know." She patted Hayley's hand. "Now let's check out pay-per-view. There has to be some trashy movie we're both dying to see."

Ten

Nicole walked into the bedroom and watched Eric pull on shorts and a T-shirt. It was still dark outside but the sun would be up soon, and with the sun, the waves.

"I have to leave at eight," she told him.

"I'll be back in time."

She nodded.

For a second they looked at each other. It seemed like there should be something to say—after all, they were married. But lately the words were few and far between.

Eric still slept in his office. So far Tyler hadn't figured it out. For the most part, Eric was up before his son and the boy was used to his dad taking naps on the futon. But still… She worried.

Not just for what Tyler might think but for what it said about their marriage. They hadn't been much of a couple for a while. Now they were roommates. She knew that his sleeping in the other room was a big part of it, yet she didn't want to be the one to invite him back into their bedroom. It felt too much like giving in. Yet wasn't a good relationship based on being willing to think more about the other person? Maybe that was what Eric was waiting for—a little give on her part.

Marriage should come with a manual, she thought as she walked to the kitchen and started coffee. Outside there was just enough light for her to see the backyard and the stone fence that was nearly as old as the house itself.

Their home was an old Spanish-style bungalow built in the 1930s. The walls were thick, the ceilings high and the rooms designed to maximize cool ocean breezes.

There had been a handful of owners. The last one—a guy in the movie industry—had redone the kitchen and a bathroom before losing everything in a film he'd backed that had flopped. He'd listed the house at 1.2 million. While it only had three bedrooms, a tiny office and two bathrooms, it was still four blocks from the beach and in Mischief Bay.

Nicole had seen it at the first open house. She'd fallen in love with the tidy little backyard, the lemon tree that provided shade and the original touches, including beamed ceilings and arched windows. But with its price tag, it might as well have been a hundred million dollars. There was simply no way.

Within a few weeks, there had been a couple of offers, a home inspection, then the revelation of the equivalent of suburban black plague: mold. Mold was found in one of the closets. The deal had fallen through and the house had been abandoned for months.

She'd watched the price drop and drop. Jokingly she'd told the real estate agent when it hit the mid-threes, she would risk it, mold and all. One day she got a call.

Armed with an experienced mold-eradicating guy, she'd faced down the enemy. He'd scraped and tested and sent samples to a lab back east. The results had stunned her. It wasn't mold. The black growing mess was instead decomposing wallpaper from the 1930s. Suddenly she had a bargain on her hands.

Using every penny she'd saved and some very creative financing, she'd bought the house. About a month after she closed escrow, the economy collapsed and the housing bubble with it. Nicole knew she never would have qualified without the loan she'd received, but she didn't care. She had the house and thanks to the faux mold, she wasn't even close to underwater on it.

She'd met Eric a few months later and the rest was history.

She turned her attention back to the kitchen and with it, her life as it was today. She would try harder, she vowed. Would reach out to her husband. His writing the screenplay was a given. But that didn't mean they couldn't be happy together. She just had to find a way to make that happen.

"You sure about this?" John asked.

Pam leaned back in her seat and watched as they drove east toward Palm Desert. "Not really, but it seemed like a good idea at the time. At least the hotel is nice."

Now that they were going to their relationship-find-the-passion-weekend, she was having some serious second thoughts. What a ridiculous idea. Yet, she was reluctant to say they should turn back. Because they needed something to add a little zing to their lives. Everything was so routine.

"I went and saw Hayley this morning," she said. "She's doing better and she'll be back at work on Monday."

"Poor kid."

"I know. It's so hard to watch her go through this." Harder still for Hayley and her husband to have to deal with it, she thought.

John reached across the console and patted her leg. "We were lucky with our kids."

"We were. Lingering morning sickness and me getting fat. That was it."

"You were never fat."

"I was a porker with Jen."

"Never. You were beautiful. Still are."

He spoke without looking at her, his attention on the road. But she had a feeling he wasn't teasing or being polite. In his mind, she *had* been beautiful. Silly man—although as far as flaws went, it was a really good one.

"I told you my friend Shannon is dating Adam Lewis."

"Did you?" He glanced at her. "I don't think I knew that. Good for her. Adam's a great guy."

"I know. I hope it works out. Shannon doesn't say much, but I get the feeling she wants to be in a serious relationship. She looks amazing, but she's close to forty and she's never been married. I know she likes kids. But to be starting at that age…"

He grimaced. "I agree. If we'd done that, Brandon would only be what? Four? To think we had all of that ahead of us."

"I wouldn't have the energy," Pam admitted. "Plus I'd worry more. When I was in my twenties, I did the best I could, but I didn't know that much."

"With years comes experience," he said. "I'm glad Jen and Kirk are starting their family now."

"Me, too. Kirk can't go with her to her first doctor's appointment, so she wants me to go with her."

"I'm glad you can be there for her."

"Me, too."

She looked at him. He was so steady, she thought. So concerned about others. A genuinely nice man. He liked sports and loved his country and his family. He was honest in business. She'd been lucky to find him, she realized, thinking of Shannon and even Nicole, who was going through hell with Eric.

"I want you to know I appreciate all you've given me," she blurted.

Her husband turned to her. "What are you talking about?" he asked before returning his attention to the road. "What have I given you?"

"A wonderful life. Three great kids. A beautiful home. Lulu."

"I didn't give you those things, Pam. We're a partnership. You've got my back and I've got yours." He reached across the console again, this time taking her hand in his. "I'm a lucky man."

"I'm lucky, too."

Palm Desert was a lush and green oasis in the middle of brown desert. Golf courses surrounded upscale communities. The shopping was elegant, the dining fine and the hotel where the retreat was being held looked like some billionaire's idea of a rustic castle.

Pam had booked them into a suite. There was a living room with a deep sofa and large fireplace. The master had a huge bed, views of the mountains and a stunning marble bath. The tub was big enough for five. Maybe using it would be one of their homework assignments, Pam thought as she stared at it. She couldn't remember the last time she and John had taken a bath together.

They unpacked, then headed down for the evening's meet-and-mingle with their fellow attendees. Signs led them to a cozy room with French doors that led onto a patio lit by glowing tiki lamps. There was a bar on one side and a light buffet on the other.

Pam held on to John's hand as they entered. Her first impression was that everyone was gorgeous. The second and more startling was that no one looked to be over thirty-five.

She turned to her husband. "Oh, no. We're the oldest people in the room."

John glanced around and then started to laugh. He tugged her close and wrapped his arm around her waist. "Then good for us."

While she applauded his attitude, she wasn't sure she could be so casual about the very obvious fact. Were the younger women looking at her? Judging her? Imagining that no man would ever want to see her naked? Except John, of course. But he loved her so did that count?

They crossed to the bar. She got a vodka tonic while he chose a Scotch. Conversation was quiet. Most of the couples were standing around awkwardly, with only a few actually mingling. About twenty minutes later, a couple in their late thirties walked in. Pam recognized them from the website.

"That's them," she whispered to John. "The ones leading the weekend."

"Hi, everyone," the woman said. "I'm Vivian and this is my husband, David. Welcome to our seminar weekend."

There were a few murmured greetings, but nothing too enthusiastic.

They were attractive. Both blond, fit and tanned. He was in jeans and a button-down shirt, while she had on a pretty summer dress.

David smiled at them. "We want this to be a safe place for you and your partner. There are no judgments, no criticisms. Just information and suggestions. We want you to have fun and we want you to learn something. And to answer the question you've all been wondering but didn't want to ask—no. You will not be performing in front of the group."

Several people chuckled.

Pam felt her mouth drop open. That question had never occurred to her. If it had, she wouldn't have signed them up in the first place. This had been a mistake, she thought as she looked around. A really stupid mistake.

"We're going to start with an easy game," Vivian said. "We'll go around the room and everyone will say their name and share one sexual fantasy."

"Just one?" one guy yelled.

Vivian grinned. "If we have time, we'll come back to you for a second one."

John leaned down and pressed his mouth to her ear. "This is going to be fun," he whispered.

Fun? This was his idea of fun? She didn't want to share a sexual fantasy with the group. She hadn't ever shared one with her husband. Did she even have any?

Her traitorous mind immediately went to Lulu's vet. No, she couldn't mention him or his dreamy eyes. Besides, her crush on Dr. Ingersoll was more mental than physical. She'd never imagined them having sex.

Vivian pointed to the couple closest. "Why don't you start?"

The woman giggled and blushed. "I'm Amanda. My fantasy is making love with two guys."

Her partner, an equally young, equally buff man, put

his arm around her. "I'm Jeff and my fantasy is two girls."

"I see we're going to have some work here," David said easily. "Nice to meet you both. Next?"

Pam tried to pay attention to the names, but was too busy frantically searching her brain for a fantasy. When it was her turn, she went totally blank.

"Um, I'm Pam and my fantasy is to, ah, make love on a beach."

Lame, she thought grimly. Totally lame. Talk about sounding like everyone's grandmother.

"I'm John and I'm happy to know my wife's fantasy wasn't about spanking."

Several people laughed.

"Because you want that for yourself?" Vivian asked with a wink.

"No. My fantasy is to do it as much as I want for a whole week."

Several of the guys clapped. David pointed to the next couple. Pam stood where she was, her drink in her hand and guilt settling over her like a thick, heavy weight.

Was that really his fantasy? It was such a small thing, she thought sadly. Because she knew what he meant. He didn't just want access, so to speak. He wanted an eager, willing partner. One who wasn't always "in her head." He wanted his wife to be excited about him, about them. Maybe this weekend would help her give him everything he wanted, in more ways than one.

Dinner at the resort was a quiet affair. Pam was relieved to discover they were going to dine as couples, rather than as a group. After she and John had eaten their fill of steak and red wine, they returned to their room. John settled in front of the TV and picked up the remote.

While he clicked channels, Pam checked her phone. Jen had texted a picture of Lulu curled up on Kirk's lap. Man and dog both looked happy.

"Pam?"

She turned and saw John staring at the TV with the strangest expression on his face. Not shock, exactly. More bewilderment.

"What is it?" she asked.

He pointed to the TV. She walked over and stared.

As her eyes focused, he turned up the sound.

A naked woman lay on a bed, while an equally naked man lay next to her, on his side. She was shaved completely bare and the camera angle gave them a clear view of her privates.

The man put his hand on the woman's thigh. The voice-over, a soft-spoken British man, continued.

"Explore your partner's genitals slowly and gently. Start at the top and go down one side, before making the return journey. Men, it is your nature to go directly for the clitoris, but women often prefer a more circuitous route.

"If your partner isn't yet swollen and wet, a lubricant can be used."

"It's not porn," Pam murmured. They'd watched porn a couple of times and while it was sort of interesting, it had never been their thing.

"Oh, there's porn."

He changed the channel and they were immediately assaulted by a shot of an incredibly huge penis sliding in and out of another man's anus.

"There's girl-on-girl and heterosexual couples," he added.

"Something for everyone." She cleared her throat. "Is there regular TV?"

"Not that I can find."

Someone knocked on their suite door. John and Pam looked at each other. John quickly turned off the TV and tossed the remote on the coffee table. He looked as guilty as a teenager caught reading *Playboy* at his grandmother's house.

She was still smiling when she opened the door to find perky Vivian standing there.

"Hi," their instructor said. "This is for you." Vivian handed over a large gift basket. "And just a reminder, there's no TV for the whole weekend. If you're looking for entertainment or inspiration, we're running several instructional videos, along with different kinds of erotic movies."

"Is that what we're calling it?" Pam asked before she could stop herself.

Vivian grinned. "Try a couple. You might surprise yourself."

"Thanks." Pam closed the door, then carried the basket over to the small dining table. "We have a gift."

John got up and walked over. "No TV?"

"I know, honey. You'll have to stream CNN on your iPad."

She untied the ribbon holding the crinkly wrap over the basket. The opaque paper fell away.

"This we can use," John said as he picked up a bottle of champagne. "I'm getting the glasses."

Pam nodded without speaking. She picked up a bottle of what she thought was some kind of ice cream topping.

Only the label showed breasts and promised a delicious, licking treat. There were also masks, blindfolds, velvet-covered handcuffs and the biggest dildo she'd ever seen in her life. Not that she'd seen very many, but still.

There were rings and balls and other things that were just plain confusing. Where did they go and what did they do when they got there?

She picked up what was obviously a vibrator. It was bright pink, in the form of a small beaver next to a large tree.

"What on earth is this?" she asked.

John handed her a glass of champagne. "Are there instructions?"

"For some things, not this."

He took it from her and turned the base. Immediately the tree began to vibrate while the beaver head moved in a circular motion. John's smile widened.

"We are so taking this for a test drive."

Eleven

"That should do it," Nolan said. "Thank you all for your hard work."

Shannon gathered her notes. The monthly senior staff meetings were always grueling. Four or five hours of every department reporting what was going on. Results were compared to benchmarks and then conversation ensued.

She minded the long meetings less than most. Her department had been in such disarray when she'd first been hired that there hadn't been anywhere to go but up. Nolan, her boss and the owner of the company, had given her free rein in hiring and firing. She'd taken advantage of both. Over the past five years, she'd cleaned out the people who couldn't or wouldn't do the job the way she wanted and brought in bright, motivated staff. The finance side of things was now a well-oiled, money-handling machine.

The receivables cycle had been reduced from over ninety days to an average of thirty-two. Loans were consolidated, interest rates negotiated down and she'd played hardball with their bank until she'd gotten the terms she wanted for all their business.

"Shannon, would you stay a second?" Nolan asked, pushing up his glasses as he spoke.

"Sure."

She smiled at her colleagues as they left. A couple gave her sympathetic glances, but she wasn't worried. She and Nolan had a good working relationship. He was brilliant when it came to software and an idiot everywhere else. The difference between him and most almost-successful entrepreneurs was that he understood that his skill set was limited. He was willing to find the best and brightest to handle the rest of the business, freeing him to do what he did best.

She knew that wasn't always the case. When she'd still worked for a large bank, she'd seen dozens of brilliant businesspeople fail because they couldn't let go of control. Every small business had potential, but to get to the tipping point of making millions, there had to be a plan. And one person couldn't do it all.

Nolan had been different. He'd started out as a client, then they'd become friends. She'd helped him write a business plan to take his company to the next level and the one after that. When he'd offered her the job as CFO, she'd taken about ten minutes to make up her mind.

Now he looked at her and grimaced. "I'm going to have to fire Ted," he grumbled.

Ted, the head of operations, had missed every target for the quarter.

"You are," she said gently. "I know it's not going to be easy."

"He's my best friend."

She nodded.

"We dropped out of college together and lived in a garage apartment while we figured out what we were going to do. I owe him."

Nolan was a good guy. A little geeky—which came with the software brilliance. He was loyal and sweet. With his millions, he could have dated a string of starlets who wouldn't care about his thick glasses and wrinkled shirts. They would have their gazes fixed on his bank account. But instead of taking advantage of the local access to those beauties, he'd married his high school sweetheart and, to the best of Shannon's knowledge, had never once looked at another woman.

"You don't have to fire him," she pointed out. "Move him laterally."

"He'll know what I'm doing."

"Yes, but then staying is his decision, not yours. He's simply in over his head right now."

Nolan sighed heavily. "You want to run operations?"

She laughed. "Thanks, but no. I would do a terrible job. I know what I'm a good at and it's not program management. I know some headhunters that can help replace him, if you want me to set up a meeting."

"Yeah, let's do that. But quietly, you know?"

"Sure. We'll do a lunch away from here. No one will need to know."

"Thanks." He gave her a smile. "You're making me feel better about all this."

"Good."

They rose and walked out of the conference room.

Shannon returned to her office. Her assistant handed her a stack of messages. Shannon took care of them, then checked her email before reviewing the latest sales projections.

She was in the middle of studying a forecast when her stomach gurgled and cramped. She ignored both and kept looking at the report. About thirty seconds later, the cramp grew, zipped through her entire intestinal track and had her running for her bathroom.

Twenty minutes later, she splashed water on her face and wondered if it was wrong to wish herself dead. The opening salvo of food poisoning was never happy news. She tried to review what she'd eaten in the past couple of days, but thinking about food wasn't a good idea. Through the closed door of her office, she heard her cell ring.

She managed to walk to her desk and grab it.

"Hello?"

"Hey," Adam said. "Are you okay?"

She pressed her hand against her stomach. "I'm not feeling that great."

"What's wrong?"

She thought about what had just happened in the bathroom. "Trust me. You don't want to know."

"I'm sorry to hear that. I was calling to see if you wanted to get dinner tonight. I'm guessing that's a no."

"I can't. I'm sorry. Rain check?"

"Absolutely. I'll touch base in a couple of days."

"That would be great." Her intestines twisted. "I gotta go."

She pushed End and dove for the bathroom.

Pam stepped into her panties, then reached for her bra. Twinges of pain rippled through her thighs as she moved. When she slipped her arms behind her back, there was a pulling sensation in her side. She laughed softly.

"What's so funny?" John asked as he walked into the bedroom.

"I hurt everywhere."

Her husband crossed to her, his eyebrows raised. "Yeah?" he asked, before pulling her close and kissing her. Not on the cheek, or casually, but on the mouth. With plenty of tongue.

She leaned into him, liking the feel of his body next to hers. His hands unfastened her bra, then slid around to her breasts. He cupped them as he deepened the kiss.

"You have to be at work in a few minutes," she murmured, even as he was backing her up toward the bed.

"I know." He was already pulling his shirttails out of his jeans. "What on earth will I use as an excuse?"

Twenty minutes later, she did her best to catch her breath. "We can't keep doing it like this," she gasped.

He rolled toward her and grinned. "How would you like to do it?"

Sunlight poured into the bedroom. It was nearly nine and any second now Steven would be calling to find out why his father was so late getting to the office. They both had a thousand things to do and she didn't care.

"I love you," she whispered, feeling the warmth deep inside.

"I love you, too, my beautiful bride."

It had been like this since the weekend, she thought happily. Between the way-too-explicit seminars, the porn and the basket of toys, she and her husband of thirty-one years had found their way back to each other.

They'd laughed, they'd tried everything in that basket and they'd made love more times in the past five days than in the previous five months.

She couldn't explain exactly what the shift was. Before

she'd looked at John and felt that she loved him and liked him. But there hadn't been that old thrill. Now she got tingly. Yesterday, he'd snuck home for lunch and they'd gone at it on the kitchen table like teenagers. She was sore and ready to do it again at the same time.

Maybe the seminar had triggered some sexual hormone surge. Maybe the change of scene and a bit of education were all they'd needed to reignite their marital spark. Whatever it was, she was grateful. And very happy.

John stood. "I have to go earn a living. But be thinking about me."

"You know I will."

He winked. "We could try phone sex."

"I think I'd rather have you in person."

He laughed. "Which is exactly why I married you."

They both dressed. He kissed her once before he left. She made the bed for the second time that morning and hummed to herself as she worked around the house. About ten thirty, her cell phone rang.

"Hello?"

"Tell me morning sickness passes," Jen said, sounding miserable. "I feel awful."

"It passes. Are you throwing up?"

"No. I just feel like I'm going to every second. All I can get down is crackers."

"It will get better. I promise. In the meantime, eat what you can. You're not going to get malnourished."

"I have to eat right for the baby."

"You have stored vitamins. Do you feel better in the afternoon?"

"By about two, I'm okay."

"Then eat better then. Your stomach will settle when the hormones do. You're doing great."

"Thanks, Mom. I'm sorry to whine."

"It's okay. All this is new."

"I can't believe you went through this three times."

"It gets easier."

Jen sighed. "I have to run. Thanks for being there."

"I always will be. Love you."

"Love you, too."

Pam hung up and looked at Lulu. "I'm going to be a grandmother."

The dog gave a tentative tail wag, as if asking if that was good or bad.

"Good," Pam told her firmly. "It wasn't before, but it is now. I just remembered I'm pretty hot, for an old lady. So I'll be a hot grandmother."

She took Lulu and they went out to run all the errands. By three she was back and putting away groceries. The weather was already warming up, even though it was only early March. Life was funny, she thought as she set out steak on the counter. The east coast was knee-deep in snow and she and John would be barbecuing for dinner.

Just thinking about her husband made her body hum. She wondered if they would make love again that night. She wanted to. Very much. She wanted the rush of desire, the thrill of having him touch her. Maybe they'd take that ridiculous beaver-tree vibrator out of the drawer and play with it again. Adult toys, it turned out, could make things really interesting.

At five, John walked into the house. After greeting Lulu, he wandered into the kitchen and smiled at Pam.

"Prepare to be amazed," he told her.

She laughed. "I already am."

He pulled a folder from behind his back. "I'm taking you on a cruise. To the Caribbean."

"What? Really? When?"

"In May. We have a spectacular cabin with a big bed and a balcony. We're visiting several islands, including Grand Cayman. I know how you want to see those turtles."

She flung herself at him. "Really? You booked it?"

He set Lulu on the floor, then cupped Pam's face in his hands. "I booked it," he told her, staring into her eyes. "I'm sorry, Pam. You've mentioned those turtles and that island to me for years. I should have listened. I should have taken you sooner."

Tears filled her eyes. "It's okay. I'm so excited we're going on a cruise. We've never been."

"I know. Think how it's going to be when we do it to the rhythm of the ocean." He wiped the tears from her cheek. "I love you."

"I love you, too."

She held on to him. Her heart was so full, she wondered how there could be a moment more perfect than this. A man more wonderful. She'd been blessed, she thought with gratitude. So very, very blessed.

Nicole stared at her list and hoped she had it all. Shannon was still swearing she wanted to help, which was going to be great. Nicole had felt obligated to point out that seven five-year-old boys were going to be loud, but her friend had only laughed and said, "That's what birthday parties are supposed to be."

They were having Tyler's party in the backyard. The rain had ended for the season and the long-range forecast was for sunny, warm weather. Pam was loaning her two folding tables, along with eight chairs.

The food was simple enough. Hot dogs and chips with cut-up fruit and birthday cupcakes. She would be decorating with all things Brad the Dragon. As he was red, that made the frosting colors easy enough.

After waffling for a couple of days, she'd sucked it up and had gone to the party store Shannon had found. Now Nicole had a trunk full of Brad the Dragon party gear.

There were the usual paper plates and napkins. She'd bought sturdy tumblers that would double as part of the goodie bag. She'd added two centerpieces, tablecloths, a custom banner and assorted B the D, as she was now calling him in her head, toys, balls and games. She'd also rented a portable fort that came with slides and other outdoor activities. Her goal was to send her guests home happy and tired.

She heard Eric's car in the driveway and looked up from her lists. Things had been okay between them over the past few days. More friendly, which she liked. She had decided to tell him she wanted him to move back into their bedroom. In fact, she would be doing that tonight.

He walked into the house and saw her in the living room.

"You're up late," he said by way of greeting.

"I'm working on Tyler's birthday party. It's coming up quick. He's growing up so fast." She held out her list. "Want to see what I have planned?"

"Sure."

He crossed to the sofa and sat down. He wasn't next to her—there was a sofa cushion between them. Still it was the closest they'd been physically in weeks.

"How many boys?"

"Seven, counting him. All the toys and plates and stuff come in packs of eight. That gives us one extra for breakage." She looked at him. "You've got the date on your calendar, right? It's on Saturday afternoon."

Eric handed her back the list. His mouth pulled into a straight line. "Why do you do that? Why do you set me up?"

Because he went to one of his critique groups on Saturday afternoons, she thought grimly. Right after she got home from her morning classes.

"It's his birthday, Eric. I'm not trying to be difficult. That is simply the day it is. I don't feel it's right to tell Tyler he can't have his party that day because you have critique group."

"And you expect me to be there?"

The question left her gaping at him. "Is that a real question?"

"You have friends," he said defensively. "I thought you said one of them was helping you with the party. A couple of the moms will probably stay. You don't need me."

It was as if he'd socked her in the stomach. All the air rushed out and she was left stunned.

"Never mind," he muttered. "You're always so dramatic."

"I didn't say anything," she snapped.

"You didn't have to. You looked at me like I'm an ax murderer. It's just a birthday party."

"Right. It's just your son turning five. Why would you want to be there?"

He stood up and faced her, his gaze accusing. "It's not like I wouldn't see him. I'll be here in the morning. I'll be here that night. I just wouldn't be here for the stupid party."

She rose and faced her son's father. "It's not stupid to him." When had this happened? When had he changed so much?

This man in front of her looked the same. Maybe his hair was a little longer, but it was still the same dark brown color. He looked the same on the outside, but on the inside, he was a stranger to her.

Every time she dared to hope they were making progress, she discovered they weren't. That he wasn't the least bit interested in being a part of their lives at all. She was starting to think the only reason he stayed was so that he didn't have to get a job to support himself. That if he ever sold that damned screenplay, he would leave.

She turned the idea over in her head and realized she wasn't sure how she felt about that. Which was incredibly sad. Shouldn't she be devastated? Broken? Begging him to—

"Earth to Nicole."

She blinked. "I'm listening."

"I said I would cancel critique group. I'll be here for the party."

"No," she told him. "Don't. Just go."

"You're not going to let me win on this, are you? So now I have to beg to attend my son's birthday party?"

"No, Eric. You don't have to beg."

"Then what do you want?"

"I want you to *want* to be there. He's your only child and he's turning five. I want you to think that sharing his birthday party is the best thing you could do with your time. I want you to be the kind of dad who wouldn't try to get out of coming." She turned away. "He'll be with his friends. I'm sure he won't notice that you're somewhere else."

He swore. "You don't have to make this so hard, you know. You could try to see things from my point of view."

"Right now I'm more interested in Tyler's point of view. You can take care of yourself."

"Because you're the wonderful mother and I'm just the asshole father. Is that it?"

She walked out of the living room and into the master bedroom. A few seconds later, she heard Eric enter his office and bang the door shut. She waited until she was sure he wasn't coming out, then crept into her son's room.

Tyler slept on his side. His breathing was slow and steady. She smoothed the covers and lightly kissed his cheek before returning to what had become *her* room. As she sat on the bed, she wondered what was happening in her marriage. How had they gotten to where they were and how on earth were they supposed to find their way back?

Twelve

Shannon suffered with food poisoning for an ugly twenty-four hours, then spent the next day recovering. She'd had her first real food—a piece of dry toast—around noon and was now thinking she would make another attempt to keep something in her stomach.

She lay on her sofa, her midsection still sore from all the vomiting and other things that had happened. She'd also discovered that the grout around her toilet and on the edges of her bathroom floor was in excellent shape.

Beside her, on the coffee table, was an assortment of liquids. Some carbonated, some flat. All there to entice her into hydrating. Soup would be very nice, she thought. If she had any. But she didn't.

Someone knocked on her door. She sat up, then groaned as her stomach muscles protested. She was wearing jeans and a T-shirt, which were presentable enough, she thought as she stood and walked slowly to the door. She pulled it open and stared.

"Adam?"

She blinked at the man standing in front of her. The

man who looked all tidy in a long-sleeved white shirt and worn jeans.

She knew the clothes meant he'd come directly from work. Despite the fact that he'd put in a long day on a construction site, he looked good enough to model underwear. Or vodka.

She ran her palm across her hair, hoping to smooth out any sticking-up bits, and wondered how pale she was and how sick she looked.

"Hi," he said as he stepped into her condo and gave her a kiss on the cheek. "I called your office about an hour ago and your assistant said you were still out sick."

He held up two shopping bags and a take-out drink container. "Two kinds of soup, crackers, Sprite and ice cream. Because once you start to feel better, you're going to need ice cream. Oh, and a couple of chick flicks I don't think you have. Don't worry. I'm not staying. I just wanted to check on you."

He stared at her earnestly, obviously concerned he'd overstepped his bounds.

But more important to her was the fact that he'd cared enough to show up. He'd bought her food and movies. He was such a good guy.

She took the bags from him and put them on her side table, then raised herself on tiptoe and wrapped her arms around him.

"Thank you," she said, holding on tight. "You've really made me feel better."

"You sure? You're not mad?"

"Why would I be mad? You went to all this trouble. You're very sweet and I'm overwhelmed."

He hugged her, then kissed her lightly. "Good, because

you being overwhelmed does it for me." He stroked her hair. "How are you feeling?"

"Better. It was food poisoning and the worst of it is over. Now I just have to wait until I'm back to normal." She released him and reached for the bags. "Soup is exactly what I was thinking I wanted tonight. So you're not just a great guy, you're a mind reader."

"I appreciate the credit, however undeserved."

"Want to stay?"

The words were out before she could think things through. Adam probably had a million things to do. Not to mention she looked like crap. Weren't things too new for them to be sharing her being sick?

But he only smiled and said, "I'd love to."

Twenty minutes later, they were sitting at her table. He'd found a frozen dinner he liked in her freezer and heated it in the microwave while she warmed her soup on the stove. He had a beer while she sipped on Sprite. It was all very domesticated, she thought. And she liked it.

"Thank you for coming by," she said. "I appreciate you taking care of me."

"Happy to do it."

She looked at him and he met her gaze. "What?" he asked.

"It's a married thing. Men who have been married are better at dealing with things like a woman getting sick or hurt."

"Are we?"

"Yes. I assume it's the practice." If Quinn had found out she'd been sick, he would have avoided her for weeks. Adam had simply shown up.

"There were a lot of things I liked about being married," he admitted. "Things that I miss."

"Do you miss her?" A risky question, but one that needed to be answered, she thought.

"No. It's over. Long over." He hesitated. "I told you she cheated, but the end of our marriage wasn't that simple. When Tabitha and I were first married, everything was fine between us. We had our fights, but we mostly got along. Then a bunch of things happened at once. We had Char and moved and my dad started talking about taking early retirement. Over the next three years we had Oliver and I was responsible for a multimillion-dollar company and sixty employees."

He reached for her hand as he spoke. As if he wanted a physical connection as he told the story.

"I always knew I'd take over the company, but I thought I'd have a couple of decades to learn to be the boss. I was scrambling to learn everything and not screw up. Work was my priority."

"Something Tabitha didn't take well?"

"No. She was pissed. She tried talking to me and when that didn't work, she threatened me. She said if I wasn't around, she was going to find someone who would be. I didn't listen and I should have."

"That's when she cheated?"

He nodded. "By the time she came clean, things were better at work. I was ready to be a part of the family again. But it was too late. I'm not saying it's my fault she cheated. She made that decision on her own. And obviously there were problems in the marriage in the first place. We were both wrong, but I take a lot of the responsibility. I wasn't there. I didn't show up."

He stared into her eyes. "I learned from my mistakes. That's why I make it a priority to be where I say I'm going to be. I call when I say I'm going to call. I'm on time to pick up my kids. I don't ever want to make anyone feel the way I made Tabitha feel. I was wrong."

No, she thought with wonder. He was perfect. Okay, not perfect, exactly, but close. Oh, so close.

She moved forward the last few inches separating them and pressed her mouth to his. "You're a good man."

"Thank you. I consider myself a work in progress, but I appreciate the compliment."

He released her hand and picked up his fork. Conversation shifted to the movie filming by the pier and the subsequent traffic nightmare.

Later, when they were curled up together on her sofa watching one of the movies he'd brought her, she allowed herself to admit the obvious. That there was nothing about Adam she didn't like. That if she were to make her fantasy list of what she wanted in a man, he would be it. All of it. So the odds of her not getting in too deep with him seemed pretty slim.

Which should have terrified her. Only this was Adam. Whatever happened, she trusted him to catch her when she fell.

"Don't be nervous," Pam said.

Her daughter looked at her and tried to smile. "I'm not sure saying it is going to help. What if I'm carrying an alien instead of a human baby? What if it has a lizard tail?"

"Did you have sex with a lizard alien?"

Jen rolled her eyes. "Of course not."

"Then unless Kirk has some very unusual relatives, you can let the lizard fears go." She patted Jen's hand. "But I get that you're scared. Every mother goes through this. Once you have your ultrasound, you'll feel much better."

"I know. I'm sorry to be a freak."

"You're not a freak. You're my pregnant daughter. That makes you spectacular."

Jen smiled, then sucked in a breath. "No offense, but I wish Kirk was here."

"None taken." Unfortunately Kirk hadn't been able to get the afternoon off work. He was part of a joint task force with the Los Angeles Police Department and they'd had a training exercise he couldn't get out of.

"He'll be here for the later appointments," Pam assured her. "And when you have the baby. If there's a crisis, you always have me."

Jen leaned against her. "Mom, I couldn't do this without you. You're always so calm. The voice of reason."

"I try. Besides, this is an exciting appointment. They're going to date your pregnancy so we'll get to know when I'm going to be a grandmother."

"Because it's all about you?"

"You know it."

Jen laughed, then started to cry. Pam put her arm around her and rode out the emotions. Some of it was the stress of not knowing how things were going with the baby. Once Jen heard everything was normal, she would feel much better. The hormones didn't help, either.

"I used to cry every time I peeled potatoes," she admitted. "Holding them, I thought about the earth and that morphed into Mother Earth, then all mothers, then babies. Your father insisted we eat rice for the rest of my pregnancy."

Jen hung on to her, both laughing and crying. "I'm a mess."

"Kind of, but I love you so I'm not overly embarrassed. Plus, Kirk's not here. That's hard."

Her daughter wiped her face. "I thought you'd tell me to suck it up and be a grown-up."

"That doesn't seem like it would be helpful. He's your husband. This is your first child. While we both understand that he feels horrible not to share this with you, it's not because he doesn't care."

"He does care. He loves me."

The tears flowed again. The receptionist gave her a sympathetic smile. Pam had a feeling the staff was well used to the rush of emotion that came with pregnancy.

"You're going to be the best grandmother," Jen told her.

"Probably."

They both laughed.

Pam continued to hold her daughter. This was what she wanted, she thought happily. A connection with her children. For the life of her, she couldn't remember why she'd been so upset when Jen had told her about the pregnancy. So she was a grandmother? Age was just a number. She had a wonderful family and a new grandbaby on the way. She was also having more sex than was probably legal for a woman her age. She and John were still going at it like rabbits. Since their sex weekend getaway, the longest they'd gone without making love had been two days. Last night they'd joked that if they were paying for condoms, they'd have to take a mortgage out on the house.

Jen grabbed her hand and held on. "Mom, I want Kirk and me to be just like you and Dad when we're your age."

Pam grinned. "I want that, too, honey. I'm just not sure you could handle it."

* * *

Nicole used her straw to stir her iced tea. Not that the drink needed stirring, but she wanted something to do with her hands. Otherwise they would flap all over and betray her nervousness.

"So we have an approximate due date," Pam was saying. "Jen feels so much better now that she's had her first ultrasound. You remember what that was like."

"Scary," Nicole admitted. "You want to know everything is okay."

"Exactly." Pam sighed happily. "I'm going to be a grandmother. I can say that and be proud."

"I would expect no less," Nicole told her, knowing it was the truth. Pam was so warm and loving. She would be a great grandmother. Nicole wouldn't have minded her as her own mother. At least then she wouldn't have been pushed to be famous. Not that she hadn't loved dancing, but she would also have liked to have the time to be a normal teen.

Which wasn't what she wanted to talk about. But her mind was swirling and she couldn't seem to figure out how to ask her friend for marital advice.

They were at Let's Do Tea, in the upstairs dining room. The original structure had been a private residence built in the 1920s. Over the years, the neighborhood had become more business than residential and eventually someone had converted the house into a restaurant. About ten years ago, it had changed hands and become Let's Do Tea.

On the first floor was a retail store that sold all things tea with a small section of imported British food. There was also a take-out counter for sandwiches and scones to go. Upstairs was the actual restaurant with a menu that offered everything from high tea to ploughman's lunches. It wasn't unusual to see mothers with their ten-year-old daughters dressed in hats and lace next to a table of businessmen. Let's Do Tea had the best shepherd's pie in the state and petits fours that had been known to save more than one troubled marriage.

Nicole wondered if she should take a box home with her and see if they would help.

They placed their order, both getting the high tea with coronation chicken sandwiches and the scones of the day. When their server left, Pam glanced over her shoulder, as if making sure they were alone.

"Okay, so you can't tell *anyone* what I'm about to say."

Nicole held up one hand. "I promise. What?"

She wasn't worried—not exactly. Pam was looking too happy for the news to be bad.

"John and I went away for the weekend a few weeks ago," she said quietly.

"Right. To Palm Desert. You told me."

"What I didn't tell you was that we didn't just go to a hotel. It was like a sex camp." Pam flushed, even as she grinned. "It was the strangest thing. How-to classes and toys and lots of porn. But it turned out to be exactly what we needed."

She looked around again, then turned back to Nicole. "We're not like you and Eric. We've been married over thirty years. I can tell you the thrill really does fade. But now, it's all new again. We're like teenagers and it's so fun."

"I'm happy for you," Nicole told her honestly. "And only a little jealous."

"Oh, please. You two are probably still doing it twice a day."

If only, Nicole thought grimly. To be honest, she couldn't remember the last time she and Eric had hugged, let alone had sex.

"Uh-oh." Pam's humor faded. "That's not a happy face. What's going on?"

"Nothing's new, if that's what you're asking," Nicole admitted. "I'm genuinely at a loss. I don't know what to say to him. We barely speak. He's doing more around the house, but the other day we had a big fight about Tyler's birthday party."

"Didn't he like the party theme you'd chosen?"

She grimaced. "He has no idea what it is. It's not that he disapproves of what I'm doing with the party. It's that he's pissed he has to be there at all. It's one of his critique group afternoons and coming to his son's fifth birthday party will cut into that."

Pam's eyes widened. "Oh, hon, I'm so sorry."

"Me, too. Okay, he has a dream. I get that. I want him to be happy and if writing a screenplay fulfills him, then go team. But what about us? We're his family. Tyler is his only son. Shouldn't he be excited about his kid's birthday?"

The server returned with their pot of lavender Earl Grey. Nicole waited until she left before continuing.

"He's gone all the time. Do you think he's having an affair?"

"Do you?"

"I don't know." Nicole watched Pam pour them each tea. She stirred in milk, then held the beautiful rose-covered china cup. "If I had to answer that question right now, I'd say no. I don't think so. It just doesn't feel like that. Wouldn't he have all this sexual energy? I mean look at you. You're glowing."

"It's the BOTOX. I look younger." Pam sipped her tea. "You would have a sense of him cheating. I really believe that. Plus, he'd feel guilty and be a lot nicer."

Nicole sat up straighter. "You're right. That makes me feel better. Now I don't have to worry about hating another woman."

"Have you read his screenplay?"

"No. That's the other thing. I've asked and asked about it. And he kept saying it wasn't ready. So I stopped begging. Then a few weeks ago, he accused me of not being interested. How is that fair? I just don't get him. He's so different from the man I married. It's like he's a stranger. Aliens have sucked out his brain and replaced it with someone else's."

"What is it with you young people and aliens? Jen went on about being afraid she was having a lizard baby. I get sweating the fingers and toes, but a lizard baby? Is it a generational thing?"

Pam asked the question so earnestly, Nicole couldn't help laughing. She put down her tea and let the tension flow out of her body. When she finally caught her breath, she inhaled and felt significantly lighter.

"I love you so much," she said easily. "You're the best."

"That's so sweet, but you didn't answer my question."

"No, I don't think lizard babies are generational."

"I don't want to seem out of step."

Nicole grinned. "You can let go of your lizard baby concerns." She picked up her tea. "I welcome any marital insights you might have."

Pam shook her head. "Eric confuses me. I'm with you on the affair. I trust your gut and I go back to the he'd feel guilty and be nicer statement I made earlier.

He's obviously obsessed with that ridiculous screenplay. I don't like that he won't let you read it. I don't suppose you want to snoop on his computer?"

"Not really."

"I wouldn't, either. What if it's horrible? Of course, it could be brilliant and that would be gratifying."

"I'm not sure I'd be able to tell the difference. I've never read a screenplay before."

"Good point." Pam paused for a moment. "Have you thought about negotiating with him? Maybe he's been secretive because he's convinced you simply want him to abandon his dream. If he knew that you were on board with him writing for a certain period of time, he might relax about it. So suggest he has six months to finish it and then he has to start bringing in money again."

"Maybe," Nicole said slowly, wondering if any kind of compromise was possible. "I'm not sure he wants to return to his regular life, but maybe we should talk about it."

"Knowing there's an end in sight would certainly help you."

"What if there isn't? What if he wants to go on like this forever?"

"Then you have to decide what you want," Pam said gently. "How long can you keep doing what you're doing?"

Their server arrived with their plates of sandwiches. There was a handful of chips on each, along with a small fruit cup.

A timely interruption, she thought ruefully. Because she didn't have an answer to her friend's question.

Thirteen

Lulu trembled as she cuddled close to Pam.

"I know," Pam murmured as she stroked her dog, careful to avoid the angry red blotches from her latest rash. "I know, sweet girl."

The dog had started scratching the day before and this morning she'd woken up with the painful rash on her side and down one leg.

"You are a delicate flower."

Lulu licked her chin, then huddled next to her. Pam knew she was cold, but she hadn't wanted to put on a T-shirt until they had the rash checked out by Dr. Ingersoll.

"Let's go back," Heidi said, holding open the door to the examination rooms.

Instead of jumping down and leading the way, Lulu stayed on Pam's lap.

"All right, pretty girl," Pam murmured as she picked up her pet. "I'll carry you."

They went through the usual steps of weight, temperature and heart rate before Heidi studied the rash on the dog's side.

"I already know the answer," she said with a sigh.

"But I have to ask. Any changes in her diet or laundry soap or bath products?"

"No. It's all the same."

Lulu tried to scramble from the table into Pam's arms. Pam held her, trying to avoid the painful rash.

"That dog," Heidi murmured sympathetically. "Okay, he'll be right in."

Less than a minute later, Dr. Ingersoll entered the examination room. He smiled at Pam.

"We had a good run this time. All right. Let's see what our girl has gotten herself into."

Lulu fearlessly jumped from Pam's arms to his. For a second Pam's hands got tangled up with the good doctor's. Personal contact, she thought with amusement and waited for her crush quiver to activate.

Only there was…nothing. Not a hint, not even a whisper. She glanced away so he wouldn't see the amusement in her gaze. She was cured. Falling madly and sexually back in love with her husband had done the trick. Knowing what she knew now, she would have tried it ten years ago.

Dr. Ingersoll examined Lulu's rash. "That looks painful," he said. "I want to use a cream that combines a painkiller and numbing agent. You didn't dress her this morning?"

"No. She whimpered when I touched her, so I didn't want to put on clothes. It's tough because I know she's cold. I gave her Benadryl."

"Good. That should help a little. You're not feeding her any table food, are you?"

Pam cleared her throat. "Maybe a little."

"You know she's delicate. She might be having a reaction to something she ate."

"It's those big eyes. They're tough to resist."

"Try harder. We'll get her back on her steroids until this calms down."

He gave Lulu a couple of shots to get things started, then filled the prescriptions Pam would need for her. After he applied the cream, he got Lulu into her T-shirt.

"Leave the same shirt after applying the cream," he said. "She's not in fashion. She doesn't have to look perfect all the time."

Pam nodded. "We can go a couple of weeks looking casual."

"Good. Any other questions?"

She looked at him and thought about how he was nice and caring and very sexy. "I have a lot of friends with age-appropriate single daughters. Are you in a relationship?"

Dr. Ingersoll stared at her for a second. He had the most peculiar look on his face. Not surprise, exactly. Chagrin? Curiosity? Confusion? She just couldn't tell.

"I am in a relationship," he told her, at last with a smile. "A committed one. And I'm gay."

Something she hadn't expected him to say, she thought, careful to keep her mouth closed. "If that changes…" she said. "The committed relationship part, I mean. I like fixing up people."

"I'll keep that in mind." He petted Lulu. "You feel better."

After paying the bill, Pam carried Lulu and the meds to the car. She got them both inside and settled behind the steering wheel. Only then did she allow herself to think about her mad crush on Dr. Ingersoll and the fact that the whole time she'd been wondering if he was in any way attracted to her, he'd been gay.

Her mouth twitched. Then she started to laugh. She was still laughing and laughing as she backed out of her parking space and drove onto the street. Life, it seemed, had quite the sense of humor.

"Okay," Shannon said, watching seven boys wait eagerly to have their turn on the fort-swing-jumpy thing Nicole had rented for Tyler's birthday party. "Best entertainment ever. They love it and they're going to be exhausted."

"Right?" Nicole studied the table they were setting. "It's the perfect twofer. Because sending your kid home exhausted is kind of expected after one of these things. Okay—the food is ready. We'll get it out in about half an hour. Then presents, then cupcakes. Does that sound right?"

Shannon touched her arm. "Relax. You did a great job of planning. You even conquered your irrational fear of Brad the Dragon."

Nicole rolled her eyes. "I don't fear him. I hate him. Well, not him, of course. His creator. If I ever meet the guy who created Brad the Dragon, I swear I'm going to back the car over him. What a money machine. He's not in it for the stories. I'll bet he's making millions off the merchandising. Selfish you-know-what."

Shannon actually didn't know what, but with so many kids within earshot, she also wasn't going to ask. Nicole was certainly carrying around a lot of energy when it came to a fictional character. Only Brad wasn't the problem. Eric was. Because while the party had started thirty minutes ago, Tyler's father was nowhere to be seen.

Nicole hadn't said anything, but Shannon had watched her grow more and more tense. She had to be upset, maybe embarrassed. Shannon thought about what Adam had talked about a few days before. How he'd been more concerned about work than his family for several years. Now he regretted what he'd lost. Maybe not his marriage to Tabitha, but the time with his kids. She wondered if Eric would feel the same way when Tyler was older. If he would look back and have regrets. She hoped so. Although having him here in the first place would be a better solution all around.

"Hey, I was here first!"

Nicole looked over to where a couple of boys were starting to push each other. "That's not good."

She hurried over. Shannon went with her. She crouched down by one of the boys.

"I can't remember. Did you say you did want a cupcake after lunch or you didn't?"

The boy, a grinning, skinny redhead, looked at her as if she was an idiot. "I want a cupcake."

"You're sure."

"Yeah."

"Good to know." She straightened and pointed to the swing. "Oh, look. There's no line."

He made a beeline for the swing. Nicole moved next to her.

"Crisis averted," her friend said. "I'm feeling the pressure. None of the other mothers stayed. It's up to us to keep things running smoothly."

"We'll be fine. I'm not above using food as a bribe." She held up both hands. "I know. It's bad, but hey. They're not my kids and it's not like the other mothers left instructions not to."

Nicole laughed. "I like your style." Then her smile faded as she glanced toward the house.

Hurry up, Eric, Shannon thought, resisting the need to look and see if the father of the birthday boy had gotten here yet. Tyler was having too much fun to miss his dad right now, but that wasn't the point.

She wished Adam was here with Oliver, but they'd had a family thing they couldn't get out of.

The back gate opened.

"Thank God," Nicole said, and stared across the backyard, only to come to a stop when Pam walked in with a large, life-size Brad the Dragon behind her. Or rather someone in a Brad the Dragon costume.

"Hi," Pam said with a wave. "I know, I should have asked, but I was afraid you'd say it was too extravagant." She lowered her voice. "He does balloon animals. Who doesn't love a balloon animal?"

Tyler looked up and his mouth dropped open. "Mommy?" he asked, his voice squeaking with excitement. "Is that for me?"

Nicole held out her hands in a gesture of surrender. "Yes, it is. You're going to have to thank Aunt Pam, though."

Tyler flew across the grass and launched himself at Pam. "You're the best."

Pam held on to him for a second, then pushed him toward the life-size character. "I think Brad here wants to wish you happy birthday, young man."

Tyler skipped over to Brad. "Hi. I'm Tyler. It's my birthday."

Pam moved toward Nicole. Shannon joined them, thinking that the extravagant gesture was pure Pam.

"I remember my boys' fifth birthdays," she was saying quietly. "It's when the other mothers stopped staying. Something about the kids being old enough for school and the moms wanting some quiet time to themselves. I got the recommendation from a neighbor's sister. Evil woman, but she gives a great kid's party. You mad?"

Shannon wanted to give Nicole a little shake in the hopes she wouldn't get upset. Sure Pam hadn't asked, but wasn't it worth it? No way Tyler would be missing his father now.

The sudden realization had her studying Pam more closely. Had the other woman guessed that Eric would resist giving up his writing group to attend his son's birthday party? She'd been married for years—she probably knew all the pitfalls. Talk about a good person to have your back.

Nicole hugged her friend. "I will owe you forever."

"You don't owe me anything. I love you both. Now watch this guy make a dragon balloon animal. It's impressive."

The party continued without incident. The boys loved the balloon animals and the fort. Shannon and Pam took charge of serving lunch so Nicole could supervise all seven boys and somewhere around the time they were going to put out the cupcakes, Eric showed up.

As soon as he stepped out of the backyard, he called for Tyler and held out his arms. His son smiled and waved, but stayed with his friends. Shannon told herself it was petty to be pleased, then decided she could live with the character flaw. Pam hid a smirk.

"Serves him right," she murmured to Shannon. "I'm going to get the ice cream."

While the boys played games with Brad, Shannon cleared the tables, dumping the paper plates into the recycling bin. She did her best not to listen to the heated conversation happening by the fence.

"Why are you pissed?" Eric demanded. "I'm here, aren't I?"

"An hour and a half late," Nicole told him. "Never mind. I don't want to talk about it now."

"Well, I'm not talking about it later."

Shannon stepped inside to help Pam.

As she walked into the house, she thought about Adam. He'd already figured out what mattered to him. He was an ordinary guy with a steady job who loved his family. He wasn't a movie star or a record producer. On the surface, he wasn't flashy. And maybe that was the best news of all.

"I honestly don't know where to put my anger," Nicole admitted from her corner of the sofa.

Pam, who sat at the other end of the couch, nodded. "I get that. I really do."

"Throw him out."

That last bit of advice was offered by Shannon, who sat on the floor, stretching out her hamstrings. She looked up and shrugged. "He deserves to sleep in the street."

"I have to admit, the idea of it makes me all tingly inside," Nicole murmured. The picture of Eric shivering and cold was more gratifying than it should have been.

The three of them had had dinner with Tyler, then his two favorite "aunties" had read him bedtime stories until he fell asleep. Talk about a five-year-old boy's idea of bliss. Now Nicole and her friends were in the living room, drinking wine and talking trash.

Pam sipped her wine. "I know it sounds good to change the locks, but it's not that easy. You're married."

Shannon straightened. "The voice of reason speaks. I get that there are complications. Yes, they're married, but how does she get through to Eric? How does she get him to see he's ignoring what's most important in his life? He's going to have regrets later. All that's lost now can't ever be made up."

"You're assuming he *is* going to care someday," Nicole said, wondering if she sounded as bitter as she felt.

"Exactly." Shannon reached for her wine. "And here's another question for our longtime married friend. Why is where we are now the starting place? Why is the assumption that this is the situation we have and we're dealing? Why can't Nicole tell him she wants things exactly as they were and *that's* the starting point for negotiations?" Shannon glanced at Nicole. "I hope it's okay that I'm speaking for you."

"Please. You're doing a great job. I should have you around when I fight with Eric. I'd do much better."

"You would have been an excellent lawyer," Pam admitted.

Shannon wrinkled her nose. "I hear what you're thinking. But not so great at relationships."

"You're wonderful at relationships," Pam corrected. "But not so much on the yielding. There are stages of life. Sometimes we know exactly what we're doing and sometimes we're starting over, even in a familiar situation. Like my daughter, Jen. She and her husband have great jobs and a good marriage. Now Jen is pregnant and everything will be new again."

Nicole nodded slowly. "It's like learning anything. You have to start in the beginners class." She considered Pam's words. "You're saying Eric and I are in a new stage and the old rules don't apply."

"You know this kind of talk makes me crazy, right?" Shannon muttered.

Pam smiled at her. "I know. And you have an excellent point."

"I didn't make one."

"You were about to."

Shannon laughed. "Okay, Miss Smarty-pants. What was it?"

"That if Nicole accepts the premise that she's starting over in her marriage, that doesn't mean she should accept disrespect or allow Eric to treat her or Tyler badly."

Shannon sighed. "Damn, you're good."

Nicole pulled her legs up and tucked her feet under her. "So I let the past go and start with where we are," she said slowly. "But with the expectation that Eric still has to be a participating member of the family and a decent husband."

Was that the answer? To begin fresh?

"I'm still mad at him," she admitted.

"You should be," Pam told her. "There's no excuse for what he did. But that's different than dwelling on what was. You are where you are."

Nicole looked at Shannon. "You still think I should kick him out?"

"I think you should do what feels right for you and Tyler. I'll love you no matter what you decide."

"Me, too," Pam agreed.

Nicole smiled at them both. Love and support, she told herself. Always welcome and right there when she needed it.

Her friends stayed a couple more hours. When they left, she headed for the bedroom, but when she got there, she realized she wasn't tired. An odd restlessness filled her. She'd already cleaned up after dinner. She could watch TV or read, but she was too restless for either. She needed to be doing something, but what?

Without thinking, she headed for Eric's office, then pushed open the door. The futon was flat, with pillows, sheets and blankets at one end. Because this was where Eric slept now. For a while she'd worried that he wasn't coming back to their bed. Now she was more sure than ever. How could she make love with a man she didn't trust, didn't know? They weren't husband and wife anymore. They were roommates who had a kid together, and barely that.

She crossed to his desk and turned on the floor lamp, then sat down. His laptop sat in the center. There were papers in stacks. Printouts of his screenplay with notes in the margin. Some were handwritten and some were from track changes in his word processing program.

She looked at the desk. It had been hers before she'd married Eric. This had been her home office. But slowly, after their marriage, he'd taken it over and she'd moved her things to her small office at the studio.

Now she opened drawers and sorted through the contents. She had no idea what she was looking for. Proof of a secret life, maybe. Receipts or phone numbers. Ridiculous. Eric would keep phone numbers on his cell. As for receipts, she paid all the bills and there hadn't ever been anything unexpected.

He went out for drinks a couple of times a week with his writing buddies, but his bills weren't extravagant. He had lunches out, but they were rarely over twenty-five dollars. If he was seeing someone else, she had modest needs. With Eric not working, it wasn't like he had extra cash to flash around. So what exactly was she looking for?

Nicole hesitated, then pushed the power button on his laptop and waited. The machine cycled through the booting process, then the main screen appeared. Her heart sank.

The last time she'd seen the wallpaper on Eric's computer it had been a picture of her and Tyler. Now she stared at pictures that had been altered with Photoshop to portray Eric holding various awards. He'd dropped himself into several pictures with famous writers and actors. They flashed across the screen in a slideshow that made her desperately uncomfortable.

She understood the power of visualization. She'd been a dancer for years and knew that seeing the performance as she wanted it to be was vital to making it happen. But this seemed different. Or maybe she was simply being critical.

She clicked the icon for his browser, then tried to log on to his email account. She was surprised when his old password still worked.

His pending emails came up. She scanned the names of who had sent them and saw a lot of names she recognized. Names of people Eric had mentioned from his classes and critique groups. She opened a couple at random and they were all about writing. Comments about revisions he'd made or changes they were making in their own work.

Relief mingled with confusion. So he wasn't cheating. Or if he was, he was doing it brilliantly. So what exactly *was* going on?

She closed the email and opened his Facebook page. The news feed loaded automatically—the password saved by the program. Which meant he wasn't hiding anything there, either.

Nicole didn't bother scanning the posts or comments. She had access to them from her own account. Not that she spent much time on Facebook these days. She was too swamped with work.

She logged out of everything. The computer returned to the main screen. She leaned back in the chair and stared at the pictures rotating through on the computer screen. Eric laughing between Cameron Diaz and Robert DeNiro. Eric with Steven Spielberg. Ridiculous images, yet ultimately harmless. And if they helped him focus on what he wanted most in life, then who was she to say anything?

She logged off his computer without bothering to open the file for his screenplay. She'd offered to read it and he'd always said no. She wasn't going to look at it behind his back. Which was a fascinating moral line to draw in the sand considering she'd just gone snooping on his computer.

When the computer screen was dark, she stood and walked to the door, then turned and glanced back at the office itself. Sadness tightened her chest, even as resolve straightened her spine.

Slowly but surely, they were drifting apart. The marriage she'd wanted was no more. As for this new version, she couldn't say where it was going or even if they were on the journey together. She only knew that she hadn't been the one to chart the course.

Latte-Da, a local coffee place by the Pacific Ocean Park, or POP, celebrated the arrival of spring with a big poster announcing they were now serving their homemade ice cream. It was the first Saturday after that illustrious event—the ice cream, not the changing of the season—and Shannon stood in line with Adam and his two kids.

Adam frowned. "I don't know, guys. It's going to be a long wait. Maybe it's not worth it."

Char—not Charlotte—as Shannon had been informed that morning, sighed. "Dad, it's totally worth it. You always do this, and then you taste the ice cream and you get it."

"I want ice cream," Oliver added.

The adorable six-year-old leaned against Shannon and smiled winningly up at her. His small, pudgy hand was in hers. Shannon knew it was exceedingly shallow of her to have a favorite, but she couldn't help it. Oliver was like a puppy. He couldn't begin to hide his emotions and when it came to Shannon, he was smitten. Char, on the other hand, was a little wary. She was still friendly enough, but there was always a distance between them.

No doubt the eight-year-old was protective of her mother and cautious about sharing her dad with another woman. Shannon could both understand and respect that. She wished she could simply take the girl aside and tell her she had no ill intentions. That she would never try to replace her mother. But assuming she could figure out how to say that, would Char even believe her?

They moved up in line.

Char looked up at her dad. "Did you talk to Mom about my birthday party?"

"I did."

"And?"

Instead of answering, he turned to Shannon. "My daughter is turning nine. She wants a..." He glanced down. "What is it called?"

"A spa party." Char's face brightened with excitement.

"It's going to be at Epic. All my friends are having spa parties. They do mani-pedis." She pressed her palms together and locked her fingers. "And there's a new service called the skin care facial. We get a facial and they talk to us about how to take care of our skin. I'm dying for that."

Shannon thought about Tyler's party with the bouncy fort and balloon animals. Boys, it seemed, were a little easier to entertain.

"Do you even know what a mani-pedi is?" Adam asked, his tone rueful.

"A manicure and pedicure," his daughter informed him. "Everybody knows that."

"Do they." He ruffled her hair. "You're growing up too fast."

Char's impatient look said it was all happening too slowly. Shannon wished there was a way to explain that she really needed to enjoy being a kid while she could. That once adulthood was reached, there was no going back.

"Are you going to talk to Mom?" Char asked.

"I will." He looked at Shannon. "I have Char for her birthday weekend this year, so I'm in charge of the party. There will be ten girls and a day to fill."

"I know the spa she's talking about," Shannon told him. "It's not too far from my office. Want me to check it out this week?"

"You wouldn't mind?" he asked.

"That would be so great!" Char said, interrupting them. "Two of my friends have had parties there but not the skin care facial. Can you ask about that, please? It would be the best."

Shannon nodded. "I don't mind. I've seen the, ah, parties they do." She had almost added the word *kids* to the sentence. Fortunately she'd stopped herself. She had a feeling Char didn't see herself as being a child. "There's usually food and cupcakes. It might be one-stop shopping, on the party front."

"And you wouldn't have to be there," Char added, beaming at her father.

"But it's your birthday. I want to be there."

Char's brown eyes widened in horror. "Da-ad."

"I want to go, too," Oliver said, smiling at Shannon. "Are you going to be there?"

Adam's phone chirped. He grabbed it. "This may be work."

Shannon tried not to smile at the pleading tone in his voice. She had a feeling he was hoping for some kind of emergency so he could have something other than Char's party to talk about.

"It's Grandma," he said as he glanced at his screen. "We're still on for dinner tonight and..." He looked at Shannon, then away. "Some other stuff."

"Is everything okay?" she asked.

"Sure."

The word sounded right, but Adam didn't look at her as he put his phone back in his pocket.

The line moved again and they were nearly at the front.

"What kind of ice cream do you like?" Oliver asked her.

"I like the fresh strawberry. What about you?"

"Chocolate. You can share mine."

"That's so sweet. Thank you."

His hand in hers was reassuring, even if everyone else in the family was acting weird.

They got to the front of the line and placed their orders. Adam asked for two empty cups to go with their cones, then they found an empty picnic table by the carousel. Shannon quickly discovered that Oliver could make a mess faster than she thought possible. In about three licks, he had ice cream all over his face. Thirty seconds later, the scoop was tottering precariously. Adam moved the empty cup into place and caught the scoop as it fell.

"You've done this before," she said with a laugh.

"I have." He whipped a spoon out of his front shirt pocket and handed it to his son.

As she studied father and son together, she felt a twinge of something in her chest. Longing, she thought. Need. Not so much her biological clock as a sense of possibility. For so long she'd told herself she couldn't have it all. That the men she met were intimidated by her career, or if they weren't, they also weren't anything close to father material.

But Adam was different. He admired her success, thought she was beautiful and sexy, and he was the kind of man she would want to have kids with. When she was with him, she dared to hope that this could be real. That finally she'd found *the one*.

"I don't need a cup," Char said proudly.

"You obviously don't." Shannon put her hand on Oliver's shoulder. It couldn't have been easy to be Char's baby brother, she thought. But he seemed to be handling it well.

After finishing the ice cream, Adam suggested the kids ride the carousel before they all walked over to the aquarium. When they were both in place and the music had started, he stepped back to stand next to Shannon.

"My mother texted me," he began, his gaze locked on Oliver.

"You mentioned that."

"Easter's coming up. It's a big thing in my family. I don't have the kids. Tabitha's taking them over spring break to visit her folks in Arizona. It's her week, so that works."

She couldn't figure out what the problem was. He still wouldn't look at her and he seemed to be shifting from foot to foot.

"It's okay to tell me you're going to be with your family for Easter," she murmured.

He swung around to face her. "My mom would like you to be there, too."

"Oh." Talk about unexpected.

"It's the fifth," he added, speaking quickly. "We have a big dinner and everyone is there. Siblings, in-laws, grandkids. It's big and loud and you'll be asked a lot of questions. Personal questions. Members of my family don't always filter well."

Understanding dawned. She tucked her arm around the crook of his elbow. "I get it. You're afraid they'll scare me off."

"No. I'm terrified. My family can be overwhelming. The more they like you, the less they worry about being strange. And trust me, they're going to like you a lot." He closed his eyes and winced. "My dad is going to want to talk about how good you look, while my mom will be so impressed by your job. It's going to be one long, humiliating lovefest."

"Sounds like fun. The only thing I can't figure out is if you want me to be there or if you don't."

"Oh, I want you to be there. I'm also concerned about the consequences."

She grinned. "What if I promise that no matter what happens, I'll see you at least one more time?"

He wasn't smiling as he looked at her. "I need you to swear that whatever happens, you won't break up with me. I like you, Shannon. A lot. I don't want that to change because of my family."

His words warmed her in places that hadn't been warm in a very long time. This wasn't about sex, it was about connecting. It was about caring and wanting to be with her. Adam was a conventional man. Taking a woman home to meet his family was an important step. And not one he would take lightly.

She stepped in front of him and took both his hands in hers. "Whatever happens with your family, I will still like you," she promised. "I swear."

"I don't want to lose you."

"You won't."

He lightly kissed her mouth. "Okay, then. It's a date."

Fourteen

Pam parked in the lot for The Original Seafood Restaurant. She felt vaguely guilty as she got out of her SUV. She and John never ate here. They were firmly Team Pescadores.

There were dozens of restaurant choices in town, but only two upscale seafood restaurants. The Original Seafood Restaurant and Pescadores. The story went that back in the day, The Original Seafood Restaurant had been started by two friends who had known each other from birth. Their fathers had been fishermen together, they lived on the same block and they'd always known they wanted to go into business together. And they had—opening their restaurant nearly twenty-five years ago.

Everything had been fine. They'd been an overnight success, had married and started their families. Then something had happened. No one knew what, although there were whispers of an affair. One day the restaurant had been open, the next it was closed—the partnership dissolved.

Everyone thought that was the end of it. The building had stood empty for months. Then one day, just down the street, Pescadores had opened. Nearly the same menu, certainly the same excellent quality. Locals had been thrilled and had flocked to the place. Six months later, The Original Seafood Restaurant had been back in business.

Residents had been torn. Who to support? Could you go to both? Discussions were heated. Some families were torn apart by the tussle. For Pam, the decision had been easy. John was friends with the owner of Pescadores, so that was where they ate. She couldn't remember being inside the rival restaurant even once in the past fifteen years.

That was all about to change.

She walked into the building and found two forty-something women waiting in the open foyer.

"Hello, Pam," Bea Gentry said warmly and shook her hand. She was a petite woman with graying hair and warm, blue eyes. "Thank you so much for coming today. This is my friend Violet."

Violet was a tall, willowy blonde. Pam shook hands with the other woman, all the while wondering what on earth they could want with her. She'd known Bea back in the day, through various sports events at the high school. Brandon, her youngest, had been friends with Bea's oldest. The two women had spent long hours on hard benches watching baseball games. But they hadn't spoken in several years. The invitation to lunch had come out of the blue.

They wore pants, shirts and jackets. Business casual in Mischief Bay. Pam had been nervous enough to eschew her usual jeans or cropped pants in favor of a simple green dress with a black blazer and low-heeled pumps. Looking at the well-groomed women as they walked to their table, she was grateful she'd taken a little extra time with her makeup.

After they were seated, there was plenty of friendly chitchat. Violet mentioned the annual wheelbarrow auctions were coming up.

Back in the late 1800s, when the town had been founded, the police had often transported drunks and criminals to jail in wheelbarrows. Over the years, several of the old pieces had been found and saved. They'd become something of a point of pride in the town. Now new and restored wheelbarrows were placed all around—in front of businesses, in parks. They were decorated. Some were used as planters, others had been converted into outdoor seating.

While the wheelbarrows were owned by the city, every year the rights to them—to decorate, name or brag about—were auctioned off. Proceeds went to everything from refurbishing older buildings to bringing the carousel to the POP. Pam and John had "bought" a wheelbarrow a few times.

"The proceeds this year are going to spruce up The Barkwalk," Violet was saying. "There are a couple of lots coming available on the east side. If they can raise the money, they want to buy the lots, tear down the houses and expand the park."

The Barkwalk was the town's dog park. The space was long and skinny—it started on the beach, then headed inland. "I'd heard that, too," Pam said. "They want to put in an area for smaller dogs and puppies."

"A worthy cause." Bea smiled at Pam. "But not why we asked you out to lunch. You must be wondering."

"I am," she admitted.

"Then let me explain it all to you." She smiled at her

friend, then turned her attention back to Pam. "Violet and I are part of a group called Moving Women Forward. We're based here in town. Our group is an angel network."

"In the business sense, I assume," Pam murmured.

They both smiled. "Exactly."

Pam knew about different kinds of funding for start-ups. An entrepreneur could have his or her own funding, get it from family and friends, get a small business loan or even approach a bank. There were also angel funds. Often they were grants or small loans given when the entrepreneur needed them most. An angel fund helped a company get to the next level.

Bea smiled. "We work with women who are starting businesses or have one that's a couple of years old. We provide funding but also mentoring. We're careful about who we take on, but once we've made a commitment to a business, we're all in. We'll discuss anything from a business plan to marketing ideas to how to hire and fire. We become a silent partner, in a way. Our success rate is impressive. We've made a difference and we want to keep on doing that."

Pam glanced between them. "I don't have a business."

"We know. We want you to join us as an angel."

Pam couldn't have been more surprised. "What? I don't have any experience. I don't know how to write a business plan." She held up her hand. "I never went to college. Not seriously. I took a few classes here and there, but I never got my degree. I'm in no way qualified."

"You're exactly who we need," Bea told her. "You worked with John for over a decade. You juggled children and helped your husband grow his business."

"I was involved," Pam admitted. "But that was a long time ago."

"You're smart, capable and you have good instincts," Violet added.

Pam shook her head. "No offense, but you've just met me."

Violet's smile returned. "We've done our research. We've asked around. We talked to several people who know you, including Steven."

"He never said anything. Neither did John."

"We didn't tell John," Bea admitted. "He adores you. He couldn't possibly be expected to keep a secret. Your son is very impressed with you, by the way. He thinks you'd be terrific."

Pam couldn't take it all in. "I'm really not qualified," she repeated.

"Some of what we do falls outside of the sphere of traditional business," Violet explained. "We offer counseling on whatever topic the women need most. You have led an extraordinarily successful life, Pam. You bring a wealth of knowledge. Don't worry that you are unfamiliar with the specifics like writing a business plan. We have a team that helps with that. Your job would be to be the point of contact. To find out what the women really need, then deliver the resources."

Violet glanced at Bea, who nodded, then back at Pam. "The work is unpaid, in the traditional sense. We don't take a salary. We do have the satisfaction of what we accomplish, of course. For some people, that's not enough. We're also asking that you contribute to the angel fund. So far all our loans have been paid back. We want to be able to do more. If you're interested in joining us, we'd ask you to put in what we did."

"How much was that?" she asked.

"Fifty thousand dollars."

Pam felt her mouth drop open. "Fifty thousand dollars?"

"You could do it over time," Bea said. "We understand there are implications when taking that much out of your investments. So ten thousand a month for five months would be fine."

Pam's breath caught in her chest. "How generous," she murmured. They expected her to give fifty thousand dollars, work with businesses *and* not get paid? Seriously?

"Think about it," Bea urged. "At least for a little while. Talk it over with John. We're making a difference, Pam. We're helping the next generation of women entrepreneurs. We could do so much more with you on board. We'd like to have both of you come down to the office and meet some of the women we've worked with. Hear their stories. It's an amazing opportunity."

She nodded because speaking was impossible. But in her head, she knew she was going to refuse them. What a ridiculous idea. And amount. She and John were comfortable, but that kind of money! It was impossible to consider. Ridiculous.

She would do what they'd requested. She would think about it and then she would tell them there was no way on this planet she would ever agree to do such a thing.

The Lewis family lived in a big house not too far from Pam's. It was two stories and sprawling. Of course, there had been five kids living there at one time, Shannon thought as Adam pulled into the driveway. Now his parents lived there alone.

On the drive from her condo, Adam had explained

some things about his family. How there were lots of
grandchildren and that his parents complained the house
was too big for just the two of them, but never could find
a place where they wanted to move. All really good information that would have made sense if she wasn't so
nervous.

She couldn't remember the last time a guy had taken
her home to meet his family. High school, maybe. Certainly not since college. Except for one of her brief en-
gagements, and that had only been one or two very
awkward meetings. It wasn't the kind of thing she usually had to face.

She'd spent more time worrying about what to wear
for this family Easter dinner than any other event in the
past two years. A dress, she'd thought. Nothing too sexy,
but she also didn't want to look frumpy.

She'd settled on a sleeveless faux wrap dress in mint
green. The front wasn't too low and the hem was only a
couple of inches above her knee. She'd added nude colored pumps and a simple straw bag.

Adam parked the car, then turned toward her and took
her hand in his.

"It's okay," he told her.

"What?"

"You're nervous. I get it. My family is big and loud
and sometimes I have trouble dealing with them."

"If you're trying to make me feel better, you need a
different strategy."

He smiled, then moved toward her and lightly kissed
her. "I think you're amazing, Shannon. Just for this conversation we'll ignore how beautiful you are and how
you blow me away every time you walk into a room."

She stared into his brown eyes and smiled. "Oh, I

don't know. I think we could talk about that for a little while."

"And we will. But right now I want you know how proud I am to be with you. Not just for how you look, but for how you are." A muscle twitched in his jaw. "I know this isn't the best timing, but I want you to know that I love you."

Her eyes widened and her mouth went dry. Those words. Some men spoke them lightly, but not Adam. He would only say them if he meant them.

"I love you, too," she whispered, feeling desperately shy and totally elated at the same moment.

"Yeah?"

She nodded.

His mouth curved into a huge smile. "Wow. That's so great. And you're hot, too."

She started to laugh.

He kissed her, gently at first, then lingeringly. She relaxed into his embrace, only to have the moment interrupted by a car honking. Behind them, a door slammed.

"Get a room," a low male voice called.

Adam drew back. "My brother," he said. "You braced?"

"I am now."

Because he loved her. She held the most delicious secret in her hands. One she would hold close and take out when she needed.

He got out of the car and walked around to her side, then opened the door. She stepped out into the sunny afternoon. From the backseat he pulled a couple of bottles of wine and the brownies she'd made that morning. They were still warm.

She might not be a whiz in the kitchen, but years ago

she'd decided she needed a go-to dish she could take any-where. She'd chosen brownies and had spent the better part of two months finding the perfect recipe. Countless attempts and five pounds later, she had found one that worked for her.

They walked in the house. The large foyer was two stories tall, with plenty of light. From there she could see into a formal living room that was empty, and the big dining room set for dinner.

Loud conversation and music and what sounded like a baseball game drifted in from various parts of the house. The scent of ham mingled with the sweetness of lilies.

"Kitchen first," he told her. "Once you meet Mom, you'll relax."

She wanted to say she already was, only the "I love you" charm didn't seem to be working as well as she would have hoped. The nerves returned and with it the hope she would measure up.

Adam led the way to a big, open kitchen. The cabinets were white, the accent colors blue and green. There was a massive island and a six-burner stove. But she focused on all the people milling around.

Mostly women, she thought, spotting the sixtysome-thing woman who must be his mother. There were also a few other women who were younger, a couple of kids and one brother or brother-in-law.

"Adam!" The older woman smiled when she spotted her son. "You're here." She crossed to him and cupped his face in her hands. "You look good."

"Thanks, Mom." He kissed her on the cheek. "Mom, this is Shannon. Shannon, my mother, Marie."

Marie was of average height. Attractive and trim. Shannon saw he got his eyes and his smile from her. As her hair was blond, he must have inherited his coloring from his father.

Marie turned to her. "So nice to meet you, Shannon. Thank you for joining us today. The whole family is here, so you're going to see us all at once. Don't worry about remembering names. I'm the important one to get to know."

Everyone laughed. Shannon felt herself relaxing.

"Thank you for inviting me," she said. "It's a pleasure to meet you."

"She made brownies," Adam told his mother.

Marie raised her eyebrows. "Did you? Impressive. Tabitha never baked."

"Mom." His voice held a warning tone. "Don't start."

"Me? I didn't say a word." Marie linked arms with Shannon and drew her close. "She cheated. Did he tell you that? A woman with two babies at home. If you're unhappy, get a divorce or take a hammer to his car. But don't cheat. It's so tacky."

Adam flushed. "Mom, I'm begging you. Stop."

Shannon held in a smile.

"I'm just being friendly, that's all. Can I help it if Tabitha didn't bake? It's not like I told her she couldn't. Not that she ever would have listened to me. All right, who haven't you met?"

The next ten minutes passed in a whirlwind of names and faces. Marie kept a firm grip on Shannon's arm as she led her through the kitchen, then into the stadium-size family room. Shannon shook hands with and smiled at all the adults. She did her best to remember which child went with which sibling.

Adam appeared at her side. He held a glass of red wine in one hand.

"Mom, Erin says the ham smells funny."

Marie went white. "What? Excuse me. I'm needed in the kitchen."

"Is everything okay?" Shannon asked anxiously.

"Sure. The ham is fine. Erin gave me a way to help you escape."

"I don't need to escape." She took the wine. "I adore your mother."

"Really?"

"Sure. She loves her family and keeps you all in line. I totally respect that."

"You do realize one day all that laser attention will be focused on you, right?"

"I should be so lucky," she said, wondering what he meant by that comment. Was he hinting at a future together? Something else she could hope for because it seemed to her that belonging to a family like this one would be a very good thing.

"I was afraid she'd scare you off."

"I'm stronger than you think."

"All right you two. Break it up."

Shannon turned and saw a pretty blonde walking toward them. "Sister," she said. "Younger and your name is something exotic and beautiful that I can't remember."

"Gabriella," she said with a laugh. "Everyone calls me Gabby. I am his younger sister." Gabby smiled at Adam. "I'm going to tell her I'm an immigration attorney. Don't correct me."

"You *are* an immigration attorney," Adam pointed out.

Gabby sighed. "If only. I'm currently the stay-at-home mom of twins. But one day they will be in school and then I'm going back to work. Not that I don't love my children, but I can't tell you how I long for adult conversation and time in an office." She looked at Shannon. "You're in business, right?"

"Yes."

"Then you know what I mean. You can go into the bathroom by yourself. No one follows you. You get to close the door and everything."

Shannon lightly touched Gabby's arm. "You have my deepest sympathy and yes, you can pee alone when you go back to work. Are you counting the days?"

"Pretty much."

More family members joined the conversation. There was plenty of teasing and laughter. Shannon had the sense that they were a very loving, close-knit family. She liked all the noise, the bustle as people moved around. There were children running everywhere. A contrast to her parents' quiet, orderly house, she thought. A place where fitting in was the ultimate goal and achieving enough to stand out was frowned upon.

Adam slipped his arm around her. She relaxed into his embrace. He loved her. He'd told her and Adam wasn't the kind of man to play with words that powerful. She could trust them, and him.

Fifteen

The studio was quiet—a welcome relief, Nicole thought. While she adored all her clients and knew that without them, she would be lost, emotionally and financially, every now and then she just wanted quiet.

She was tired of fighting, she thought sadly. She was tired of not understanding Eric, of being disappointed by him. She would guess he was equally weary of their lack of connection and her refusal to be as excited by his dream as he was.

Sometimes she thought that divorce was the only option. She whispered the word in her head and turned it over in her mind. Still, she couldn't imagine saying it out loud. She and Eric were *married*.

But what were the alternatives? Really splitting up? When she considered the logistics, the reality of being a single mom, of possibly having to pay alimony to Eric so he could keep writing his stupid screenplay, she got so angry and so afraid, she couldn't breathe. The thought of going through that, of tearing apart their lives—it was awful. And worse, truly much, much worse, was what a divorce would do to Tyler. While he wasn't as close to his dad as she would like, Eric was his father. She couldn't separate them. Couldn't force her son to travel from home to home, spending weekends with one and weekdays with the other. How could they make that work?

She looked at the names on the paper in her hand. Two were for therapists and one was for an attorney. The first two came from Pam and the latter from Shannon. It had been Shannon who had explained the grim reality of community property.

The house wasn't an issue. It was in Nicole's name and she'd never added Eric to the deed. He'd never asked, which only helped her case. Even more important, over the past year or so, she'd been the only one bringing in money. So whatever happened, she would keep her home.

But the business was more complicated. While it was in her name, they'd bought it with joint assets. So he had a claim there. Shannon had started to explain about business valuation, but Nicole's eyes had glazed over. She wasn't ready to know that much. She wasn't ready to go there.

Nicole fingered the paper. She knew she had to make a choice, one way or the other. Which was it to be?

She drew in a breath and picked up her cell phone, then dialed the first number. Therapy, she thought as the call connected. She went right to voice mail, as Pam had told her she would. The psychologist would call her back and set up an appointment.

Pam had explained how she and John had seen the woman while they were dealing with Brandon's difficult stage. There had been family counseling, of course, but she and John had wanted to see someone different. Someone who was in it for them and their marriage.

"Every marriage has its ups and downs," Pam had

told her. "Dealing with Brandon's drinking and drug use had been so awful. John and I had ended up fighting all the time. Seeing the therapist helped us see that we were taking our fear out on each other instead of using each other for support. She's great. You'll love her."

Pam had also provided the name of a male therapist in case Nicole talked Eric into couples counseling. Most guys were more comfortable with a man, she'd said. Wise advice, but then Pam was always ready with the upbeat and practical suggestion.

Nicole left her name and number and mentioned Pam as the person who referred her, then hung up. She drew in a breath and noticed she wasn't as tense as she'd been. The knot in her stomach was a little smaller and her breath came easier.

"Okay," she whispered to herself. "I made the right choice. Therapy."

She had no idea how she was going to pay for it, but that was a problem for later. This was good—she had a direction. She would fix things with Eric. They would be a family.

A direction chosen and some small amount of faith restored, she turned her attention back to her computer. There were monthly bills to be paid.

She got out her business checkbook, then went on to her bank's website and used the bill-pay function. For a small fee they would even produce paychecks for her employees—a real gift. Because payroll for those not blessed with the accounting gene was a nightmare.

After paying the bills and generating the paychecks, she updated her balance. Talk about a virtuous hour, she thought. She had another hour until her next class. She could go get a coffee or she could stretch and do a mini-workout for herself. That would feel good.

She rose and started for the mats against the wall. As she walked toward them, someone knocked on her locked front door.

She changed direction, then slowed when she saw Eric. She couldn't remember the last time he'd come to the office. The knot returned when she got closer and saw his face.

He was wide-eyed and flushed. Everything about his body language told her something had happened. Her heart felt as though it actually stopped as she fumbled with the lock.

"Is it Tyler?" she demanded the second the door was open.

"What? No. He's fine. He's at day care. Why would you think something was wrong with him?"

"Because something's happened."

Eric surprised her by laughing, then he grabbed her hands. "I forget that you know me. Of course you'd guess." He spun her around. "Nicole, you're not going to believe it. I can't believe it. I did it. I swear to God, I did it."

"Did what?"

"I sold the screenplay. I have an offer and it's incredible." He kissed her on the mouth, then stepped back, as if he couldn't possibly stay still.

"You know I've been in meetings, right?" He walked to the door, then turned and moved toward her. "I can't believe it."

She was stunned. More than stunned. A little chagrined. She hadn't known he'd finished the screenplay.

Not that he ever told her much lately, but still. Sold. He'd done it.

"I'm really proud of you," she told him. "You had a dream and you made it happen."

"I know. I'm still trying to figure it all out." He laughed again. "The money. Want to know how much they offered?"

"Sure."

"Guess how much."

"I have no way of knowing. Honey, it's not about the money. You sold a screenplay. No matter what, you'll have that for the rest of your life. It's incredible."

"A million dollars."

The room seemed to tilt a little. She shook her head, confident she hadn't heard right. "What?"

He threw back his head and yelled, "I sold my screenplay for a million dollars." He raced toward her, caught her in his arms and spun her around. "One million dollars. My agent's negotiating for more, but screw that. It's fantastic. Do you know what this means? I'll be helping again. Paying the bills, buying food. You want a new car, because you can have one. A Mercedes."

He put her down and kissed her. "I gotta go. I have to meet with my agent and then the studio wants to talk to me." He was beaming. He kissed her again. "I couldn't have done it without you, Nicole. I hope you know that. You're the best. I'll be late tonight because my critique group's taking me out. But you and I will celebrate soon. This weekend. I promise. I love you."

And then he was gone.

She stood alone in the quiet of her studio and didn't know what to feel. What to think. Eric had sold his screenplay for a million dollars?

She sank onto the floor and drew in a steadying breath. When had that happened? How? And why hadn't she known it was possible? Of course the news was wonderful. Amazing and good for him. Of course she appreciated that money wouldn't be tight now. And he'd said he loved her. She hadn't heard those words in months. It was all wonderful and exciting.

But it wasn't anything they were doing together. Once again he was gone and she had no idea when she would see him again.

No, she told herself. Everything would be fine. He needed time to celebrate. He'd earned it. Good for him. And later, they would figure it all out together.

"It's ridiculous," Pam said firmly. "And I'm done having this conversation."

"You wouldn't say that if they'd come to me," Steven told her.

"It's a group that supports women," she pointed out, trying not to let her annoyance bleed into her voice. Why on earth her family couldn't let this go was beyond her. "They wouldn't have come to you."

"I can be very supportive of women."

Pam rolled her eyes. "Are you really going to go there? Because we can talk about how I took care of you after you were circumcised."

Her twenty-six-year-old son held up both hands in a gesture of surrender. "Sorry, Mom. I'll do anything if you don't talk about my penis."

She relaxed. Order was restored, she thought happily. "As long as you remember, I have ultimate power."

"Always and forever. You are the queen of this family and we worship at your feet."

"That's going a little far, but I accept your fealty."

They were in the kitchen, where all important conversations took place. It had been a couple of weeks since her meeting with Bea and Violet and for reasons she couldn't understand, no one in the family was letting it go.

She'd told John, expecting him to be as shocked and outraged as she had been, but he'd told her they could afford it and she should consider it. Forty-eight hours later, she'd still been openmouthed.

"It's fifty thousand dollars," she reminded Steven as she got up to get more coffee.

"You have the money. Besides, you're not blowing it. You're paying it forward in a really cool way. Come on, Mom, you could make a big difference. You know how you love taking care of all of us. Imagine what you could do in the real world."

"I don't have the business experience."

"You're selling yourself short."

Just what John had said, she thought, both pleased and frustrated by her family's faith in her. Of course, Steven was just like his dad. They were both over six feet, with dark blond hair and blue eyes. Strong men with good heads and gentle hearts. The difference being John had married young and settled down and Steven's idea of a long-term relationship was six weeks.

"Are you seeing anyone special?" she asked as she returned to the table and handed him his coffee.

"You know we don't talk about my love life."

"We don't talk about your sex life. There's a difference. Don't you want to fall in love?"

"Sure. One day. But for now, variety is the spice of life."

Part of the problem was Steven had it easy with women, she thought with both pride and concern. He was handsome and charming.

She held her mug in both hands. "If you're worried about it getting boring with just one person, it doesn't have to. Sure there are times when things get routine, but there are also ways to break out of that. Your father and I still find each other exciting."

Her son froze, his mug raised halfway to his mouth. The color left his face and his eyes widened. "Mom, I beg you. Stop. Honest to God, I would rather talk about my penis than this."

Pam's mouth twitched. "I'm just trying to reassure you."

"I know and it's great that you and Dad still do that kind of stuff. But I don't want to know. Seriously. Don't take this wrong, but it's gross."

"All right. We'll talk about your penis instead."

The mug slammed onto the table and coffee spilled over the edge. Steven sprang to his feet.

"Okay, that's it. I'm out of here."

He circled the table, kissed her cheek and called out a goodbye to Lulu.

"We're still doing it like rabbits," Pam called after him.

"I can't hear you."

The front door slammed shut.

She chuckled as she cleaned up the mess and put his mug in the dishwasher. Sometimes her kids were so easy to rattle. It almost wasn't a sport.

She glanced at the clock, then pulled out the ingredients for meat loaf. She could prepare it now and still give Lulu a bath before John got home.

She was looking forward to seeing her husband more than usual. Not just because thinking about him still gave her a little thrill, but because of what Nicole had said when she'd called earlier. Eric had sold his screenplay for a million dollars.

Nicole was still in shock, which made sense to Pam. Who knew he was that talented? That he was making that much progress? Good for him and the family, but still, very strange.

The rest of the afternoon passed quickly. Pam finished her chores and popped the meat loaf in the oven. Lulu strutted around in her pink T-shirt, all fresh and happy after her bath. Her rash was better, so she wasn't quite so uncomfortable.

Pam got out the bag of potatoes and put a couple in a bowl. She had just reached for the peeler when she heard the garage door open.

Lulu barked and headed for the side door. Pam's stomach gave a little *ping* of excitement. Oh, yeah, it was good to be her.

"How's my best little girl?" John asked as he walked into the house. Lulu yipped with happiness as the pack was restored to its full glory.

"And how's my best big girl?" he asked as he came into the kitchen. He smiled at her, the dog still in his hands. "Meat loaf," he said just before he kissed her. "My favorite. You spoil me."

"Always." She stepped into his embrace.

Lulu was caught between them. The dog alternated who got puppy kisses while Pam and John did some adult kissing of their own. When they came up for air, he patted her butt.

"How was your day?" he asked.

"Good. Yours?"

"Not bad."

She took the dog and gave him a little push toward the family room. "Go. I know very well there's a Dodger game on even as we speak. Go and watch it. I'll call you when dinner's ready."

He paused to drop another kiss on her cheek. "Have I told you how lucky I am?"

"You have and you're going to get even luckier later tonight."

He chuckled, then walked toward the family room.

Pam set Lulu on the floor. The dog trotted away to join John. Not that she was all that interested in baseball, but she did enjoy a snooze on a warm lap.

Pam continued her preparations for dinner. She set the table while the potatoes and carrots cooked, then opened a bottle of wine. Lulu trotted back into the kitchen and stared at her.

"What?" Pam asked. "You've already eaten, remember?"

Lulu stared at her for a second, then barked.

"What?"

The dog looked toward the family room.

"John? Is everything okay?"

There was no answer.

Pam followed Lulu through the doorway. John was stretched out on his recliner, his eyes closed. The game played softly in the background.

"He's sleeping," she told the dog. "Silly girl. John, honey, it's nearly time for dinner."

John didn't stir.

Pam walked close and shook his arm. "John? John? Wake up. John!"

Sixteen

The Eiland house was full of people Shannon didn't know. Somber strangers who were mostly dressed in black, murmuring about how unexpected it had been. How shocking. Poor Pam. The kids were mentioned by name. No one had seen it coming. He'd been so strong, so healthy. How would she survive?

All great questions, Shannon thought as she walked through the formal living room and picked up abandoned plates and cups. She carried them to the kitchen, where Nicole and a woman named Hayley were loading the dishwasher.

The caterer had offered to arrange for staff to assist with cleanup and putting out the food, but Shannon and Nicole had said they would handle it. Because somehow it felt like helping in a time when there was genuinely nothing to do. Hayley, who had introduced herself as John's secretary, obviously felt the same way. Every fifteen minutes she carried a coffeepot throughout the room of mourners, offering refills.

"Hey," Adam said as he came up and put his arm around her. "How are you holding up?"

"Okay. I was just thinking how we all get caught up in ridiculous tasks at a time like this. I can't stop cleaning up after people. Hayley's obsessed with the coffee and Nicole keeps topping up all the buffet items."

He squeezed her close. "No one saw this coming. We're all in shock. John was a great guy. From what my dad told me, there was no evidence of any heart trouble. His blood pressure was low and he was plenty active on the job. It was just one of those things."

Shannon knew what he meant but doubted Pam saw it that way.

She visually searched the room until she spotted Pam standing surrounded by her kids and a few friends. She was pale and seemed to have lost weight. Impossible considering it had only been three days, and yet she looked gaunt and drawn.

Shannon saw that everyone else was talking, except Pam. She stood in the middle of the group and yet entirely alone. Her hands shook as she balanced a plate of uneaten food. The half sandwich and scoop of mac and cheese trembled.

Jen, Pam's oldest, started to cry. Her husband led her to the largest sofa. Several guests moved to make room.

Jen was pregnant, Shannon thought, remembering when Pam had told her the news. The stress couldn't be good for her or the baby. Nor was the realization that her child would never know his or her grandfather. Was Pam thinking that? Was she aware she was going to be a grandmother alone?

Shannon couldn't grasp what it must feel like to have been with someone for over thirty years, yet imagining the loss was somehow easier. Maybe because pain was universal. Whatever the cause, everyone had felt it in some form or another.

She wanted to say something to her friend, to offer comfort. A ridiculous need. Because there was no comfort to offer. Pam had been married longer than Nicole had been alive. She'd just lost her husband. She had defined herself, lived her life, planned her day, raised her kids, all of it as John's wife. He was the rhythm of her days. And now he was gone and she was expected to go on? Impossible.

"I feel so bad for her," she said, not sure how to articulate any of it.

"Me, too. It's horrible."

She touched his arm, then stepped away. "I need to get back to my compulsive cleaning."

"Sure. I'll call you later tonight."

She nodded and allowed herself a moment to savor the fact that he would call. That she could depend on him. That at the end of every call, every date now, he told her he loved her. He said it clearly, looking into her eyes, with an intensity that chased away any doubts.

She walked through the family room and picked up a few plates and cups, then returned to the kitchen.

Nicole was alone, leaning against the counter. Shannon walked up to her and they hugged.

"It's so awful," Nicole said. "I feel sick to my stomach. I never told Pam, but sometimes I would pretend they were my parents. When things were bad, it was nice to think I wasn't alone, you know? So in a way, it's like I lost a part of my family. Not that I would tell her that. Am I making sense?"

"You are. We're all rattled. It's horrible for everyone."

"Especially Pam," Nicole said with a sigh. "She must be terrified."

"I think she's still in shock."

"I would be and I'm used to Eric being gone a lot. John was home every night, though. She's not used to that."

Shannon nodded without commenting on Eric. He'd been at the funeral, but then had left. Nicole had ridden back to Pam's in Shannon's car. Nicole had said something about him taking a meeting.

They watched the people move through the buffet line. There were several hot dishes, along with sandwiches and salads. On the island were the coffeemaker, pitchers with different kinds of juice and a plastic container filled with ice and sodas in cans. Open bottles of wine stood next to long-stemmed glasses. Cupcakes, cookies and brownies were on a smaller table by the door to the family room.

"Jen and her husband are staying with Pam tonight," Shannon said. "Steven mentioned he would be moving in for a week or so."

Nicole nodded. "That's nice of him, but then what? She has to figure out how everything is going to be different."

"I know. I was thinking we'd back off for the next couple of weeks. She'll have plenty of friends and family around. What if you and I agree to hang out with her after that? Through the time when everyone returns to their regular lives and she's still in shock."

Nicole nodded as tears filled her eyes. "That's perfect. I want to do that with you. We'll make a schedule or something. Because Pam's always been there for me."

"Yes," Nicole said firmly so the woman on the other end of the phone wouldn't know she was nervous. "I'm confirming my account balance."

Because Eric had received payment on his screenplay and she couldn't quite grasp that much money was sitting in their checking account.

She waited while the woman typed.

"You have five hundred and fifty-one thousand dollars in your account."

Nicole exhaled slowly. "Okay. Great. Thank you."

She hung up, then tossed her cell phone onto the sofa. Hysterical laughter and tears both threatened. It was real. Totally and completely real. The contract had been signed and Eric had been paid. Fifteen percent had gone to his agent and he'd told her he was going to send off thirty percent to the government, so they wouldn't have to worry about that. Talk about being responsible. Just as startling, he'd put the balance of the money into their joint account.

Until this second, until she'd known for sure he would, she'd been half expecting him to take the money and run. Shannon's talk about community property be damned.

But he hadn't and now Nicole was left feeling pretty crummy about herself. Sure, Eric was busy a lot and he could be difficult and he wasn't always there for her and Tyler. But he obviously hadn't been secretly waiting to disappear from their marriage.

That was good, right?

Despicable Me 2 played on as Tyler cuddled next to her. In the distance the sound of the shower continued. She closed her eyes and told herself it *was* good. She had to look on the bright side and a few other clichés. Because as far as she could tell, selling the screenplay might have put money in their checking account but it hadn't changed anything else.

Eric was still gone all the time. He had meetings. Actually he was *taking* meetings. He had a rewrite due and was working on that. He was still surfing most mornings.

The sound of the shower turned off and she opened her eyes. For a second she wanted to hide her cell phone, which was ridiculous. Why would Eric care that she'd called the bank? He would probably think it was funny. It wasn't like he knew she'd been worried he would simply disappear with his windfall.

"Are we going to the park tomorrow, Mommy?" Tyler asked.

"We are. I get home at noon, then we're going to have lunch and go out all afternoon."

Her son smiled up at her. "I like the park."

"Me, too. After we're done with the park I thought we'd go see Auntie Pam and Lulu." Because she and Shannon were starting their plan of visiting their friend regularly.

So far Pam hadn't returned to class. She also wasn't very talkative whenever Nicole phoned to check in on her. Not a surprise— How could you get over losing a husband of over thirty years? Nicole was sure Pam couldn't remember what life was like without him.

Eric walked into the living room. He'd dressed casually—new jeans and a shirt she didn't remember seeing. Both looked expensive. Not that she was going to ask.

"What's the meeting tonight?" she asked.

"Jacob."

She nodded, although she had no idea who Jacob was. There were too many new people in her husband's life these days.

"I shouldn't be late," he added, then smiled at Tyler before returning his attention to her. "Can we talk in the kitchen for a second?"

"Sure." She kissed Tyler's forehead. "I'll be right back."

He nodded as he watched the minions having fun on what looked like a tropical island.

Nicole followed Eric into their small kitchen.

It was clean for once, mostly because she'd spent an hour after dinner scrubbing it. Since selling his screenplay Eric hadn't bothered with any of the household chores. Something she was going to have to discuss with him. But she saw him so rarely these days and fighting about chores seemed...

She couldn't say what. Uncomfortable wasn't right. She had a bad feeling that because he'd scored such a huge paycheck, she felt she didn't have the right to bug him about stuff around the house. A ridiculous concept that suggested contribution was only valued if it was monetary. Applying that theory, then before he'd sold the screenplay, he should have been doing everything. And he hadn't. Nor had she expected him to.

"About Tyler," he began, then checked his watch. It was gold and she couldn't remember seeing it before. "I'm going to be busy with my rewrites and meetings. There's no way I can be taking him to day care and picking him up."

She opened her mouth to protest, but he shook his head. "Let me finish."

"All right." She folded her arms across her chest and told herself she wasn't going to give in to anger. That the pissy feeling would pass.

"I want us to get some help around here. Like I said, I'm going to be busy and you have responsibilities with your business. Now that we have the money, it's ridiculous not to use it to make things easier. I think we should get a nanny to pick up Tyler and a cleaning service to come in once a week."

Talk about reasonable, she thought, oddly resentful and not sure why. "That would help a lot."

"Good. Do you want me to ask around for suggestions? Maybe we could get a housekeeper who is also a nanny. It would be nice if you didn't have to always be scrambling to cook dinner."

"I, ah, okay. I wouldn't know where to start with something like that," she admitted. A part-time housekeeper-slash-nanny-slash-cook? In her world? Was this really happening?

"I'll get some names and you can interview them."

"Thank you." She drew in a breath. "Eric, I appreciate that you're concerned about the logistics of our life. Thanks for that. But what about us?"

He stared at her blankly. "What do you mean?"

"You're gone a lot, which is fine. You have to be right now. We both have responsibilities. But you and I never spend any time together. We never talk. I'm worried about us."

Several emotions chased across his face. They were too quick for her to catch and read, so she was left wondering what he was thinking.

"I know," he said. "You're right. We need to find some time. And we will." He kissed her. "I gotta run. I'll see you later."

And with that, he was gone. Nicole stood in her kitchen and hoped he meant what he said. That he was paying more than lip service to the cracked vessel that was their marriage. Because if they weren't careful, it was going to shatter and fall apart completely.

* * *

Pam wasn't sure when the house had become the enemy. She would have said she knew every inch of it. She'd lived through remodels, understood the idiosyncrasies of the various systems. She was at peace in her house. Or she had been.

Now it was a torture chamber, a prison filled with memories. A mocking, living creature that held her captive with the simple reality that she had nowhere else to go.

John had lived in this house. John had talked and laughed and slept and made love and ultimately died in this house. She wandered from room to room, searching for something. Him, most likely, because even though her head knew the truth, her heart was still waiting to hear his footsteps, his voice. Her body longed to be held, to be comforted. Because only he could understand how she grieved.

The phone rang. Pam ignored it. She didn't want to take any calls, didn't want to hear the platitudes. Time did not heal. The gray skies were not going to turn blue. She wouldn't find closure. What the hell was closure? How could there be closure? She wasn't recovering from something small. Something simple. Every time she woke up, she remembered that the very essence of her being had been ripped from her. She was like one of those people who accidentally survived a horrific accident. She was parts, not a person, and she should have been left by the side of the road to die.

But no matter how she wished that to be true, she lived. She breathed, she walked through her house and knew that nothing was ever going to be the same again.

She stood in the center of her kitchen and shivered.

Not from cold, but from a lack of warmth. A lack of comfort. She shivered with the realization that there was no deal to be made, there was nothing she could sell or offer. No authority would listen to her begging and respond with compassion. John was dead. He was never coming back.

She heard the click of Lulu's nails as her dog circled her anxiously. She reached down and gathered the small animal in her arms. For the past three weeks Lulu had been her silent companion. Except for the funeral, Pam hadn't left the house and Lulu hadn't left her side. At night, when Pam curled up in John's old recliner, Lulu curled up with her.

Her cell phone rang. Strains of "Footloose" filled the kitchen, which meant she could ignore the call. When her kids called, the phone ringtone was Michael Jackson's "Thriller." Not that she loved the song so much, but they all claimed it made them crazy, so it was a family joke that she'd chosen it.

She'd been careful to always take their calls so they wouldn't worry. She was able to do that much, at least. Let her children believe that she was healing. A ridiculous thought, but one they seemed to think was important.

John would have wanted that, she thought, still holding Lulu close and letting the dog's small body warm her. They would have discussed how well Brandon was doing in medical school and how he didn't need more to worry about. That Steven was struggling to fill his father's shoes at the business. And Jen had to stay calm because of the baby. So many reasons that none of her children could know how she woke every morning only to watch her heart bleed out yet again.

Her stomach rumbled. She looked at the clock. It was nearly four in the afternoon. She wasn't sure of the day. Time had started blurring. She knew at some point she had to eat, but the thought of food made her want to vomit. It didn't matter how hungry she was, she simply couldn't stand to chew and swallow. Every few days she threw out the casseroles that were in the refrigerator and pulled a few more out of the freezer. She fed Lulu when the dog told her it was time. She let her out in the yard, collected the mail every day, paid the bills that arrived and when she thought she might have been in the same clothes for several days, she showered and changed them.

The first week had been different. People had been with her all the time. They had guided the rhythm of her now broken life. But one by one they'd left. There were other things to be tended to, other places to be. Jen had stayed the longest, but after four or five days, she, too, had returned home.

Pam didn't mind the solitude. She bled whether someone was here or not. The nights didn't bother her, mostly because there was little sleep to be had. When she was alone, she could cry or scream or simply stand in the middle of the room and do nothing.

The doorbell rang. Lulu barked and struggled to get down. Pam put her on the floor and the little dog took off to announce that someone had arrived.

Pam followed more slowly. She wasn't completely sure of the day, so didn't know if her visitor was as simple as the UPS man or as complicated as anyone else.

She opened the door and saw Shannon standing there. Nicole and Tyler were beside her.

"You're not answering your phone," Shannon said

by way of greeting. "That's going to get people to worrying."

"I don't want to talk to anyone," Pam admitted, trying to remember if she'd invited the three of them over. She didn't think so. "Why are you here?"

"Because we love you. Now let us in."

Pam stepped aside because it was easier. Tyler rushed toward her and Pam instinctively bent down to hug the small boy. For that brief second when she held him, she could breathe. Then she straightened and the hell returned.

Nicole smiled sympathetically. "Hey," she said softly. "We're all here for you."

Pam nodded, knowing she meant well, but that no company, no words, could possibly help. Shannon walked in, a large pizza box in her hand. The smell of cheese and tomato sauce made her stomach growl again. This time it cramped, as well, and she swayed a little on her feet.

"Are you okay?" Shannon asked. She closed the door behind herself and set the pizza box on the foyer table. After hanging her purse and jacket, she scooped up Lulu. "Hey, pretty girl. How's your mom?"

"I'm all right." Pam spoke deliberately, thinking about each word. Planning them so they came out in the right sequence. Normal conversation seemed impossible right now. How did people know what to say next?

"I'm going to get Tyler settled in the family room," Nicole said. "We brought movies."

Tyler went with her obediently. Because he was still at an age when being around Mom and Dad was the best part of the day. Pam remembered what that had been like—when all three kids had competed for her attention. That had been nice. Of course, John had still been with her.

Shannon put down the dog and picked up the box. "Come on. Let's eat. I'm starving. I missed lunch. Usually my department is a well-oiled machine but every now and then we screw up as much as everyone else. It's so discouraging. All is well now. I've chastised the ones who made the mistake and they are suitably afraid of me once again. Order is restored."

Pam listened to the words and wondered if any of them were funny. Should she laugh? Was that the right thing to do? She wasn't sure about anything anymore.

Following Shannon seemed like the easiest course of action, so she did. Once in the kitchen, her friend set the box from The Slice Is Right on the kitchen table and got out four plates.

"Have you been eating at all?" Shannon asked as she moved around the kitchen.

Pam thought about lying, but what was the point? Did it matter if anyone other than her children knew the truth? "No."

"I didn't think so. You've lost weight. Come on. Have a seat."

Pam walked over to the chair Shannon had pulled out and sat down. Her friend put a slice of mushroom and green pepper pizza—Pam's favorite—on a plate.

"What about Lulu?"

Pam stared at the melted cheese, the roasted vegetables, and her mouth watered. In that moment, she could see herself biting, chewing, then swallowing. In that moment, there wasn't the knowledge that her throat had sealed so tight she could never eat anything again.

"I feed her when she says it's time."

"I'll take care of her dinner," Shannon said. "Just take a bite. It's delicious."

Nicole walked into the kitchen. "Tyler says the cheese side only, please."

"I've already put his slice on a plate." Shannon pointed to a plate on the counter.

They continued to talk. Pam listened, but much of the time, their words didn't make sense. They came from far away—almost as if from under water.

She reached for her own pizza slice. It was heavy. Substantial. She took a small bite. It was still hot, but not burning. Flavors exploded on her tongue. The slight bite of the sauce, the hint of sweetness in the dough, the smooth, creamy tang of the cheese. The grilled vegetables offered a subtle counterpoint of tastes, with the peppers adding crunch.

Shannon set down a glass of orange juice. The small TV in the corner clicked on and channels switched. The sound of a shopping show chased away the quiet of the afternoon.

Pam chewed carefully and swallowed. She waited for her body to revolt, as it had every time she'd tried to eat since...

Her mind shied away from the ugliness, so she thought only of the pizza. She took another bite as carefully as she had the first, chewed and swallowed.

Behind her came the sound of Shannon feeding Lulu and Nicole's quiet conversation. Pam didn't bother to turn around or participate. She focused only on the food and her careful, deliberate eating.

Every time she swallowed, her stomach ached a little less. Her head cleared and she wasn't quite so cold. She tried the juice and was surprised at how good it tasted.

She finished the glass, then got up to get more. She was surprised to find herself alone in the kitchen. Had her friends left?

Lulu had finished her canned food and now chomped on her special extrasoft kibble. She looked up at Pam and wagged her tail. Pam's face pulled in way that made her uncomfortable. She touched her cheek and realized she'd smiled.

Horror washed through her. She clutched her stomach and waited to throw up all she'd eaten. Only she didn't. Her stomach grumbled for more food while her parched throat begged for juice.

She'd smiled! How could she have done that? She was never going to smile again. Never laugh, never not ache. It wasn't right. It wasn't allowed.

The room dipped and swayed as she struggled to breathe, to understand what was happening to her. The phone began to ring.

She wanted to ignore it, the way she always did. But with friends in the house—and where had the women gone?—she couldn't. She picked up the receiver.

"Hello?"

"Mrs. Eiland?"

"Yes."

"This is Dr. Altman's office. I'm calling to confirm your consultation tomorrow at three thirty."

Pam shook her head. "What? I'm sorry. I have no idea what you're talking about."

"Your consultation. For your face-lift."

The cold returned. A face-lift? "No," Pam said clearly. "I'm not getting a face-lift. My husband died. John is dead and who cares if I look old or not? How ridiculous." She started to cry. "How could it matter now?"

"I've got it," Nicole said gently, taking the phone from her. "Hello? I'm Pam's friend. Yes, it's all right. You had no way of knowing. It was sudden. Just a few weeks ago. Please cancel the appointment. Thank you."

Pam leaned against the island as tears poured down her cheeks. She wanted to vomit, to empty herself of anything that would sustain life, but her body refused to cooperate. Nicole put the phone on the counter, then returned to her side.

"Hey," she said gently. "Come here."

Warm arms held on tight. Pam clung to her, but it wasn't the same. It wasn't John. It would never be John.

She wasn't sure how long she cried. Eventually she straightened and reached for the box of tissue. She wiped her eyes and blew her nose.

"I'm sorry," she managed to say, even though she wasn't.

"It's okay. That's why we came by. To be with you." Nicole led her back to the table. "Try to eat a little more. I've got a load of laundry in and Shannon's changing the sheets."

"You don't have to do that."

"I know, but we want to." She sat across from her and squeezed her hand.

"You have lives, too."

Nicole shrugged. Her blond ponytail moved with the gesture. "Sure, but you're a part of that. I want to be here. I don't know how to help, but I do know how to do laundry. So that's what I'm going to do."

Pam nodded. Her friend rose, hugged her again, then headed out of the kitchen. Pam reached for the pizza box, then pulled her hands away. In the distance she heard the chugging sound of the washer. On the TV some woman

explained why the blazer she was selling was perfect for
spring. Pam rested her arms on the table and her head on
her hands. Then she breathed in the pain that was missing John and let it fill her until there was nothing else.

"It was brutal," Shannon admitted, still stunned by
Pam's grief. "Her pain is a living being. There's no es-
caping it. I'm not sure how she's getting through the day."

She sat on her sofa, her feet tucked under her. Adam
was next to her, angled toward her. He held her hand
in his.

"They were together a long time," he said. "That's
really rough. My mom keeps talking about how she
couldn't survive losing my dad. That she would never
be as strong as Pam."

"That's how I feel, too. But I'm sure that's what Pam
would have told everyone. We have no way of knowing
what we'd do. I just wish I could help."

"You were there for her. That means a lot."

Shannon wasn't so sure. "Nicole and I did stuff, but
does it really matter that she had clean sheets? There's
still plenty of food. People brought it by and one of her
friends arranged for groceries to be delivered for a few
weeks." She wrinkled her nose. "I got rid of the last of the
flowers. They'd reached the point where they just smelled
awful. I don't know if she noticed, or if she didn't want
to let go of the reminders of the funeral."

She didn't have a lot of experience with this kind of
suffering. She'd never known anyone close who had died.

"You did a good thing," Adam pointed out. "Taking
care of her. Your plan with Nicole is a good one. You'll
be there for her and make sure she heals."

Shannon nodded. Assuming a person could heal from

this sort of thing, she thought sadly. "She's so raw. I never expected that. I hate to admit this, but it's hard to be around her." She bit her lower lip.

Adam shifted closer. "Don't beat yourself up for being scared of all that emotion. It's hard to watch someone grieve. You stayed with her. That's what matters."

"I hope so. I just can't begin to imagine what it must be like." She'd been through breakups before, but nothing like this. She supposed that part of it was that she'd never loved anyone for that long. She'd been hurt, but never devastated. No one had ever been her world.

"Was it like that for you when your marriage broke up?" she asked him.

Adam shook his head. "No. We were living separate lives. I was angry and upset, but I wasn't grieving. Not the way she is. That's the difference. While I never would have chosen to get a divorce, I was part of the problem. Pam's the innocent party in what's happening to her."

She studied his face as he spoke, taking in the way his mouth moved and how he always looked at her when he talked. He was in the moment.

She'd seen him with his family. He was understanding with his parents and caring with his siblings. He adored his kids and did all he could to be the best dad possible. She loved him and for the first time in her life, she knew she could finally have it all. The dream—a career *and* a family. A man who loved her, kids, maybe even a dog.

"I'm turning forty soon," she said slowly, because talking about her birthday was so much easier than saying what was really on her mind.

He grinned. "I know. That's going to be some party."

"I hope so, but it's really not all that important. I have goals in my life. I've accomplished a lot of them. My career, where I live, the travel. But there's a lot more to being happy than a job and money."

His smile faded, as he nodded slowly. "You're right. There is. There's connecting with someone. Shannon, you're important to me. You know that, right?"

"Yes."

They both paused as the weight of the moment hit her. They were getting in deep, she thought, and she was both excited and terrified. This was the place she'd mostly avoided because she'd never seen it working out before. She'd never thought she wanted to grow old with someone. Except for Adam. She'd met his dad, had watched his parents interact, and she wanted that, too.

The thought of being a stepparent scared her. Oliver was easy, but Char was more of a challenge. Not that he was proposing, but what if he did? Did she want to say yes?

She cleared her throat. "You're important to me, too."

He gave her a rueful smile. "Now we're both dancing around the elephant in the room. It's too soon to take this to the next logical step, but I want you to know I'm thinking about it. A lot. You're so special to me. I love you and I respect you. I need you to tell me if you're thinking the same thing."

Something of a challenge, she thought as butterflies dive-bombed her stomach, considering they weren't saying what *it* was. They'd both said they loved each other, which meant the elephant was very possibly getting married.

"I hope we are," she murmured, shyness making her wanting to duck her head. She forced herself to keep meeting his gaze. "I want to be with you. I want us to be a family."

He leaned in and kissed her. "I want that, too. I'm glad you feel the same way."

In for a penny, she thought ruefully. "I want to have a baby."

Adam pulled back so quickly, she thought he might snap a bone. The warmth in his eyes faded and his mouth twisted into a not-happy expression. "You mean get pregnant?"

The question sounded a lot like an accusation. Shannon quickly folded her arms across her chest and tucked herself more firmly into the corner of the sofa.

Something an awful lot like shame chilled her. She told herself she'd done nothing wrong. She was being honest and if Adam couldn't handle that, then maybe she was all wrong about him.

She raised her chin. "Getting pregnant is the traditional way to have a child, so yes."

"Shannon, I can't. I've had a vasectomy. I thought you knew."

Seventeen

Pam hung on to Lulu as if the small dog were the only thing keeping her safe in an otherwise not-to-be-trusted world. At Steven's insistence, she'd made her way to the office to meet with him and the company's lawyer. Not anything she wanted to deal with, but she'd recognized her son's stubborn tone. He'd said if it was too much for her to deal with, he and the lawyer would come to her. Which seemed like a generous offer, but it meant that Pam wasn't in control. If she went there, she got to decide when to leave.

But now that she was in the building that she and John had bought together so many years ago, now that she had to face the polite yet sad smiles of his employees, she knew it had been a mistake. There was no way she could get through whatever conversation Steven wanted to have without screaming. And if she started to scream, he would guess she wasn't as together as she pretended.

Maybe that wasn't a bad thing, she thought as Steven fussed with his fancy Keurig coffeemaker and brewed her a cup. Maybe someone should lock her up in a mental ward somewhere. As long as they drugged her, she wouldn't mind. Oblivion sounded really nice these days. She didn't want to have to think, didn't want to have to feel. Didn't want to deal with anything.

"I'd take you with me," she whispered to Lulu, not wanting the dog to think she was being left behind.

Steven handed her a tall mug with the company logo. Pam did her best to keep her fingers from trembling. She remembered when she and John had chosen the mugs. They had gotten so many samples, they'd ended up having a dessert and coffee party with their friends. Everyone had taken away a sample mug with them. There'd been a lot of trading between guests for colors and sizes. They'd had so much fun that night.

Her eyes burned with the familiar pressure of tears. She drew in a breath and reminded herself that when she got home later, she would be alone. She could curl up in John's chair and do nothing but breathe. There would be no expectations, no conversations.

Steven got his own coffee and sat down at his desk. She studied his face, taking in the shadows under his eyes and the tension in his shoulders. The physical manifestations of his grief reminded her she wasn't the only one suffering.

"How are you?" she asked.

"Okay. Tired. Sad." Steven cleared his throat. "It's hard to be here every day without him."

"Oh, honey, I'm sorry. Of course it is. I have my ghosts at the house, but you have as many here."

He nodded. "Everything is exactly the same and totally different." He glanced toward the closed office door and lowered his voice. "I called that counselor you mentioned. The one you and Dad saw when Brandon was having his trouble."

She nodded. "I gave her name to a friend of mine, too. She's getting a lot of business from me these days. Did it help?"

"Yeah. I didn't think it would, but talking about what happened was good. I know it's going to take time to get that he's really gone. He was a good man."

Pam nodded and told herself they were talking about someone other than *her* John. If she could convince herself the conversation wasn't personal, she could survive this. She could fake her way through the meeting and then escape. That was what she had to focus on. Being not here.

"You remember Ashleigh from high school?" he asked.

Pam sipped her coffee and tried to recall the name. "She was your girlfriend. A sweet girl. You broke up with her because she wouldn't sleep with you."

"Mom!"

Pam shrugged. "Did I get it wrong?"

He flushed. "You weren't supposed to know that."

"I was your mother. You didn't have any secrets from me. I always respected her for not putting out. Why do you mention her?"

"We ran in to each other the other day. She's back in Mischief Bay. She's a nurse at the hospital. Pediatrics. She looked good. Still sweet, you know."

"You mean not your type?"

"Exactly."

He flashed her a grin that was so like John's. Pain sliced through her. She instinctively pressed her hand to her stomach to hold in whatever blood she could. Only there wasn't a visible wound. Just the kind that only mattered to her.

"We're going out this weekend. I don't know. It's just when I was talking to her I kept thinking how much Dad would have liked her."

Pam thought about pointing out that was a silly reason to date someone. But maybe losing his father would help Steven mature when it came to his romantic life. She thought about saying that, but exhaustion descended and the conversation would require more than she had.

"It's getting late," she said, putting her mug on the table. "I should go."

"Mom, we haven't talked about the money yet," her son said gently. "It's why I asked you to come by. Jason is going to meet us here in a few minutes."

She stared at him blankly.

"Jason is our lawyer," Steven added.

Because there were complications with the business. Finances. "Can't you handle it?" she asked. "Do I have to be here?"

"You do."

Someone knocked on the door, then opened it. Hayley smiled at her. "Hi, Pam."

Pam did her best to smile back.

"Jason's here," Hayley told Steven.

A tall man with blond hair and blue eyes walked into the office. Pam clutched Lulu and tried to remember if she'd met him before, then decided it wasn't worth the effort. So what if she had or hadn't?

He was probably in his forties. She vaguely recalled something about working with his father, before he retired.

Jason sat next to her. "I'm so sorry for your loss, Pam. John was a great man. I always admired him for his business sense and how he loved his family. I hope in time you'll find comfort in knowing how respected and admired he was in the community."

"Thank you," she murmured, telling herself than in ten minutes she was leaving, no matter what. Or she would start rocking and keening and they could lock her up and get the good drugs going in an IV.

"I'm not sure how familiar you are with the business structure of the company," Jason continued. "While you and John owned the majority of it, you also set up profit sharing and employee ownership."

Pam bit hard on her lower lip, trying to distract herself from her need to sob. Because sharing the good times with those who had worked for him for years had been important to John. He'd been so proud to be able to provide a way for his employees to have a stake in their own future.

"The corporation had something called a key man insurance policy," Jason continued. "In the event that something happened to John, the corporation received the proceeds from the policy. That money is to be used to buy you, Jennifer and Brandon out of the company."

"I don't understand," she admitted.

Steven cleared his throat. His eyes had a sheen, as if he, too, were holding back tears. "You know Dad always talked about leaving me the business."

She nodded. "Of course. You're the only one who was interested. Your father was so happy when you said you wanted to work with him."

"Yeah. I remember." Her son swallowed hard. "He, ah, wanted to make sure everyone was taken care of. The key man policy does that. Dad leaves me the company in his will and the insurance money buys everyone else out. Jen and Brandon have a chunk of cash to put away and you're taken care of for the rest of your life."

"And you're not saddled with a lot of debt as you run things here," Pam whispered, then gave in to the inevitable and let the tears free. They ran down her cheeks, almost certainly smudging the bit of makeup she'd managed to slap on.

Someone pushed a box of tissues into her hand. She grabbed a couple and wiped her face. No doubt she looked hideous, but who cared? Lulu licked her chin and watched her with worried eyes.

"He took care of everyone," she said, her voice thick with pain. "Even after he's gone, he's taking care of everyone. He was such a good man."

She clutched Lulu and let the shuddering sobs wash through her. She could feel the two men watching her, clearly worried about her emotional state, but she couldn't bring herself to care.

"He loved you so much, Mom. The way he talked about you. There was something in his voice."

She raised her head. "What are you talking about?"

Her normally totally cool son actually blushed. "I don't know," he said, avoiding her gaze. "It didn't matter what the subject was. When he said your name he got this tone. Love, I guess. I can't describe it but I heard it all the time. We all heard it. That's why I haven't been serious about anyone. I want to wait until I hear that in my voice, too. I want what you and Dad had. I want to be that in love after thirty years."

He got up and came around the desk, then crouched in front of her. His arm encircled her. For a second she wondered if she could pretend he was John, but there was no way. No one could fill in. No one could make up for what had been lost. What *she* had lost.

She knew the only way to get out of here was to survive the rest of the meeting. She gathered what little strength she had left and raised her head.

"Thank you for telling me that," she said and forced a smile. "It helps a lot."

"I'm glad."

He rose and returned to his seat.

Jason glanced between them. "Your share of the proceeds is substantial, Mrs. Eiland. Do you have a financial advisor?"

She nodded.

"I know who he is," Steven said. "I'll call him later today and let him know what's happening. If that's okay with you, Mom."

"Thank you. I don't want to deal with any of it right now. Just do what you have to. I won't make any rash decisions." Or any decisions at all, she thought.

Steven watched her carefully. "You know, Mom, he really wanted you to join that angel fund you were talking about. You still could."

She gathered her bag and Lulu and stood. The alternative was to blurt out the truth. The alternative was to tell him that there was no way she ever wanted to do anything again. She was barely hanging on. Couldn't anyone see that? Didn't they know how every moment, every breath, was an effort? That just living took everything she had? She barely had the strength to eat or shower, let alone leave the house.

"I need to go," she said, as both men came to their feet.

"Mom, we need to—"

She cut him off with a shake of her head. "No, we

don't. You've told me what you had to. I'm glad everyone
is taken care of financially. Now if you'll excuse me."

She walked out into the hallway. Although she'd been
to the office a million times, she suddenly couldn't remember which way to turn to find the exit. The walls
seemed to be moving and the hallway got too narrow.
She was trapped. Her chest tightened until breathing
was impossible. Fear built up inside until the only thing
left, the only possible way to escape was to scream and
scream until—

"Pam?"

She turned and saw Hayley walking toward her. Instantly the hallway returned to normal and she could
breathe again.

"All done with your meeting?"

"I am," Pam admitted. "They might not be."

"They'll survive. Do you have time for a cup of tea?"

The alternative was to go home and be in that house.
Something Pam found comforting, only she'd always
liked Hayley.

"Sure."

They went into the break room. It was big, with lots
of windows that looked out onto a small walled garden.
There were tables and chairs in both areas and when the
weather was nice, the staff ate outside.

Hayley put a kettle on a burner of the small stove.
There was also a microwave and refrigerator, along with
several cupboards. Lockers lined the far wall. Pam remembered picking out the colors on the walls and all the
appliances when the offices had been remodeled. Before
that, she'd worked here, on and off, when she and John
had first been married.

So many memories, she thought sadly. She kept expecting to see him walk in the door and smile at her. There was simply no way to escape. Not that she wanted to, she reminded herself. In the moments when the pain receded just enough that she could think, she knew that while she was devastated, she was totally connected to him. Healing wasn't an option. Healing was too much like letting him go.

Hayley sat across from her. Pam noticed the other woman's eyes were red, as if she, too, had been crying.

"I won't ask how you're feeling," Hayley said. "People always ask me that after a miscarriage and I just want to scream at them. I can't tell them how I really feel, which is like shit. As if my hopes and dreams have been ripped from me." She raised one shoulder. "I can't begin to imagine what you're dealing with."

Pam appreciated the understanding. "It's hard," she said, thinking that didn't begin to describe what she was feeling. "I thought it would get easier, but it doesn't. Ever."

The kettle whistled. Lulu perked up her ears, as if not sure what strange creature was invading her space. Hayley walked to the stove and pulled it off the burner.

"It's okay, baby girl," Pam told Lulu quietly. "It's okay."

Hayley fixed two mugs of tea and returned to the table. "I'm going to be working for Steven now. Linda, his assistant, has been toying with the idea of moving somewhere exotic. She got offered a job in Dubai and is going to take it."

"What? Dubai? Seriously?"

"I know." Hayley gave her a sad smile. "Steven and I get along, which is great. He reminds me a lot of his dad, which is both good and bad. I think he and I can do well."

"I know you can," Pam told her. "He's going to need a lot of help making the transition. He always knew he was going to take over, but not this soon."

Steven walked into the break room. "Mom, I know this may be a bad time, but several of the people here want to come by and offer condolences. Can you stand that?"

Pam shuddered. Listening to people she knew tell her how wonderful John had been to them was both heaven and hell. She was so tired, so lonely, so sad and so broken. There was almost nothing left of her. Where was she supposed to find the strength?

But this wasn't about her, she reminded herself. This was about John. They had loved him and while they couldn't say that to him anymore, they could say it to her.

"Of course," she said as she pushed away the tea and passed Lulu to Hayley. "That would be nice."

She stood and braced herself for the emotional dump. Soon she would be home, she told herself. Soon she could sit alone in the silence, cradled in John's old chair. Soon she could cry and scream and wait for the exhaustion to claim her. All so she could start it all again in the morning.

Shannon finished reviewing the report and typed in her initials on the margin. The good news was her hyperfocusing allowed her to sail through her work at a quicker than normal pace. The bad news was every time she surfaced, she had a split second of wondering what was wrong, followed by the dull thud of reality.

It had been two days since she'd seen Adam. He'd sent her a couple of texts, but they hadn't talked and she didn't know when they would.

Now she turned in her chair so she could stare out at the view from her office. She could see the businesses and houses of Mischief Bay, with the Pacific Ocean beyond. A killer view that she'd been so damned proud of back when Nolan had hired her. She'd taken pictures and sent them to her friends. Not to her parents, of course. They wouldn't get the thrill and would instead focus on the fact that she was bragging. In the Rigg family, that wasn't allowed. You never talked about the good things, you never tried too hard, you never strived. And if you somehow, despite the goal of mediocrity, succeeded, you never mentioned that success to others.

Probably why she didn't spend all that much time visiting her parents, despite the fact that they were less than seventy miles away. Every time she went home, she counted the seconds until she could leave. She and her parents had nothing in common. Adding to that was the fact that she knew she was a disappointment to them. She'd never followed a traditional path. She'd majored in finance rather than studying something more acceptable—like teaching or nursing. She'd always wanted more and in her family, that was a cardinal sin.

She closed her eyes against the beauty outside her window. She knew that she was still feeling the effects of her last conversation with Adam. The shock of what he'd told her still had the power to make her second-guess the path she'd chosen. It seemed grossly unfair that she'd finally met a terrific man—a man she loved and trusted—and he'd chosen not to have more children.

She knew that for the average married guy with a couple of kids, getting a vasectomy was a no-brainer. It solved the birth control issue in a quick and permanent way. Why wouldn't he have done that? But from her position, it was a statement that went beyond that. It said he didn't want any more children.

The logical side of her brain pointed out that Adam had acted responsibly and had assumed he wouldn't get a divorce, so why not? Her heart questioned why he hadn't guessed he could fall in love with her someday. Logic returned with the fact that he'd used a condom every time they'd had sex. Obviously that had been about protection from things other than pregnancy.

She was being idiotic, she told herself. And yet in the absence of other information, she was hard-pressed to not feel crappy about the whole thing. But what happened now? Was she expected to give up her dream of having a family? Was she simply to accept the possibility of being a stepmother and go no further?

Difficult questions, she thought. Ones without easy answers. She turned back to her computer, doing her best not to think about the fact that Adam wasn't overly eager to speak with her again. He hadn't set up another date and a couple of texts did not a relationship make.

Her office phone buzzed.

"Yes?"

"There's a gentleman here to see you," her assistant said. "He doesn't have an appointment but he seems pretty confident you'll see him."

Her heart melted as her doubts faded. Because Adam was here. Which was just like him. He wasn't the guy to ignore the problem or leave her in limbo. He would get things taken care of.

"He's right," she said. "Give me a second and I'll be out."

She hung up the phone, then stood and smoothed the front of her dress. She opened the small closet and checked her makeup in the mirror before walking out into her assistant's office only to come to a stop.

The man standing there was familiar enough, but he wasn't Adam.

Quinn smiled when he saw her. "Gorgeous."

Both a greeting and a compliment, she thought, stunned to see him. She and Quinn seldom saw each other outside of his place. Sometimes he came to hers, but rarely. As for being together in a nonbedroom situation...she couldn't remember the last time.

"What are you doing here?"

"I had a couple of meetings and remembered your office was nearby. I thought I'd take you to lunch." He winked at her assistant. "If you can spare her."

Molly, a happily married woman in her late fifties, practically swooned. "Of course. You don't have any appointments until later this afternoon."

"How convenient," Quinn murmured, moving toward her and kissing her cheek. "So lunch?"

She led him into her office. When they were out of earshot, she picked up her handbag and raised her eyebrows. "Are we actually talking lunch?"

"Sure. We can talk." He held up a hand. "We're capable of having a regular conversation."

"Without sex."

"Yes."

"I'm in. Do you know where you want to go?"

"Gary's Café. They have the best burger on the beach."

"I know several businesses that would disagree with you on that."

"Then they're just plain wrong."

They agreed to take his car with the understanding he would drop her off after lunch and go on to his next meeting. Today Quinn was driving a dark blue Maserati GranTurismo. A ridiculous car that totally suited him. She had to admit it was nice to sit in, but she would rather have the money to pay down her mortgage. Not that anyone was offering her either choice.

They drove to Gary's Café and Quinn easily found parking in the lot. When they went inside, several heads turned. Shannon would like to think it was because she looked especially nice that day, but she knew the truth. Quinn might not be a rock star, but he still had that indefinable I'm-famous quality about him. People generally assumed he was "someone" and in his case, they were right.

They were seated in a booth by the front window. It was still early, not yet noon, and there were plenty of empty seats. A few old men sat in a row at the counter, and a couple of mothers with young children were in the back of the restaurant. The chalkboard on the wall detailed the special.

Quinn didn't bother with the menu. Shannon scanned hers and decided she was going to live large today, as well. Maybe it was wrong to medicate herself with food, but so what?

Their server—a young woman in her early twenties—walked over. She only had eyes for Quinn and tried a couple of ponytail tosses to get his attention.

"Hi," she said breathlessly. "I'm April. I'll be helping you today."

Quinn gave her his easy, sexy smile. "Great." He motioned to Shannon. "All right, love of my life, what are you having?"

April visibly deflated. She glanced at Shannon, then back at Quinn, and sighed heavily.

Shannon smiled. "I'll have the burger special, no cheese. And an iced tea."

"Same for me," Quinn said, then stretched out his arm across the booth and took her hand.

Their server glared at Shannon before flouncing off.

"Love of my life?" Shannon asked when they were alone. "Seriously?"

"I wanted to get the point across without hurting her feelings."

Something she could nearly believe. Quinn had many flaws but being cruel wasn't one of them.

"I haven't seen you in a while," he said. "You've been ignoring me."

There had been a couple of texts she hadn't answered. "A lot's going on. A friend of mine lost her husband."

"Not why you're avoiding me."

His voice was low. Quiet, but not suggestive. This was the Quinn she rarely saw. The regular guy who was her friend.

Funny how she wasn't sure which side of him was real and which was used simply because it worked for him. The smooth, handsome Quinn who charmed as easily as most people breathed was the one she had met. Sexy, slightly aggressive, thirty ways to please a woman Quinn was the man she had sex with. But they were rarely simply people sharing a normal conversation.

She wondered what part of her truth to share with him. He took the decision out of her hands by smiling and saying, "You're seeing someone."

"I am."

"And?"

"I'm in love with him."

One dark eyebrow rose. "As simple as that?"

"It's not simple. There are unexpected complications."

"He's gay?"

Shannon laughed. "You'd like that."

"Ouch. Why would you say that?"

"Because then I'd want to continue having sex with you and never press you for more."

"You don't press me for more."

Their server returned with their drinks and stalked away. Shannon busied herself with the wrapping on her straw.

"Good point," she murmured. "Why is that?"

"You don't want more," he said simply.

"Not true. I want what everyone else has. A husband and a family."

"I don't have a husband and a family."

"You know what I mean. I want a traditional happy relationship. I want something I can count on."

"Which you could never have with me," he pointed out.

"You don't want that?" she asked. "Not ever?"

One shoulder rose and fell. His too-long hair added to the appeal of the man, she thought, watching him. The hooded blue eyes both promised and withdrew. An irresistible combination.

They'd met at a party. She didn't do a lot of Hollywood events, but a friend had asked her to tag along and Shannon had just been through yet another hideous day at the bank where her boss had made it clear because she didn't have a penis, she couldn't possibly have enough of a brain to get where she wanted to at the firm. Not that he was above taking credit for her work.

She'd dressed to kill in the skimpiest LBD she owned and then had proceeded to ignore every man who had tried to come on to her. All the while she'd been aware of Quinn, who simply watched.

At the time she'd had no idea who he was. She'd kept track of him, watched the people who moved in and out of his orbit. Those he'd spoken to and those he'd ignored. She'd wondered about him, but told herself she didn't care enough to speak to him.

After one too many cocktails, she'd gone out on the patio of the excessively large Bel Air mansion. The cool night had helped her catch her breath. Quinn had joined her then.

"What has your panties in a bunch?"

The unexpected question had gotten through far more than any of the compliments.

"Why do men assume being a woman is the same as being stupid?" she'd asked.

"Because they're threatened. Work issue?"

"My boss."

"He knows you're going to be *his* boss in less than three years and that scares the hell out of him."

"Yeah, right. I can't get anywhere with him in the way."

"Then force him out or leave."

Until that second, she'd never thought about leaving the bank. Getting through college and getting a job with upward mobility had violated every rule she'd been raised with. She had been so proud of herself, so smug. But she'd never once thought she should leave the bank and go find something better. Which was ridiculous.

"Understanding dawns," Quinn murmured.

She glared at him. "Who are you?"

"I'm crushed you don't already know." He took her drink from her and set it on a patio table, then took her hand in his and pulled her back inside. "Come on. We'll find your friend and you'll explain you're coming home with me."

"What? No way. I don't even know your name."

"You're not interested in my name. You're pissed and a little drunk and you can't screw the boss the way you want, but you can screw me however you'd like."

Shannon let herself be pulled along. She hadn't decided what she was going to do, but going home with the stranger was getting more intriguing by the second. She'd been so good for so long. Didn't she deserve a single night of being irresponsible?

"There's your friend," he said as he pointed. "It's Quinn, by the way."

"Shannon."

"I already know that."

She'd gone home with him that night. It had been the first of many times she'd visited his house in Malibu. She hadn't tried to fool herself into thinking they were anything but part-time lovers. Sometimes she contacted him but mostly he got in touch with her. If she was available and in the mood, she went over.

They talked music. He gave her CDs and MP3 files from new artists he'd found. She'd steered him toward a couple of excellent investment bankers she knew. But their relationship never went beyond that.

"Why wasn't there more between us?" she asked as she pulled her glass of iced tea toward her.

"You only play at relationships."

Harsh but possibly true, she thought. "Now that you've identified my flaw, what's wrong with you?"

"I'm afraid to fall in love."

"As easy as that?"

"It's not easy. It's hell. The pleasure isn't worth the potential pain. How do you do that? How do you simply hand over your heart knowing there's a better than even chance it's going to be returned to you in smaller slices than coleslaw?"

"One day you're going to have to take that leap of faith."

"Why? I'm perfectly happy."

She wondered if that were true. Or even possible. Pam and John would have been the closest she'd known and look what had happened there.

"Is he a good guy?" Quinn asked. "The one you're in love with?"

"He is."

"Then what's the problem?"

"I want children and he had a vasectomy."

"So adopt."

"The conversation didn't get that far. He left. We haven't spoken much since."

Quinn studied her. "You're breaking up with me regardless."

A statement or a question? And then she knew. "I am." Because whether or not things worked out with Adam, Quinn was no longer good for her.

"We still going to have lunch? Because I've had a hankering for this burger for weeks."

She smiled. "I would never deprive you of a burger, my friend."

"Good to know."

Eighteen

Pam sat in the recliner. It was early still. Light barely crept into the house. Lulu was curled up on her lap, asleep. Her baby girl had been faithful, she thought, careful not to move so she wouldn't disturb the canine's sleep. Lulu had stayed with her every second of every day. Night after night, the little dog had been her only source of warmth. A gentle beating heart to keep her going until dawn.

Pam looked at the bottle of wine on the table next to her. It was nearly finished. She'd taken to having a glass or three late in the evening. It helped her get sleepy. Nothing helped her stay asleep. She woke up every couple of hours to find herself crying. The fiery ache of missing John never faded, never wavered. It was as constant as the rotation of the earth.

This past night had been better than most. Not because she'd slept, but because she'd been alone. She hadn't had to pretend.

Shannon and Nicole had made good on their promise to keep her company. They dropped by after work, stayed for dinner and sometimes spent the night. She knew they had her best interests at heart, but most of the time she simply wanted them to go away and leave her alone.

Lulu stirred and opened her eyes. When she saw Pam looking at her, she wagged her tail, then rolled onto her back to show her belly.

"Good morning, sweet girl," Pam murmured. She stroked the bare skin of her stomach, then rubbed her chest. "How are you?"

Lulu scrambled to her feet, planted her front paws on Pam's chest, then lavished her with puppy kisses.

"Yes, it is a new day." Something that always made Lulu happy.

Pam lifted her to the floor, then stood herself. She felt stiff and creaky. Sleeping in the chair wasn't comfortable, but she couldn't possibly face her big bed. She took a step and groaned when her back and hips protested. Maybe she could try sleeping in the guest room, she thought. Maybe that would be better.

She made her way to the kitchen and let out the dog, then started her coffee. After collecting plates and ingredients for Lulu's breakfast, she let her girl back in, then prepared her food. By the time the coffee was done, so was Lulu. Together they went into the master bath.

Pam stared at her face. She looked old, she thought. Pale and lost. She hadn't been doing any of her usual skin care. There were flakes and dullness to prove it. She'd managed to put on makeup a few days before, but had never washed it off. Old mascara collected under her eyes. Not that it mattered. Who was there to impress?

She got through a shower and dried off. Lulu licked her damp feet, helping as best she could. Pam slipped on her robe and together they walked into the closet.

She stood and stared at the racks of clothes. The closet

was divided between her things and John's. He'd taken about a third of the space, leaving her with the rest. She stared at the neatly hung shirts, the pants, the jeans. His shoes all in a row on a shelf.

She reached for one shirt, not sure what she was going to do with it. Roll it into a ball? Put it on? Regardless, it fell to the floor.

Lulu immediately jumped on it, thinking they were playing a game. Pam pulled another shirt off a hanger. It fell on the dog and she yipped with excitement.

Shirt after shirt was tossed. Pants and jeans followed, then ties and jackets. Lulu stood to the side and barked with excitement, then jumped on the giant pile. She started digging and soon was lost in the mass of clothing.

Pam quickly dressed. She changed Lulu into a light sweater, then opened the hatch of her small SUV and began carting the clothes to the back. She didn't fold them or organize them in any way. She simply stuffed them inside and when she was done, she got in her car and drove to the Goodwill.

She waited an hour for the donation center to open. A nice young man helped her take everything out, then offered her a receipt. She said that wasn't necessary.

She returned home to her quiet house and crawled into the recliner. Lulu curled up on her lap. Pam held the dog and waited for time to pass. Because that was all she had. The knowledge that time passed, however slowly.

By three Pam was shaking and by three thirty, she knew she couldn't manage any of this alone. She dug her cell phone out of her bag and scrolled through all the listings.

Not her kids. They were just getting back into their

lives. They didn't need to know she was falling apart. Name after name flashed by and not one of them seemed right.

Nicole's name came up next and Pam felt the tension in her chest ease. She pushed the number to make the call.

"Hi," Nicole said. "I was just thinking about you. Tyler and I were thinking about coming by later. I talked to Shannon earlier and she'd like to stop by, too. Would that work?"

Pam closed her eyes and nodded in gratitude. "I'd like that."

"I'm bringing dinner. What are you in the mood for?"

"Anything."

"I'm on my way home now. Tyler and I will be there by five."

"Don't you have class at five?"

"Not anymore. I've hired another instructor. I'll tell you all about it when I get there."

"Thank you," Pam breathed.

"Of course. We miss you. See you soon."

Pam hung up. She patted Lulu. "You're going to have Tyler to play with."

Lulu wagged her tail.

Pam got up and studied the family room. There were plates with food on them, glasses and empty wine bottles everywhere. The kitchen was worse, she thought, remembering the partially eaten casseroles she'd left out, the stack of dirty dog food dishes.

"There's a mess," she told the dog. "I'd better get cleaning."

She moved slowly at first, carrying each dish individually back to the kitchen. But the more trips she made, the more she was able to carry. She loaded the dishwasher, then started the cycle. She took out the trash and saw the can was nearly full. Because Steven had stopped coming by to take out the can for her.

She stood there, breathing hard, knowing that there would be a million other moments like this. Moments when she would be forced to remember that she was alone. John was gone and he was never coming back.

"Stop it," she told herself. "Just stop it."

She had to learn to function. She had to start doing better. Or at least faking it better. Because healing was something she knew would never happen. The alternative was to fake enough not to frighten anyone. John would want that, at the very least.

She ignored the fact that he would also want her to keep moving forward, to have a life, to be happy. All impossible concepts when faced with a full trash barrel.

She tried to figure out what day it was and then remember when the trash came. It overwhelmed her, so she retreated to the house, where she at least knew what she was doing.

With the family room and kitchen looking reasonably presentable, she went into the master bath to do the same with herself. She washed her face and was shocked at how her skin was peeling like a snake. She quickly pulled out an exfoliating mask and used it, then slathered on moisturizer before applying light makeup. When she'd done all she could to be presentable, she let out Lulu for a potty run. While the dog was doing her thing, she collected three days' worth of mail before returning to the house.

She'd barely sorted the envelopes into piles—bills, condolence cards, crap—when the doorbell rang. Lulu barked with excitement and raced toward the front of the house. Pam followed, surprisingly eager for her company.

She opened the door and nearly started to cry again. Nicole stood with a take-out bag in one hand and a roller bag suitcase handle in the other. Tyler had a Brad the Dragon backpack over his shoulders.

"Hi," Nicole said. "We decided we wanted to spend the night. I hope that's okay."

Pam opened her arms. Nicole stepped into her embrace and hung on like she was never going to let go. Tyler grabbed Pam's leg and hugged tight, too. Pam breathed deeply for the first time in days and thought maybe, just maybe, this night was going to be easier.

Nicole sipped from her wineglass. "I miss you in class," she admitted, not sure if that was okay to say. Her decision to come visit her friend had been sudden. Driven as much by her need to get out of her house as to help Pam. But now that she was here, she wished she'd come by sooner.

The death of a husband had to be devastating, but even knowing that, she'd been unprepared for Pam's appearance. Her normally well-groomed, classy friend was disheveled at best. She'd lost weight and looked drawn. In the past month, she'd aged at least ten years.

Shannon had looked equally shocked when she'd arrived an hour later. She'd brought cupcakes and wine, along with her overnight tote. So far the two of them hadn't had a chance to go off together and compare impressions, but Nicole knew there was plenty to say. Pam wasn't doing well at all.

More upsetting than her friend's change in appearance was her lack of energy. It wasn't just how slowly she moved, it was the dullness in her eyes. The way she seemed to have difficulty following the conversation. She wasn't totally with it. Nicole hoped it was just grief and not something more troubling like pills or other drugs.

"Steven told me that you were invited to join Moving Women Forward," she said, then waited for Pam to catch up with the subject change. "Did I ever tell you that they helped me when I first bought the studio?"

"I didn't know that," Shannon said.

"I couldn't have gone into business for myself without their help. But I couldn't have stayed in business without your help and advice, Pam. I don't know what I would've done without you. You should really think about accepting their invitation."

"I need to get back into exercising," Pam admitted, missing the point but at least engaging in the conversation at last. "I'm so tired and sore all the time. I'm sure it would help."

"Whenever you're ready, we want you back," Shannon said. "It's not as fun without you. You're the glue that holds us all together."

"I'm not sure I'd be much fun now," Pam said. "Or glue-like. I can't remember the last time I laughed."

Nicole touched her arm. "We're not looking for a stand-up routine. Having you around would be enough."

They were in the large family room. In addition to John's recliner, there was a huge sectional sofa. Rather than separate into various bedrooms, they'd decided they were all going to sleep here. Tyler was already zonked out on the floor. He'd been thrilled with the chance to use his B the D sleeping bag. Nicole and Shannon would sleep on the sectional and Pam would settle in John's recliner.

Nicole wondered if that was where she slept now. To

feel closer to him, maybe. Or to avoid their bed. Because they'd spent the past thirty-plus years sharing a bed, she thought, aware that *her* husband still slept in his office. She was beginning to think he was never coming back into their bedroom.

Pam sipped her wine. "Enough about me and my troubles. How are you two doing?"

"I'm fine," Shannon said brightly. "Everything's great. Nicole, how are things with Eric? With the new screenplay?"

Nicole wasn't going to mention her romantic separation from her husband, but there was plenty of other news.

"It's been a whirlwind. He spends his days either doing rewrites or taking meetings."

"He's still the big-shot writer?" Pam asked.

"You know it. But I'm just as bad. Do you know I've actually been interviewing nannies? I can't believe it. But with him gone so much and all his strange hours, there's no way I can count on him to take Tyler to preschool or pick him up. And while I really like having another instructor, she's only part-time and that means I'm still the one mostly responsible for the classes. There's no way I can be running around with Tyler."

She didn't mention that she was also talking to the various women she'd interviewed about their willingness to do housework, laundry and cooking. Because Eric insisted they have a full-service nanny.

"Two months ago, we were struggling to pay the bills," she continued. "Now I'm interviewing nannies. It's surreal."

"Have you found anyone?" Shannon asked.

Nicole wrinkled her nose. "A woman named Greta.

She's worked with two people Eric knows and they speak very highly of her. She's in her early fifties, she's never been married. She loves children and whenever I'm around her, I feel inadequate."

Pam smiled. "I doubt that."

"No, I do. She believes in a totally organic kitchen. She's a vegan but thinks meat is good for growing children. She bakes her own bread, does windows and looks at me like I'm an idiot. Should I hire someone who intimidates me?"

"What does Tyler think of her?" Shannon asked. "Because that matters the most."

"He adores her."

"We all make sacrifices for our children," Pam murmured.

"You think it's funny that she scares me."

"A little."

Nicole sighed. "I should probably just be grateful she comes so highly recommended." She shifted so she could sit cross-legged on the sofa. "Eric is turning into a total Hollywood type. He's reading *Variety* every day and quotes articles to me."

"More surreal moments?" Shannon asked.

"Daily. I'm trying to be supportive and at the same time, I'm completely uncomfortable."

Pam's expression turned sad. "Everything's different. You don't know where you are or how to find your balance. Life makes us start over again and again. Of course you feel different. Anyone would."

Nicole wanted to slap herself. She was supposed to be helping her friend, not making things worse. "I'm sorry," she murmured. "I'm not helping."

"You're wrong. Having you here is a great help. I really appreciate it." Pam turned to Shannon. "It's nice to have my friends with me."

"You sure?" Shannon asked.

"I swear." She managed a shaky smile. "And in the morning we'll have nonorganic calorie-filled pancakes and sausage for breakfast."

Nicole grinned. "You sure know how to show us a good time."

"I try."

The Goodwill store was big and bright, with high ceilings and more of a crowd than Pam would have expected on a Thursday morning. She pushed her cart through the aisles of clothing. She didn't have a plan, exactly. She was simply here to collect what was hers. Or more correctly, John's.

She'd tried to fill in the empty space in the closet by spreading out her things. She'd told herself it was for the better, that she had to start moving on. But the words didn't seem to help. She still felt she'd given away something precious and now she had to get it back.

What she hadn't expected was the sheer size of the men's department. There were dozens of racks of clothing, maybe hundreds. How was she supposed to find what had belonged to John? What if all the shirts looked the same and she couldn't tell which were his?

She reached the first rack of shirts and started flipping through it. The shirts were arranged first by color and then by size. She knew the brands he favored, so that would help. She also knew the collar size and sleeve length. But as she studied shirt after shirt after shirt, she began to wonder if she could know for sure she'd found one of his.

She turned and saw the jeans section was even bigger. White shirts seemed to go on for miles. The store was massive and there were so many people pawing through what could be her things.

The tightness in her chest began almost before she realized what was happening. Her breathing became labored and then the first cold claws of panic reached for her soft belly and ripped it open. She gasped and clutched her midsection just as the tears began to fall.

She gripped her cart, hoping to stay upright, but it was too much. All of it. The overhead lights, the chatter of conversation, the smell of fresh soap combined with the scent of guilt and fear. She gave in to it all and slowly sank to the ground.

Around her she heard a few murmurs as the nearest shoppers scattered. No doubt they were worried she was some crazy person who was going to brandish a knife or something.

"I just want to find John's things," she whispered.

"Ma'am? Are you all right?"

She raised her head and stared at the tall, thin, dark-haired woman standing by her cart.

"No," Pam admitted. "I'm not."

"What's wrong? Are you sick? Do you want me to call an ambulance?"

Pam sniffed. "You must really have to deal with a lot of things here. I'm not sick." She sniffed, then struggled to her feet. "I brought my husband's clothes in a few days ago. Now I'm trying to find them to buy them back."

"Did you have a fight?"

"No. He's gone. He died. I miss him so much." The tears started up again. "I don't know how to be without him." She noticed that two security guards were heading in her direction. "Are you going to ask me to leave the store?"

"No. Of course not. I'm going to help you find your husband's things. When did you make the donations?"

"Three days ago."

"Then they're probably not out yet. Come on back to the sorting area and we'll see what we can find."

Pam pushed her cart along and followed her through to the back of the store. "Thank you for being so nice."

"We all have to deal with something. I know that to be true. They say God never gives us more than we can handle, but I say sometimes He assumes we're stronger than we are. Life is a challenge."

She pushed through swinging doors. Pam left the cart in the store and went with her into a huge back room. There were dozens of people sorting through thousands of donations. There were televisions and furniture, household goods, pots, pans, dishes and clothes. Mountains of clothes.

The piles were higher than a basketball player's head. They were impossibly large. It was as if every single person in the Los Angeles metro area had donated the same day she had.

The woman at her side was talking, explaining about where the clothes would be, given when Pam had dropped them off. And then she knew the truth—that discovering a shirt or a jacket would in no way bring John back. He was gone.

There was no bargaining, no mourning, no begging that would bring him back. He was lost to her forever.

"Thank you for your help," she told the woman and started to leave.

"You don't want to look?"

Pam glanced back at her. "He's not there."

She walked to her car and got inside. As she leaned back in her seat and closed her eyes, she remembered watching a movie with John. One he'd really liked—*The Shawshank Redemption*. Morgan Freeman's character had said something in the movie. That it was time to get busy living or get busy dying.

She probably had the line wrong, but that was the heart of it, she thought. Maybe her problem was she hadn't made a decision yet, and until she did, she was trapped in a world of pain and suffering with no possible way to escape.

Nineteen

The Friday night crowd at Pescadores was loud and happy. Conversation flowed easily and there was plenty of laughter. In the bar, a baseball game played silently on several televisions. Shannon caught sight of the occasional play out of the corner of her eye. She'd never noticed the TVs before, but then she'd never felt the weight of silence when she'd been out with Adam before.

This was their first P-V-R date. P-V-R aka post vasectomy reveal. They'd gone from texting to a couple of quick calls, the last of which had been him inviting her out to dinner tonight at a place they generally enjoyed.

She'd accepted because she loved him and missed him, but also with a sense of dread. Because there was a part of her expecting this to be where he told her he was done with her. That she wanted impossible things, that his love wasn't the forever, I want children with you kind. That he'd been more interested in getting laid than happily ever after.

Even as she'd wrestled with her fears, she'd told herself she was being unfair. That Adam had been nothing but sweet and kind and open and attentive. That she shouldn't assume the worst about him or them. But she was scared. After years of thinking she could never "have it all," she'd finally found someone who saw who she was and still loved her. She'd allowed herself to hope and now this.

She'd had a late meeting so they'd met at the restaurant instead of him picking her up. Not as convenient, she thought, but if things went south, at least she would be able to get away without a hideously awkward ride home.

Not that the meal was going any better, she mused. Since being seated, they'd discussed the weather and how the Dodgers were off to a good start on the season but were likely to disappoint later in the summer.

They'd ordered wine and an appetizer and now were left on their own. Which was turning out not to be a good thing.

She glanced at him, liking the shape of his face and the kindness in his eyes. He was such a great guy, she thought wistfully. She'd known there were going to be issues they had to deal with but had assumed they would be about her getting involved with his kids or getting along with his ex-wife. For some reason, she'd never once thought they would be on different sides of the "I want kids" debate.

He reached across the table and touched the back of her hand. "We should talk about it."

She nodded. "We should. I'm sorry I sprang the topic of more kids on you without warning. It never occurred to me that you'd feel differently. Foolish, but there we are."

"My vasectomy doesn't meant I don't want kids," he began, then stopped himself. "At least, it…" Another pause.

She really wanted to pull her hand back, but that seemed hostile. In truth, she felt the need to protect herself rather than withdraw. She wanted to curl up in a ball or have some layer of armor between her and him. Not that all the steel in the world would be enough to protect her from what he was trying too hard not to say.

"I get it," she said quietly. "You had your family and you were happy with Oliver and Char. You didn't expect to get a divorce so why not? And even knowing you were going to be single again, you still had your complete family. I'm not there yet. I may not have made all the right decisions in the past, but that doesn't mean I'm willing to give up on being a mother."

"You shouldn't," he told her. "You'd be a great mom."

"That's yet to be proven."

He smiled and withdrew his hand. "I have faith in you."

She pressed her now-free arm against her stomach. "I wish I could say the same about myself. I guess I'll have to figure out that one later."

"I don't want to lose you," Adam told her. "The kid thing came up suddenly."

"I know. I didn't mean to scare you. We haven't been dating that long."

"Long enough. I love you, Shannon. I want this to work. Can we keep moving forward with the idea we'll be talking about our future and coming up with a plan that works for both of us?"

She nodded because it was the mature thing to do. But in her head, she was less agreeable. How were they supposed to fix the problem? Was it possible for him to get his vasectomy reversed? She understood there were other options but wasn't sure what he meant by coming up with a plan.

She opened her mouth to ask him to be more specific, then pressed her lips together. Their relationship was too new, she thought. There was too much going on too soon. They didn't have the history needed to get through it all.

They weren't going to make it, she thought suddenly. By bringing up children, she'd sent them down the road to the end. There was no fixing things now, she thought sadly. There was only getting through it all.

"We do need time," she said, doing her best to keep her mouth from trembling as she fought against the pain of the inevitable. She hadn't met anyone like Adam ever. She'd been so sure he was the one. Yet here they were.

"You won't give up on me?" he asked.

"No," she promised, knowing it was the truth. She wouldn't be giving up on him. But it was just a matter of time until he gave up on her.

"Come shopping with me," Eric said with a grin. "Come on, you've got time. Tyler's at preschool and Greta will pick him up when he's done. You don't have class until four. I'll get you back in time."

Nicole couldn't say what surprised her more. The invitation or the fact that Eric had shown up at her studio. He never came here. Sometimes she wondered if he remembered where it was.

She hadn't seen much of him in the past few weeks. He'd been busy starting his new life as a successful screenwriter. They'd hired the slightly scary Greta and she'd started on Monday. So far things seemed to be going fine. Tyler liked her and Nicole was determined not to be intimidated by her.

She thought about all the things she had to do, then told herself they could wait. She and Eric needed some time alone together.

"Shopping, it is," she said, grabbing her bag. "Where are we going?"

"Where else?"

"Not Beverly Hills," she said. "That's ridiculous. It's so expensive."

Eric opened the passenger side door of his new red BMW convertible. "Only the best for us. Only the best."

They headed toward the 405 freeway, then got on going north.

Traffic was light in the middle of the day. The temperature was warm and the sky a perfect California blue. Eric turned on the radio to a popular pop station, then surprised her by reaching across the console and taking her hand in his.

"I've finished the first round of revisions on my screenplay," he said. "There were a lot of notes. I'm expecting another go-round, but Jacob said with what I've done, he's ready to move forward."

"That's great."

She knew Jacob was the producer who had bought Eric's screenplay. He wanted to get it into production as quickly as possible. Nicole wasn't sure of all the steps involved, nor did she understand who the players were. From what she'd been able to piece together, Eric's sale had been something of a lightning strike. Instead of going through the usual channels and having it take forever, he'd gotten lucky.

A member of his critique group was neighbors with Jacob. While Jacob hadn't been interested in his buddy comedy, he'd been intrigued when told about Eric's techno-thriller. They'd had a meeting, Jacob had read the screenplay and had made the impossible offer.

Now they were moving forward with making a movie. From what she heard, most screenplays got optioned first. Those that were bought generally languished and were never made. Talk about a roller coaster.

"You must be so proud of yourself," she said. "What you've done is impressive."

He smiled at her. "I couldn't have done it without your support."

"I don't think I was very supportive. I yelled a lot."

"I deserved it. I should have been more clear about what I wanted. I should have made you a part of things. I'm sorry about that. But it's going to be different now. You'll see."

A promise she wanted to believe. And while part of her was willing to accept that he was right, she couldn't be completely sure. Chasing dreams took time—she got that. But she still had the sense of being on the outside, looking in.

They exited the freeway and headed east into Beverly Hills. Eric talked about what it would take to get the movie into production, how they would be filming in Vancouver and London and who would be in the starring roles.

"Jacob and I have talked about an unknown for the female lead. Like a young Jennifer Lawrence."

Nicole laughed. "She's only what? Twenty-five. How young are you thinking?"

"Okay, not young, but undiscovered. The male lead would go to someone who can bring in the audience. There's a spot."

He pulled into a lot and parked. They got out and walked toward the sidewalk.

Nicole couldn't remember the last time she'd been in Beverly Hills. When she was little, her mother used to bring her here every few weeks. They would window-shop and study the rich women who strolled so casually.

"One day you'll be famous," her mother had promised. "You'll shop here. You'll buy the most expensive clothes and jewelry. Everyone will know who you are."

At first that dream had sounded fun but as Nicole had learned what it took to be successful as an actress or a dancer, she'd begun to wonder if it was worth all the effort. Of course, that had been before she'd discovered she didn't have the talent.

Now she lived what most would consider an ordinary life. She didn't have any regrets about how things had gone. Wouldn't it be funny if the whole dream her mother had for her was fulfilled by Eric?

"Here we are," Eric said, pointing to the front of a store.

She studied the big windows and the display mannequins in suits and more casual clothes. The styles were the right combination of trendy and timeless, with impeccable tailoring and beautiful fabrics. It took money to look that good, she thought, slightly startled and totally bemused.

Of course, she thought, doing her best not to laugh as they entered the European-based menswear store. Why would she have thought otherwise? Because when Eric had asked her to go shopping, she'd assumed it was for her. And she'd been completely wrong.

"Good afternoon," a middle-aged well-dressed salesman said as he approached. "How may I help you?"

"I'm looking for a few new looks," Eric told him. "Hollywood casual. Clothes I can wear to meetings and to parties." He turned to Nicole. "Maybe one suit and a tux. What do you think?"

"That sounds about right, although I'm not sure you need a tux right now. I'd wait until award season and get something then."

"Good point," Eric said, and kissed her cheek. He turned back to the salesman. "No tux."

"As you wish. I'm Phillip. And you are?"

Introductions were made all around.

"Why don't you come this way and we'll get started," Phillip said. "Would either of you like a glass of champagne?"

"We both would," Eric said easily, as if shopping with champagne was an everyday occurrence.

Nicole followed them to the back of the store. She was seated on a comfortable love seat. An assistant brought out two glasses of champagne on a silver tray while Phillip took Eric's measurements, then asked him a few questions about where he would need the clothing.

"You're in the business?" Phillip asked.

No need to clarify. There was only the one business in Los Angeles.

"Screenwriter."

Phillip's expression remained impassive. "You've sold it?"

"A seven-figure deal."

Phillip got a whole lot friendlier. "Excellent. Congratulations. We have everything you're going to need. You'll want to look fashionable, but without trying too hard. Casual but not sloppy. The focus is on you, not what you're wearing. One suit for now. Navy, I think. It will all be about the tailoring. Prada, perhaps. The Italians know what they're doing with a suit. Give me a few minutes to collect some samples. I'll be right back."

Two hours later, they left the store. They were each carrying bags. Eric had bought everything from socks to a leather bomber jacket. Most of the pants, along with the suit, required tailoring and he would pick them up later.

"I need to get you home," he said as he stored everything in the trunk. "Then get to my meeting." He walked around to the passenger side and held open her door. "You should take yourself shopping when you get a chance. Buy some new things."

She nodded as she got in. The message was clear. He wouldn't be going with her. After all, watching her shop wouldn't help his career. Perhaps a harsh judgment, she told herself. But was it inaccurate?

She'd long known that the Eric she'd married was gone. What about this new guy? Did they have anything in common? Because if they didn't, she didn't see how their marriage was ever going to work.

Riverside was less than ninety miles from Mischief Bay, but in terms of life, purpose and style, it was another galaxy in distance. Or maybe that was unfair, Shannon thought as she sat in her parents' backyard on a hot and sunny Saturday afternoon. Maybe the real distance was simply between her life and her parents'.

Her dad had gone golfing with a few of his friends. To the public course, he'd been careful to say before he left. Because he would never join a country club of any kind. She was pretty sure her parents could afford it and as much as her dad golfed these days, it made sense. But to do so was to cross that invisible line of being too much or having too much. You bought things because they were necessary. A golf club membership wasn't ever going to be necessary.

"It warmed up early this year," her mother said.

"It did. Your roses look beautiful."

"Sally's are much nicer, but I'm happy with how these came out. I've been working with them."

The backyard was a testament to her mother's love of and talent with all things plant-based. There were lush bushes, blooming flowers, artfully arranged and elegantly displayed. Shannon had never shared her mother's affection for the outdoors, but she'd still spent many happy hours on this small patio, reading while her mother gardened.

"Your father's thinking of retiring," her mother said.

"Good for him."

"He's sixty-six. It's past the retirement age."

Shannon understood that retiring could be mistaken for being lazy. Or not working hard enough. "He's earned this. What about you, Mom? Thinking about letting the kids teach themselves?"

Her mother, also a natural redhead whose only vanity was to color her hair ever four weeks, shook her head. "Shannon, I don't know where you get your strange ideas. Children can't teach themselves. I don't know how much longer I'll work. Your father and I have been thinking about buying an RV. A small one, of course. It's just the two of us. Used. We've been looking around and there are some bargains."

"That sounds like fun," Shannon said as she picked up her lemonade and sipped it. What she really wanted to say was "Go wild. Get a big one. Or even a medium-size one. And hey, look at a new one!"

But she wouldn't. Not only couldn't she possibly change their minds, but they would also be uncomfortable at what they perceived as waste.

Shannon told herself to respect their frugal natures. They'd been raised by depression-era parents who had taught them to squeeze every penny until it was reduced to its base elements. Saving was good for families and good for the economy. But, like anything worthy, it could be taken to the extreme.

And it wasn't the savings she took issue with, she thought. It was the attitude that went with it. The constant apology if something was new, or nice. That her mother couldn't simply accept a compliment about the roses—she had to say someone else's were nicer and that she'd worked hard to get them that way.

"I hope you and Dad get an RV," she said instead. "You've always wanted to travel."

"I have. And it's not like we're going to Europe. That would be so extravagant."

"It doesn't have to be," Shannon said gently. "There are discount trips…"

Her mother was already shaking her head. "We're not like you, Shannon. We don't believe in that sort of thing."

"Seeing the world?"

"Wasting money like that. You always wanted more. You were never content with what you had."

Shannon remembered being eight or nine. It had been close to Christmas and she'd seen a pair of red patent leather shoes in the store.

They had been the most beautiful shoes she'd ever seen in her life and she wanted them with a fiery desperation. Of course, her parents had told her no. That she already had her school shoes and her play shoes. If she needed something fancy, which was unlikely, she could borrow a pair from one of her friends. Come summer, she would get a pair of sandals and maybe they could be red.

She hadn't been appeased by the thought because she knew that come summer, she would get brown sandals. Brown was practical. Brown went with everything.

She'd tried begging, bargaining, and had even attempted to sell some of her toys to neighborhood kids. But no one would pay for her modest playthings. Christmas morning had come and gone. She'd gotten three presents, and no red patent leather shoes.

Years later, she'd started babysitting. She'd saved until she had enough and then she'd bought a pair of ridiculous high-heeled patent leather pumps. Her parents had been horrified. She was supposed to be saving for her future. She told them she'd been dreaming about red patent leather shoes for six years. She was past due.

Later she'd realized the pumps she'd bought were more suitable for someone who dabbled in prostitution than a high school sophomore. She'd only ever worn them a couple of times. But they'd represented something significant: she'd wanted them and she had bought them herself. Buying those shoes had represented possibilities and freedom.

Her mother would say they'd been her first step down the dark path and maybe they had been. But Shannon had decided then and there she was going to make enough money to buy whatever she wanted, whenever she wanted. No one was ever going to tell her no again.

"You do know I have a savings account, right?" she asked her mother. "And a 401K."

"I hope it's enough."

"Mom, I work in finance. I'm the CFO in a billion-dollar company. I know how to handle money."

Her mother glanced around, as if concerned someone would overhear them. "Keep your voice down. There's no reason to go bragging to the whole neighborhood. That sort of thing is private."

Right. Because aside from not spending money, her parents never talked about it, either. To this day she had no idea what either of them made. She could guess, but she didn't know. Of course they didn't know what she made either. She had a feeling they would faint with shock at her mid-six-figure salary.

"Maybe you could plan to go to Europe for your sixty-fifth birthday," she said. "That gives you a couple of years to save for it. It could be your present."

For a second her mother's expression turned wistful. "That would be nice," she admitted, before shaking her head. "Your father would never agree it was a good idea."

Shannon only nodded. No point in getting into it with her mom now. But later, she would drop a hint or two to her father. Maybe if she suggested it and offered to pay half as her gift to her mom, she could make it happen. Or maybe it would all blow up in her face with her father accusing her of bragging. It was difficult to know with them.

For the four hundred millionth time, she wished they could be different. An impossible request, of course, but she couldn't shake the feeling of sadness when she thought of her parents. They chose to live such small lives. They could afford to do more and wouldn't. If they didn't want to travel, then she could understand them choosing to stay home. Only they did. Or at least her mother did.

Shannon knew her love of exotic places came from the times when she and her mom would check out travel books from the library. They would pore over the color pictures and talk about going there…someday.

Shannon had learned that for her parents "someday" really meant never. Once she'd broken free and bought her red shoes, she'd also decided she was going to see the world. And she had. She supposed for her mother, the RV was enough.

Shannon wondered if the concept of enough should be one she embraced. But she wanted more—at least when it came to her personal life. A problem she and Adam had yet to resolve.

"Mom, why didn't you and Dad have more kids?"

Her mother picked up her drink and took a sip. "Are you sorry you're an only child?"

"It's all I know. I can try to imagine what it would have been like with siblings, but at this point, I'm not sure what difference it would make."

"We talked about having more children," her mother admitted. "But then it never happened."

The obvious question was why. Had there been problems getting pregnant? Problems in the marriage? Or had her parents simply made the sensible choice? The one to only have a single child so they wouldn't stretch their budget?

"I want to have a baby," Shannon confessed.

Her mother turned to her, her eyebrows raised, her mouth twisted in judgment. "Shannon, no. You can't. You're too old."

An unexpected slap, she thought, trying not to react, at least on the outside. "I'm going to be forty."

"I know how old you are. And you'd be close to sixty

when your child graduated from high school. Are you sure you could even get pregnant at this age? Besides, you're not even married." Her mother's eyes widened. "You're not going to go adopt a foreign child on your own, are you?"

"I might." Because the stubborn kid in her thought defying her mother sounded pretty damned good right about now.

"I have no idea what your father would say about that."

Shannon wanted to find her way to the golf course and tell him that second. In front of his friends. Then she drew a breath and let the urge wash over her and away.

It was usually like this when she came home, she thought. She and her mother talked while her father disappeared somewhere. Conversation took a turn and she found herself on the teenaged side of parental disapproval.

She knew she was a disappointment. She hadn't followed the family rules. She wasn't modest enough or average enough or traditional enough. She'd been too driven, too flashy. Although her parents knew about her beachfront condo, they'd never seen it. No doubt their senior hearts couldn't stand the strain.

She told herself that love came in many forms. That she should be grateful she still had her parents and that while they couldn't be more different, if something bad happened, they would be there for her. She was only staying for a few more hours. She could afford to be gracious.

"You've raised some good points," she said gently. "I'm going to have to think about them. And I won't say anything to Dad."

Her mother relaxed. "He loves you very much. We both do. It's just sometimes…"

"I know, Mom. I don't make it easy."

Twenty

Nicole stared at the foil-covered glass casserole dish. The instructions were very clear. Thirty minutes in a 350-degree oven. Greta's writing was like the woman herself—precise and deliberate. Okay, and maybe just a little bit scary.

In addition to the prepared entrée, there was a salad for her and Eric, along with a weird blue smoothie drink in a child-size cup for Tyler. One he claimed to have had before and really liked. Nicole was sure all the ingredients were organic and locally sourced, wherever possible. That the meal couldn't be more healthy and that she would sleep better because of it.

All things to be grateful for, if only she could get over the weirdness of it all.

Two years ago, she'd been going along with her life. She had a husband and a son and a new business. All of which was still true, but somehow it all felt different. As if the traditional painting that was her life had been redone by Picasso. All that was missing were the flying goats.

Not that she was complaining. The changes had happened gradually. But when she looked back at how much things had changed, she felt a little strange about it all.

She turned on the oven to preheat it. There wasn't much else for her to do. The laundry was done, the kitchen clean. Even the bathroom towels had a just-washed scent and softness. Tyler informed her that Greta had already given him a bath that afternoon *and* read him his favorite B the D book twice.

Nicole realized that she didn't have anything to do. Not cleaning, not getting dinner ready beyond the back-breaking task of turning on the oven, not anything. She was tired from a long day at work and she could simply relax with her son.

"Let's play while dinner's heating," she said.

Tyler shouted his pleasure and made a beeline for his room.

She followed and soon they were busy working on a puzzle. When the oven beeped it was hot enough, she put in the casserole, then returned to the fun. By six, they were sitting down to eat.

For once there was time to find a nice classical station on the radio and even pour a glass of wine. Tyler enjoyed his strange blue drink and didn't seem to notice the vegetables Greta had hidden in the casserole.

When they were done, they cleaned the kitchen together, then went into the living room to watch one of his movies. Movies that had been put away on their shelf... in alphabetical order.

The evening continued to pass smoothly. Nicole wasn't sure when Eric would be home, but that was true most nights. He was kept busy with his movie and starting a new screenplay. She only knew that last bit because she'd overheard him talking about it with Jacob. As for the current one, he still hadn't given it to her to read, despite her asking.

At eight, she put Tyler to bed and then wandered through her clean, organized house. She picked up a book she'd been wanting to read for at least two years and settled down to sink into the story. It was a weekend night and here she was—reading.

Somewhere around nine, Eric walked into the house.

"Hi," he said when he saw her. "How was your day?"

She looked up from her book. "Good. How was—"
She stared at the man she'd married. The clothes were new, but then she'd been there when he'd bought them. But they weren't what startled her. She stared at his hair, taking in the blond ends of his new sticky-up style.

"Do you have highlights?" she asked, unable to grasp the possibility.

"Yeah. Do you like them?"

Sure, this was L.A. but highlights? Who did he think he was? Brad Pitt?

"Um, sure. They're, um, great." She closed her book. "Did you eat? There's a chicken casserole in the fridge. Greta outdid herself again."

"I ate, but thanks." He sat at the other end of the sofa. "We're getting serious about casting. That's been interesting. I'm learning a lot from Jacob."

"I'll bet. It's great that he's involving you in so much of the movie."

Eric leaned forward, his clasped hands dangling between his knees. "I know. We're becoming good friends. Most writers don't get to see all the magic happen. We've been brainstorming my next project. I'm going to have to take a few months to write it, but I want to stay with the movie as long as I can. Then I'll hole up and get the writing done. It's hectic, but fun."

She studied his face. He looked happy, she thought. Relaxed. The highlights would take some getting used to, but she could probably live with them.

"I'm glad it's all going so well." She paused, not sure what she wanted to tell him. "You're gone a lot."

"I know. It's tough, right? All this work. It comes with the business. I'm sure you can imagine. Jacob's going to be out of town for a few days. So the three of us can do something Sunday. Maybe go to the POP and hang out."

"Tyler would like that a lot. He misses you."

"I miss him, too." Eric rose. "I'm going to catch up on email."

"I miss you, too," she added.

Her husband nodded and gave her a kiss on the cheek. But instead of speaking, he headed for his office.

When she was alone again, she leaned back against the sofa. Had he noticed that he didn't say he missed her? They'd drifted so far apart. It had happened slowly at first, but now the chasm between them was wider and deeper every week.

She couldn't tell if he was excluding her deliberately or if it was simply happening through circumstance. While she was glad Eric was happy with his work, where did it leave their relationship?

What did he want from her and what did she want from him? And if they were rarely in the same room at the same time, how were they ever supposed to have that conversation?

Shannon hesitated only a second before walking into Latte-Da. It was ten in the morning on a Tuesday and there wasn't much of a crowd. She spotted Adam right away. He had two to-go cups in front of him and when he saw her, he stood and carried the cups over to her.

"Thanks for coming," he said, as he approached.

"You said it was important." She took one of the cups. "Thank you for my latte."

"You're welcome. Let's go outside and walk along the boardwalk."

Shannon held on to her coffee with both hands. Adam had called a half hour before and told her they had to talk. She knew he was right—they had things they needed to talk about. Her solution for dealing with the tough stuff had been to avoid him as much as possible. Not the mature response and not one she was proud of. So when he'd asked to get together, she'd cleared her calendar to meet with him.

She'd never been dumped by the POP, she thought as they walked across the street and stepped onto the cement path that stretched from Pacific Palisades to Santa Monica. And somehow she'd assumed that if her relationship with Adam ended, she would be the one saying goodbye.

But it hadn't happened that way. They'd reached an impasse. They wanted different things and there was no easy solution. Maybe if they'd been together longer, she thought sadly. Maybe they would have a chance.

She wasn't sure how she was going to deal with losing him. He was a great guy and she had fallen in love with him. Foolishly, she'd allowed herself to believe she was finally going to get to have it all. Marriage, kids and growing old with someone.

When she'd realized that wasn't going to happen, she'd put off the inevitable as long as possible. Now that it was here, she promised herself she would be reasonable. Even kind. She wouldn't cry. Not in front of him. When they were done, she would go back to her office and finish her day. But that night—all bets were off.

She wondered how long it would take to stop missing him. How long until she was able to think about seeing someone else. How long until thinking about him didn't cause a physical ache.

"You've been avoiding me," he said as they turned north.

"I have."

She wondered how they looked from the outside. A successful couple, she thought. Adam might be in jeans, a long-sleeved shirt and work boots, but he had an air of confidence about him. No one would be surprised to learn he ran an eight-figure construction project.

She had on one of her business suits. It was California-inspired—less structured than a traditional suit, but with all the pieces. Her high heels clicked on the cement path.

"If we don't talk, we can't fix the problem," he told her. "Something this big could get in the way of what we want." He pulled her to a stop and stared into her eyes. "Shannon, I love you. That hasn't changed. I don't want to lose you, but I don't know what you're thinking. Are you still in this with me or are you already gone?"

She stared into his eyes and read the truth there. He wasn't done with her. He wasn't breaking up with her. He was trying to fix things between them. He was acting like the grown-up in the room.

"I'm not gone," she whispered.

"Promise?"

She nodded.

He exhaled. "Thank you for saying that. I was really worried. Especially when you disappeared. I know this is hard. I'm working on it. Can you give me some time? I'm not talking years or even months, but I need a few weeks to get my head around things."

Because he took her seriously, she thought, amazed and grateful. Because he wanted her to be happy.

"Take as long as you need."

He smiled and touched her cheek. "I appreciate the offer. I want to work this out. I can't believe I found you. I don't want to blow it."

"Me, either."

"Then promise me you won't disappear on me again. If you're mad, say so. We can fight about it. We can search for solutions. I'm good at that. What I can't deal with is being shut out."

Something she hadn't thought about before, but now that she did, it made sense. Of course he didn't want to be excluded. He knew the price of doing that. It was one of the reasons he'd ended up divorced.

"I promise."

A skateboarder in shorts and a T-shirt whizzed past them. Adam ignored the guy as he leaned toward her and kissed her mouth.

"Thank you," he whispered. "For what it's worth, I'm not the only one who's missed you. The kids have been asking about you. Char keeps saying how she wants to make sure you're at her party."

Ah, the infamous birthday bash at Epic, Shannon thought. "Why do I know that's more about her fear that you're staying than her excitement at having me there?"

"Whatever works," he said with a smile.

She kissed him and felt the hardness in her heart crack. "You're right. Whatever works. I don't want lose you, either. Thank you for not giving up on me."

"Never."

* * *

"I don't understand," Jen said, holding up a tiny onesie. "How can clothing be organic?"

"Maybe it's the cotton they use. Or the dying process." In today's world, Pam half expected to see a gluten-free sign over a bag of socks.

"I guess when Kirk and I register for the baby, we'll have to decide about organic fabrics."

Which would make them wildly popular with their friends, Pam thought. Not that she would say anything. Jen had invited her to lunch followed by an afternoon of wandering at South Bay Galleria. While Pam generally preferred the odd little stores in Mischief Bay, every now and then she enjoyed hanging out at the mall. These days having a reason to leave the house was good. She knew she was spending too much time on her own. While Lulu was a faithful companion, she wasn't much for conversation.

She knew it would be better if in addition to feeling she *needed* to get out, that she also *wanted* to get out. But that wasn't happening. Her days were still cold and empty, with the realization she would never be happy again. She still drank too much, didn't eat enough and had long given up ever feeling normal.

She knew down to the minute how long ago John had died. She resented him for dying and ached for him in equal measures. She was lost and alone and yet had apparently learned to fake it so well, no one bothered to ask her how she was doing in that worried tone she'd grown used to. Even Jen had barely mentioned John.

People moved on, she told herself. People healed. Not her, but then she had been his wife. Their relationship was different. No one else had marked the passage of time by his comings and goings.

"You don't have to decide anything now," Pam pointed out. "You have a lot of time until you need to register."

Jen nodded and linked arms with her. "You're right. Thanks. I'm not even showing. I'm still in all my regular pants." Jen wrinkled her nose. "Not the skinny day ones, but all the others."

Pam heard the impatience in her daughter's voice. Because like nearly every other expectant mother-to-be, she was ready to proclaim her baby to the world. She thought maternity clothes would be cool and fun.

Pam remembered her own excitement when she'd been pregnant. The thrill of knowing there was going to be a baby. The terror that she didn't know how to be a mother with the first one and the worry about exhaustion with the second and third.

"You'll be showing soon enough," she told her daughter. "Trust me, when it's finally time to have your baby, you'll be thrilled to get on the road to getting your body back."

"I guess."

"You sound doubtful. We'll have another conversation about this in seven months. I'll be the one saying 'I told you so.'"

Jen laughed. "You'd never say that."

They walked out of the store and headed for California Pizza Kitchen for lunch. Jen had suggested the place, admitting she was desperate for pizza. Pam had agreed because she generally liked their food and these days what did it matter? She ate because she had to. Her stomach cramped and she felt light-headed if she didn't. But there was no pleasure in it.

They were seated at a booth. Jen eagerly opened the menu and studied the options. Pam looked at her daughter. Overhead light caught a few strands of Jen's sleek hair. Her skin looked firm and flush with good health.

At night, when she couldn't sleep, she thought about her children and wished them long and happy lives. If only she could spare them from future unhappiness, she thought. Because that was all she had to give them. Wishes and hopes. There wasn't much of anything else left. Not inside of her.

She knew that on the surface, she was doing fine. Quieter than usual, sure. But getting through the days. She'd figured out when the trash had to go out and was paying her bills. She answered the phone because if she didn't, people worried. Shannon and Nicole stopped by faithfully and she pretended to be excited to see them. But despite the physical actions, she wasn't fine. She was barely getting by.

Most nights, she couldn't sleep. She drank more than she should. She lost hours just sitting and thinking about John. Sometimes she would look up and be surprised to discover it was dark outside.

But those were *her* secrets. She protected her pain from outside scrutiny. She no longer thought she should be locked up, but she certainly wasn't ready to give up the daily grief that connected her so completely with John.

"Barbecue chicken pizza," her daughter said firmly as she closed the menu. "What about you, Mom?"

"I'm getting that soup I like."

"Dakota smashed pea and barley?"

"That's the one."

"Is it enough? Do you want a sandwich to go with that?"

"No, thanks." She pushed the menu aside. "I take it Kirk's working today."

"He is. He's been taking extra hours when he can. To pad our savings."

Pam thought about the sale of the business. "You'll be getting money from your father," she said. "Won't that be enough?"

Jen's easy smile faded. "We're saving that, Mom. For the kids' college. Our retirement. That's not money we'd spend."

Because her daughter was sensible, Pam thought with pride. "You're taking a long-term view. That's good."

"I can't help it. Somehow it seems wrong to spend it on a vacation or carpeting. I want it put away. There will be expenses later." She rested her elbows on the table. "Everything's different now that we're having a baby. Like we can't be frivolous. We're going to get a will, if you can believe it."

Jen paused. "Is it okay I say that?"

"Of course." Pam forced a smile. "You're going to have a child of your own. Things change with that. When that happens, we're all forced to be the adult in the room. Harder for some than others. You've always made smart decisions."

"I wish that were true, but thanks for the compliment. I worry, though. About Kirk. He's in a dangerous line of work. What if something happened to him? I'm not like you, Mom. I couldn't be that strong."

Pam thought about the long nights, the crying, the way every single breath hurt. She wasn't nearly as strong as they all thought, but sharing that wouldn't help anyone.

"We all do what we have to," she said instead. "You'd

get by because there isn't an alternative. But I suspect you and Kirk will be together for a long, long time."

Jen's eyes filled with tears. "Thanks for saying that. I hope you're right. I miss Daddy a lot."

Pam nodded. Her throat tightened and she found herself longing to be home. Lulu never brought up John. Pam was the one who decided what she could stand and what she couldn't.

"He's never going to see his first grandchild." Tears spilled down Jen's cheeks. "I think about that all the time. It's so unfair."

Pam wanted to shriek at her that Jen couldn't begin to understand what was unfair. That Pam's loss was greater. Harder. Sharper.

Parents were older. They were expected to die at some point. But not a husband. Not so soon. She hadn't been ready.

But she didn't say any of that. Instead, she pulled out the stash of tissues she kept with her and passed a couple across the table. Jen took one and wiped her eyes.

"Sorry."

"Don't be. I cry all the time. I try not to do it outside the house, but it's still happening."

Jen nodded and sniffed. "Mom, if you want to come stay with us, you know you can, right?"

For the first time in days, Pam smiled spontaneously. "I love you like you're my own daughter, but moving in with you and Kirk is my own version of hell."

Jen laughed. "I figured, but you're always welcome."

"Don't take it personally."

"I won't. You'd hate living with the boys even more."

"You got that right."

Jen squared her shoulders. "Enough of my emotions.

How are you doing? Really? Tell me the truth. Is it better than it was?"

Pam thought about the long nights, the hideously lonely days. She thought about how she wandered from room to room, waiting for someone who would never return. She thought about the pain, the tears, the bottles of wine she consumed. Then she looked into her daughter's beautiful face and knew lying offered the most kindness.

"It's better. Not great. But it's better."

Twenty-One

"We should do something today," Eric said.

It was nine on Sunday morning. Nicole had yet to shower, let alone dress. She had been looking forward to a long day of doing nothing. With Greta taking care of things like grocery shopping and cleaning, Nicole's free time had taken a turn for the open and she was excited about that.

"What did you have in mind?" she asked as she thought about getting another cup of coffee. But that would mean getting up and walking across the kitchen. "I could look online. I'm sure the California Science Center has something fun going on."

It was also one place Tyler had a good time. He was still too young for the other museums. "Oh, there's also the La Brea Tar Pits. He'd like that."

"Not a museum," Eric told her. "I was thinking we'd have a party. Here."

"A party? Today?"

"Sure. Just a few people over. We'll grill burgers. It'll be great."

Nicole watched as her vision of a do-nothing day evaporated like mist. On the bright side, Eric hadn't been interested in socializing outside of his writer friends for months, which meant there were a lot of people she hadn't seen, either. Their friends were mostly couple friends. And with her and Eric not acting like a couple lately, they'd been turning down invitations regularly.

"You're right," she said firmly. She got up and walked to the coffeepot. "We should invite all our friends over. I'm sure some are busy, but we'll take who we can get. It'll be good for us to hang out with them."

Eric got a pad of paper and started making a list. It got up to twenty people pretty quickly, but Nicole figured they'd be lucky to get half that to attend. Once the list was made, they divided it and started texting people.

Within the hour they had seven yeses and a grocery list. Two of the couples would bring kids. So fourteen adults, two kids, plus them.

"That's nineteen people," Nicole said, double-checking her math.

"We'll get everything at Costco," Eric told her. "Burgers, buns, a couple of salads, beer and juice for the kids."

"It won't be organic," Nicole pointed out. "You don't think Greta will be able to smell it when she shows up tomorrow morning?"

Her husband laughed. "Leave Greta to me. I appreciate that she's looking out for Tyler, but sometimes you have to go with the flow and have a little fun."

"You say that now, but wait until she's staring you down."

"I can handle her."

Nicole savored the moment of happiness. This was the Eric she remembered, she thought with contentment. The fun, sweet man who wanted to spend time with his family and hang out with his friends. Maybe she'd been too judgmental about what he was doing and how things had changed. Maybe she should take his advice and go with the flow.

"While you deal with Costco, I'll take Tyler to Patty Cakes and get the cupcakes. We'll get home first, so I'll get out the folding tables and wash them down."

"This is going to be fun," he told her as he got up and circled around the table. He dropped a kiss on the top of her head.

"It is," she whispered when he'd left the kitchen.

"Oh, my God! I can't believe it." Julie clapped her hands together. "When we found out Eric had sold his screenplay, we were stunned. I mean we've known the two of you forever. And to think you're like a famous Hollywood couple now."

Nicole was careful to keep smiling as she put condiments on a tray to take outside. Smiling was important, she thought. Because the party was fun and these were her friends. Only things weren't going exactly the way she'd thought they would. Rather than spending time catching up, all anyone wanted to talk about was Eric's screenplay deal.

She was okay with him having the attention. He'd worked hard and he deserved to get credit for that. But she'd wanted to spend time with their friends, not have an event in celebration of him.

Julie sighed. "I wish Shane would do something like that. It would be so cool."

"You love Shane. He's a great guy."

Julie grinned. "I'd love him more if he was famous, that's for sure." She leaned in and lowered her voice. "I can't believe he's going to read part of it to us later. I'm so excited."

"What?"

Her friend nodded her head. "He told me he's going to read a couple of scenes. It's totally insider info. I can't wait."

Nicole did her best not to look as shocked as she felt. Reading part of his screenplay? Out loud? Wasn't that taking things a bit too far?

"What was your favorite part?" Julie asked. "You must be tired of it by now, so thanks for indulging the rest of us."

Nicole managed to keep smiling, even though she felt a little sick to her stomach. She didn't have a favorite part of Eric's screenplay because she hadn't read any of it. He'd never let her. Not once, no matter how many times she asked. But he was going to read a couple of scenes to their friends?

She handed Julie the condiments. "Would you take these out, please? I want to check on the drink supply. We want to make sure we have enough for everyone to toast Eric later."

"Oh, right. Sure."

Julie walked through the open back door and into the yard.

Nicole leaned against the counter. Everything was going to be fine, she told herself. At least she didn't have to worry about being bored during the reading. But as she stood alone in the kitchen, she wondered what was going on. Had Eric forgotten she hadn't read his screenplay? Was this a giant snub?

She told herself she would deal with it later. That right now there was a party and she wanted to have a good time. She checked on the drinks, then took out a container of potato salad and carried it to the patio.

The three boys had already exhausted themselves running around and were now flopped down on a blanket in the shade of a tree playing with plastic dump trucks. Eric and a couple of the guys stood by the grill. Everyone else was either on folding chairs or on blankets on the grass. Music played from wireless speakers.

Bits of conversation drifted to her.

"No, really, have you met anyone famous?"

"I heard it was like a million dollars. I wonder if they'll move."

"They have a nanny now, you know. Must be nice."

Nicole looked at their guests and realized how long it had been since she'd seen any of them. Eric had chosen to bury himself in his screenplay, but what was her excuse? She'd let the friendships wither. Sure she'd been busy, but that was hardly a reason. If she wanted people in her life, she had to make time for them.

She put more potato salad into the bowl, then carried the empty container back into the kitchen.

Mark, a friend of Eric's at the software company where they had both worked, followed her inside.

"Everyone's talking about Eric's deal," he said.

"I heard."

"It's fun for all of us. Maybe you'll get to go to an award show and we can see you on TV."

"Maybe. I haven't seen you and Paige in forever. How are things going? Tell me everything."

Mark's gaze shifted away. "We're fine."

"What?" she demanded. "Is everything okay?"

Mark smiled. "Everything is great. Don't worry." He stepped toward her. "Can you keep a secret?"

"Sure. What?"

"Paige is pregnant. Three months. We were going to start telling people today, in fact, but then we got the text. This is about Eric and we don't want to steal the spotlight. But we're both really happy."

"Congratulations," Nicole told him. "That's wonderful. I wish you would tell everyone. It's wonderful, happy news."

"Next time," Mark said, then glanced back outside. "Oh, look. Eric's going to read from his screenplay. I don't want to miss that."

Nicole watched him walk away, then slowly followed. Shouldn't news of a baby trump a screenplay reading? What was going on here? Maybe it was her, she told herself. She was overly sensitive. She had a thing against fame and anything remotely entertainment-related because of how her mother had pushed her. But she couldn't shake the sense of being swept away by something she couldn't control and didn't completely understand.

"That's a lot of pink," Adam said.

"*Overwhelming* is the word you're looking for." Shannon stood next to him in the "party room" at Epic Salon and told herself that the paint wasn't really vibrating on the walls. It just seemed that way.

Whoever had designed the space had gone all out. While the front part of the salon was quiet and elegant, done in grays and lavenders, back here it was all pink, all the time. The walls, the tables, the chairs, the tablecloths, even the window coverings were shades of pink. Balloons in tones from palest rose to lipstick floated near the ceiling. Pink lemonade filled pitchers on tables. The cupcakes were iced in pink.

"Now I'm scared about the pizza," he admitted. "And woozy. Can too much of a color make you light-headed?"

"I think your testosterone is worried about being over-whelmed."

"Rightfully so." He looked around. "This isn't nor-mal, right? I'm afraid for a reason?"

"You are, but you're going to have to deal. This is what you agreed to for your daughter's birthday party." Shannon patted his arm. "Don't worry. You're not stay-ing and I doubt a few minutes in this hostile environ-ment is going to be enough to turn you into a woman."

"You're mocking me."

"Right now you're kind of mockable."

Adam pulled her close and kissed her. "I can't tell you how glad I am you're here to save my butt."

"It's a nice butt and well worth saving."

He grinned. "You're irresistible and as soon as I re-turn my children to their mother's I'm going to prove it five times over."

"Five times, huh? That's quite an offer."

"How about I throw in dinner, too?"

"Sold."

He released her and circled the room. "There's not much for me to do."

She nodded, guessing that was the point. Epic pro-vided a full-service birthday party for the younger set. First the girls would have a mani-pedi, then they would adjourn to the back room for the actual party. Pizza, drinks and cupcakes were provided, along with the dec-orations. For a guy like Adam, it was a godsend. All he had to do was make the reservation and cough up the credit card. Pretty brilliant marketing, she thought.

"You're sure you're going to be okay?" he asked.

"I'll be fine," she assured him, thinking that a group of nine-year-old girls couldn't be that scary. And if she was wrong, she had a bottle of wine waiting back at her place.

"Because I can stay."

"You're adorable for offering, but I can see the fear in your eyes. It will be fine." She pushed him toward the door. "Go pay the nice lady for the party. The girls will be arriving soon."

Adam nodded and headed toward the front of the store. Shannon circled the room one more time, making sure everything was in place. There was a table for gifts, and another table with the small goodie bags prepared by the salon. Inside was a bottle of nail polish, several temporary tattoos and some plastic costume jewelry.

There was no present from her father at the party. He would be giving that to her tonight at dinner. Shannon had declined to attend. She had a feeling that a three-hour party was going to be more than enough family time for one day.

She walked up front to confirm that everything looked good and found Char in tears and Adam looking frustrated.

"She won't say what's wrong," he said. "Char, if you don't tell me, I can't help."

"It doesn't matter," his daughter told him. "Just go. I'm fine."

"I can't leave you like this. Your party starts in a few minutes. Tell me?"

Char sniffed. "Dad, I'm okay. I'm going to have a good party. I promise. Just go."

Adam hesitated, then looked at Shannon. "You'll call me if you need help?"

"In a heartbeat," she promised.

Char stepped close to her. "Shannon's here, Dad. I'm fine. You should go pick up Oliver."

Because her younger brother was at a friend's house.

Adam glanced at the door, then back. "Okay, but you know how to reach me." He kissed them both on the cheek, then left.

When he was gone, Shannon pointed to the chairs in the waiting area. "We have a few minutes before your guests arrive. Why don't you tell me what's wrong?"

Char sat and her eyes filled with tears again. "It's the party. I wanted the skin-care facial and my dad said no. That he wouldn't pay for it. But when Bree had her party here, we had the skin-care facial and everyone loved it. He says the party is already expensive. But all my friends are going to laugh at me."

Shannon felt the hit straight to her gut. She knew Adam had been against the facial from the beginning. She kind of saw his point. Char was only nine and a facial sounded pretty adult. But she hated seeing Char so upset right before her party.

"I'm sorry Char, but I can't help with something your dad specifically said he didn't want you to have," she said.

"I know." Char hung her head. "You can't go behind his back, even though it's my birthday."

Shannon recognized the attempt to guilt her. No way she was going to fall for it. But she still felt like crap.

"Is there something we could add to the mani-pedi package that would be different from the other parties?" she asked, confident she was both weak and being played, but unable to help herself.

Char brightened immediately. "Nail art. No one's had

that." She pointed to the signs on the wall. "The glitter package."

Shannon saw that there was indeed a glitter package for the parties. The price made her wince, but it was too late to back out now.

She stood and walked to the receptionist. "Then let's get this party started."

Ninety minutes later, Shannon was fighting a killer headache. She'd had no idea ten nine-year-old girls could make so much noise. And at such a high pitch.

The party itself was brilliant. The salon partnered with a nearby beauty school. The technicians brought in for the event were students. Epic didn't tie up staff with clients who would not become regulars for at least another decade and the students had an opportunity to practice.

The glitter package had been a hit. Now, as they waited for their lunch of pizza to arrive, the girls ran around showing off their manicures and pedicures.

Shannon was kept busy circling the room and making sure everyone had drinks. She'd thought at least a couple of the mothers would stay, but they'd all taken off immediately. Leaving her as the only adult who wasn't hired by the salon. A fact that made it difficult for her to completely relax.

There were presents stacked on the table. They were to be opened after lunch but before the cupcakes, Char had informed her. And after the cupcakes, everyone went home. Hallelujah.

"We're out of soda," Char informed her. "Could you see about that?"

Shannon hesitated. While the pitchers were empty, there was something in the girl's tone that gave her pause. An imperiousness that was incredibly annoying.

"Sure," Shannon said, telling herself Char was simply running on adrenaline. It was her party, after all.

She went and mentioned they needed more soda to the party coordinator and returned to the back room in time to hear Adam's daughter say, "Oh, she's not my stepmother. She's just someone my dad's dating. I don't think they're even boyfriend and girlfriend."

"But you like her," one of the girls said. "She's really nice."

Char shrugged. "She's okay. We're not friends or anything. I would never hang out with her."

"At least your dad just dates one woman at a time. My dad doesn't. It's gross."

Shannon turned and walked out of the room. The party coordinator was hurrying toward her, a full pitcher in each hand.

"Oh, I'll help with that," Shannon said, and blindly took one. Because all she could do was keep moving. If she stopped, she would have to think about what Char had said. She would have to admit the truth. That while she'd been looking to get to know Adam's daughter, Char had only been interested in using her to get a better party.

Once back in the room, she poured soda into glasses and made sure she was smiling. She admired the glitter polish and told herself she would wallow in being a fool later. That she only had an hour or so left before she could make her escape.

A few minutes later the party coordinator walked in with several pizza boxes from The Slice Is Right. Shannon helped her set out the food. The girls found seats.

Char sat at the head of the table. "I go first," she announced loudly, and studied the open pizza boxes. She pointed to the pepperoni pizza. "I want a slice of that. Shannon, would you get it for me?"

Every girl turned to look at her. Some seemed shocked by the request. A couple looked gleeful. As if this had been planned. Or maybe they were simply enjoying the opportunity to watch an adult squirm.

Shannon chuckled, as if Char was making a joke. "You're nine, not ninety. You can get your own pizza."

"But it's my birthday."

"Happy birthday to you." Shannon scanned the table. "We need more napkins. I'm going to get them."

She practically bolted from the room. Once outside, she leaned against the wall.

Had she handled that right? Should she have just handed her the pizza? She wished she knew the right thing to do. Maybe she was overreacting to what she'd heard—letting her own insecurities color her view of things.

"Here are extra napkins."

The party coordinator pressed them into her hand.

"Thanks."

Shannon sucked in a breath and then walked back into the party. The girls were deep in conversation and didn't seem to notice.

After the food, Char insisted everyone sit in a circle and pass her the presents, one by one. She opened them and thanked everyone, but also made a few digs about the choices. It was a side of her Shannon hadn't seen before.

She told herself to keep quiet and simply get through the rest of the party. When the guests had left, she collected Adam's receipt along with her own and carried the presents to the car.

When the gifts were stacked in the backseat, Char fastened her seat belt and sighed.

"That was the best party ever!"

"I'm glad you enjoyed it."

Char looked at her. "What?" she demanded. "Why did you say it like that? Didn't you have fun?"

"I wasn't there as a guest," Shannon said. No, she'd been there as some girl her father was dating. Not that she was going to get into that. Simply get the kid home, she told herself. Don't fight about it. Walk away.

All good advice, except for one problem. She wasn't just someone Adam was dating. She was in love with him and they were talking about having a future together. If she let Char's behavior go, didn't that make her an accessory to it? Or at the very least, someone who condoned it?

She wasn't sure of her place in the situation. What was expected? What was allowed? No one had given her a manual or even basic instructions.

"I knew you'd be this way," Char said with a heavy sigh. "I knew you wouldn't be happy for me."

"What are you talking about?"

The girl glared at her. "You don't really like me. You're just doing stuff so my dad will think you do."

Shannon had no idea where the accusation was coming from. "Char, if I didn't like you, why would I have tried to make your party better? Your dad wasn't there. He doesn't know what I did. I did it for you." She angled toward her. "I have to say, I'm really disappointed by all this. I thought you and I were friends. I'm sorry I'm wrong."

Char turned away. "Why are you doing this? Why are you ruining my birthday? You wanted me to have a bad time. I know it."

"You're not making sense. You got everything you wanted. You wanted me to pay for the glitter package and I did."

Char swung back to face her. "You offered. That's not my fault. Besides, it's my birthday. I get to say. You wouldn't even hand me a slice of pizza. That was mean."

"No," Shannon told her. "What was mean was when you told Madison that her gift wasn't expensive enough and that you weren't sure you could be friends with her anymore."

Char flushed. "She bought me socks. That's a grandma gift."

"They were cute and in your favorite colors. You don't get to judge a gift, Char. That's the point. People want to show they care. By complaining about it, you're showing that you're the one who doesn't care. You embarrassed your friend in front of everyone. Whatever you remember from today, she's going to remember feeling sick to her stomach and wishing she could be anywhere but at your party. It's one thing to be the center of attention on your birthday. It's another to hurt people in the process."

Char's face went pale, then flushed again. Her mouth twisted as tears filled her eyes.

"I hate you," she breathed. "You ruined everything. I'm going to tell my dad what you did and he's never going to see you again."

"Very possibly," Shannon murmured. "Very possibly."

They drove back to Adam's place without talking. The only noise was the car engine and Char's choked sobs. When Shannon pulled into the driveway, Char bolted from the car and ran into the house. Shannon turned off the engine and rested her head on the steering wheel. She honestly didn't see a good outcome in her future.

She'd just loaded up with the presents when Adam burst out of the house.

"What the hell happened?" he demanded. "Char's shrieking that her party was ruined and that it's your fault."

"That's not exactly how it went. There were a few bumps in the road."

Adam expression hardened. "I need you to tell me exactly what happened. What did you say to upset her? Jesus, Shannon, it's my daughter's birthday. Why is she inside crying as if her heart is broken?"

She thrust the presents at him. "Well, for starters, she's mad because she didn't get her way. Oh, don't get me wrong. She played me like a pro. I paid for the glitter package for the mani-pedis. But that wasn't enough. She wanted to be the center of attention. Fine. It's her birthday. But I refused to serve her pizza and there was some other stuff."

He stared at her. "What are you talking about? This is because you didn't want to hand a nine-year-old a slice of pizza?"

"No. Not exactly. It's more than that. She was mean to some of her friends and—"

"She was mean to you? Shannon, she's a kid. You're the adult. Communication is your responsibility. I have to admit, I'm really disappointed by all of this. I thought it would go better. I thought I could trust you."

She felt the jab all the way down to her heart. Talk about a perfectly placed blow. Because there was nothing she could say in return. He had a crying birthday girl in the house and his girlfriend on the outside. When push came to shove, she knew exactly where his loyalties would lie.

"You're missing the point," she told him.

"Am I? This is why I'm usually so careful about introducing my children to anyone I'm dating. You don't have a family of your own, so you wouldn't understand. But it sucks. She's upset, I still don't know what happened and I'll be dealing with this all weekend. Then I have to explain to her mother how my girlfriend let this happen. All I wanted was to make sure my daughter had a good birthday."

She glared at him. "What makes you think I wanted anything different? You weren't there, Adam. Be careful with your accusations and assumptions. Because some things can't be unsaid."

He threw up his hands. "If you'll excuse me, I have to go fix things with Char."

He turned and walked back to the house. Shannon stood there and watched him go. She told herself to stay in the moment, to feel the feelings, to integrate that this was how it was going to be, should she and Adam stay together. That his children would always come first. That whatever the circumstances, they would be the ones he believed, while she was suspect.

She got in her car and told herself not to jump to conclusions. That he would figure out she wasn't the bad guy. That he would be sorry and they would get through this.

As she drove away, she wondered how long it would take for him to realize that Char wasn't the only person he had to fix things with. Or if he would realize it at all.

Twenty-Two

Pam sat at her small desk in the study and waited for her laptop to boot. She'd had a good night, sleeping for several hours in a row. This was the most rested she'd felt in weeks, which meant it was time to tackle one of the difficult tasks she'd been putting off: John's email.

Ever thoughtful, he'd kept a list of user names and passwords in his desk drawer. They had been there in case she needed to access something while he was at work, but had turned out to be helpful after his death.

The paperwork and logistics that went with a spouse's passing were ongoing and onerous. Steven and Jen had helped with some, but after the first couple of weeks, they'd returned to their lives. Pam had slowly been dealing with the rest.

There were bank accounts to change, investment accounts. Acquaintances to notify, subscriptions and memberships to cancel. Every time she turned around, there was something else she had to deal with. Some other forgotten element of his life that had to be tidied.

She carefully drew in a deep, calming breath before

logging on to his email account, then shook her head when she saw well over a hundred emails waiting.

The spam was easy. She forwarded anything that needed answering to her own account. There were a few political notices, some ads from the car dealership he used and something from a cruise line.

Her gaze drifted to the subject line. She froze in her seat. Pain hit her hard, front and back, stealing her breath and making it impossible to fight back tears.

New information for Booking...

The actual number blurred, as did the email when she opened it. She sat there and let the tears flow down her cheeks.

The cruise. The cruise she and John had been so excited to go on. He'd made the reservations right after their sex-retreat weekend, when they were doing it like rabbits three times a day.

She covered her face with her hands. They'd talked about all the places they were going to have sex. How they would go visit the turtles in Grand Cayman and float down a river in Jamaica. They'd made plans and now he was gone.

Small paws touched her thigh. She looked down and saw Lulu standing on her back legs, looking up at Pam anxiously.

"I'm sorry, baby girl," she said as she picked up her dog and cradled her. Lulu licked her cheek.

"I know it's hard when I get like this," Pam murmured. "You hate to see me so sad. It's just I can't help it. I miss your dad so much."

Lulu's ears perked up. She struggled to get down. When Pam set her on the carpet, the little dog raced toward the garage door, barking as she went.

Sobs ripped through Pam. She'd said "Dad." Lulu thought John was finally coming home.

"He's not," she whispered, even though she knew Lulu couldn't hear her. "He's never coming home. We're never going to see him again."

She rested her elbows on the desk and covered her face with her hands again. This had to stop, she thought. She couldn't keep doing this to herself. Suffering day after day. Everyone said things would get easier with time, but they weren't. Everyone promised she would start to heal, but so far there had been nothing but the hell of knowing John was never coming home.

She dropped her hands to her lap and stared sightlessly at the computer screen. From deep in her chest came a primal scream of protest, and in the background, the steady beating of her heart.

Because while she might be falling apart emotionally, physically she was fine. She came from a long line of women who lived well into their eighties. She was facing the next thirty years without John and for the life of her, she couldn't figure out the point of that.

Lulu returned to the study. Her fluffy head hung in defeat. Her tail was tucked between her legs. Pam picked her up and held on tight.

"I know," she whispered. "It hurts so much."

She wiped her face and turned back to the computer screen. She was going to have to call the cruise company and cancel. Or maybe find out if she could send Jen and Kirk. Although they were both working and saving any extra time off for after the baby was born. No, she would cancel. It wasn't as if she was going to take a cruise by herself. That would be beyond depressing.

For a second she tried to imagine herself on the ship—

a pathetic figure wandering aimlessly from place to place. She couldn't do it. Certainly didn't want to even try. The way she was feeling, she would end up throwing herself off the ship at some point.

Pam turned her attention back to the screen. There had to be a contact number somewhere. She started to scan the email, then realized what she'd thought just seconds before.

She could throw herself off the ship.

She set Lulu on the floor and placed her hands on the keyboard of her laptop. No, that was ridiculous. She wasn't going to kill herself. It was wrong and selfish.

People fell off ships all the time. She was forever hearing about it on the news. Lost at sea.

No, she couldn't do that to her children. Losing a parent unexpectedly was one thing, but to know that she had killed herself would be another. They would be devastated. They would think she didn't love them. And she did. Desperately. It was just they didn't understand how hard it was to be without John. They didn't know about the empty nights, the life that stretched before her.

Still, they were her children and she loved them. She would never hurt them.

What if they thought it was an accident?

Pam turned that idea over in her head. If it was an accident, then they would miss her, but there wouldn't be any sense of having been abandoned. Could she do that? Could she make them think she was fine and then simply jump off the ship?

She looked at the email again. In addition to the tickets, there was information on the itinerary and various shore excursions. She scanned the ports and saw that Friday was a day at sea.

The cruise started on Saturday. If she showed up at different activities, talking to people, pretended to be having a good time, no one would suspect. She could be memorable enough that when questioned, everyone would say she had been sad about her husband, but obviously healing. Then on Thursday night she would slip over the edge and never have to feel the loss of her husband again.

It was the perfect solution, she thought with more than a little surprise. And exactly what she needed to do.

She let the idea sit in her brain for a few seconds. There was no horror, no revulsion. Only a sense of rightness. She couldn't live without him, so she wouldn't.

She printed out the tickets. While the printer hummed away, she used the hotlink in the email to go look at the various excursions. It only took a few minutes to find the ones she wanted.

Her goal was to be visible and make friends. For the day in Jamaica she booked the Shaw Park Gardens, Dunn's River Falls and Beach trip. Her chest tightened a little when she went to look at trips in Grand Cayman. She'd wanted to see the turtle farm there for as long as she could remember. John had always teased her about it.

She squared her shoulders, then booked herself on the Turtle Farm, Hell, Tortuga Rum Cake and Scenic Drive tour. For the island of Cozumel, she chose the Tulum Mayan Ruins and Playa del Carmen trip.

Once it was all done, she printed out her confirmations, then turned off her computer and stood. Thousands of thoughts flitted in and out of her head. There was so much to do, she thought. She was filled with purpose in a way she hadn't been for weeks. A thousand details to manage. She wanted to get everything completely in order, down to the tiniest detail. She had a plan and she was determined to see it through.

"Sorry," Nicole said as she walked back in the living room. "I just wanted to make sure Tyler was asleep. Once he's out, he's gone until morning, but every now and then it can take him a bit to get to that point."

Shannon nodded. "I'm sure me showing up like this didn't help."

"He adores you." She sat across from her friend. "Want to talk about it?" she asked gently. It wasn't that she minded the company. Having Shannon stop by was great. It was just the sadness she saw in her eyes, not to mention the grocery bag with about five different flavors of Ben & Jerry's. There were a limited number of reasons for them to need that kind of emotional help.

Shannon pulled her knees to her chest and wrapped her arms around her shins. "It's Adam," she admitted. "We had a huge fight. I'm angry, he's angry. It was so awful."

She tucked her long red hair behind her ear and pressed her lips together. "It's the kid thing. Or rather the lack of kid thing. I don't have children. I get that. But why did he assume the worst about me? I'm not a bad person. I wanted Char to have a good time. But would he listen? Of course not. He played the parent card."

She held up one hand. "He's the parent. I know that. And I get that being a parent means having responsibilities. But I would never hurt Char or Oliver. She was horrible and he didn't want to listen. He simply assumed I'd done something awful and I was a bad person." Shannon shook her head. "I'm not a bad person."

Nicole did her best to sort through the information.

"Okay, it would really help if I knew what happened with you and the kids. Was it Char's birthday party?"

"Yes. It was nowhere near as cool as Tyler's. Give me Brad the Dragon any day over a bunch of little girls at a spa."

Shannon explained about the glitter add-on and how Char had been rude and imperious.

"I wanted her birthday to be special," Shannon told her. "I wanted her to be happy and excited. But there was something else going on. It's like she had something to prove."

"Has she been like that before? Some kids are just obnoxious."

"I know what you're saying and I want to say that no, she's been more difficult than Oliver, but not in a bad way. I think she's really protective of her mom, and that's admirable. She's generally pleasant and normal. At the party, it's like she was possessed by some evil narcissist."

Shannon leaned her head against the back of the sofa. "I can't get over what Adam said to me. That he was disappointed. It was like he was scolding me. I really didn't like that at all. And why didn't he want to talk to me about what happened?"

Nicole raised her eyebrows. "You still haven't spoken to him?"

"No. I'm not calling and apparently he's not calling, either. What do you think?"

"That you're sweet and kind and he should find out the facts before assigning blame." Nicole thought about the people she knew who were divorced. No one in their inner circle of friends, she thought. A couple of clients had been through it.

"Being a single parent has to be hard," she admitted. "There's guilt and stress. But he should know you well enough to confirm what happened. I could forgive being upset in the moment, but not letting it go on for several days."

Shannon blinked several times, then stared at the ceiling, as if willing back tears. "Yeah," she said after clearing her throat. "That's what I thought, too. The longer I don't hear from him, the worse I think it is between us. He was so angry and he didn't want to hear my side. I love him, but I also know he's wrong about this. He should have talked to me."

Nicole thought maybe she was right. She couldn't imagine someone else telling Tyler what to do. He was hers. Hers and Eric's. But with Eric, it was different. As much as he was gone, she was confident he loved his son. But someone else in the mix would just be a mess.

"Dealing with stepkids can't be easy," Nicole admitted. "You get a lot of responsibility with little or no say in what happens. Talk about a minefield."

"They're not even my stepkids and I'm dealing with this," Shannon said glumly. "I thought he was the one. I thought we were going to work it out. But now I just don't know where we are. Does he even care that we're not talking? Is it over?"

"You could call him," Nicole said gently.

"And what should I say? Ask if he's ready to apologize?"

Nicole didn't have an answer. In her heart, she thought maybe reaching out was a good first step. Especially if Shannon wanted the relationship to work. But she got why her friend felt Adam should be the one to make the move. But if neither of them did anything, they would stay stuck.

Kind of like her and Eric. They were stuck—married but not actually a couple. Not for a long time now. The money problems had been solved, but nothing else was better. He was still gone a lot and moving in a direction that didn't seem to include them.

"I wish I had better advice," Nicole said.

"I don't think there's an answer right now. I think Adam and I both need time."

Nicole nodded. "Want some ice cream?"

"Yes."

"And tequila?"

Shannon smiled. "You sure know how to show a girl a good time."

Pam signed her name over and over. There were dozens of little stickers with an arrow on them, pointing to where she should sign her name. She went from page to page, feeling her sense of satisfaction grow with each signature.

"Excellent," Dan, her financial advisor, told her. "I'm impressed, Pam. At our first couple of meetings after you lost John, I was worried about you. But you're doing really well."

"Thank you," she murmured, careful to stare at the paperwork as she spoke. Dan was a friend of the family. She was afraid that if she actually looked him in the eye, he would quickly figure out something was up.

She wasn't doing well at all. It was impossible to draw a breath without wanting to scream for missing John. But her decision had given her energy. More important, she had a purpose. There were things to be done to prepare for her upcoming trip…and subsequent lack of return.

She might not be willing to live with her grief, but she wasn't going to be a burden to her children in the process.

He took back the papers and flipped through them, checking to make sure all the signatures were in place. She waited patiently.

Several years ago she and John had put everything into a trust. It was the easiest way to transfer assets within the family without having to worry about sibling disagreements and huge tax bills. Since finding out about the key man policy and the buyout of her share of the business, she'd known she had to do something. Once she'd decided to kill herself, she'd been motivated to take the next financial step.

She'd divided the after-tax amount from the sale of the business into two equal halves. One had been put into her trust, the other half had been set aside for the children.

When she was declared lost at sea, aka dead, Dan would manage the trust for her estate. The kids would get their money with minimal hassle and waiting.

The house was also part of the trust. She thought it was possible that Jen and Kirk might want it. They would have enough to buy out Steven and Brandon. If no one wanted it, the house would be sold and the proceeds then split between the siblings.

She finished with Dan and then left his upscale office. Her next stop was to see Hayley. She and John's assistant were having lunch together.

She arrived at Gary's Café with five minutes to spare. When she got home, she would have to take Lulu for a long walk on the beach to make up for spending the morning alone. As she entered the restaurant, she thought that it would be hard to leave her little girl behind. Not just for the cruise. Lulu would miss her so much.

She briefly acknowledged that thinking about the dog was much easier than thinking about her children. That she truly *hadn't* thought about her children. About how all this would impact them. Losing two parents so close together would be devastating. She understood that. But she also knew she was making the right decision. She simply couldn't go on without John. People had to understand that.

She was seated in a booth and glanced at the chalkboard specials on the wall. Gary's Café had been established sometime in the 1950s and it hadn't changed much since. It had been refurbished several times but each new version looked exactly like the old one. There were red booths, Formica tables and a jukebox in the corner. The food wasn't fancy, but it was delicious and honest. Unlike the places that advertised no microwaves as a way to show the food was healthy, Gary's Café didn't use microwaves because they hadn't had them, back in the day.

Hayley walked in and spotted her. Pam stood and hugged the other woman, then slid back into the booth. Hayley settled across from her.

"How are you feeling?" Pam asked, studying her friend. The shadows under Hayley's eyes were gone. When she smiled, it reached all the way to her eyes. The air of sadness had faded. All signs that Hayley was healing from her latest miscarriage.

"I'm fine," the pretty blonde said. "And I should be asking that of you. How's it going?"

Pam brushed away the question. "I'm doing okay. It's hard, but I get through."

Hayley leaned toward her and smiled. "I'm so glad about you going on the trip. Getting away will help."

"I know. That's what I think, too. I love my house,

but it's impossible to escape there. I see John in every corner. I feel him with every breath. On the ship, I'll be scared and lonely, but I think it will be better. If that makes sense."

"It does. You'll make friends. Don't they have meet-and-greets with single people?" Hayley winced. "Sorry, I don't mean to make it sound like you'll be dating, but you know what I mean. You can meet other women traveling together. Make friends."

Which all sounded like a nightmare, Pam thought. But she wasn't going to get on with her life. She was going to end it. And part of her plan was to make enough friends that people remembered her.

"That's what I thought, too," she lied. "A change of scene will do me good."

Their waitress stopped by the table and took their drink orders. They both glanced at the menu.

"I'm still a few pounds underweight," Hayley said cheerfully. "I'm having a burger and fries."

"Me, too," Pam told her. Why not? It wasn't as if she had to worry about her cholesterol. People always said to live like you were dying. That it changed everything. She had to admit that they were right.

"I have the instructions for the last time I watched Lulu," Hayley said. "Is her food still the same?"

"It is. I have a new sunscreen we're using."

Hayley giggled. "I know it makes me weird, but I love that I have to put sunscreen on her." The humor faded. "Damn, it's because I see her as a baby. Which I can live with. She's sweet and having her cuddle with me is the best."

"What does Rob think about her?"

Hayley rolled her eyes. "He loves her more than me,

if you can believe it. And you know Lulu dotes on him." Her smile broadened. "I've already warned him that I'm your puppy guardian. If anything happens to you, we are so keeping Lulu."

Information Pam had wanted to ask, but hadn't been sure how. She and Hayley had discussed that point every time Pam had left Lulu with her. Jen had been her backup, but with a baby on the way, that wasn't going to work.

Of course, Hayley could get pregnant, too. Pam remembered her friend's miscarriages and knew she couldn't mention anything about babies at this point. She would simply have to trust Hayley to handle Lulu and a child.

"There's money for her medical care," Pam said, careful to keep her voice sounding teasing. "It should last her whole life."

The "take care of Lulu" clause had been in the will since she and John had brought the little dog home. There were also some individual bequests and a large amount to be given to her favorite charities.

Hayley shook her head. "I'm honestly not worried. Nothing's going to happen to you. And if it does, I'll be there for your little angel. I promise."

Pam blinked against sudden tears. "You're a good person. I appreciate all you've done for us over the years."

"I haven't done anything."

"You took care of John. I always trusted you to do that."

Hayley's mouth twisted. "You're going to get me crying. I loved John. He was a rock and the nicest man. Steven's great. I like working for him, but I miss John every day."

Pam nodded. "Me, too."

Their waitress returned with their drinks and glanced between them. "You two okay?"

"We will be," Pam told her. "After our burgers."

"They do have magical powers," the server said. "You want fries with that?"

"Of course," Pam told her. "We're living large."

Shannon told herself that being the bigger person had value. That she could savor the moment of maturity, of being gracious. That, in karmic terms, she was taking care of her future. But it was all crap. The truth was she was hurt and frustrated and thinking that falling in love with Adam had been a huge mistake because he was nothing but a super butt head.

She walked up to the front door of Adam's house and knocked. Seconds later, he answered.

"Hi. Thanks for coming by."

He looked good and wasn't that just grossly unfair? A little rumpled, a lot tired and shaggy. Like he needed a haircut. Her fingers itched to sweep his hair off his forehead and then linger. Because touching Adam was always fun.

His dark gaze swept over her and in that moment, she could swear she heard his impressed "Wow!" like when they'd first met. Because whatever else might go wrong between them, he'd always thought she was the hottest thing that moved.

"You okay?" he asked.

"I don't know."

"You're still mad."

"Are you asking or telling?"

"Both."

"Quite the trick."

He stepped back. "Please come in."

When he'd called and asked to see her, she hadn't known if she wanted to. A week had gone by. A week of brief texts between them. His had been along the lines of "I need some time with this." And hers had been edited from "Go fuck yourself" to a more generous "Fine."

But as she stepped into his house, something inside of her shifted. She let herself remember how much she'd missed him, despite her attempts not to. She thought about how he made her laugh and how he was one of the most emotionally generous men she knew. Until the incident with Char, she would have said being with Adam always made her feel better about herself. And that was hard to find.

"You and I need to talk," he said. "But Char would like to speak to you, as well."

Char? Shannon came to a stop in the living room, then forced herself to keep walking. Saying she wanted nothing to do with his daughter wasn't an actual solution to their problem. If things were going to work out between the two of them, she had to figure out how to navigate the difficulties of dealing with his kids.

He had to do the same, but right now she was more concerned with her own reaction to hearing the girl's name.

They continued to the family room. Char sat on the edge of the oversize sectional. Her shoulders were slumped and she seemed smaller than Shannon remembered. As the girl raised her head, Shannon saw that she'd been crying.

She came to a stop and pulled Adam close. "Are you making her talk to me?"

"This is completely her idea." One corner of his mouth twisted. "Actually it's hers and her mother's, if you can believe it. She went home last night and today Tabitha called me to say Char wanted to talk to you."

Shannon glanced at the nine-year-old, who slowly stood. Her lower lip trembled and a single tear slipped down her cheek.

If it was an act, it was a good one, Shannon thought, the wall around her heart cracking just a little.

"Thank you for talking to me," Char whispered.

"You're welcome."

Shannon crossed to the lounge side of the sectional and sat down. Char sat in the middle of the sofa part and faced her. Adam hovered, looking both hopeful and worried.

Char twisted her fingers together in front of her. She kept her head down and when she started to speak, Shannon could barely hear her.

"I'm sorry," the girl whispered. "About the party. I wanted it to be the best one and my friends wanted that, too. None of our parents would get the glitter package so we talked about how to make it happen at my party."

Shannon told herself not to react. While being played by several nine-year-old girls wasn't exactly a point of pride, she had been out of her element. And inexperienced. Which made Adam's comments about her not being their mother not only true, but also something she would have to consider later.

"You thought I'd be easy to manipulate?" she asked, careful to keep her tone neutral.

Char nodded. "I knew you liked my dad a lot and if you made me happy, he would like you more. Plus, a couple of my friends have divorced parents and they said that I needed to be careful with you. That I had to act a certain way so you would do what I said."

Shannon was about to ask her to explain that confusing statement more, when Adam spoke.

"What are you talking about?" he asked sharply. "How did you act?"

Char looked at her father. Tears ran down her cheeks. "Bratty. Like I was the boss of her and she had to do what I said. I made her get me stuff and I wasn't nice. I'm sorry, Daddy."

Adam shoved his hand through his hair. "Seriously?" He looked at Shannon and shook his head. "I had no idea."

She wanted to point out that was because he wouldn't listen, only she thought maybe this was a good time to be quiet.

Char seemed to physically shrink. "I didn't want to be mean. I didn't like it when I was doing it, but once I started, I couldn't stop myself. And everyone was having a good time at the party and I wanted it to go on."

She looked at Shannon. "I felt so bad when I talked to my dad, but I couldn't tell him the truth. So I waited until I saw my mom last night and I told her everything. She was really disappointed in me. For acting that way and for lying to my dad." Char turned to him. "I'm sorry, Daddy. I thought if you knew how bad I'd been, you'd punish me and you always punish way worse than Mom."

Adam muttered something under his breath.

Char bit her lower lip. "I was scared. Because of Shannon. I know you like her and if you believed her, you'd be so mad. But now I'm afraid you won't like me anymore and you'll go away and my dad will be sad and I'll miss you, too."

Shannon struggled to follow the logic. Her first thought was to wonder why Char would worry about her father leaving. Then she got the girl meant her.

The relief was instant. With an explanation in place, she could understand how things had gotten out of hand. Kids made mistakes, right?

Adam circled around to the front of the sofa and sat down. He held out his arms. Char rushed into them and hung on. Her whole body shook with her sobs.

"Now Tabitha's comments make sense," he said over his daughter's head. "She wanted me to call later. She said that we needed to talk about getting Char into some different activities so she could make new friends." He stroked his daughter's back. "She also said we needed to come up with a punishment plan together, so the consequences for messing up were the same at both houses. Now I know why."

Char straightened and faced her. "I don't want you to go away," she admitted. "I don't want you to be mad at me. I'm sorry, Shannon. It's nice when you're here. Sometimes I get scared because I like you and you're not my mom."

Shannon's chest tightened a little. She was doing just fine until that last bit, she thought grimly.

"I like you, too," she told the girl.

Adam squeezed his daughter. "Okay, you've said what you wanted to. Now I'm going to take you back to your mom's."

Because it wasn't his weekend to have her, Shannon thought. "Tabitha wanted her to do this today?"

"Yeah," Adam said. "She felt it had festered long enough. I'm going to run her home and come right back. Can you wait?"

She nodded. When he'd gone, she stayed on the sofa. Too much had happened, she thought. Their relationship had too many sharp edges and if she wasn't careful, she was going to end up cut and bruised.

Stepchildren were a complication. One she didn't know how to deal with. She loved Adam—that hadn't changed. But this part of his life—she didn't know how to deal. Having children with him, or anyone, was going to be different than she imagined. Hard. Worthwhile, she was sure, but not easy.

He was back as quickly as promised. He walked over to her and pulled her to her feet, then kissed her on the mouth.

"I'm sorry," he said, holding her close. "I was so incredibly wrong about all of it. Can we talk about it?"

"Sure."

They sat down. He kept her hand in his. "After the party I was mad. Char was crying and saying you'd ruined her birthday. I hadn't been there. I felt guilty and angry."

"You didn't trust me," Shannon said, remembering how betrayed she'd felt. "You didn't bother to listen to what had happened."

"She was crying. I had to deal with that."

"Why? She wasn't bleeding. You could have taken two minutes to let me explain what was wrong. But you didn't even consider that. You listened to half of what I had to say, assumed I'd hurt her and went to make it better."

He released her hand. "I never thought you'd hurt her."

"Yeah, you did. I appreciate the apology, Adam. Don't get me wrong. But it's not just what she did to me. She was horrible to Madison. She didn't like the girl's gift and she tormented her about it. I'm not saying that's a punishable offense, but it needs to be addressed. If she acts like that with all her friends, she's not going to have any left in a few months."

A muscle in his jaw tightened. "Shannon, I'm trying to make this right. I need you to get off Char and talk about us. I'll deal with Char later. Tabitha and I are going to talk about her and what happened. I'll ask about Madison. Now can we please talk about you and me?"

A reasonable request, she told herself. Because there was nothing she could do about Char. Char wasn't her business. He had Tabitha for that. A circumstance that was never going to change.

There was no instant family here. No way for her to step in and play at belonging. Adam, Oliver, Char and Tabitha already were a family. They might live in different places, but they were a unit. They had a history. No matter what, for the rest of her life, she would never be a part of that. If she and Adam stayed together, she would always feel like in some ways, she was on the outside, looking in.

She could make her own memories with the kids. She could love Adam, even marry him. But they would always be two separate circles with only a small area that intersected. A large part of who he was wouldn't belong to her.

"No," he said firmly, grabbing both her hands this time. "Don't do it, Shannon. Don't disappear on me."

"I'm right here."

"You're going away. I can feel it. I screwed up, okay? I'm going to make mistakes. But I love you."

"I love you, too," she admitted. "But loving each other didn't prevent the problem. It didn't make things go easier with Char."

"She did some things wrong. We all did. That has to be something we can survive. I want to talk about it. I want to set up some strategies so this doesn't happen again."

He held her gaze with his own. She could feel him willing her to understand. The thing was, she did understand. Even more than he did. Because she saw all the places where they could fail.

"I'm not going away," she told him, feeling her way as she spoke. "But I need to think this through. Your kids change things between us."

"For the better?" he asked hopefully.

She pulled a hand free and touched his face. "I really want this to work."

"I really want to believe you."

She kissed him. The pressure of his mouth against hers felt good. Right. She did love him, but the kid thing confused her.

"We're new at this," she said. "Give us some time to get better at it."

"I'm not worried about me running away. I'm worried about you."

"I won't run."

"You promise?"

"Yes."

She wasn't going to run, but she, like him, was going to take a little time to figure out exactly what she wanted. Adam was a package deal. She couldn't pick and choose the parts she liked. It was all or nothing.

She had thought the only question mark was whether he would be willing to have another child, and what she would do if he said no. But there was more to it than that. And while in the past she'd been the kind of woman who simply went for it, now she knew there was more on the line. Care was required. Not just to protect Adam and his children, but to protect herself, as well.

Twenty-Three

Nicole was surprised to find her husband up and sipping coffee. Normally Eric was in bed long after she'd left for her morning classes, but for some reason today he was awake and sitting at the kitchen table.

"Morning," she said. "I didn't hear you come in."

"It was late. I was going over the revised script with Jacob. He says we're a go."

"That's great. You must be excited. Congratulations."

"Thanks."

She put her travel mug on the counter. She would fill it right before she left and drink it on the way to the studio. It was early—barely five thirty. She had ten minutes to eat her breakfast and pour her coffee. Then she had a ten-minute drive to the studio and ten more minutes to get ready for class. One day she promised herself she would graduate to the place where she could live her life in fifteen-minute increments. Or even twenty.

Ah, the dreams we dream, she thought with a chuckle.

"What's so funny?" he asked.

She got a Greek yogurt out of the refrigerator and sprinkled on some of her organic granola. "Just thinking about how I live my day. Speaking of which, what do you have going on now that you've finished with the script?"

"Going back to the next one."

"Impressive dedication."

She told herself it was enough that they were having a conversation. That it didn't matter that they could have been commuters, exchanging pleasantries about the weather, for all the depth in their conversation.

"There's a party next weekend," he said. "I'd like you to go with me."

She walked over and sat across from him. "Really?" He hadn't asked her to attend anything. This was progress, she thought happily. "I'd like that."

"I'm glad. It's Saturday. Can you talk to Greta about working that night? Or get a sitter?"

"Sure."

He smiled. "I'm glad you're excited. This party is going to be so great. It's all industry, so you'll recognize some faces. You'll need to act cool. No staring."

Her good mood had been like bubbles filling the spaces in her heart. A few of them popped.

"Cool it is," she said, determined to find the good in this moment. "So what kind of party? Cocktail? Meet and mingle?"

The smile widened. "Both. There's going to be a water bar. Can you believe it?"

"A what?"

"A water bar." He stared at her like she was an idiot. "With water?"

"Okay," she said slowly. "That's interesting."

"There will be different types of water, from all over the world. You can do a tasting."

Of water? This was why it was probably for the best

that she'd never gotten famous. There was no way she would appreciate all the glorious things that went with it.

"Sounds like fun."

He looked away. "You just don't get it."

"Eric, come on. It's water. But I'll be excited if that makes you happy."

"Just don't embarrass me."

"I'd never do that."

"You need to wear something nice. Not like how you usually dress. I hope you can manage that." He stood and walked out of the kitchen.

She rose as well and tossed out her yogurt, then filled her to-go mug and walked out of the house.

Pam stood in front of the ship terminal, waiting for her turn to register, or whatever it was called, before she could get on the ship. She'd arrived in Fort Lauderdale the evening before and after she'd collected her luggage, she'd been met by an older woman with a Princess Cruises clipboard.

More people had joined them and they'd eventually been whisked to a nice hotel. This morning she'd had a tour of the town and then been taken to the terminal.

While she and John had vacationed, they'd never taken a cruise. She'd underestimated how incredibly large the ships were. The Caribbean Princess rose like a beautiful, gliding superbuilding. There were rows and rows of balconies and windows and what felt like an entire village of people trying to board within a few hours of each other.

The line moved forward. She had her passport in hand. Her luggage was being handled for her, so she only had her carry-on bags. Around her happy couples and families laughed and talked. She didn't see anyone else who was alone. She was the only one.

For a second she thought about turning back. She still could. She could get a cab back to the airport and then buy a ticket home. She could figure out the luggage problem later. She could return to her life and go on, hoping one day she would heal. Or at least be able to breathe without feeling that she was being ripped apart by grief.

Behind her a man laughed. The sound was so familiar, so wonderful, she turned. John! There'd been a miracle. A reprieve. A—

Her gaze settled on an older couple. The man was short and heavy, with dark hair and glasses. He laughed again. Pain squeezed her heart in a vicious grip that would never let go. She faced front and moved forward a few steps.

This was the answer, she reminded herself. Only a few more days and she was never going to hurt again.

The lines moved quickly. Check-in turned out to be a template of efficiency. She handed over her credit card for any additional charges, got her room key and a map, then paused to get her picture taken with several other happy people.

Proof, she told herself as she smiled broadly. Proof she'd been here, proof she was excited. Later, her children would see that picture and tell themselves that she'd been having fun. They would be fooled and that was the greatest kindness she could give them.

Even as the thought formed, a small, quiet voice whispered the greatest kindness might be to return home. To slog through the swamp that was her life without John. To be a mother and grandmother. To go when it was her time.

She shook her head and walked more quickly toward the ship. She'd made up her mind. She wasn't going to change it now.

John had booked them into a minisuite. Pam explored the efficient and comfortable space. There was a bathroom and nice-size closet, a king-size bed and beyond that a small desk and a sofa. She opened the door that led to the balcony and stepped into the warm, tropical air.

She lived in Southern California, only a few blocks from the beach. Yet somehow being on the water in Florida was completely different. Something to do with the more shallow water, she thought. Or just one of those things that nonscientific types couldn't explain.

She went back inside and quickly unpacked. There was a schedule of events for the evening, and information about their first stop at Princess Cays in the Bahamas, the next day.

She scanned what there was to do that night and decided she would go to the welcome reception and the live entertainment. In the meantime, there was a ship to explore.

Pam took her handbag with her and tucked the ship's map in the back pocket of her white cropped pants. She walked along the narrow passageway until she found her way to a bank of elevators.

She went down to the sixth floor—Plaza Deck. People filled the open space. She circled around the elevators and found herself in a huge atrium that went up several stories. There was a woman playing piano, a small café, a bar, a wine bar and a gallery with paintings and sculptures.

She wandered around, smiling and nodding as she explored. A display of pastries caught her attention.

"The éclairs are heavenly," an older woman said, then wiped her mouth with a small napkin. "I've already had two."

"Okay, then. Éclairs it is." Pam nodded at the young woman behind the counter. "An éclair."

She put it on a small plate and handed it to Pam. "Anything else?"

"I think this is plenty to ruin my dinner."

Pam paused a second, expecting the server to ask for money, then remembered that she was on a cruise. Nearly everything was included. She took a bite of the éclair and savored the sweet flavors. The crispy lightness of the pastry, along with the sweet, creamy filling, all surrounded by a whisper of chocolate.

Definitely something to have again, she thought.

She went up a couple of decks and did some window shopping. A sign said the shops would open after the ship sailed. She noted several familiar cosmetic brands and some jewelry that looked interesting. She would make sure to get everyone a souvenir, she thought. Her things would be returned to her family. Which made her think she had to make sure to send chatty emails over the next few days. Happy notes so her children would think she was having a great time.

She went back to the elevator, then up to Deck 16, the Sun Deck. She stepped into a party in progress. As the ship pulled away, live music played and people cheered. Pam sipped a tropical mai tai and smiled until her face hurt.

The sun was warm, the breeze gentle and all around her people laughed and waved and talked about the start of their vacation of a lifetime. Pam tried to join in. She spoke for a few minutes to a young couple from Great Britain and reunited an overly excited toddler with his mother. But it all seemed to happen from a great distance. She was there, but not there. As the moments ticked along, she felt her strength fading.

The crowd was too much, she thought. The noise. All of it.

She set her drink on an empty table, then hurried forward. She found a bank of elevators and took one down to her floor, then ran to her stateroom and ducked inside.

The thick plastic covering that had protected the bedspread from her suitcase was gone. Her room had been tidied and on the table in front of the sofa was a beautiful arrangement of pink roses.

Her legs started to give way. Pam had to hang on to the wall to stay upright. She staggered to the sofa and sank down, then reached for the card tucked into the flowers. Her fingers trembled as she opened the small envelope.

Beautiful flowers for my beautiful bride. I love you more every day. J

Not a message from the great beyond, she thought sadly. He would have ordered them when he booked the cruise. Because that was the kind of man he was.

She touched one of the rose petals, then dropped her chin to her chest and gave in to the emotion. Missing him hurt, she thought as she cried. Being without him was torture.

She collapsed onto her side and sobbed out her pain. Soon, she promised herself as she gasped for breath. Soon.

* * *

Nicole wasn't sure which shocked her more. How much her dress had cost or how little there was to it. The style was beautiful—she could easily admit that. The Alexander McQueen pleated leaf crepe dress was the most beautiful thing she'd ever worn, and that included her wedding gown. The squared-off sweetheart neckline was cut low enough to be supersexy without showing too much. The dress itself was fitted to her hips, then flared out before it ended well above her knee. But the dress had cost over twenty-three hundred *dollars*! You could get a used car for that.

She studied herself in the mirror for another second, before shrugging. Eric had rejected the first two dresses she'd brought home as not being special enough. He'd finally insisted on accompanying her to the store where she'd tried on over a dozen cocktail dresses until they'd settled on this one. When he'd gone to pay for it, she'd half expected to hear their credit card shriek in protest. Of course, when compared to what he'd been spending on clothes, the dress was completely reasonable. Which only went to show how their world had changed in the past few weeks.

She picked up the tiny clutch and then joined Eric in the living room.

Tyler smiled at her. "Mommy, you're beautiful!"

"Thank you, sweetie."

"I will have him in bed by eight," Greta promised. "You do look lovely."

"Thanks." Nicole turned to Eric. "Ready?"

"Uh-huh. Let's go."

She hugged Tyler and then followed her husband out of the house. For a second, she thought about pleading a headache. Nothing about this party sounded appealing. But she'd promised to go. Besides, she and Eric needed some time together. Not just the party, she thought. But after.

Because they weren't sure how late they were going to be, Greta was staying the night. Nicole had spent part of the afternoon tidying the guest bedroom and washing the sheets. She and Eric had booked a room at the Beverly Hills Hotel. They would be going there after the party. Their overnight bags were already in the trunk.

She wondered about their sleeping arrangements that night. She and Eric hadn't shared a bed in months. Obviously that was going to change. Would they make love, as well? She missed their intimacy, their connection. Maybe tonight would be when all that shifted back.

They went directly to the hotel and checked in. Nicole kind of wanted to see the room, but Eric was anxious to get to the party.

They drove through Beverly Hills. She lost track of where they were going, but Eric had been to the house before. It was owned by a friend of Jacob's.

They pulled into a wide, long driveway, flanked by open gates. A valet took their car and handed Eric a ticket. A second valet opened Nicole's door for her.

She got out and stared up at the three-story house. The style was Southern California Spanish, with a tiled roof and plenty of wrought iron. Floodlights illuminated the lush garden and the scent of night-blooming jasmine filled the air.

"Ready?" Eric asked as he put his hand on the small of her back.

She nodded.

They went up the front steps and into the big, open

two-story foyer. Music spilled from hidden speakers. Guests mingled and servers walked around with trays of appetizers and glasses of champagne.

Everyone was above average in the looks department, she thought uneasily. Talk about a gathering of the beautiful people. She saw several stars from TV she recognized and a couple of members of One Direction. To the left, in the living room, she would swear Sandra Bullock was talking to Eric's producer friend, Jacob.

Eric took two glasses and handed her one. She thought about mentioning the "water bar" but doubted she could say the words without sounding sarcastic. She wanted tonight to go well. She was going to be the perfect party companion.

After sipping the champagne, she slipped her arm through the crook of her husband's elbow. "Let's make a circuit of the room and see who's here. Then you'll have a better idea of who you want to make sure you talk to and who can wait for later."

His brows rose. "Excellent plan."

"Thank you. I have skills."

He flashed her a smile. "Mad skills."

She laughed.

His gaze lingered on her. "You look beautiful tonight."

"I'm glad you think so." She squared her shoulders. "If anyone asks, I'm here with the hottest new writer since Matt Damon and Ben Affleck wrote *Good Will Hunting*."

"You got that right."

They plunged into the crowd. Nicole hadn't known what to expect from the party. She'd assumed it would be crowded, loud and filled with those trying to prove they belonged, while the super "in" crowd was determined to show they were too cool to have to try. That part was right. But what she hadn't expected was how easily Eric fit in with everything going on.

They did as she suggested and made a circuit of the party. She helped him keep track of who was where. Then they ranked the list in order of importance and started the serious mingling.

Jacob came first. Nicole had briefly met the older man. He was tall, fit and well-dressed. Now he greeted her as if they'd known each other forever and kissed her on both cheeks.

"You must be proud of your husband," he said when he straightened.

"I am. Very."

"Me, too. There's a lot of people who want to be in this town. Far fewer are willing to do the work. Eric came up with a great story and turned it into an even better screenplay. We're going to have a winner with this one."

"Congratulations."

Jacob put his arm around Eric. "I have a couple of people I want you to meet." He smiled at Nicole. "Five minutes, I swear."

"No problem."

She instinctively stepped back, giving them privacy, or maybe room to walk away. They stayed close by, talking intently. Jacob gestured toward a group of young women. Two of them broke free and came over.

The casting call, Nicole thought, watching them shake hands with Eric and then stand just a little too close. There was plenty of preening and breast thrusting as they talked. Eric seemed flattered but not interested. She turned her attention to Jacob.

He was smooth, she thought, as she watched him dismiss the girls when he was done with them. He dressed

well and had a confidence about him that was appealing. She could see why Eric was happy to have him as
his mentor.

She finished her champagne and replaced it with a
full glass, then glanced around at the other guests. Her
mother would have loved this party, she thought. Between the industry heavyweights and the stars, she would
have been running around and getting autographs—
which would have humiliated Eric.

Her mother had wanted this for her. How ironic it was
happening to her son-in-law instead.

Nicole talked to a nice couple who were costume de-
signers, then joined a conversation with a couple of other
wives who had also been asked to wait "just a couple of
minutes."

But even as she told them about Eric's screenplay and
listened to them brag about their husbands, a part of her
wished she was home reading Tyler his before-bedtime
story. This simply wasn't her thing. She'd been influ-
enced by her mother's dreams for her, but in her own
heart, she hadn't wanted fame. Fortune, sure. Who turned
that down? But the idea of being well-known, of having
strangers come up to her or want her autograph? No,
thanks. Which meant Eric had the best of both worlds—
he was part of the in crowd, but could go to the grocery
store in peace.

The "few minutes" with Jacob turned into over an
hour. When Eric finally returned to her side, they circu-
lated through the party, talking to people he knew. Jacob
came by and introduced them to Steven Spielberg and his
wife. Nicole listened to the conversation without joining
in. She doubted Mr. Spielberg would want to hear that
she'd loved *E.T.* since she was a toddler.

Sometime after midnight two guys from One Direction joined with a couple of other singers in an impromptu jam session. Nicole found herself at the water bar, where she participated in a taste test. The ridiculousness of the concept had her giggling. Or maybe it was the champagne on an empty stomach.

By two in the morning, her butt was dragging. She'd been up since five thirty and had taught four classes. Her feet hurt, she was hungry and all she wanted to do was go home.

She searched for her husband and found him talking to Jacob. Not sure if she should join them or not, she hung back, then sank into an overstuffed chair by the French doors leading to the palatial backyard. As soon as she settled in the chair, she realized how much her feet hurt from her heels and her back ached from standing. She struggled to keep from yawning.

"Your beautiful wife is exhausted," Jacob said, smiling at her. "You should take her home." He winked at her. "If any of my wives had been half so lovely…"

She struggled to her feet. "You're too kind." She walked over to Eric and leaned against him. "Sorry," she said, yawning again. "My days start early."

Jacob nodded. "You have a boy?"

"Tyler. He's five. Full of energy."

Jacob patted Eric's shoulder. "You're a lucky man. We'll talk on Monday. Progress was made tonight. It's all good." He waved and walked away.

Eric stared after him for a second, then turned to her. "You ready to leave?"

There was something in his tone. "Not if you're not."

"There's no point in staying now." He headed for the front door.

Nicole trailed after him. She could tell he was upset, but had no idea why. From what she'd seen, the party had been a success.

"Did you try the water bar?" she asked as they waited for the valet to bring their car. "It was interesting. The various waters really did taste different. My favorite one was from Finland. Who knew?"

Eric didn't answer. When the valet pulled up with their car, he got inside without speaking.

The short drive back to the hotel was accomplished in silence. Nicole decided to wait until they were in the hotel room to figure out what was wrong with him.

When he opened the door to their room, he pushed in without waiting for her. The closing door nearly hit her in the face. She put down her bag, stepped out of her heels, then put her hands on her hips.

"What on earth is wrong with you?" she demanded.

Eric spun toward her, his face tight with rage. "You humiliated me in front of Jacob."

"What? Are you on crack? I did no such thing."

"You were practically sleeping in that chair. You walked away from him more than once, as if to prove how uninteresting you found him. Do you know how lucky I am that he's taken me on? Do you know how unlikely it was for him to buy my script? The least you could have done was *pretend* interest, but no. That was too much for you."

She felt her mouth drop open. "You are a hundred percent wrong. I never walked away. I was giving you space. Privacy. I didn't know what you were going to talk about. I thought if I clung to you, I would be in the way. I was being polite."

"Is that what it's called?"

"Yes, and if you could take a second and breathe, you'd see I mean what I said. Eric, I was proud of you. I was happy to be with you. I wanted to make this evening special. I did what I thought you wanted."

"By snoring in a chair?"

"I yawned. I was up early and I worked this morning. I was tired. Is that so unforgivable?" She paced to the window, then faced him again. "I'm confused. I really tried to make you happy. I mingled, I was friendly, I tried the water bar. I wasn't ignoring you or Jacob. You have to know that. What's actually going on here?"

She kept her voice gentle. She didn't want to fight with him. This was a misunderstanding. He had to know her well enough to believe she wouldn't ever try to humiliate him.

"You had your chance," he told her. "All those years ago. You had your chance and you couldn't make it. So you settled. Now you see me getting my dream and you can't stand it. You resent me for being successful."

She'd run out of ways to express shock, she thought as she gaped at him. "That isn't true. I love my life. I have the business and you and Tyler. I don't want to be in the industry. I don't want what you have but I certainly don't resent you for what you've accomplished."

"You sure didn't make it easy. You hounded me to get a job. You wanted me to stop writing."

"You quit your job without discussing it with me and then basically disappeared. You wouldn't help with anything. I had to be responsible for everything, including paying the bills."

"It's the price of art. This is who I am now."

Weariness tugged at her until all she wanted to do was collapse on a bed and sleep. She didn't want to be having this argument on what was supposed to be a special evening. She'd thought tonight might be a chance for them to make a positive change. Instead, it had turned into a disaster.

"I don't know what you want," she admitted. "I know you're angry, but I don't understand why. I'm not the bad guy here, Eric. I thought I did the right thing at the party. I'm sorry you don't agree."

She sat on the edge of the bed and shook her head. "You're so different these days. It's confusing."

"And you're exactly the same."

She raised her head. "What does that mean?"

"I've changed and you haven't. You don't want to. You like how things were. If it was up to you, you'd want things back the way they were."

"I did," she admitted. "Not anymore. You're obviously happier now. You've found your passion. You should pursue it. You—"

His words replayed in her mind. He'd changed and she hadn't. He saw her as stuck in the past and she saw him as only caring about himself. They'd reached the point where they couldn't retreat and they couldn't go forward. Not together.

For weeks she'd wondered what it would be like if she and Eric split up. She'd played with the *D* word, but hadn't actually believed it. Not in a way that meant anything.

For the first time, she stared down into the chasm that was divorce and wondered what would happen if she was forced to the other side.

"You don't want to be married to me anymore," she whispered.

His gaze met hers, his stare unflinching. She saw

emotions flashing through his dark eyes and none of them were soft or loving.

"No, I don't."

Just like that. She forced herself to keep breathing, to focus on the moment. Reality would slap her hard soon enough. There was no reason to rush it.

"Is there someone else?" she asked.

"No. It's just that I don't want to be with you." He hesitated. "I'm not sure I ever loved you."

He stood there for a second, then turned to the door. "I'll go get another room for the night. You can take a cab home in the morning. I'll be by at some point to get my things."

And then he was gone.

Nicole sat on the bed and breathed slowly, staying in the moment. Because to leave it was to acknowledge that her world had just crumbled around her.

Twenty-Four

The singles mingle was the last thing Pam wanted to attend. Despite calls of sun and sand, she hadn't gone on shore that day. Her balcony faced the island and she had watched the small ships—tenders, she thought they were called—take happy people across the water.

She promised herself she was going ashore in Jamaica. She had her tour all lined up and her plan to be happy and outgoing. She would ask people to take a picture with her, knowing that in return they would ask the same. That way, there would be a photographic record for later.

Planning a suicide to look like an accidental death was a lot harder than she would have thought. There were lots of complications and details to be worked out. But it had been good for her, too. She had to think about something other than how much she missed John. Which was probably the weirdest, most twisted thing ever.

She glanced at her watch and realized it was time. She got her small cross-body bag and her map, then headed out to be friendly and outgoing at the event.

She arrived at Skywalkers nightclub a few minutes later. This was one of the highest points on the ship and the view was spectacular. A bird's-eye 360-degree view of the island they'd left and the Caribbean beyond. Both sky and water were beautifully blue.

The room itself was big, with plenty of seating and, of course, floor-to-ceiling windows. The carpet was a brightly colored swirl pattern. There were sofas and tables, lots of chairs. Music played at a comfortable pitch but she had a feeling that later in the night, it would be a whole lot louder.

Pam stopped just inside the nightclub and looked around. At first she couldn't figure out what was wrong, then the truth sank in. The meet-and-mingle she'd come to wasn't for people to meet and make friends as much as it was for singles. As in men and women. She'd been hoping for a few women her own age. Maybe someone she could make friends with.

Instead, there were lots of people in their twenties and thirties. Women in short, flirty dresses and men prowling around, eyeing the offerings.

An older man caught her gaze and winked. She immediately turned away. She couldn't do this, she thought. She had to get out of here.

She hurried to the bank of elevators and frantically pushed the down button. None of the doors opened. She pushed again and again, desperate to get out. To get away. To get back to her room. What had she been thinking? This was wrong—all of it.

The elevator doors opened. Before she could throw herself inside, she had to wait for the people already on it to exit. There were a couple of younger men who walked past her without giving her a glance, followed by three older women.

Pam practically stumbled as she rushed into the elevator. She jammed the button for her floor, pushing it over and over again. The doors couldn't close fast enough. At the last second, one of the older women stepped into the elevator with her.

"Are you all right?" she asked, her tone concerned.

"I'm fine. I don't feel well." She just had to get back to her room, she thought. Where she could sob in peace.

"Those two statements don't go together. I think it's more than that."

The elevator began to move.

The stranger moved closer. "I'm Olimpia. And you are?"

"Pam. Pam Eiland." She turned to the other woman and saw she was being watched with a combination of sympathy and understanding.

"Are you by yourself?" Olimpia asked.

Pam nodded.

"A recent widow?"

"How did you know?"

"I recognize the look. You came to the meet-and-greet thinking you could make some friends and instead you found supermodels and horndogs."

In spite of everything, Pam smiled. "Horndogs?"

"Those horrible men trying to get laid." Olimpia shuddered. "Why do men have to be like that? Why do they have to assume we want to have sex with them before we even know them? I know it's popular with young people today, but I don't understand it. Why would you want to touch a penis before you know where it's been?"

"I never thought about it like that," Pam admitted, really looking at Olimpia for the first time.

She was small, maybe five feet, and thin. She wore white cropped pants and a yellow T-shirt with a rhinestone pink flamingo on the front. Her hair was short and dark, with a couple of red highlights. Pam would guess she was in her late fifties.

They reached Pam's floor. Several people got on. Pam started to say it had been nice to meet her when Olimpia grabbed her wrist and held her in place.

"Sixteen, please," she said to the man standing by the elevator. She turned back to Pam. "Come back upstairs with me and meet my friends. We'll go get a drink and introduce ourselves. They're nice girls. You'll like them."

Pam hesitated, then the elevator doors closed and she was on her way up again.

"The widows" as Pam thought of her new friends, turned out to be interesting women. Olimpia lived in Florida—Vero Beach. She was very proud of the fact that one of her neighbors was a famous novelist—Debbie Macomber. "The nicest woman you'd ever want to meet." Olimpia didn't have any children, but was an avid volunteer—helping out with everything from adult literacy to animal welfare.

Laura, a tall and full-figured redhead, lived in Roanoke, Virginia. She hated the winters there, but was close to her four children and nine grandchildren, so moving wasn't an option. She lived in a condo with three cats and a Swarovski figurine collection that apparently rivaled any in the country.

Eugenia was from Dallas, Texas. She had big hair, a thick accent and an ability to drink anyone under the table. She, too, wanted to move, but stayed where she was because of her children and grandchildren.

All three of them were older than Pam, but each had

been widowed. They'd met on cruises and now took two or three trips together each year.

"The Caribbean, Alaska or Mexico, then somewhere exotic," Eugenia drawled. "Last year we did a river cruise in Germany. Lots of good wine. Plus on the river, the ride's real smooth."

After Olimpia had taken Pam back upstairs and introduced her to her friends, Pam had found herself having a drink with them in the Explorers Lounge. The fact that it was the middle of the afternoon didn't seem to bother anyone. That evening she'd joined them for dinner.

Their entrées had been cleared and now they lingered over a shared chocolate soufflé and decaf coffee.

Laura nodded. "That was a good one. We're still planning our last cruise for this year. I say Italy."

Olimpia shook her head. "No way. I'm still upset about what they did to Amanda Knox."

Pam frowned. "Who?"

Eugenia rolled her eyes. "That American girl accused of murdering her roommate. The trial was all over the news. They released her, then convicted her again."

Pam glanced at Olimpia. "You know her?"

"She's never met her, or anyone in her family," Laura said. "Olimpia, honey, you're beyond weird. You know that, right? Not that I don't love you like a sister, but you are desperately strange."

"I'm old. I can be strange if I want. I'm not going to Italy."

"It's a beautiful country." Eugenia sighed. "My Roger and I had a wonderful time there. Great wine, great sex." She smiled. "The perfect combination. The people were so warm and friendly."

"You go without me," Olimpia said, and picked up her coffee. "I'll be fine on my own."

Pam wasn't sure what to make of the trio. They had obviously been friends for a long time. There was an affection and a history. She liked that.

"Roger is?" she asked cautiously.

"My late husband. It's been five years now." Eugenia smiled sadly. "He was a wonderful man. I still miss him." She nodded at the other two. "We're all widows. How long has your husband been gone?"

Pam blinked. "Nearly two months."

"He booked the cruise before he died, I'll bet," Laura murmured. "You took it, anyway." She tilted her head. "Same thing happened to me. That's how I met Olimpia."

The petite woman nodded. "I was the first. My husband died almost twenty years ago. I was supposed to go on a cruise with a girlfriend and she backed out at the last minute. I said the hell with it, and went by myself. I was lonely and I still had a good time. I went back every year until I met these two. Now we travel together. Cruises are comfortable for women our age. No luggage to carry, no worries about the hotel being safe."

Pam couldn't imagine such a thing, and yet it made perfect sense. They were able to get away, to have fun. To just be themselves. Not someone's mother or grandmother. Not that she minded either, but what she most wanted was to be John's wife again and that was impossible.

"We have a lot of fun things planned for this week," Laura said cheerfully. "You'll join us."

"Are you asking or telling?" Eugenia raised her eyebrows. "It sounded like an order to me."

"I think it was." Laura laughed. "What do you say, Pam? Want to join the widows club?"

Pam thought about her plan. Meeting these three would make it easy. She would have a visible presence on the ship. People would know her and remember her. It was perfect.

"I do," she told them, raising her cup of decaf. "To the widows club."

Nicole pressed her hand to her chest. She told herself that feeling as if she couldn't breathe wasn't the same as not being able to catch her breath. That the problem was anxiety—there wasn't anything physically wrong. Only her body didn't seem to be listening to her brain as the sense of panic increased, the sense of impending death grew, too.

She gasped, trying to draw air into her lungs. Shannon walked in from the kitchen, a bottle of wine in her hand.

"What?" she demanded the second she saw Nicole.

"I'm having a panic attack," Nicole gasped. "I can't breathe."

Shannon set the open bottle on the coffee table. "Stand up and start walking. You have to burn off the chemicals pouring into your body. Talk to me."

Nicole shook her head. She wasn't going to talk. She could barely breathe. Even though she was sucking in air, it felt as if it wasn't getting into her lungs.

"Talk," Shannon said firmly. "If you can talk, you can breathe."

"I can't," Nicole blurted, her voice a little strangled. "I can't."

But the words came a little easier.

She sucked in more air. "I'm talking. This is me talking." As she spoke, she circled the living room. "I'm a total mess."

"You're not. You're under a whole lot of stress. Which is perfectly understandable. Who wouldn't be? First you had to deal with Eric writing the screenplay and doing nothing else. Then he sold it and now this."

Nicole nodded. The vise around her chest loosened and she thought maybe she wasn't breathing so hard. She circled back to the sofa and sat down.

"Everything's a disaster," she admitted as she took the glass of wine Shannon offered. "My life, my marriage."

"Not everything," Shannon told her firmly. "You have a business you really like and you have Tyler."

Nicole sipped the wine. "You're right. Work keeps me sane. It's where I have to be every morning. It's an anchor. Tyler's just great." His happy smile and his excitement about every part of his day made putting one foot in front of the other possible. Now it felt as though Tyler was all she had and that was way too much to put on a five-year-old.

She looked at Shannon. "Eric's gone. He's really gone. I haven't heard from him in two days. He hasn't been by, we haven't spoken. He sent a text saying he was finding his own place and that he'd be in touch."

"What about the money?"

Shannon's question surprised her. "What do you mean?"

"Your joint checking account. Did he clean it out?"

The question was completely unexpected, but the implications were terrifying.

"I don't know."

Shannon pointed toward the study. "Let's go find out."

"He wouldn't do that," Nicole said, even as she got to her feet and walked across the living room to the hallway.

"Three days ago you would have said he wouldn't leave, and he has. I'm sorry to be harsh, but I've had friends go through a divorce. It's never easy and things get ugly fast. He made a lot of money selling his screenplay. Half of that is yours."

"I don't want it," Nicole said automatically.

"Sure you do. You're going to have expenses. This house for one."

The house that was only in her name, she thought. But Shannon was right. There were expenses. Greta. And even if she didn't keep the full-time nanny, there was going to be day care. She worked. With Eric gone, Tyler was solely her responsibility.

She opened her browser, then entered the address for the bank. After logging in, she checked the balance, then the history.

"He pulled out fifty thousand dollars, but the rest of it is there."

"When did he take out the money?"

"This morning."

"Tomorrow you go open a personal account and do the same. Take out exactly what he did." Shannon sat in the spare chair. "You're going to need to talk to a lawyer. I can talk you through some basics, but you need someone who knows the law. Someone who's on your side. California is a community property state. That means everything goes into a bucket and the bucket is split in half. If you had assets before the marriage or he did, then those are separate. But everything else is up for grabs. His money from the screenplay, your business."

Shannon paused, then gentled her tone. "I'm sorry," she whispered. "I know this is hard."

It was only then that Nicole realized she was crying. She brushed away the tears. "I never thought this would happen. I never thought we'd get a divorce. But he said he didn't love me." She pressed her lips together. "No. That's not true. He said he never loved me. Things have been so horrible between us lately. I thought maybe we weren't going to make it, but that was in my head, you know? Not real. Now he's gone. I haven't told Tyler. Eric spends so much time on work, he hasn't really noticed. Greta helps with that. She knows. She hasn't said anything, but I'm sure she does."

The slightly scary nanny had been more kind than usual in the past couple of days.

"I kept thinking I'd be okay on my own. That getting a divorce might not be so bad. Now I want to go back and fix things. Only I can't."

How could she fix a relationship when her husband had never wanted it in the first place?

"I'm here for you," Shannon told her. "Do you want me to stay with you for a couple of days?"

Nicole sniffed. "No. I'm not scared to be alone." She thought about what Shannon had said earlier about the community property. "Do you think I should talk to a lawyer?"

"I do. I can get some names for you in the morning. You need to know what your rights are. You need to understand what each of you can legally do. I'm not saying Eric's a bad guy, but I don't want him taking more than he's allowed. I don't want you getting screwed."

Nicole appreciated the support even as she wished it wasn't necessary. She'd been sick to her stomach for three days now. Unable to fully grasp what had happened. Eric was gone. Their marriage was over. Even back when she'd thought things were fine, he hadn't been happy.

Which made her wonder if everything about their relationship had been a lie. He'd obviously been going through the motions and she'd been completely fooled.

Shannon pulled into the church parking lot and wished that Pam was back from her trip. While she was glad her friend was away and hopefully having a good time, right now a little wise counsel sounded good.

Before John had died, everything had been going so well for all of them, Shannon thought as she stared at the building in front of her. Eric had just sold his screenplay, things were great with Adam and Pam was her normal, happy, stable self. Then it had all gone to hell.

Nicole was in shock about Eric leaving. Shannon was surprised things had unraveled so quickly, but not totally stunned by the outcome. Adding to that was the reality that when one partner hit it big in nearly any field, there were stresses added to the relationship. In this case the million-dollar deal was both a blessing and curse. Now Eric could afford to walk away. He didn't need to be supported.

Shannon told herself there had to be other reasons for the breakup. Obviously there had been other problems. Every couple had them. Look at her and Adam. Or maybe it was better not to look.

She was avoiding him. He'd tried to set up dinner or even just a walk on the beach, but she kept saying she needed time. Which was true. She wasn't sure where their relationship was going. Despite his apologies and explanations about what had happened with Char, she wasn't sure she could do it. Be a part of his family.

Some of it was getting involved with a family that already existed. She wasn't sure where she would fit. Learning the rules, being "the other," all frightened her.

There were other considerations, as well. In truth, she'd spent the past twenty years only being responsible for herself. She'd done what she wanted, when she wanted. She'd made her own rules. Some of her decisions had been bad or wrong, but the only consequences were to herself.

If she stayed with Adam, if they kept going on their current path, then she wasn't going to be the only one in the room. There would be other considerations. Other people who had to be consulted, and not just the children. Tabitha would be a part of her life. This woman that Shannon had yet to meet would get one of the votes.

If she stayed with Adam, she would be the second wife. Whatever they did, he would have done it before with someone else. A wedding, a honeymoon, even having a child. She knew he wouldn't ever say it, but she wondered if he would be thinking it. Been there, done that.

She got out of the car and headed into the church. An easel with a sign pointed her down the hall. She entered what looked like a multipurpose room. A few high windows and a dozen or so chairs set out in a circle.

There were about ten women in the room already. They were talking to each other. A few stood together while others had already taken a seat. Shannon approached the woman behind the desk near the door.

"Hi," she said. "I'm Shannon Rigg. I called."

"Of course. Welcome." The woman's name tag said

Alice. "You're welcome to be a guest at two meetings. We ask that you observe without speaking." Alice shrugged. "We've had problems with people showing up, dominating the time to get their questions answered, then disappearing."

"Sure. That makes sense." Shannon could respect the concept of having to earn her way into the group. Assuming she wanted to belong.

"Once you join, you'll be given access to our resource network. There's an annual fee that covers maintaining the website and the referral service."

All of which Shannon already knew. She took the name tag Alice offered her, then got a cup of coffee from the tray in the back of the room. She walked over to the circle and settled in a chair.

The women in the room were all in their thirties and forties. One of them had a sleeping baby in her arms. The others watched the baby with varying expressions of longing. Madge, the group leader she'd spoken to on the phone, had explained that some women stayed on, even after having a child. They had made friendships that were important to them.

Shannon sipped her coffee and waited for the meeting to start. She didn't think she would join. She was here to observe and learn. While she was figuring things out when it came to her relationship with Adam, she'd thought maybe it was time to figure out a few things for herself. Like why hadn't she had a child on her own?

She'd been so determined to have it all or not have any of it. What was up with that? Part of her attempt to answer that question had been to come here. To a support group for women over thirty-five trying to have a child. Some were married with fertility problems, others were single. The topics included traditional pregnancy, surrogacy and adoption.

A tall woman in a business suit walked over and sat next to Shannon.

"I'm Madge," she said with a welcoming smile. "Nice to meet you in person. I'm glad you could make it to our meeting."

"Me, too."

Madge nodded at the woman with the baby. "She used a surrogate. We were all excited when she finally got her daughter."

"I can imagine."

Shannon braced herself for the inevitable and awkward questions. Why hadn't she had a baby before now? Had she considered adoption, or just getting pregnant by some random guy? But Madge didn't go there. Instead, she addressed the women and asked them to take their seats.

"We have a guest tonight. This is Shannon."

Several people called out a greeting.

Madge leaned back in her chair. "Who has something to report?"

A dark-haired woman in her forties smiled. "We've heard that we've been approved for our adoption in Ethiopia. We're flying out next week."

Everyone applauded.

She went on to talk about the process—how long it would take and what was involved. Several of the other women mentioned where they were in the process. Someone else gave an update on her IVF.

By the end of the hour, the sun had set and Shannon had a lot more information about what it would mean to have a baby on her own.

She thanked Madge for letting her visit and promised to think about joining the group. First she would have to figure out what she wanted and whether or not her interest in having a baby had anything to do with her relationship with Adam.

If she had a baby on her own, she would be dealing with a lot of logistical issues. Finding someone like Greta, for one. And if she was alone and working her usual fifty hours a week, should she really have a child? When would she see him or her?

There would be massive lifestyle changes. Was she willing to make them? To cut back on her hours? To talk to Nolan about working from home a couple of days a week?

If she stayed with Adam, then he would need to be part of the decision. There was his vasectomy to work through, assuming he was even interested in having a child with her. She was also very close to forty. Could she get pregnant the old-fashioned way?

She walked to her car and got in. Questions swirled, threatening to overwhelm her. She needed someone to talk to and at that moment, she couldn't think of a single person she could call. Pam was gone, Nicole was dealing with Eric leaving her, and Adam, well, she was confused about him.

As if wanting to help, her phone rang. She glanced at the screen and saw the familiar skull and crossbones.

Quinn, she thought. A man with no answers, but an impressive way of distracting her from whatever was wrong in her life.

"Hello?"

"Gorgeous."

"Hey. What's up?"

"Funny you should ask. I know we said we weren't going to do this anymore, but I wondered if I could change your mind."

There was something in his voice, she thought with surprise. A kind of vulnerability. Or maybe she was hearing what she wanted to hear.

Going over to Quinn's wouldn't solve anything, but it would make her feel better. She could lose herself in the moment, maybe put a little distance between herself and Adam. Emotionally if not physically.

Except it would be wrong, she thought with surprise. She and Adam were in a relationship. Things might be uncomfortable between them, but they were still together. She hadn't broken up with him. If she slept with Quinn, she would be cheating.

"That difficult a question?" he asked.

"It kind of is."

She thought about how feeling good would be followed by the drive of shame. She thought about how her nights with Quinn could very well be a metaphor for her life. Fun in the moment, but without direction or purpose, and always with more than a hint of regret at the end.

She didn't want regret. She wasn't sure where she stood on the baby front, but spending the night with Quinn didn't answer any of the questions. Even more important, she didn't like what a night with Quinn said about *her.*

"No," she told him. "I'm sorry, but I can't see you."

"Okay. You take care."

"You, too."

He hung up. She dropped her phone into her purse and

started the engine. She might not know exactly where she was going to be in five years, but for tonight, she was going home.

Twenty-Five

Pam was surprised to discover that a busy social schedule made fitting in a suicide kind of difficult.

The week of the cruise had flown by. Once she made friends with Olimpia, Laura and Eugenia, she'd been busy nearly every second of every day. Together the three of them had explored Jamaica, including a very fun river cruise on a small flat-bottomed boat. Laura had brought lemon-flavored vodka for all of them and they'd ended up singing "Born to Be Wild" and frightening their tour guide.

When they'd stopped in Grand Cayman, they'd visited the turtle farm and Pam had discovered that not only did rum cake get you drunk, but if you ate enough, it could also give you a hangover. Now it was the last day—the day at sea, when she was supposed to do the deed. But so far she hadn't found a single moment to get herself ready, let alone fling herself off the ship.

She'd seen ruins in Mexico and had bought silly souvenirs for her kids. She'd attended an art auction and had actually bought a couple of pieces. There'd been movies, live shows and laughter. She'd nearly forgotten what it felt like to laugh.

The week had been so much better than she'd hoped, but it was nearly over and she had to remember why she'd come in the first place. She was going to end her life.

She couldn't do it without organizing her thoughts and making sure her room was tidy. All she needed was an hour, she told herself. She would sneak away and get it done.

But morning had turned into afternoon and now it was only an hour or so from dinner. Maybe that was better, she thought. In the dark no one would see her falling. That way it would take them longer to miss her. After dinner. She would have a last meal with her friends.

Eugenia waved a piece of paper. "Do you know how hard it is to plan a tour in Europe without going to Italy? Especially when everyone else *wants* to go to Italy?"

They sat, as they always did, in the Explorers Lounge. They even had "their" table. They'd met for cocktails before dinner.

"I'm ignoring the parts about Italy," Olimpia said. "What did you find?"

"A glorious cruise. It leaves September sixth. We start in Amsterdam and finish up in Istanbul." Eugenia looked at Laura. "That's in Turkey."

"I know where Istanbul is," Laura told her. "Wasn't there a song?"

Olimpia leaned toward Pam. "Music is where Laura gets all her information."

"I'll have ya'll know, I was very talented at one time."

"You're still talented," Pam pointed out. Because she'd learned that Laura was a classically trained pianist. And that Eugenia had published five novels. And that Olimpia had kept her husband's business going for nearly a decade after his death.

These women weren't just widows. They were bright and funny and loyal. She enjoyed their company. They had helped her get through what could have been a horrible week and she would always be grateful. In a way, she wished she could leave them a note, telling them what they meant to her. But she couldn't. Her death was supposed to be an accident.

"Back to the cruise," Eugenia said. "Are we interested?"

"We are," Olimpia said, then winked at Pam. "She always gets like this when it's her turn to plan things. Completely imperious."

Pam smiled. She'd learned that each year one of them was responsible for making the arrangements for their three cruises.

"I'm ignoring you," Eugenia said.

"Then there's no point in voicing my opinion," Olimpia murmured with a sly smile. "You'll have to vote without me."

"Not a problem," Laura said cheerfully. "Three votes is a majority. What do you think, Pam?"

Eugenia passed her the itinerary. "I've checked. There are four staterooms still available."

Pam took the piece of paper and stared blindly at it. Her go with them? That had never been discussed. Oh, there had been comments made. "You'll love Alaska." Or "Would you be willing to go to Italy? We can leave Olimpia at the airport." But she'd thought they were just being nice.

She tried to bring the tiny print into focus. Laura passed over a pair of reading glasses.

Pam slipped them on. "I've never been to Malta," she whispered, looking at the exotic-sounding ports. "That would be nice."

"Then it's decided," Eugenia said. "I'll email all of you the information as soon as I'm home." She waved at one of the servers, and gestured that they wanted another round. "Are we eating at Sabatini's tonight?"

"We are," Olimpia said. "I made reservations. Six thirty."

Sabatini's was one of the premium restaurants on the ship. Pam had forgotten they were going there. The evening would be lovely—good food and caring company. And then... Well, she would think about that later.

By the time the four of them had finished dinner and giggled through the last night of karaoke and had a nightcap, it was close to midnight. With every passing second, Pam was aware of the ship getting closer and closer to Florida.

The evening had gone by so quickly, she thought. She'd laughed and talked and while she'd still missed John with every breath, the pain was less intense than it had been. It seemed almost...manageable.

How could that be? She'd lost her husband—she needed to be suffering. Not only to feel closer to him, but also to prove her love. Even as those thoughts appeared, she understood the wrongness of them. But that didn't take away their power.

She'd come on this cruise for only one reason and her window of opportunity was closing.

"I should get to bed," she said as she stood.

The three women exchanged a look, then Olimpia

rose. "I'll walk with you." She picked up her bag. "We're all clear on where we're meeting in the morning?"

Laura wiggled her fingers. "You've told us fifteen times. We'll be there, to say our goodbyes. Until September, right Pam?"

Pam bit her lower lip and nodded. She wanted to hug each of them. To tell them how much she'd appreciated them taking her under their collective wing. They'd made her feel welcome and they'd reminded her that life did indeed go on. She might not be willing to go through the pain of healing, but they'd allowed her to see the possibilities.

But to admit any of that would mean telling them too much. So there would be no goodbyes, no last hugs, no thanking them. Instead, she simply said, "Good night" and walked with Olimpia to the elevators.

"I've never been to Mischief Bay," Olimpia said as they waited for the elevator. "What's it like?"

"A small town tucked in the middle of Los Angeles. The weather is great."

"You're near the beach?"

"Only a few blocks away."

They stepped into the elevator. Pam pushed her floor.

"Maybe I'll come out for a visit this August," Olimpia said. "By then the humidity is making me think about relocating." She flashed a smile. "Not that I would, but I do complain and threaten."

They got off on Pam's floor. She thought about pointing out that her friend was on a different deck, but figured she wouldn't mind a little company. It wasn't that she was having second thoughts, exactly. It was just the thought of throwing herself off the ship was a little harder than she'd expected.

They got to Pam's room and stepped inside. Olimpia headed for the sofa and sat on one cushion.

"You must be excited about seeing your kids," she said as Pam set down her bag and took the chair opposite.

"I am. Of course."

"Jen's what? Four months' pregnant?"

"Yes."

Olimpia smiled. "You'll know the sex of the baby soon. That's so fun. I don't suppose twins run in your family."

"No, and don't let Jen hear you say that. She would freak out."

"Twins would be difficult. But she'll have you. And soon Steven will meet someone and settle down. Plus Brandon will be graduating. A doctor. You must be so proud."

Pam nodded because it was expected, but what she was thinking was that she wanted Olimpia to stop talking. All this conversation about her children was making her sad. She didn't want to think about all they would accomplish or experience without her being there to see it. She didn't want to imagine not holding her first grandchild, or her second or tenth.

But she had to do this, she reminded herself. It was the only thing that made sense. She had to...

"I'm not leaving," Olimpia said quietly, her gaze steady. "If I think I can't stay awake, I'm going to call Laura or Eugenia and they'll come sit with you."

Pam eyes widened. Her face flushed and she stood. "I don't know what you're talking about."

"You do, and it's all right. We've felt what you feel, Pam. We've had the long nights, the empty days, the horror that the missing won't go away and the terror that it will. We've all wrestled with going on and the knowledge that sometimes it seemed so much easier not to."

She smiled sadly. "If you want to do it, I can't stop you. But it won't be tonight. Not on our watch. We care about you and want you to be around to travel with us."

Pam sank back in the chair. "I'm sorry."

"You don't have to be. We understand better than most. It does get better. It's never easy, it never feels completely right, but you do heal. And move on."

Pam wasn't sure what to feel. Embarrassment, maybe. Shame. Or defiance. Emotions swirled through her, none of them staying long enough to be defined.

"I didn't know how to survive without him," she admitted.

"You'll learn. And when it gets hard, remember, John wouldn't have wanted this. He would have wanted you to be happy."

Olimpia was right, she thought, a little dazed by the revelation. John *would* have wanted her to keep moving forward. To find her place in life.

In life, she repeated to herself. Because that was the whole point of every person's journey. To be alive. To live and to keep moving forward.

"I'm not sure I'm ready for this," Adam said. "So I appreciate the company."

"Not to mention the extra free labor," Shannon added.

He grinned. "That, too."

He'd called the previous day and explained he was painting Oliver's bedroom. His son had decided he was old enough to let go of his Brad the Dragon motif and move toward "big boy" decor. According to Adam, that meant light blue walls and new bedding.

By the time she'd arrived at his house that morning, Adam had already taken the dragon bed out and loaded it into a company pickup. He would be dropping it off at Nicole's later for a very thrilled Tyler.

The dresser and desk had been pushed to the center of the room and covered with plastic. The windows and doors were taped off, as were the baseboards.

"I can cut in around the ceiling," he said. "Unless you want to."

"I've painted exactly once before in my life," she admitted. "You should give me the jobs I can't mess up."

"A novice," he said, stepping close to her. "So I get to show you the ropes."

"There are ropes? I thought we used brushes."

"Very funny."

He put his hands on her hips and drew her against him. He was casually dressed in jeans and a paint-spattered T-shirt. Both looked good on him, as did his choice not to shave that morning.

She rested her fingers on his broad chest. He was warm and being close to him made her breath hitch. She'd missed him, she thought. She'd kept herself busy enough that she wouldn't notice, but she had. So when he'd called, she'd wanted to say yes.

She still wasn't sure where they were going, but somehow being without Adam had become more difficult.

"It's nice to have you here," he said, right before he kissed her.

His mouth settled on hers. Wanting settled low in her belly. She raised her arms and wrapped them around his neck. Her breasts nestled against his chest.

They fit, she thought. In so many ways. But what about everything else?

She drew back enough to see into his eyes. She needed to put herself out there. To take a risk in love and see it through. "I don't know if I can be a good stepmother."

She ignored the fact that he hadn't asked. They were supposed to be a couple. It was the next logical step.

"Is it something you're willing to talk about?" he asked.

"I think so. I want things to work out, but I'm not sure. You and Tabitha were a family. I'll never have equal footing. I'll always be the other one. You'll want me to care about the kids as much as you do but I won't have the same say in what happens with them."

His dark gaze never wavered. "That doesn't sound very fair."

"It's not, but do you think it's untrue?"

"No." He touched her cheek. "I can't change what I bring to the table."

"I don't want you to. I'm just not sure how to make it all work. What if I want a baby from Ethiopia?"

"Do you?"

"Maybe. I'm not sure. Did Tabitha work when you had the kids?"

"No. She stayed home until Oliver was three."

Shannon tried to imagine giving up her career. She loved her work, loved her lifestyle. But was it enough? She had a feeling she already knew the answer.

"I could see taking a six-week leave. Or even a couple of months," she said slowly. But not more. She didn't want to give up that much of who she was.

Had that been the issue all along? Had she not wanted

children, but been afraid to admit it? Afraid it made her a bad person? So she'd pretended it was because she couldn't find *the one*?

"I love you," Adam told her and kissed her. "Whatever you decide, I want to be with you. Losing you isn't an option." He smiled. "I mean that in a nonscary way."

He leaned his forehead against hers. "I know what happened with Char was frustrating. I'm to blame for a lot of that. You're the first woman they've met."

She straightened. "I'm pretty sure they've met other women, Adam. At the grocery store, at the park."

He groaned. "Fine. You're the first woman I've been dating that they've met. It's going to take some time for us all to figure it out." He grabbed her hand. "I want to make it work. My sister Gabby and I were talking about this. She thought maybe family counseling would help. First you and me, then with the kids. To establish ground rules that are fair for everyone. What you said before about being the outsider? I know that there are pieces of that I can't change, but I want to make it right for you. However I can."

She believed him. Because he was listening and accepting and because he was a good guy. Would there be mistakes? Sure—by both of them. That came with being human. But with some effort, and maybe a little professional help, they could make it work.

She flung herself at him. "I love you."

"I love you, too."

His mouth settled on hers. She pressed her body to his and gave herself over to the passion they generated. When he started nudging her backward, toward his bedroom, she went willingly. Because while they might not have all the answers, as long as they were willing to search for them, they were going to be just fine.

The *click-click-click* of Lulu's nails on the kitchen floor was a familiar sound. Pam reached down and picked up her little dog.

"I missed you," she told Lulu. "Was I silly to think I could leave you or what?"

Lulu kissed her chin, then snuggled close. The dog hadn't left her side in the three days she'd been home. It had always been this way when they traveled, Pam thought. Only this time she'd been the only one to come home.

The last night of the cruise had gone just as Olimpia had promised. She hadn't left Pam alone. They'd talked for hours and had fallen asleep in their chairs sometime after two. There'd been a rush for the early morning departure with plenty of hugs and promises to stay in touch.

Since she'd been home, she'd already heard from all three of them. Even more important, she'd made her reservation for the European cruise they were taking in September. It wasn't like having John back, nowhere close. But it wasn't the hell it had been. Maybe she couldn't see the light at the end of the tunnel just yet, but she knew it was there. Her job was to keep moving.

Now, with Lulu in her arms, she walked through the big house she'd lived in for so long. She went from room to room, studying the furnishings, the mementos.

In the living room was a family portrait taken about ten years ago. Brandon looked impossibly young. John was so handsome. In his study was the baseball he'd caught at a Dodger game. There were candid photos of all the kids and several of her. The mug he'd used and casually placed on the bookcase the weekend before he died was exactly where he'd left it.

The dining room held other memories. Family dinners. She and Jen had had their worst fight ever at that table. Her daughter had been seventeen and wanting to be respected as an adult while cared for as a child. Pam had wondered if they would ever get through that time where every word was misunderstood and each encounter seemed to lead to angry words and door slamming. John had been her rock through it all. He'd assured her Jen would once again become the daughter they remembered, and in time, she had.

In the hallway, Pam paused by what had been Brandon's door. How many nights had she and John stood there, not sure what to do or say as their youngest experimented with drugs and alcohol. They'd spent hundreds of hours worrying and fearing the future. But he'd gotten through it.

In the hall bath, behind the door, were the lines marking Steven's various heights. At nine, he'd been frantic he wouldn't be big enough to play professional baseball, only to discover that while he enjoyed the game, he wasn't interested in making it his entire life.

So many memories. So many good times. She'd been blessed. And while losing John would be a wound she would carry with her always, she was beginning to see that maybe, just maybe, she had the strength to go on.

"Hi, Mom. It's me!"

Lulu struggled to get down. Pam set her on the floor and the little dog went running to greet Jen. All three kids were coming by that night for a rare midweek dinner. Pam had chili in the Crock-Pot and her famous cheddar biscuits ready to bake.

She went toward the kitchen and found her daughter holding Lulu.

"Mom!" Jen put down the dog and hurried to greet her. "I'm so glad you had a good time on the cruise, but I missed you. It was hard having you gone."

They hugged. Jen hung on a little tighter than usual. Pam gave a brief prayer of thanks for whatever angel had arranged for her to meet her three friends. Without them, she wouldn't have made it back. She knew that. And what a waste of a blessed life.

Pam cupped her daughter's face in her hands. "Look at you. You really are glowing. You've always been beautiful, but now it's kind of unfair to the rest of us."

"Oh, Mom." Jen's eyes filled with tears. "I had my ultrasound while you were gone. Kirk was with me. The baby is healthy and I'm doing well. You're the first to know, aside from Kirk, of course. We're having a boy."

Warm, bubbling happiness filled her. Pam hung on to it, even as the pain of loss tempered the edges of the joy. It would always be like this, she thought. But it was okay. There would be good days and bad days. And John would always be in her heart.

"Congratulations. A boy. Kirk must be thrilled. He's always had that macho streak."

Jen laughed. "I know. He's really excited." Her daughter sniffed. "We want to call him John, if you're okay with that."

Pam had to take a breath before she could speak. "That would be wonderful, but you know you don't have to."

"I know. We want to. I miss Daddy so much. Not like you do, I'm sure."

They walked into the family room and sat down on the sofa. Lulu jumped up and settled between them. She curled up against Pam but kept her gaze on Jen, as if making sure no one was going anywhere.

"I'm glad you made friends on your cruise," Jen said. "Those three ladies sound great."

"They are. I'm joining them in September. We're going to Europe together. The four of us."

"Wow. Impressive. Look at you, traveling the world."

Pam smiled. "I'll be nervous, but I won't be alone. Then I'm staying put until you have your baby."

"Good, because I want you with me for every second the whole first year."

"You say that now, but you'll do great. Of course, I'll help when you need it, but I'm not worried about you." She looked around at the big room, the giant TV John had loved so much. "I want to talk to you about something."

Jen's eyes widened. "What? Are you okay?"

"I'm fine. I've just been thinking. This house is so big and—"

The tears returned to Jen's eyes. "No, Mom. You can't sell it. We need this house in our family. The memories. Don't all the books say you have to wait a year before doing anything big? Wait. We'll help. Didn't Steven do a spreadsheet for maintenance and stuff? We can all pitch in."

Pam shook her head. "Hear me out. It's okay. Yes, your brother put together a spreadsheet of what has to happen when. I have a list of vendors to call. I can take care of the house—I just don't want to anymore. I've talked to your brothers about this and they agree with you. The house has to stay in the family."

Jen shot to her feet. "Is Steven taking it? Because he would not treat this house right. He's a single guy. There's no way Brandon would want it."

Pam patted the sofa. "Sit. Listen."

Jen's mouth twitched. "Now you're talking to me like I'm Lulu."

"She is better behaved than you."

Jen laughed and sat. "Okay. I'm listening."

"The boys agree that the house should stay in the family. We have so many memories here. Like the Memorial Day barbecue in a couple of weeks." An annual tradition where friends and family came over for a big celebration of the start of summer. On the flight home Pam had realized she had to continue the tradition. At least this one last time.

"You're right about Brandon and Steven not wanting the house. But you do. You and Kirk."

Jen's eyes widened. "Mom, that would be incredible, but there is no way we can afford it. I'm a public school teacher and Kirk's a cop. On our best day, we barely make the rent on our apartment."

"I know. If you want the house, you can have it. Think of it as an early inheritance. I would transfer title to you and Kirk. I would put an amount equal to the value of the house into the boys' trusts."

"What would you do?"

"Buy a condo. My friend Shannon has a lovely place right on the beach. I'm going to look in her building. I'd be five minutes away." She smiled at her daughter. "You think about it and talk to Kirk. I'd love to see you two and your children here. But it means hosting the family events and carrying on traditions. I'd help with the cooking, but the bulk of it would fall to you."

Jen hugged her. Lulu wiggled between the two of them and gave plenty of kisses.

"Mom, I don't know what to say. I'd love it. I'll talk

to Kirk, but I'm pretty sure he'll agree. This house is so amazing." She drew back. "But not right away. You have to think about it, too. You and Daddy lived here for so long. You have to be sure you want to give that up."

"It's okay," Pam told her. "Wherever I go, John is with me. We had a wonderful life here. There's a lot of good energy in these walls. A lot of happiness. I know he'd want this for all of us."

Twenty-Six

Pam waited until both Shannon and Nicole had their Cosmos before raising her glass. "To friends. Thank you both for being there for me after John died. I don't think I ever thanked you."

"You did," Shannon told her.

"You're being kind."

Shannon wrinkled her nose. "Not possible. I'm a career-driven harpy. Haven't you heard?"

Despite her words, Shannon was practically floating. Her eyes were bright and her skin glowed. There was a softness about her and an air of mystery. She was keeping secrets, Pam thought. The good kind.

"Another article on successful women breaking barriers?" Nicole asked.

"You know it," Shannon said and took a sip of her drink. "There's an entire paragraph on my unmarried and childless state."

"Fuck 'em if they can't take a joke," Pam said.

Both women stared at her.

"I've never heard you say the *F* word," Nicole admitted. "It makes me like you so much more."

Pam grinned at her, even as she worried about her friend. Shannon had already called and told her about what happened with Eric. While Shannon was all happy smiles, Nicole seemed smaller somehow, and shell-shocked. As if the reality of what was happening hadn't set in yet.

Pam knew the feeling. She'd felt like the walking dead for a couple of months after John's death. Pretty much until the cruise, she thought. Most of her heart was still in hibernation, but there was the hint of coming spring. A bud or two. And for now, that was enough.

"Tell us about the cruise," Shannon said. "It sounded like you had a good time."

"I did. Better than I expected."

They were in the bar at Pescadores. Their reservation for dinner was in an hour, giving them plenty of time to chat at a quiet table in the back of the bar. It was relatively early on a Wednesday evening. There weren't many other patrons. Even so Pam lowered her voice as she spoke.

"I'm not going to share this with anyone else, but I want you two to know the truth." She sipped her drink. "I went on the cruise to kill myself. I thought I couldn't survive losing John."

Both Nicole and Shannon stared at her.

"Oh, my God," Shannon murmured. "Pam, I had no idea. I'm sorry you felt so alone."

"No. Don't blame yourself. I meant what I said before. You were both there for me. Everyone was willing to help the first couple of weeks, but you two went so beyond that. I wouldn't have made it through without you." She rested her elbows on the table and told them about how she'd picked the day and the means.

"It's hard to explain. The loss, I mean. I haven't been

anyone but John's wife for thirty years. I didn't want to try to find out what being on my own would be like. I was selfish and weak. John would have been so ashamed of me."

She thought about the man who had been the best part of her. He wouldn't have understood, she thought. "This may sound strange, but I'm so grateful for what I went through. I'm glad I came up with the ridiculous plan and tried to see it through. To be honest, I have no idea if I could have done it or not. What I do know is I was extraordinarily fortunate to meet the women I did on that ship. That last night, when Olimpia wouldn't leave me on my own, I felt as if God touched me."

She wrinkled her nose. "I don't mean that in a weird way. Just that I was given another chance. It's not any easier without John, but somehow I can deal with it better. I can breathe. I couldn't breathe before. Jen's going to have a baby. One day Steven will fall in love. Brandon is going to be a wonderful doctor. I want to see all that."

She turned to Shannon. "I want to see what happens with Adam and watch you continue to kick business ass." She touched Nicole's arm. "I want to be around as Tyler grows up and you figure out what's next. But mostly I want to thank you for being my friends."

"I am not crying," Shannon said firmly. "You're not going to make me."

Nicole wiped away tears. "I'm not even trying not to. Pam, I've said this before and I hope you know it's a compliment, but I so want to be you when I grow up."

"Aim higher," Pam told her.

Nicole shook her head. "Not possible."

* * *

"I need you to prepare a list of all your assets and all your debts, both personally and for the business."

"Should I be taking notes?" Nicole asked.

Her lawyer, Nancy, a sensible-looking woman in a suit, shook her head. "No. I'll be sending you home with a lot of paperwork for you to look over. There are some information sheets and a list of what you'll bring to the next meeting."

Nicole didn't understand how she'd gotten here. Oh, not to the meeting itself. That was simple. Pam had driven her. But to this place in her life. She and Eric were getting a divorce.

They still hadn't talked. Nor had she seen him. He'd been by a couple of times to pick up clothing and his computer. She only knew because Greta mentioned it. Three days ago he'd sent a text saying he was retaining a lawyer and suggesting she do the same.

Shouldn't they have a conversation? Talk about what had gone wrong or even try to fix it? His answer was easy to figure out, she thought, still too surprised by everything happening to feel anything. She moved through her days as if her life was happening to someone else and she was just the observer.

"Nicole owns her own business," Pam said. "And Eric recently sold a screenplay for a sizeable sum."

"Everything comes into play," the lawyer said. "California is a community property state. That means all joint assets are shared. Did you own anything before you were married?"

"My house," Nicole murmured. "I bought it myself and Eric isn't on the title."

"Did he put any money down on it or pay for any improvements?"

She shook her head.

"Eric hasn't worked in over a year," Pam told the lawyer. "He quit his job to write his screenplay. Nicole's been paying all the bills."

"That helps," Nancy said as she took notes. "You'll need to prepare a P-and-L for your business."

Nicole looked at Pam. "A what?"

"Profit-and-loss statement," her friend told her. "It's in your bookkeeping program. I'll show you. It's not hard. Basically everything will be added up. The value of your business, less any debts, what you owe on credit cards and how much money you have. Life insurance and the like. Then it's split down the middle."

"Exactly," the lawyer said with a smile. "You've been through this before."

"Not personally," Pam told her. "But a few friends had difficult divorces."

Nancy nodded and looked at Nicole. "What about your son?" She glanced at her notes. "Tyler."

Nicole shrugged. "Eric and I haven't talked. He hasn't seen Tyler since he moved out. I want to retain custody. We have a nanny—Greta. I don't think I can afford her on my own, but without her, there will be day-care expenses. Could Eric help with that?"

The last thing she wanted was her son having even more disruptions.

"Absolutely. Once I meet with his attorney, I'll know what he expects as far as custody. His abandonment of the family works in your favor."

Nicole wondered if it had to be phrased that way. Eric

had left them. Wasn't that different? Or maybe when it came to a divorce, it didn't matter.

"If you're the custodial parent, he'll be paying child support. With your share of his screenwriting money and child support, you should be able to afford Greta, or some other arrangement." Nancy gave her a sympathetic smile. "I know this is overwhelming. You need to understand it's going to get worse before it gets better. Divorce isn't easy, but it is survivable. You have a support network. I suggest you take advantage of that. This is the time to reach out to your friends."

Pam squeezed her hand. "We're all here for you."

"Thank you."

Nancy returned to her notes. "Don't make any major purchases. It's fine to buy food and replace clothing, but don't get a new car. Also, I'll need copies of all recent bank statements. Neither of you is allowed to transfer out money from the joint account beyond necessities for living expenses. You're not still having sex with Eric, are you?"

Nicole blinked. "Ah, no."

"Good. Keep it that way. It's possible he may try to get back into the marriage bed as a way to manipulate you into agreeing to a lesser settlement."

The idea was practically comical, Nicole thought. Eric hadn't slept with her for months. No way would he try to do it now, she thought.

"I think I'm pretty safe," she said. "But I'll remember your advice."

They discussed more logistics, then wrapped up the meeting. Nancy handed over paperwork and Nicole gave her a check to retain her services.

When they were in the office building parking lot, Pam gave her a hug.

"I won't ask how you're doing."

"Good, because I don't have an answer," Nicole admitted. "None of this is real. Everything happened so fast. We were struggling, then Eric sold his screenplay and now we're getting a divorce. How is that possible?"

"I only have clichés to offer. People change and grow apart. It's not your fault."

While Nicole appreciated the vote of confidence, she was less sure. For things to fall apart so quickly, there had to have been underlying problems. Things she hadn't noticed or maybe hadn't wanted to see. While it took two to make a relationship successful, she had a feeling that it also took two for it to fail. So where had she gone wrong?

"You are the weirdest man," Shannon said.

"You love that I'm weird," Adam told her, his voice cheerful.

He was right, she thought, looking into his dark eyes and knowing that whatever course they chose, she wanted them on it together.

She still didn't have answers to the kid question. Nor was she a hundred-percent sure she was decent step-mother material. But she was willing to try. With patience and maybe some outside help, they could make it.

It was Sunday morning. The warm temperatures had meant breakfast out on her deck overlooking the POP and the ocean beyond. Already joggers and cyclists were out, earnestly exercising. In the distance, she could see a couple of dogs in the dog park.

Adam had spent the night. They had a lazy afternoon planned, then dinner with friends. The kids were with their mother this weekend. If she and Adam stayed together, this would be what it was like, she thought. Every other weekend would be just the two of them. Unless they had a baby. Or adopted.

"Why are you frowning?" he asked. "I walked three miles in the snow to get you croissants."

She laughed. "There is no snow and Latte-Da is two blocks away."

"Still. I hunted and brought you back my prize kill."

She raised her latte and toasted him. "I appreciate it."

"So why the frown?"

"I don't know what to think about having a baby," she admitted. "I'm very capable. If I wanted children, wouldn't I have taken care of that by now? Yet, if I don't do something soon, I won't have the chance later. It's complicated. I want to make the right decision and I don't know what that is."

He surprised her by standing. "Hold that thought."

He disappeared into her condo, only to return a couple of seconds later with a briefcase. He sat across from her and started pulling out folders.

He handed her one. "Information from my urologist."

She stared at him. "You have a urologist?"

"I do now. I've been to see him about reversing the vasectomy. Because my vasectomy is less than ten years old, the expected success rate is ninety percent. It's an outpatient procedure with an easy recovery." He shrugged. "No sex for three weeks, but then we can go for it."

"You'd do that for me?"

"Of course. I love you, Shannon." He nodded at the folder. "All the information is in there."

He pulled out a second folder. "International adoption. I talked to my sister Gabby."

"She's an immigration lawyer."

"Right, but she has friends who handle adoption. There are a lot of opportunities, and not just in Ethiopia. Although if that's your favorite country, we should go for it."

She opened her mouth, then closed it. Speech was impossible. This man, this amazing man, only wanted to make her happy. She pressed her lips together.

"It doesn't have to be Ethiopia."

"Good to know."

He set a third folder on the pile. "This is kind of from left field, but hear me out. You love your work. You want kids, but I don't see you taking off six months to do the stay-at-home mom thing." He held up both hands. "An observation, not a judgment."

"Keep talking."

He tapped the folder. "Foster kids. There are hundreds who need a home. We could provide that. A place for them to feel safe. Maybe even adopt a couple. We'd have our own family, you'd get to be a mom and it would be good for Char and Oliver. Plus, if we went with older kids, you wouldn't have to give up any part of your career. Everybody wins."

Foster children? The idea had never crossed her mind. "We'd have to get approved or certified or whatever first."

"Sure, but I think we'd make it through the process." He reached in his briefcase again and pulled out a turquoise blue jewelry box.

Her gaze locked on it, then slowly rose to his face. He smiled at her. "I love you, Shannon. I swear, the first time

I saw you, I couldn't believe I was that lucky. As I got to know you, I realized that the beautiful package on the outside was nothing when compared to who you are on the inside. You're smart, funny, caring and for reasons that delight me constantly, you love me. And every time I'm with you, I'm more sure of my love for you. I want to spend the rest of my life being with you. I want us to create a family that makes you happy and I don't care what form it takes. As long as you're with me."

He drew in a breath. "I come with some baggage and I'm not saying it will be easy. But I promise to be there, no matter what. Will you marry me?"

She didn't remember standing, but suddenly she was on her feet and circling the table. He pulled her into his arms and held her close.

"Yes," she whispered. "I love you and I want to marry you, Adam. I'm all in."

Twenty-Seven

"It's all very fair," Nancy said. "I'll admit it. Eric surprised me."

"Me, too," Nicole murmured.

Her lawyer glanced at her. "I won't ask if you're okay. But do you need a minute?"

Nicole shook her head. There was nothing left to think about. It was done.

She thought about reading the documents one more time, but didn't have it in her. She trusted her lawyer and even if she didn't, she was too exhausted and numb to fight.

Eric had agreed to divide everything down the middle. The house was hers, because it always had been. The modest value of her business had been added to the money he'd made on his screenplay, less taxes and agent fees. Their debts had been subtracted from that amount and that final amount had been divided in two.

From her half, Nicole had bought him out of her business. The final lump sum would be deposited in her new only-hers checking account. She now owned her business herself and soon would have a nest egg sitting in a money market.

Of that two hundred thousand dollars, she would put half away for Tyler's college and keep the other half for herself. It wasn't enough to live on forever. Not even close. But it was there. A nice, comfortable safety net.

In addition, they'd agreed on child support payments. The amount allowed Nicole to keep Greta. Eric would see Tyler every other weekend, while she retained full custody.

Nancy had brought up asking for alimony, but Nicole had refused. She was young and healthy. She could support herself. Asking for anything else seemed greedy.

She signed the documents where Nancy indicated. In a matter of minutes it was done. Her divorce would be final, according to the state of California, in six months. But she knew the marriage had been over for years.

She thanked her attorney and headed for home. Eric had said he would come by at two to get his things and she wanted to be there.

When she rounded the corner, his car was already in the driveway. She parked across the street and walked toward the house.

"It's me," she called as she walked in the front door. "I'm back here."

From the sound of his voice, she would guess he was in his office.

There were just the two of them in the house. She'd asked Greta to take Tyler out for the afternoon so they wouldn't be here. Not that Nicole was expecting anything to happen. Even so there was no need for their son to witness the last gasps of their failed marriage.

She went down the hall. The door to Eric's office

stood open. He was putting books into boxes. He glanced up and smiled at her.

"Hi. I shouldn't be too long."

"When's the truck coming?"

"What truck?"

"The moving truck. For your things. Aren't you taking some of the furniture?"

He looked around at the small office. "No. I don't need it. The only thing I bought was that." He nodded at the futon. "While it has sentimental value, I'm not interested in finding a place for it. Let me know if you need help getting rid of it."

She'd thought he would want at least some of the furniture. Now that she thought about it, she realized they'd never discussed what he would and wouldn't need for his new place.

"You have things for the kitchen and a sofa and stuff?" she asked.

"I'm living in a furnished place. I'm not sure where I want to settle. I'm close to the studio, so convenient for now, but after I sell my next screenplay, I might move to the Hills."

Hollywood Hills, she thought. Where houses perched like eagles' nests had views from downtown to the ocean.

"You'll want lots of entertaining space," she said quietly. "For your movie-star parties."

He grinned. "You know it."

Nothing about this felt like it was really happening, she thought as he picked up the full box and carried it out to his car. Not him leaving, not the empty space that separated them. She honestly couldn't think of a single thing to say to him. How could they have been married for less than six years and have already run out of words?

Not sure what else to do, she filled a second box with the rest of his books.

"Thanks," he said, when he returned. "I still have a few things in the bedroom."

She took one of the boxes, walked out of the office and into the living room. She'd already sorted the DVDs and Blu-ray disks. She put them in the box, then collected a couple of magazines, and a plate Tyler had decorated for him last Father's Day.

In the kitchen, she added a couple of pens from the junk drawer and a few pictures of him and Tyler.

There were some T-shirts and board shorts stacked on the washer. She got those and added them to the box, along with an iPod and headphones.

He walked into the kitchen. "I think I have everything."

She pointed to the box. "You'll want that."

He glanced inside. "Thank you."

They stared at each other. Although he looked exactly the same as he had the last time she'd seen him, and the time before, in so many ways, he was a stranger. She no longer knew him and wondered if she ever had. Their relationship had been nothing but an illusion. They'd both played at being in love, and neither of them had done a very good job.

"If you want to see Tyler more, just call me and we'll set something up."

"I'm going to be busy," he said, picking up the last box. "The every other weekend thing is about all I can handle and I might need you to understand if I have to miss a few times."

She wanted to protest—to point out that a boy needed his father. That Tyler missed him. Only Eric had started leaving long before he'd moved out. So much so that their son barely mentioned him. Tyler had friends and preschool. Come September he would be in kindergarten. Eric would matter less and less.

One day Eric might regret that. One day he might try to reconcile with his son. Until then, her job was to give Tyler the most stable home she could. To love him so much he wouldn't notice the absent father.

"I have a meeting," Eric told her. "I have to go. Once my lawyer gets the signed papers, he'll arrange to have the money sent over to your account."

She nodded.

He gave her a quick, impersonal smile. "Okay, then. I'll see you."

He walked out of the kitchen. Seconds later, the front door closed.

She stood in the quiet house and steadied her breathing. It was done. The paperwork was signed. In six months the lawyers would go to court and a judge would sign some papers and she would be divorced.

She looked around the kitchen, at the painted cabinets and the tile she'd chosen shortly after she'd bought the house. Through the window she could see the backyard. All the plants she'd nursed back to health and the ones she's bought. She'd always loved this house. The bright colors, the light, how she'd decorated…

Nicole slowly turned in a circle, taking in every corner of the kitchen. There was the stove she'd replaced and the door handles she'd bought. In the laundry room were the washer and dryer that had been replaced just before Eric had quit. A washer and dryer she'd bought on her own because he didn't care about that kind of thing.

She ran into the living room and stared at the sofa, the

chairs, even the TV. She'd picked them all. In the bedroom was the set she'd bought at an estate sale the same month she'd closed on the house. It had taken her two months to refinish the wood and stain it. She'd been so proud of the outcome and when Eric had first seen them, he'd been impressed by her hard work.

Slowly, she walked to Eric's office. Even there she'd been the one to find the old desk at the Habitat for Humanity store. Eric had liked it fine, but he hadn't picked it. No wonder he'd only needed a few boxes to move out. There was nothing of him in this house.

She leaned against the hall wall and slowly sank to the floor. After pulling her legs up to her chest, she rested her head on her knees and told herself to keep breathing.

But the truth was insistent. Like a lonely dog determined to be petted, it nudged at her, slipping in when she let down her guard.

She and Eric had never known each other. Not really. And because she hadn't known him, she couldn't love him. Not really. Not in a way that was meaningful to him.

He'd been the one to leave. He'd been the one to step away from their marriage, but she hadn't given him any reason to stay. The past six years of his life fit in a handful of boxes. No part of their life had been his.

She was to blame, she thought, her stomach twisting until she was afraid she was going to throw up. Not completely, but she had a pretty equal share.

She'd never seen it. Making everything his fault had been so very easy. She'd never noticed how she was also responsible. She wasn't sure she wanted to be married to Eric anymore, but by her actions, she hadn't given either of them a choice.

Now it was done. There was no going back. There was

only moving forward. Right now that unknown path was more than a little terrifying. And the kicker was, she'd done it to herself.

The sun flooded the backyard with warmth and light. Pam had made sure there were plenty of chairs in the shade, not that anyone was using them, she thought happily. Her guests were too busy laughing and talking to do something as mundane as sit.

She'd already made a pest of herself with the sunscreen, especially for the children. It was the first unofficial day of summer. She didn't want anyone getting a sunburn. Brandon had taken her aside and told her to lighten up. He'd then kissed her cheek and handed her a margarita. She'd decided to take his advice.

The Eiland family Memorial Day barbecue was a tradition. It had started two weeks after she and John had moved into this house. She'd been pregnant with Brandon, exhausted from unpacking and too big to sleep more than thirty minutes at a stretch and tired of not being able to see her feet. She'd been swollen, achy and the last thing she'd wanted was a party.

But John had promised he would handle everything and to her surprise, he had. When the guests had arrived, they'd swarmed the house and seen to the last of the unpacking. In less than an hour the books were in the bookcase, the baby-to-be's room was in order and all the boxes were lying flattened in the garage. A good thing, because right after the burgers had been served, her water had broken. Six hours later, Brandon entered the world.

The following year, they'd had the party again. Mostly to thank their guests who had cleaned up after the party and put the leftovers in the refrigerator.

And so it had begun.

The party had grown as she and John had made new friends. Later, their children's friends had joined in. Some people had moved away or found traditions of their own. But the core of the party, the celebration of friends and summer and all that went with both, had continued.

Pam stood in front of the kitchen window, watching her guests and sipping her margarita. Eugenia had called that morning to confirm the travel arrangements to London. The four women were meeting there for three days of sightseeing, before leaving for Amsterdam, where they would start their cruise.

Pam was already checking out the Chico's website for their easy travel clothes. Hayley would take Lulu for the three weeks Pam would be gone.

Jen walked into the kitchen. Her daughter glowed in a simple red T-shirt and shorts. She was showing already and counting the days until summer vacation started.

"Kirk says he's starving," Jen said with a laugh. "That man can eat. I'm going to take out the burgers so the boys can get started cooking."

The boys being her brothers, Pam thought. She put down her margarita. "Let me help."

"Mom, I can carry a platter of meat."

"Yes, and I'll take care of the chicken and the ribs. You be sure to wash your hands when you're done."

"Oh, Mom."

The words were filled with a combination of affection and frustration. Because Pam would always be a worrier and her family would have to live with that fact.

Come mid-July, Jen and Kirk would move into the big house. The title was in the process of being transferred. Pam still had to decide how much furniture she was taking with her and how much she was going to buy. She thought a combination of familiar and new would be best.

Pam and Jen walked out into the backyard. Shannon and Adam stood talking with Gabby, Adam's sister. Char, Adam's daughter, leaned against Shannon. Shannon absently stroked the girl's hair.

They were a family now, Pam thought, glancing at the other woman's sparkling diamond engagement ring. Shannon had used her business-honed efficiency to plan a wedding for the last week of June. Three days before, escrow would close on Shannon's beachfront condo. While they were on their honeymoon, Pam would move Shannon's things into Adam's house and her own things into Shannon's former, aka her new, condo. Once engaged, Shannon had wanted to sell and Pam had wanted to buy. Taking care of the move was her wedding gift to her friend.

Jen handed the plate of burgers to her husband. "Better?" she asked.

Kirk kissed her. "Now that you're here."

Pam set the chicken and ribs by the barbecue. Her children were happy, she thought with pleasure. Brandon was gearing up for finals, but enjoying every second of medical school. Steven had come into his own with the business. There were days when the responsibility weighed on him, but he got through it.

She watched him talk to Hayley. Rob, Hayley's husband, was traveling on business.

Steven tucked a strand of hair behind Hayley's ear as he laughed at something she said. Pam watched them, wondering if there was something going on, then dismissed the notion. Hayley was married. Steven would never get in the way of that.

She turned her attention to the rest of her guests. Fraser Ingersoll and his partner talked with a couple of guys from John's business. Lulu cuddled happily in her vet's arms. Children ran through the trees, laughing and shrieking. Tyler was with them.

Pam looked for Nicole. She stood with several other women. Although she nodded and smiled, there was still a sadness in her eyes. She'd gotten thinner since Eric had moved out. Quieter. Pam didn't know what it was like to get a divorce, but she knew plenty about grieving. She would be there for her friend. Help her as best she could.

Violet and Bea, from the angel fund, were part of the group of women. Pam had committed to join them. She still couldn't believe how much money she was putting on the line, yet she knew she'd made the right decision. She wanted to be a part of something bigger than herself.

So much had changed, she thought. She was moving, she was going to travel, she would be working several days a week.

In a perfect world, John would still with her. He would be standing at the barbecue, cooking the burgers and telling jokes. He would catch her eye and wink at her and she would smile back.

She thought about all that had happened since his death. All he had missed. The nights without him and how she still thought she had to call and tell him something, only to remember she couldn't. Not anymore.

She would give anything to have him back, even for a minute. Just one more hug, she thought. One more whisper of his voice. She would give anything, but that wasn't an option. So she had begun to heal. To move forward. Because it was what he would have wanted.

Sometimes life was hard, she thought, walking across

the grass to be with her friends. Just when you least expected it, you had to start over. There was pain in that, but also satisfaction. With or without her wanting it to, life moved on. And she would, too.

* * * * *

Reader's Discussion Guide

Bookclub Menu Suggestion:

To Drink: A California Chardonnay
To Eat: The Farm Table's Chicken-Spinach Salad with
Strawberries and Maple Vinaigrette (recipe follows)

1. Nicole, Shannon and Pam are very different. Why do you think they're friends? What do they have in common? Do you think age matters when it comes to friendship? Do you have a close friend from a different generation? What makes your friendship work?

2. What did you think of the setting of Mischief Bay, California? Did the setting affect the characters and the story and, if so, how?

3. Nicole was angry with her husband for quitting his job in order to pursue his dream of writing a screenplay. Did she have a right to be angry? Did your feelings change as the story progressed? How should Nicole and Eric have handled things differently?

4. As you were reading, did you feel that Shannon really wanted children? Why or why not? How would you have handled Char at her birthday party?

5. Pam does something surprising to breathe new life into her marriage with John. What did you think of the couple's retreat? How did their relationship change after that? Would you ever sign up for a weekend like that?

6. What did you think of Pam's plan when she went on the cruise that John had booked? What surprised you about the cruise?

7. Which heroine did you relate to the most, Nicole, Shannon or Pam? Why?

8. How did each woman change by the end of the book? What were the turning points that prompted these changes?

9. Susan Mallery's working title for this book was *The Beginners Class*. "Every time you learn something new, you have to start in the beginners class," Nicole says in Chapter Thirteen. How is this relevant to each woman's story? How is it relevant in your life?

10. Nicole will be a main character in the next Mischief Bay novel. What do you hope will happen?

The Farm Table's Chicken-Spinach Salad with Strawberries and Maple Vinaigrette

Vinaigrette:
1/3 cup vegetable oil
1/3 cup maple syrup
3 tbsp. balsamic vinegar
1 tbsp. Dijon mustard
1 tbsp. lemon juice
1/2 tsp. salt
1/4 tsp. pepper

Salad:
1 lb. boneless, skinless chicken breasts
5 oz. baby spinach
8 oz. strawberries, quartered
4 green onions, sliced
1/2 cup slivered almonds, roasted 30 seconds
in a dry pan

Whisk together the vinaigrette ingredients and refrigerate.

Grill the chicken breasts until thoroughly cooked. Slice on the diagonal. Mix all salad ingredients in a bowl. Serve with maple vinaigrette. Makes 4-6 main dish salads.

Find more recipes from the restaurants of Mischief Bay at www.mischiefbay.com!

To experience more of Susan's trademark humor,
friendship and romance,
turn the page for a sneak peek of
THE FRIENDS WE KEEP,
the next story in Mischief Bay.
Available from MIRA Books.

One

Was it wrong to want to pee alone? Gabriella Schaefer considered the question for maybe the four hundredth time in the past couple of months. In truth, she loved everything about her life. Her husband, her five-year-old twin daughters, her pets, her house. All of it was an amazing gift. She got that. She'd been blessed. But every now and then…okay, at least once a day, she desperately wanted to be able to go to the bathroom, like a normal person. To sit down and pee. Undisturbed.

Not with someone pushing open the door to complain that she was hungry or that Kenzie had taken her doll. Not with Andrew wandering in, a pair of socks in each hand, to ask her which one was the better choice. Not with a pink-toed cat paw stretching under the door or a basset hound moaning softly on the other side, begging to be let in. Alone. Oh, to be alone for those thirty or forty seconds. To actually be able to finish and flush and wash her hands *by herself.*

Gabby signaled as she got into the left lane, then slowed to wait for her turn. Fifty-seven days, she reminded herself. She had fifty-seven days until the twins started kindergarten and she went back to work. Sure, it was only going to be part-time, but still. It would be magical. And what she would never share with anyone was that she was most excited about being able to pee by herself.

"What's so funny?" Kenzie asked from the backseat. "Why are you smiling?"

"Are you telling a joke?" Kennedy asked. "Can I know?"

Because at their age, they were all about the questions, Gabby thought, keeping her gaze firmly on the road. When there was a break in the oncoming traffic, she turned into the parking lot and drove toward the end of the strip mall. There were still a couple of spots directly in front of Supper's in the Bag. She pulled into one and turned off her SUV's engine.

"I'm thinking funny thoughts," she told her girls. "I don't have any jokes."

Kennedy wrinkled her nose. "Okay."

Her voice was laced with disappointment. Both girls knew that what grown-ups thought was funny and what was *really* funny were usually two different things.

Gabby grabbed her handbag—a small cross-body with an extra-long strap—and got out of the car. She walked to the rear driver's-side door and opened it.

"Ready?" she asked.

Both girls nodded. They were already undoing the safety straps on their car seats.

Getting them out of their seats was never the problem. Getting them into them was another matter. Despite the fact that the seats were rated for kids up to sixty pounds, both girls wanted booster seats rather than their car seats. Car seats were for babies, she'd been informed several times already. The fact that car seats were safer didn't seem to be making an impact on the discussion.

She and Andrew were going to have to figure out a better strategy, she thought as she helped Kennedy jump to the ground. Kenzie followed. Gabby couldn't keep having the same fight every day. Plus the arguments were taking longer and she was having to build an extra five or ten minutes into her routine just to get to appointments on time.

The problem was both girls took after their father, she thought humorously. He was a highly skilled sales executive with the gift of verbal charm. Even at five, the twins were starting to try to talk themselves out of being in trouble.

"Is Tyler going to be here?" Kennedy asked.

Gabby brushed the girl's hair out of her eyes. Her blond bangs needed trimming. Again. "He is."

The girls cheered. Tyler, her friend Nicole's son, was six and soon to be in the first grade. In the eyes of two girls who were excited and a little nervous about kindergarten, Tyler was very much a man of the world. He knew things and they both adored him.

Gabby reached past the troublemaking car seats for the empty tote bags that came with her membership. The bright green bags were covered with the Supper's in the Bag logo. Every two weeks she joined a couple of her friends for a three-hour session at Supper's in the Bag and when she left, she would have six meals for her family. Meals that could be thrown in the oven or grilled on the barbecue. They were seasoned, portioned and ready to be prepared.

The premise of Supper's in the Bag was simple. Each session took about three hours. In the large, industrial kitchen-like space were eight stations, each dedicated to a different entrée. By following the clearly marked instructions, you portioned meat, added spices and vegetables into recyclable containers, basically doing whatever was needed to get the meal ready for cooking.

At first Gabby had felt guilty about signing up for the service. She was a stay-at-home mom. Surely she could get her act together enough to cook for her family. *And yet*, she thought, handing the empty bags to her daughters and then guiding them to the store. The days slipped away from her. Fortunately for her, the owner of Supper's in the Bag was the sister of a close friend. Telling herself that she was supporting a local business helped with the guilt.

Because Andrew was one of the good guys, he encouraged her to use the service. They went out to dinner at least once a week, so with the six meals she prepped here, that meant she only had to come up with six meals on her own.

The store was big and open, with the kitchen stations set up on the perimeter of the room. Industrial racks filled with pantry items stood in the center area. There was a cash register by the door and shelves for purses and the bags they all brought. The counters were stainless steel, as were the sinks.

To the left was a small seating area where clients could linger and talk, if they wanted. To the right was a small partitioned area that had been painted bright colors and set up with kid-sized tables and chairs. There were a few toys, lots of boxes of crayons and plenty of coloring books. Cecelia, the resident sitter, was already there. The petite, curly-haired college student grinned when she saw the twins.

"I was hoping you two would be by today," she said, waving at them. "We're going to have so much fun."

"Cece!"

The twins dropped their tote bags and ran to greet the teen. There were hugs all around.

"Is Tyler coming?" Kenzie asked anxiously.

"He is. I'm sure he and his mom are running late." Cecelia guided the girls toward a table. "Let's start on a picture, while your mom gets going on her meals," she said.

Gabby used the distraction to head for the aprons by the check-in area. She picked up her sheet, telling her which stations she would be using, and in what order.

Supper's in the Bag wasn't a unique idea. There were several businesses like it around the country. While Gabby had never been a fan of Morgan, the woman who owned the place, she had to give her kudos for wringing every dollar out of her clients.

Children were welcome for the price of five dollars per child per hour. For Gabby, that meant an extra thirty bucks, but it beat having to find a sitter herself. There were wine selections offered with each entrée, available for an extra charge. Gabby guessed the mark-up was a restaurant quality 100 percent. After-prep wine and appetizers were available, again for a cost.

Morgan's sister, Gabby's friend Hayley, came in early several days a week to prep the food. She did much of the dicing and slicing, the opening of spice bottles and tomato cans. Gabby happened to know that Hayley worked in exchange for meals.

While Hayley said she was getting the better end of the deal, Gabby had her doubts. No matter the situation, Morgan always seemed to come out ahead. Gabby doubted the arrangement with Hayley was any different.

Several more women walked into the store. Each session could handle thirty-two customers, although the daytime sessions generally had more like twenty-five. Supper's in the Bag was also open Thursday through Sunday evenings, from four until eight-thirty. She spotted Hayley, Nicole and Nicole's son Tyler. Nicole dropped her son off with Cecelia and they all met by the hand-washing sink.

"Hi," Gabby said as she hugged her friends.

Nicole was tall, blonde and enviably willowy. Gabby wasn't sure how much of her fit body was genetic and how much of it came from the fact that she taught exercise classes for a living. Gabby kept promising herself she was going to sign up for one. She was still carrying around an extra twenty-five pounds from her pregnancy, but given that the twins were starting kindergarten, she needed to either do something about the extra weight or stop blaming her daughters.

Hayley was also thin but in a way that made Gabby worry. As usual, her friend was pale with dark circles under her eyes, but for once she seemed filled with energy.

"I'm excited about the meals tonight," Hayley said. "The veggies were extra fresh and I think the new enchilada recipe is going to be a winner."

"You seem happy," Gabby said as she put on a green Supper's in the Bag apron. "What's going on?"

"Nothing much."

Gabby wondered if that was true. Hayley's life was a physical and emotional roller coaster as she tried desperately to carry a pregnancy to term. Her last miscarriage had only been a few months before and she was taking a break—on doctor's orders.

Nicole pulled her long hair back into a ponytail. "You sure?" she asked. "You're very bouncy."

Hayley laughed. "I don't think that's a flattering description."

The three friends stopped at their first station. Directions were written on laminated cards. The ingredients for layering the casserole were stored in bowls and bags. Spices were clearly labeled.

Each of them took a foil pan. "I can't believe it's already the middle of July," Nicole said as she layered corn tortillas on the bottom of the pan. "I was hoping to take Tyler away for a few days, but I don't see that happening. Between work and taking care of him, I'm constantly running."

"You own a business," Gabby said, ignoring yet another stab of guilt. She should own a business, she thought. Or be going back to work more than twenty hours a week. And cooking all her dinners from scratch. Honestly, she had no idea where her day went. The twins were in a summer program from eight until one every day. Makayla, her fifteen-year-old stepdaughter, was in a different camp that went from eight until four. Surely she could get her errands run, laundry finished, meals prepped and cooked, *and* do something to help the world. But it didn't seem to happen.

"There's always Disneyland," Hayley offered as she scooped chunks of chicken into her casserole. Rather than using a single nine-by-thirteen pan, Hayley used two eight-by-eights. Which doubled her number of meals. Of course it was just her and Rob.

"Tyler loves Disneyland," Nicole said. "It just seems like cheating."

"Be grateful it's close," Gabby told her.

The massive amusement park was only about thirty miles away from Mischief Bay. Less than an hour by car, if the traffic gods were on your side.

Gabby put her arm around Nicole. "It could be worse. There could be Brad the Dragon Land. Then you'd be totally screwed."

Nicole grinned. "I'd be tempted to set it on fire."

Hayley and Gabby laughed.

Brad the Dragon was a popular children's book series. Many young boys, Tyler included, loved B the D, as he was known by intimates. For reasons Gabby had never understood, Nicole disliked the character and had a serious loathing for the author. She claimed that she'd read an article once that said Jairus Sterenberg was only in it for the money, that he was evil and most likely responsible for any coming zombie apocalypse headed their way. Gabby was less sure about those claims. Of course there were plenty of parents who were desperately tired of all things *Frozen* or *Minion*.

"Was Hawaii amazing?" Nicole asked.

Gabby nodded as she remembered the ten days she, Andrew and the twins had spent in a condo on Maui last month. It had just been the four of them. Makayla had stayed with her mother.

"It was gorgeous! Beautiful weather and plenty to do. The girls had a fantastic time."

"How did Makayla do at her mom's while you were gone?" Hayley asked.

Gabby sighed. "Okay. Her mom doesn't love having her around more than a weekend at a time, so that makes things difficult. I don't get it. Makayla's fifteen. Sure, she can be a bit mouthy, but she's her kid. You're supposed to love your kid."

"She's back with you?" Nicole asked.

"Her mom dropped her off the first night we were home."

"Too bad you couldn't take her with you," Hayley said.

"Uh-huh," Gabby murmured neutrally, sprinkling cheese on her finished casserole before securing the plastic lid. Because while she probably *should* have wished Makayla could have gone with them, in truth she'd been grateful for the break from her stepdaughter.

Their first meal finished, they took their pans over to the wall of refrigerators and placed their entrées on their assigned shelves, then moved on to the next station. Hayley began pulling down spice bottles while Gabby and Nicole scanned the directions.

"Stew is interesting," Nicole said, her tone doubtful. "The Crock-Pot information is good."

"You don't sound convinced," Gabby murmured, her voice low.

"It's summer. I don't want to have to use the Crock-Pot in the summer." Nicole shook her head. "A classic first-world problem, right? But Tyler loves stew, which means a dinner that's easy and he'll eat. I'm in."

"Excellent attitude," Gabby told her, with a wink. "You get a gold star today."

"I live for gold stars."

Hayley pointed to the spice jars she'd lined up. "This is going to be delicious," she promised. "You'll love it. And the next station is all about grilling over fire."

"You *are* in a happy mood," Nicole said. "What's up? Your boss give you a raise?"

"No, and that's okay." Hayley opened one of the gallon plastic bags and began measuring the spices. "Gabby mentioned my mood, too. Am I usually crabby all the time?"

"Not at all," Gabby said quickly, not sure how to explain that for once, Hayley seemed happy and relaxed. If she hadn't known the other woman was on hiatus from trying to conceive, she would have wondered if her friend was expecting. Before she could figure out if she should ask anyway, Hayley picked up the bottle of red wine on the table, measured out a half cup and poured it into her bag.

Nope, Gabby told herself. Not pregnant. But there *was* something.

They worked through the rest of the stations, then loaded their meals into their totes. Gabby packed up the car before going back to get her girls.

"You ready?" she asked.

Kenzie and Kennedy looked at each other before nodding at her.

"They were great," Cecelia told her.

"We were very good," Kenzie added.

"I'm sure you were."

The twins were at that age where they were angelic with everyone but her. She'd read dozens of books on child rearing and from what the experts said, the need to be more independent battled with the need for Mom. So while everyone else got smiles and good behavior, she got pushback and tears.

She waited while her girls hugged Cecelia goodbye. They were growing fast, she thought with contentment. They were bright, inquisitive and loving. Given how right everything was in her life, she could deal with a little pushback now and then.

They left the child-care area and headed toward the

front door. Today they'd chosen matching clothes. Blue shorts and blue-and-white T-shirts with little kittens on them. They'd lost that toddler chubbiness and were now looking like little girls.

They were fraternal twins, but so close in appearance that most people thought they were identical. They both had big hazel eyes and strawberry blond hair. They sounded alike and were both energetic.

But there were also differences. The shape of their chins. Kennedy had thicker, slightly curlier hair. Kenzie was a bit taller. School was going to be interesting, Gabby mused. Kennedy was more outgoing, but Kenzie had a level of patience her sister didn't. She wasn't sure which characteristics would mean success.

They reached her SUV and she opened the rear door on the driver's side.

"In you go."

The girls didn't budge.

"We want booster seats," Kennedy said firmly. "Car seats are for babies. Mommy, we're starting kindergarten."

"That means we're not babies anymore," Kenzie added.

Gabby didn't know which kid at their summer camp had said something about booster seats versus car seats, but she really wished he or she hadn't.

She thought about the bottles of wine waiting back inside Supper's in the Bag. She could give the girls back to Cecelia, have a couple of glasses and then phone Andrew to drive them all home. She could bang her head against the side of the SUV until that pain was bigger than the argument. Or she could suck it up, remind herself that she was blessed and lucky and every other good thing, and simply deal.

Despite the fact that the wine scenario was really appealing, she went with the latter.

"You are growing," she said, keeping her voice gentle. "And I love you very much. That's why I want to keep you safe. Please get in your seats so we can go home and get dinner ready for your dad."

The twins stayed stubbornly in place.

Gabby held in a sigh. Where was the win in this fight? She wasn't going to be blackmailed by five-year-olds. "Boomer and Jasmine are waiting for their dinners, too. I want to go home. Please get in your car seats now."

"We won't." Kennedy crossed her arms over her chest. Kenzie followed, because Kenzie always followed.

"For every minute we wait here, you will lose fifteen minutes of your television time," she told the girls. Kind of a big deal because TV was limited in the Schaefer household.

The twins glanced at each other, then back at her. Kenzie leaned over to her sister.

"Fifteen minutes is a *long* time."

Kennedy sighed heavily, then got in the SUV. Kenzie did the same. Gabby vowed that later she would talk to her husband and they would brainstorm a solution. Or at the very least have a glass of wine and remind themselves that in ten years, when the twins wanted to start dating, they would look back on the car-seat fights and tell themselves these were the good old days.

Don't miss the rest! The Friends We Keep
is available wherever books are sold.

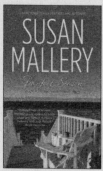  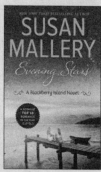

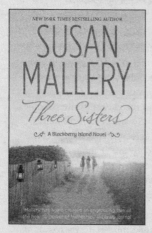

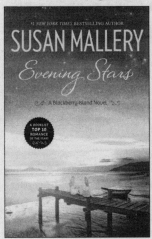

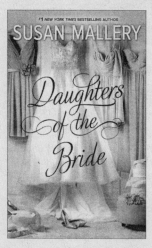

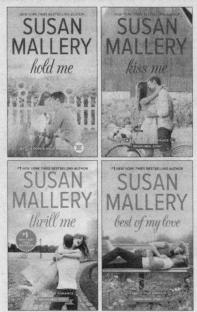

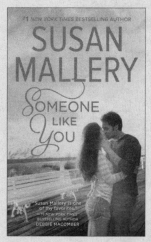